S T A

$\mathcal{G}$ULF OF MEXICO

Brownsville
Matamoros

Monterrey

Tampico

Mérida

Querétaro

Río Frio

Yucatán

Mexico
City

IXTACCIHUATL

Puebla

Vera Cruz

Cuernavaca

Paso del Macho

Córdoba

Orizaba

Oaxaca

Acapulco

GUATEMALA

OCEAN

map by palacios

CATHERINE GAVIN, who was born and educated in Scotland, has been a university lecturer in history, a candidate for Parliament, and a war correspondent in World War II. THE CACTUS AND THE CROWN is her tenth published work.

Married to an American businessman, Dr. Gavin spent ten years in the United States and is well known in the American lecture field. She and her husband now have a home in London, their base for extensive travel on both sides of the Atlantic.

THE CACTUS AND THE CROWN

Catherine Gavin

THE CACTUS
AND
THE CROWN

Doubleday & Company, Inc.
Garden City, New York

With the exception of actual historical person-
ages, the characters are entirely the product of
the author's imagination and have no relation to
any person in real life.

To Margaret Collingwood

CONTENTS

THE CACTUS AND THE CROWN

A DOCUMENT OF STATE

A TALL MAN, with a red-gold beard, stood at his study window high above the Adriatic and focussed his glass on the vessels lying at anchor between Trieste harbor and his castle of Miramar. Beneath his window sill the castle's limestone walls sparkled in the sun, and April flowers were breaking into waves of color round the marble fountains and terraces which he had designed for Charlotte when Miramar became their home. It was a time of day he usually enjoyed, when he could pause before starting work on his latest travel diaries or the catalogue of his butterfly collections to watch Charlotte and her ladies enjoying their morning stroll among the flowers. Today the gardens were deserted. Since the Emperor arrived the life of Miramar was concentrated indoors, and swollen with the influx of archdukes, cabinet ministers, soldiers and policemen by the score. But for once courtiers and guards were not grouped only round the Emperor. In a hush of anticipation they waited at the very threshold of the quiet room where his younger brother stood face to face with the great decision of his life.

Maximilian von Hapsburg, archduke of Austria, had been offered a crown. His brother said "Take it!" His wife said "Take it!" and only his irresolute heart, for days and months past, had hesitated at the final step. Ever since the ships he watched through his glass had finished coaling at the Trieste jetties and begun slipping out quietly to lie between the castle and the town, he had felt himself being pushed inexorably towards an affirmative choice. The convoy forming beneath his eyes had come from many European ports to escort a new sovereign across the Atlantic. Its guns would thunder the first salute to Maximilian, Emperor of Mexico.

He counted them over: the French frigate *Themis,* the Austrian gunboat *Bellona,* the Imperial yacht *Phantasie,* and six cruisers of the Austrian Navy, of which Maximilian had once been the High Admiral. His glass dwelt longest upon *Novara,* which he had been proud to call his flagship. When Charlotte and he came first to Miramar, after the Austrian defeat in Italy, it had suited his nostalgic fancy to furnish his study exactly like the commander's cabin in *Novara.* He had not expected then that he might one day be piped aboard *Novara* with Charlotte by his side, to set sail for Vera Cruz.

Maximilian closed the glass with a sigh. Across the blue water he could see the sunshine reflected in the city windows of Trieste, and wondered if the lens of another spyglass might be blinking there. The Mexican envoys, preparing to put on the finery for which French money had paid, were certain to be keeping a close watch on Miramar. They must have known of Charlotte's hasty journey to Vienna and her return; they must have seen the imperial standard broken from the castle tower when Franz Josef arrived by special train at eight o'clock that morning. Had they interpreted the Emperor's unheralded arrival as flattering to themselves and their momentous errand? Or what other construction had the eloquent Señores Almonte, Gutierrez and Hidalgo had the wits to put upon it?

An hour had passed since Franz Josef entered the castle and, as always the prisoner of his own routine, announced that he would breakfast alone with his staff. The complex daily organization of the Austro-Hungarian Empire would be continued in the guest chambers of little Miramar as calmly as if the Emperor were in his vast apartments at the Hofburg. It had the effect—perhaps a calculated one—of making Maximilian and his anguished indecision over the crown of Mexico seem of no more importance than the promotion to postmaster of some ambitious mail carrier in Tirol.

At a sound behind him Maximilian turned from the window with a start, expecting to see the chamberlain's gold lace and white wand, and hear the announcement that the Emperor was now free to deal with the small matter of Mexico. But it was his wife, Charlotte, who had closed the door, putting her back against the oak panels and in her scarcely controlled excitement almost hissing out the words:

"He has dismissed his secretaries. He will join us here in five minutes!"

She added, with a change of tone, "Why are you standing there staring at the sea?"

Her imperative voice jarred upon her husband for a moment. Then, with a charming gesture, he held out his hand to her and smiled as he sketched a light kiss on her hand.

"I was wishing we could play truant and row out to *Phantasie*," he said. "Don't you think this would be a perfect day to sail down to Lacroma and see how the new house is coming along?"

"There are palaces waiting for us in the City of Mexico," said Charlotte reproachfully. There was never a trace of humor in her young face, withered by a long agony of ambition, envy and secret humiliation, nor in her wary eyes. They were strange eyes, with a flickering light in them, and of a vivid unexpected green. A dusting of pearl powder failed to hide a rising fever blister on Charlotte's upper lip. Her lower lip showed the marks of teeth.

"His Imperial Majesty!"

The Archduke and Archduchess were ready with their second bow and curtsy of the morning as Franz Josef entered, tall and correct in the white tunic and dark trousers of his army uniform. He wore a dress sword with a tasseled hilt and ornamented scabbard which clattered on the carpet as he sat down stiffly behind the desk copied from the commander's desk aboard *Novara*.

"Max!" said the Emperor affably, "Charlotte! My apologies for keeping you waiting. How very well you both look."

He surveyed them with a slightly sarcastic smile. Max in a black frock coat, with a row of medals, and the Order of the Golden Fleece on a jeweled collar round his neck. Charlotte in what appeared to be evening dress, a white lace crinoline gown with an ornate parure of opals, and her bare shoulders only partly covered by a silk scarf of the anticipated imperial purple. She had enough tact to wear no diadem, but her dark hair had been dressed in an elaborate coronal of puffs and braids which seemed to imitate a crown. That was the Coburg upstart in her, of course; it often dominated Charlotte's Bourbon blood! The Emperor memorized the details for the amusement of his lovely Sissi, who could look like the empress she was in country cotton, with a wreath of daisies in her hair.

"Very fine!" he repeated. "Are those Hungarian opals, Charlotte?"

"The Mexican envoys sent them to me, in honor of today," she answered haughtily. "These are fire-opals of the first water, from the new Esperanza mine at Querétaro, and much finer than anything Hungary can show."

"So the new Mexican mine is called 'Hope,' " Franz Josef commented with a smile. "What a happy omen for the beginning of your reign!"

Maximilian's hand went to his golden beard. When he was ill at ease he had a trick of twisting it into two points, and at thirty-one he was very often uneasy in the presence of the brother who had been for fifteen years his sovereign and autocrat.

"I haven't yet made up my mind to accept the crown," he blurted out.

Franz Josef raised his eyebrows.

"Don't tell me you anticipate a counterattack by Benito Juarez? His forces are in full retreat on every front. The French have complete control of the situation, and the republic has to all intents and purposes ceased to exist."

"Oh—Juarez!" said the Archduke vaguely. "They say he's taken flight toward the Río Grande. No, I'm not afraid of Juarez."

"Then isn't it rather late to be uncertain? You've been conferring with the Mexicans since October 1861—that's two and a half years ago. You've been to Paris, and accepted all the terms the Emperor Napoleon offered—"

"That was before I heard *your* terms, Franz," said Maximilian.

The Emperor raised his eyebrows.

"I gave Charlotte an amended copy of the Compact," he said. "Where is it?"

"On the desk close by your hand."

Franz Josef took up the roll of parchment, untied the red tape round the blank outer page and flattened the stiff sheets beneath a paperweight.

"This was sent back to you as the final version of the Family Compact," he said gravely, "which you must sign before I, as your sovereign, can consent to your becoming Emperor of Mexico. It contains the concessions I made during my talk with Charlotte a few days ago, namely to continue your personal allowance of one hundred and fifty thousand gulden per annum, and to send an Austrian Legion of six thousand men to support you in Mexico. With the twenty-five thousand French troops Napoleon III has promised to maintain in Mexico, plus eight thousand of his Foreign Legion, you should have an extremely adequate force to rely on until the Mexican Imperial Army can be organized."

He paused, pressing his finger tips judicially together.

"Now after Charlotte went away the other day—in tears, I'm sorry to say—I considered the clauses of the Family Compact once again."

"And—?" said Maximilian hoarsely.

"And I decided I had better come to Miramar in person, to direct this matter of the signature," said Franz Josef. "Even the most carefully prepared, most secret document can leave a loophole for misunderstanding between its words. I want you to understand from me, Maximilian—with no possibility of evasion, or any interpretations by your wife, or your wife's grandmother, or mamma, or any other of your petticoat confidantes—that before you accept the Crown of Mexico today you must give up the right of succession, after my son Rudolf, to the throne. You must agree that if I die while Rudolf is a minor, the regency shall pass to brother Ludwig, and not to you."

"Then you only came to tell us what we already knew?" The Archduchess Charlotte touched a cambric handkerchief to her tortured lips. "In spite of all I said to you at the Hofburg, you haven't changed your mind about the succession?"

"You only confirmed my intentions, Charlotte dear."

"Then I say your intentions are infamous!" cried Maximilian. His voice, a pleasant tenor, rose and cracked. There was a drop of saliva on the full, red lower lip above the golden beard. "You want to hound me out of the Family, Franz—in God's name, why? Why did you wait until the very end of the negotiations, when you thought me too far committed to turn back, to spring your trap on me? Are you jealous of my popularity with the Viennese? Do you call it brotherly affection, to make me give up my rights as a Hapsburg—not only for myself, but for my heirs?"

"What heirs?"

The question, in Franz Josef's icy voice, cut like a lash across the younger man's tirade.

"In seven years of marriage you've never even had the hope of a child," the Emperor said. "That's an additional reason why the guardianship of Rudolf should pass to Ludwig. Poor Ludi, with all his faults, understands children, and has two fine boys of his own already."

Charlotte met his gaze. He was torturing her and he knew it, but the strange green eyes did not waver from his own.

"Your child . . . if after all you have a child, will have a rich inheritance in Mexico," said Franz Josef. "Be content with that, for I won't divide the empire to satisfy your ambitions, Maximilian! Go to Mexico or stay at Miramar—it's a matter of indifference to me. But if you mean to stay, have the goodness to give me time to leave for Vienna before you receive the delegation. I don't propose to be here when the Mexicans realize they've backed a loser."

He rose with a glance at the clock. "The Chancellor is waiting for me," he said to his brother's averted head.

"Thank you for your exposition, Sire," said the Archduchess Charlotte. "You may care to know that I had a dispatch from Brussels late last night. My father expresses his agreement with you. He urges Maximilian to sign the Family Compact."

"Quite so!" Franz Josef looked down at her with a half-smile on his handsome face. "I was sure King Leopold would prefer the substance to the shadow. Remember, Mexico is your substance and Austria your shadow, Charlotte. I intend to live to a great age, and see Rudolf's sons grown men before I die."

He held out his white-gloved hand and Charlotte compelled herself to touch it with her own.

"I leave him to you," he said significantly, with a glance at Maximilian. "And I hope that next time I greet you it will be by a new title—La Emperatriz Carlóta Amalia!"

The strange eyes blazed as she swept him a curtsy fit for a ball at the Hofburg, and Franz Josef left the study as near to laughing as a man without gaiety ever came. He had chosen the key words and the right moment. He knew that he had done well to leave Maximilian to his wife.

But Maximilian, when the door was shut, turned on her with a weak man's bluster.

"You're on *his* side now? You and your father think I should sign away my rights to a place among the Hapsburgs?"

"We want you to be the leader of men you used to be, and ought to be again—"

"And you want an imperial crown for your own lovely head, don't you, my dear?"

"Yes!" she said, driven beyond herself. "Yes! And do you know why? Because I'm sick of playing second fiddle to every woman who wears a crown in Europe! My cousin Victoria is nothing but a little dumpy *Hausfrau,* with fewer brains in her head than I have in my little finger—but she's the Queen of

England, and can condescend to poor dear Charlotte, who arranges flowers so beautifully! Eugénie de Montíjo was fair game for any man while that disreputable old mother was peddling her round all the spas of Europe, but now she's Empress of the French, and I must kiss her hand and be oh! so grateful for her interest in us! I'm buried here at Miramar while Sissi is the first lady of the land. Do you think I enjoy hearing that crazy Wittelsbach girl cheered as Empress of Austria, praised for her beauty, complimented on her—on her lovely children . . ."

She hid her face on her husband's breast, and burst into a storm of crying.

His arms went round her as he whispered, "Franz Josef shouldn't have said that—about the children. He doesn't know how much it hurts you."

Charlotte laughed hysterically.

"What would Franz Josef say if he knew the truth? What would any of the Hapsburgs say? Franzl and Sissi, so proud of Rudolf and their little girls; Ludwig with his two fine boys already; all the Family so sorry for poor Maxl, saddled with a barren wife! What if I told them just one story, Max—the story of your infidelity?"

His eyes fell before hers. He was shaken by an old guilt and pity as she went on remorselessly, "Don't you think you owe me something, Max?"

"Carla, Carlotta *mia!*" the man said pleadingly, and her lips trembled as she heard the tender diminutives of their Italian honeymoon, when she adored him and believed him to be in love with her. "I owe you everything. I would be lost without you. I'll do anything you want. We'll go to Mexico, and I will try to rule there like a Christian prince, so that God in His mercy may relent, and send a child to us . . ."

"A son!" she said. "A son to rule over a far greater land than Austria; a Central American empire stretching from the Río Grande to the frontiers of Brazil . . ."

He stared at her slack-lipped, carried away as often before by the visions she knew so well how to conjure up for him.

"But in the meantime you must sign this," she said, and slipped out of his loose clasp to reach for the paper on the desk.

"It is a document of state," he said. "It must be signed in the presence of witnesses."

"Franz will be glad to spare the Chancellor." She was actually laughing, though her face was still stained with tears, as she stretched out her hand to the beaded crimson bellrope. But she was watching him, too. She saw the wistfulness of the last look he threw at the ships he loved and the gardens he had made.

"It means power and glory," she prompted him. "It means you will go down in history as the greatest of all the Hapsburg emperors."

"It means I can never go home again," he said.

Chapter One

FRENCHMAN'S GRAVEYARD

I

THE AMERICAN steamer lay off the harbor of Vera Cruz
with her engines rung down to Stop, her captain in conference
with the quarantine officials, and all her white passengers in their
cabins, drowsing through their last siesta aboard the *Jupiter*. It
was a day at the end of February, when the tropical sun was
already high above the Tierra Caliente, and only the Negro passengers, already grasping bags and bundles, had come out of
their steerage quarters and clustered at the rail.

Their voices, keyed to anxiety, drifted up to the passenger
deck, where a grizzled sugarbroker from Havana was taking his
ease in a long rattan chair. Mr. Jonas Wilkinson was a seasoned
traveler, who hardly turned his head to glance at the irregular
shoreline he knew all too well. The desolate sand dunes and
scrub palms, broken only by the cluster of adobe buildings which
was the town of Vera Cruz, was as familiar to him as the graveyard of the Isla de Sacrificios and the jail of San Juan de Ulúa,
between which all vessels had to pass to reach the port. He was a
great deal more interested in a girl who stood alone at the ship's
rail, looking at the fever belt of Mexico as if it were the Promised
Land.

He wasn't surprised, he said to himself, that Miss Sally
Lorimer was the first of the whole dismal company of Southern
exiles to come on deck for a closer look at the land they had
chosen for their own. In fact he was prepared to bet that she had
slipped away while old mother Ayres, her self-appointed chap-

erone, was snoring in their overcrowded cabin, because she had neither hat nor parasol, gloves, fan, reticule—none of the impedimenta which the two giggling Ayres girls usually trailed on deck. Not very tall, but still too slender for her height, she stood there graceful and erect in her plain black dress with its single hoop, and the sun cast a tawny light on the rich brown hair she had brushed and coiled into a smooth chignon.

It was the first time Jonas Wilkinson had left Havana since the Civil War ended in America ten months before, and the voyage, though short, had been far more irksome than any of his many business trips to Mexico. Nearly all the passengers embarked at New Orleans were members of a group going out to a new colony in Mexico under the leadership of Matthew Maury, one of the great men of the Confederacy, who had persuaded the Emperor Maximilian to make a grant of land near Córdoba to Confederate veterans who found life intolerable in the defeated South. Mr. Wilkinson was Northern by birth and sentiment. He rejoiced in the victory of the Union, but he had resided in Cuba since 1848, deplored the civil strife at home, and like the few other businessmen aboard the *Jupiter* wanted the hatchet to be buried as soon as possible. This, the Maury colonists were by no means prepared to do.

"I do declare," Mr. Wilkinson had said more than once to the gentleman from Portland, Maine, who shared his cabin, "those plantation gentry are all set up with grievances for a lifetime. They'll be too busy cussing out Phil Sheridan to make any sort of show at growing oranges. I tho't it was Sherman the Rebs hated most, but not this crowd! What drove 'em crazy was Phil Sheridan at New Orleans, making them take an oath never to return to the United States before he let 'em go aboard the *Jupiter*."

"He did it at Secretary Seward's orders," the Portland man pointed out.

"Sure he did, but the Secretary's a civilian, when all's said and done, and snug in his office at Washington. Phil was one of the generals who whipped 'em, and when they came face to face

with Phil at New Orleans, the fireworks started. Without the oath
of no return, they might hev been no worse company than a
bunch of deaf mutes at a funeral. The way things are, we might
as well hev had a bunch of rattlesnakes for shipmates."

And the women, Mr. Wilkinson reflected, were worse rat-
tlers than the men. They had a venomous way of looking at you,
when they weren't looking through you, and only Sally Lorimer
had been willing to talk to him, whenever she could escape the
vigilance of Mrs. Ayres and that surly dog her brother. Young
Lorimer—Dr. Lorimer, no less—was not one of the Maury group,
being on his way to take up a practice in the City of Mexico. His
sympathies, however, were entirely with the settlers, for he too
had been forced to take the oath of no return imposed upon
them by the federal government.

Mr. Wilkinson threw away his cheroot and levered himself
stiffly out of the rattan chair.

"Good afternoon to you, Miss Sally!"

She turned round quickly, with a charming smile of greeting,
but without the little fluttering exclamation, the How you startled
me! expected by convention.

"Oh, can you tell me—can that possibly be the Peak of
Orizaba?"

He followed the direction of her eyes. Many miles inland,
high above the pestilential port and the fever belt, a rose of snow
flowered above the trailing mists which hid the lesser ranges of
the Tierra Caliente.

"Yes, that's Orizaba. We're mighty lucky to get a sight of it
on a sticky afternoon like this."

"I didn't know it could be seen at all from Vera Cruz."

The man took her gently by the elbow. "Better come underneath the awning since you haven't got a parasol. You don't
want to get a sunstroke before you go ashore. Not now, when
you're looking just as fresh as paint!"

It was true. The light filtering through the frayed red awning
stretched above the deck gave color to Sally's rather pale face,
and her eyes, neither brown nor hazel, had a lively sparkle in

their depths. At present her appeal lay in this fresh and piquant look. Hers was not the oval face and rosebud lips of the admired Southern belle; haughty nose, determined chin and generous mouth were the features of a woman of character, as yet only predicted in a young girl's face. Might be a raving tearing beauty one of these days, was Mr. Wilkinson's silent judgment. Or turn as sour as any New England schoolmarm, if the world don't treat her right.

"'Tisn't every traveler gets a sight of Orizaba on his first time in to Vera Cruz," prosed Mr. Wilkinson. "Don't know as I've seen the Peak myself since the day Emperor Max and his lady landed here, two years ago come June."

"Oh, and did they think it was wonderful, sir?"

Her voice was unusually incisive for a girl from North Carolina. Every consonant was given its value, particularly the letter R, for Sally had spent the first eighteen years of her life close to her Scots-born father, in a parish on the Cape Fear River where the Scottish heritage was strong.

"I didn't hear what they thought," said the Yankee drily. "Guess Max was too fretted by the poor reception they got to set much store by mountains. I was standing not ten yards from the gangway when the *Novara* berthed, and I can tell you Madame Carlóta's face was a study when she looked about her at the empty wharf."

"Do you mean nobody had come to meet them?"

"Nobody that they thought counted, and the two or three officials who did turn out brought news that made Max laugh on the wrong side of his face. You see, they'd tho't the South was bound to win the war, and support a new emperor in Mexico. Lee was going great guns when they left Europe, and 'twasn't until Vera Cruz they heard that U. S. Grant had taken command of all the Union armies, and was tearing ahead into the Wilderness." He recollected, just too late, that Sally Lorimer was a Southern girl.

"I remember when Grant crossed the Rapidan," she said composedly. "It seems like a hundred years ago instead of less

than two . . . Mr. Wilkinson, do you think there will be long to
wait before we berth?"

"You're anxious to be on land again, and I don't wonder.
But it won't be long now. The *Juno* had the speed of us, as you
know. You can see her lying at her berth beside the Customs
House. The port authorities should've given us clearance next,
but a French troopship, outward bound, claimed the priority—or
so the first mate said. Howsomever, they've come aboard us now;
if you look down instead of up, my dear, you'll see the cutter."

Sally obeyed him. She saw first, and on the steerage deck, a
row of bent dark heads. The emancipated Negroes whom the
Maury settlers had brought out with them as "apprentices,"
bound for seven years to their former owners, were also looking
down in silence at a rowboat which Mexican oarsmen, in the
ragged semblance of a uniform, were holding steady at the
Jupiter's side.

"They'll clear us faster than they cleared the Frenchman,"
said Mr. Wilkinson. "Seems the Army sent aboard so many
stretcher cases, the Mexican Customs turned suspicious. They
thought the French might be smuggling jewels and silver ingots
out of the country, it's been done that way before."

"And were they?"

"Nothing beneath the bandages but blood."

He regretted his bluntness as soon as he had spoken. But
there was no flinching in the steady face before him.

"Has the French ship sailed yet? Can we see her go?"

From where the *Jupiter* lay it was not easy to distinguish all
the shipping in the harbor. Although trade had fallen off in the
two years of Maximilian's reign, Vera Cruz was still the most
important port in his empire and thronged with European vessels. It was the sudden yell of joy, ringing across the water, that
told them the French troops were bidding farewell to Mexico.

Sally looked nervously around as a number of the *Jupiter's*
passengers, yawning and heavy-eyed after the siesta, began to
make their appearance on the deck. But neither her brother nor
Mrs. Ayres was among them; no imperative voice called her

away from her Yankee friend as the French ship passed Fort San Juan and came rapidly up to starboard. Shading her eyes against the sun, which fell in dazzling bars across the heat miasma rising from the water, Sally could at first see nothing but a blur of blue, white, and red. Blue of cutaway tunics, white of pipe-clayed gaiters, red of knee-length trousers—and then above all the fluttering of hundreds of neckcloths as the French soldiers waved their képis in the air. The sound of cheering came across the water, mingled with the singing of the *Chant du Départ*.

"Glad to go," said Jonas Wilkinson. "That's the entire garrison of Chihuahua, leaving Mexico for good. The mate says General Billot and his boys got a bad mauling from the Juaristas when they withdrew. Guess they think they're well out of the Frenchman's Graveyard . . . Can your young eyes read that boat's name, my dear?"

"It's the *Eugénie*," she said after a moment's hesitation. "Yes, the *Impératrice Eugénie*. And the home port, St. Nazaire."

Mr. Wilkinson whistled. "That's the Pereires' crack mail steamer. If they've turned her into a military transport it looks as if someone mighty high up at Paris put the squeeze on Pereire Brothers. Maybe Emperor Nap means to keep his last promise to his so-called Parliament, and leave Emperor Max to paddle his own canoe."

"Or maybe somebody very high up at Washington, perhaps Mr. Seward himself, used strong persuasions on the Emperor of the French?" suggested Sally.

"I wasn't going to mention the Secretary, seeing how most folk on this boat foam at the mouth when they hear his name, but—yes, I guess that's about the strength of it, Miss Sally. Uncle Sam won't stand for a foreign archduke posing as an emperor south of the Rio Grande—though Lord knows the title is about all he's got, poor devil! The ports, a telegraph wire, a passel of French bayonets . . . that and his lifeline, the highway from Chihuahua down through Mexico, down to Vera Cruz."

The Yankee spoke as he would have spoken to the Portland man who shared his cabin, and with the same assurance of being understood. He had thought more than once that this girl, just past her nineteenth birthday, had a better grasp of the situation in Mexico than any of Mr. Maury's recruits, fluent and opinionated though they were. She was quick, too; she seized on the essential, and said:

"But if the Chihuahua garrison has been evacuated, that means the northern section of the road is undefended. And if General Escobedo has a sufficient force to harass General Billot and the French, then he must be strong enough to protect Benito Juarez, if Juarez decides to come back across the border. So?"

"How do you know so much about the Juaristas, Miss Sally?"

"I read the Washington papers, sir. I know, in spite of all Mr. Maury has told the settlers to the contrary, that the war in Mexico is a long way from being won."

"You mustn't call it a war, Miss Sally. It's Napoleon's boast that he hasn't fought a war for seven years. When he fights in Algeria it's called Pacification; and when he fights in Mexico he calls it Intervention. The French "intervened" to support the claims of a rascally financier called Jecker, who was hand in glove with Napoleon's bast— his half-brother; but they're not at war. Not though three thousand of their lads lie buried on the Isle of Sacrifices yonder. All dead from yellow fever, which is why they call Vera Cruz the Frenchman's Graveyard; and that's not counting thousands more who fell upcountry, when they were pushing Juarez across the Rio Grande."

"When Juarez crossed into Texas last fall," said Sally, "my brother and I had just heard of our inheritance. We thought it was a good omen—that with Juarez gone there might be peace in Mexico."

"But Diaz and Escobedo went on fighting, and the Juaristas plucked up heart again; now they're everywhere."

"Even in Mexico City, sir?"

"Say Mexico, my dear, only the greenhorns say Mexico City. No, they're not in Mexico, nor in the Valley of Mexico . . . nor anywhere, so far, between the capital and Acapulco."

She looked up at him quickly. Her lips were tightly shut, but her eyes invited the sugarbroker to go on. After a brief hesitation the old man said:

"Your hacienda lies in that direction—down at Cuernavaca?"

"About two miles from Cuernavaca."

"And there's a garrison at the Cortés barracks in the town. That should be safe enough—once you get there."

Sally smiled. "We'll get there."

"We?" said Jonas Wilkinson interrogatively. "You'll hev to pardon me, Miss Sally. Since you were good enough to confide in me last night, I've thought of nothing but your situation. My dear, I've girls of my own, so you'll forgive me if I take a liberty —I don't think you have any idea of the trouble you'll encounter if you try to run a sugar hacienda. It would be difficult enough for a lady to handle if there were peace in Mexico. In the present state of the country, I would call it hopeless."

"My uncle bequeathed me the hacienda," she said with a touch of defiance. "If he hadn't wanted me to keep it in operation he could have sold it, couldn't he?"

"Your late respected uncle should hev known better than lay such a burden on your shoulders. Running a sugar plantation is a man's job, and a man bred up to the business from a boy. Your brother has his own profession—he can't help; and you can't live alone on a hacienda with your overseer, can you now? I would say, sell the place at once and get what you can while it's still a going concern. The risks in Mexican real estate are tremendous these days, when most foreigners are scared to stay on in the country."

"But we've got nothing to be scared of!" The strong little jaw stiffened as Sally's dark eyes scanned his lean and interested face. "We don't intend to get involved in politics! My uncle emigrated from Scotland long before my father did. He practiced medicine in Mexico for forty years, through Santa Anna's wars and all the revolutions, and died respected by everyone who knew him. Why shouldn't my brother be able to do the same?"

"He could, I suppose, but does he want to? I don't want you to think I've been eavesdropping, but these young fellows talk pretty freely in the saloon when the womenfolk retire and the wine goes round, and I certainly got the impression that the doctor means to change his plans and head for Córdoba with the Maury crowd. That wouldn't suit you very well, I fancy?"

"I'd rather stand up to any Juaristas than join the colony at Córdoba."

He grunted. "I could see you didn't cotton to the Maury lot. I didn't know it was that bad."

Sally said nothing, but with one swift, eloquent gesture she indicated the silent Negroes on the deck below.

"So that's it!" said the man, enlightened. "You think they're wrong to bring their slaves with them—all right, their freedmen, then, and your brother doesn't see it as you do? I should say not! I've heard him ranting against Negro suffrage with that Captain Ayres—"

"If you please," Sally interrupted, and a flush which had nothing to do with the sunlit awning colored her pale face, "I must remind you that you hardly know my brother, sir. He's very bitter against the North, but then he saw all the suffering and pain of the war when he was a surgeon at the front, and lost so many of his friends. And what he can't accept and can't forget, is my sister Helen's death in the siege of Vicksburg. That—that changed him terribly."

"Ah now," said Mr. Wilkinson, "that was a bad business, Vicksburg. Your sister was caught inside the town, was she? I didn't know you had a sister."

"It's very hard to talk about Helen." Sally faltered, and tears filled her eyes. "She was so sweet, and so much more than a sister to me, because our mother died when I was born. And she got frightened, alone on her husband's plantation, when he was a prisoner of war at Rock Island. So she went to stay with his aunts in Vicksburg, about the time Sherman was defeated at Chickasaw Bluffs. But when General Grant laid siege to Vicksburg the Miss Cartwrights were terrified and insisted on taking refuge in the caves . . . and Helen died there with her little baby."

"I'm sorry, my dear," said the sugarbroker awkwardly, and patted her hand. "Believe me now, I'm truly sorry for your loss. It's a vile business, making war on women, but don't you cry. Look, the quarantine officers are getting ready to go: you don't want the Mexes to see you crying, do you?"

It was not only the Mexican officials, preparing to leave the ship at the orders of a bored French officer in Bonaparte green, who were looking curiously at the pair. The sailors dragging trunks on deck were staring; some of the women passengers seemed ready to intervene. But Sally dried her eyes with the heel of her hand, like a boy, and said unsteadily:

"I must go back to the cabin. I'm sure Mrs. Ayres is awake by now."

The brown hand, veined and wrinkled, which had patted Sally's hand in sympathy, closed about her wrist.

"Now listen to me," said the sugarbroker, so quietly that none of the passengers thronging the deck could hear, "if you do go on with your sugar plantation, and need any help, you be sure and write to me. Jonas Wilkinson, at Havana, Cuba— that'll find me at my office; I believe I'm as well known as any man in town. My house is called Vista del Mar, and Mrs. Wilkinson and the girls will admire to see you, if ever you care to accept our hospitality."

"I do appreciate your kindness, sir," said Sally gratefully. Jonas Wilkinson kept her hand imprisoned,

"I'm an old enough man to tell you, and no nonsense about it, that you're a mighty sweet girl, Miss Sally. But are you enough of a woman to take a word of advice from someone who'd like to see you cut loose from the slaving gentry? Try to handle your brother right. Try hard to keep your temper when he loses his. You're a smart scholar, I know. You've read all about the Spanish Conquest of Mexico and how Cortés burned his ships right here at Vera Cruz, which is an event Mr. Maury's settlers hev mostly never heard of, and I've seen you studying your

Spanish grammar while the Miss Ayreses were making cat's
cradle of their tatting. But it's going to take more than book
learning to get the doctor and you to drive in double harness as
far as Mexico. You see, an average smart woman can always
handle a smart man. But it takes the smartest woman who ever
stepped to handle a dog with a burned tail!"

II

MATTHEW MAURY gave a dinner in Vera Cruz that night
to celebrate the arrival of the *Juno* and her sister ship the
Jupiter, and though the walls of the posada were two feet thick
Sally could hear the sound of applause long after the ladies had
left the dingy dining room. They were drinking healths, she supposed, as she changed her black dress for a thin wrap and took
the pins from her heavy coil of hair. She knew the rhythm of it:
first the sound of a single voice, emotional, blurred by distance,
then the scrape of chairs, the determined cheering for President
Davis, General Lee, Beauregard, Longstreet, Stuart—it might
very well go on till midnight. Sally brushed her hair until the
tawny strands crackled with electricity.

When she was ready for bed she knelt on the broad white-
washed window sill of the wretched room which her first attempts
at Spanish had secured for herself alone, and dragged the window open. The hot pall of night lay over Vera Cruz, and there
were beads of perspiration on Sally's forehead as she pressed
against the heavy Spanish grille and looked into the street below. It was no more than an alley between the posada and the
adobe wall of the next building, and feebly lighted by a creosote
flare which burned in an iron socket at the corner. Against the
wall lay the motionless figures of the homeless, with thin bright
serapes drawn across their faces. Among the men lay a sleeping
woman, slack-jawed and limp from fever, whose hand mechanically twitched at the rebozo which covered the dark head of the
infant on her breast. The only sound was the slow tread of a
sentry of the wharf patrol. Sally saw the man as he passed below

the light at the corner of the alley: he was a tall Nubian of the Egyptian Legion lent by the Khedive to support the French in Mexico. They had garrisoned Vera Cruz for three years—the only troops under European command who could resist yellow fever and support life in the Frenchman's Graveyard.

Sally shivered. She was not daunted by the sordid scene or the discomfort of an inn apparently built round a dunghill. But with every hour since their disembarkation she had become more dismayed at the identification of her brother and herself with the Maury colonists. She had felt drawn to Mr. Maury, for all young people instinctively liked the short, limping Virginian with the ruddy face and clear blue eyes of a boy. He had been a famous American before becoming a famous Confederate, for he had been Superintendent of the U. S. Naval Observatory until the Civil War began, and his studies in marine geography were expected to lead, before long, to the opening of a new transatlantic cable. But he now appeared perfectly happy as Maximilian's Director of Immigration in Mexico, and his faith in his colony impressed Sally in spite of herself. It was his son Richard whom she feared, for Captain Dick Maury, the first settler in Mexico under the Maury plan, had come to Vera Cruz with his father to welcome the new arrivals. He was a war hero who had lost a leg on the battlefield, and for most of the guests at dinner he personified the South—gallant and indomitable in an undeserved defeat. Captain Maury had made Andrew Lorimer sit next to him at table, and their heads had been close together all night long.

On this her first night in Mexico, Sally Lorimer felt as if her life had been pared down to the bone, stripped of all its old memories and graces, just as her personal possessions had been reduced to a trunk, portmanteau and dressing bag, and the few treasures spread between two candles on the crate covered with tawdry lace which did duty as a dressing table. A leather case which had belonged to her mother and contained some pieces of old-fashioned jewelry, her father's Greek Testament, a Spanish grammar, a selection of poems by Browning and a moneybelt holding a few hundred dollars from the sale of the home furniture, composed Sally's slender equipment for her new life. That, and a strong, driving ambition which might still be shattered against the rock of her brother's obstinacy.

Sally and Andrew Lorimer were the surviving children of a Scots minister, who about the time of his marriage in 1833 had received a call from a Presbyterian church in North Carolina, and emigrated with his bride. His manse in the piney woods not far from Fayetteville had been Sally's home for the first eighteen years of her life, where the affection of Helen and their father had made up for the mother she never knew, and Andrew, as a medical student at Harvard, satisfied her need for hero-worship. But Sally's lively, inquiring mind soon outpaced Helen's limited powers of teaching. At twelve, she was sent to a famous ladies' seminary "at the North," from which, after only two years' schooling, she was brought home much against her will at the outbreak of the Civil War. From that time all was changed. For a brief period she was satisfied by Helen's romance with Charles Cartwright, the wealthy Mississippi planter whom the war had brought their way; then that vicarious happiness was laid aside with the bridesmaid's dress, and the adolescent girl, with views on the justice of the war developed by her Hartford teachers, was soon in conflict with her brother. When the young field surgeon came home on leave they began to argue States' Rights and Emancipation—even Woman Suffrage; and Andrew heard his little sister taunt him that a man was not infallible because he was a man, nor himself all-wise because he was a doctor. Helen's death at Vicksburg shocked and quieted them both, but in the last year of the war they were at loggerheads again, and finally, when Fayetteville was captured by the Union troops, a quarrel broke out between them which was still unhealed at the time of their father's death. The Sally of Vera Cruz turned shudderingly away from that memory. It was pleasanter to remember the Andrew of the earlier times than the stern, embittered man who came back from the war and assumed the guardianship of his young sister as an unwelcome duty.

There was no money, he said, to send Sally to the women's college at Mount Holyoke, and he refused to allow her to look for employment as a governess. She was to live with him at a boardinghouse in Fayetteville, where he had been hired as assistant to one of the older doctors, and remember—if she could —that she was a lady, born and bred. Remember that on their mother's side she was the granddaughter of the Scottish peer whom Andrew, with inverted snobbery, always referred to as Lord S. That awareness of a Lord S. in her background was not enough to keep a lively, intelligent girl from moping to death in a parlor-bedroom did not occur to the young doctor. He had his own troubles. The field surgeon, twice cited by Lee for bravery under fire, was not a conspicuous success in civilian practice. Work fell off, and Andrew began to kill idle hours over a jug of bourbon with other veterans, as the humid summer afternoons of 1865 passed in futile protests against the enforcement of Negro suffrage in North Carolina. But this stalemate in two lives was not fated to last long. A Raleigh lawyer called on the Lorimers one day in early fall with documents from the British Legation in Mexico, where their father's brother, a bachelor, had lived for many years. Dr. Lorimer, the elder, had left his whole estate to his niece and nephew—the Hacienda de las Flores at Cuernavaca to Sally, and to Andrew his medical practice and what the attorney described as "a town house in a fashionable square."

At once all Sally's vitality and enthusiasm were concentrated on this new start in life. She had read her Humboldt and her Prescott, fallen in love with Mexico, begun the study of Spanish and packed their clothes twice over before Andrew could make up his slower mind to leave Fayetteville, or be persuaded that this was the right thing for them to do. His devotion to the South was absolute. He had hoped to live and die in North Carolina— but she managed to fire him with some of her own eagerness before they set out on the first stage of their journey across the war-disrupted railroad system leading to the Gulf of Mexico. She hadn't counted—and she set her teeth at the thought of it—

on two undeserved pieces of bad luck: their arrival at New Orleans at the very moment when the Government had decided to
penalize the Southern emigrants to Mexico; and the meeting
with a group of men and women as determined as Andrew himself to keep alive the memories of the Lost Cause.

"A dog with a burned tail"—the stinging words seemed to echo
in the room, and with the echo came not only resentment
but a sense of guilt. Sally Lorimer had been brought up in
the strictest Calvinist traditions. Uncompromising honesty, demanded by her father, had been heavily stressed in the curricu-
lum at Hartford, where young ladies were taught to search their
consciences and make public confession of their faults. They
were also urged to help their schoolmates by frankly pointing
out the faults of others. "Tell the truth and shame the Devil"
was a favorite maxim at the school, and the most downright
young ladies of New England were forced to admit that Miss
Lorimer was their equal in plain speaking, and their superior in
the prompt statement of an unpleasant truth. They knew nothing of the struggles of conscience which their outspoken class-
mate was to undergo when she went back to the South at war, or
of the painful heart-searching which would be hers on the night
she arrived in Mexico.

I was dishonest, at the end, with Mr. Wilkinson, she told
herself, with her hot forehead on her knees and her slim back
gracefully arched in the candlelight. I should not have let him
think of me as a friend of the Negroes—I, who didn't do one
thing to make the voyage easier or more pleasant for them, or
denounce their so-called apprenticeship to a single one of their
masters and mistresses. I am a coward! And I'm a cheat, too,
because I only told Mr. Wilkinson Helen's story to make him
sorry for us and better disposed to Andrew. I didn't tell him
that my conduct, and not Helen's death, was what had made
my brother bitter—that he will get over Helen before he will ever
be brought round to forgiving *me*.

Lost in her own thoughts, Sally did not hear her brother's
footsteps in the stone corridor. But she recognized the irritable

knock as soon as his hand fell on the door, and scrambled up to open it; her heart was beating fast. "Keep your head! Keep your temper!" she said to herself, and let him in.

"Am I disturbing you?" he said formally. "I was afraid you might have gone to bed."

"Oh no, not yet. Can you find a place to sit down?"

"Sit down?" he said. "There's hardly a place to stand. What are you doing all by yourself in this hole? Why aren't you sharing a room with the Ayres girls?"

"I'm tired of the smell of stale cologne water, that's why."

"Talk about smells!" said Dr. Lorimer. He brushed his sister aside and closed the window on the nauseating alley. "After all the stuff you've read about Mexico, don't you know enough to keep your window shut at night? Vera Cruz is rotten with fever; I've warned Mr. Maury that he'd better get those people up to Córdoba without delay."

Andrew Lorimer sat down on the bed, which creaked beneath his weight. He was a tall man of twenty-eight, nearly ten years older than Sally, with a well-shaped head—the dark red hair worn fashionably long—set on broad shoulders. His handsome face, with high, harsh Scottish cheekbones, was already marked by two vertical lines between his brows. His voice was all North Carolina, drawling and deceptively sweet.

"Let me take your coat, Andrew. You look so tired."

He watched her hang the black coat carefully behind the door. Another man, not an exasperated brother, might have found Sally charming then, when the wide sleeves of the white cambric wrap fell back from her slender arms and the tawny hair swung in a heavy wave across her shoulders. But Andrew's ideal of a woman's charm had been fixed by his mother and his sister Helen; he had laughed at Sally's looks in the days when she was like a baby bird, all beak and golden eyes, and he was still blind to the promise of her beauty.

Sally sat down again on her window sill with her hands folded demurely in her lap.

"Well," she said, "I suppose the discussion has come to an end, downstairs?"

"Yes—not quite in disorder, you'll be sorry to hear."

"Why should there be disorder?"

"Oh—they had an argument about naming the new colony. Matthew Maury is too modest; he doesn't want it to be called Mauryville, as I think it ought to be."

"Did they decide on any name?"

"Carlóta, for the Empress of Mexico."

"They must all have worked very hard last winter," said Sally carefully, "to have increased the value of the land, as Mr. Maury says, a hundredfold already."

Andrew grunted. "He makes the place sound like an earthly paradise. My God, I hope he's right! Vera Cruz hasn't been much of an introduction to Mexico. I walked as far as the plaza with Jack Avery before dark, and we agreed we'd never seen— never imagined—such filth and squalor in a town. And those damned great vultures hanging in the air above the shops, above the houses, ready to scavenge carrion everywhere—it's worse than any battlefield."

"But Mexico itself is beautiful," said Sally. "I'm sure Uncle Andrew's house has a lovely garden, with roses and a fountain; and don't you suppose there'll be a patio, like the pictures in that book I showed you? You know there's a big stable, where you'll keep your carriage horses, and when you're famous—"

"Famous in Mexico City!" said Andrew. There had been many occasions when the carriage and the patio had fired his own imagination, but obviously this was not to be one of them. He leaned forward with his elbows on his knees, and ran his hands wearily through his red hair.

"We may be taking a big risk by going on to Mexico," he said. "Dick Maury says the highway is in bad repair between Puebla and the capital. He claims it's well policed, at least, by French patrols and units of Maximilian's new army, but Jack Avery's bankers told us a different story. They say one coach out of every four, more or less, is stopped by bandits, capable of everything from robbery under arms to actual murder, and the only safe way to travel is in a convoy with the silver mule trains going and coming from the coast. God knows how that can be arranged . . . I tell you, I felt so down tonight before dinner that if it weren't for that damnable oath they made me take never to return to the United States, I'd have booked our passage on the first steamer back to New Orleans."

"You worry too much about Seward and the oath. I'm sure it was only done to catch votes at the Congressional election. It'll be repealed in two years time—you'll see."

"I do hate to hear a woman babbling about elections. Especially when she's a minor and not affected by the oath. I'm the one who has to live with the knowledge that I can't go home again!"

Sally was silent. Her brother looked up at her with something like appeal in his eyes. They were slate-blue, the color of northern seas, now faintly bloodshot from the nights of drink and talk aboard the *Jupiter*.

"Sally, here's a suggestion I've been asked to make. An idea Mr. Maury had. He says it can be dangerous for women to go straight up to the Cold Country from Vera Cruz, because of the altitude. He feels you might like to break your journey and spend a while at Carlóta Colony on the way."

It was not the proposal she had dreaded hearing, and Sally was taken unawares.

"That was very kind of Mr. Maury," she said slowly. "But where would you be while I was at Carlóta?"

"In Mexico City, of course, looking the practice over. But before very long, I'd be coming back again to the settlement."

"Why? Could you leave the practice easily, once you'd looked it over?"

"I could sell it, Sally."

"Sell Uncle Andrew's practice?"

"If I thought it was my duty to settle at Carlóta, yes."

He saw her discomfiture, and sat straighter on the bed, pinching the disordered ruffles of his shirt into neat folds.

"Sally, in Córdoba province there's a growing community of our own people. Mr. Maury—and Dick—made me realize to-night that the Southerners in Mexico are real pioneers, with nearly as many hardships to face as the people who crossed the Rockies twenty years ago. They've got homes and orange groves, yes, but they haven't got a school yet, nor any sort of hospital, and in sickness they've had to rely on home nursing, unless they wanted to try the herb remedies some old Mexican witch doctor peddles round the settlement. Maybe it's up to me to provide the medical care our own friends need, instead of going among strangers in the city. Oh, I admit it's not a new idea. Jack Avery, and Fothergill, and some of the others, proposed it on the boat. But it took Matthew Maury to make me see that it might be my duty to give my services to American exiles like ourselves."

"I don't think of myself as an exile!" said Sally, starting up. "We're moving on, that's all, just as father and mother moved on when they were young! Father never called himself an exile! He became an American and a loyal one, but often, when he told how far he and Uncle Andrew had traveled from their old home, he'd say to me, 'The Scots are the wayfarers of the world, Sally—remember that!' "

"You make my father sound like the Wandering Jew," said Andrew.

"*You* make us sound like refugees."

"Well," said Andrew, "God knows I never expect anything but opposition from you, but I was just simple enough to think that you mightn't be against the idea of settling at Carlóta, among people of our own sort."

"They may be your sort of people, Andrew; they certainly aren't mine."

"That's a reflection on you, then—not on them. Some of them come from the finest families in the South, and every one of them, man or woman, has been a great deal kinder to you than you deserve. Or than they would be, if they knew you as well as I do."

She chose to ignore his last words and clasped her hands, with an earnestness which might have melted him.

"They *are* charming, I know that, and I've tried to be nice to them—"

"Nice? To Mrs. Avery and Blanche, for instance? I've seen you deliberately walk away from them on deck or in the saloon —of course you much preferred the company of that old Yankee from Havana. You consistently snubbed Jack Avery, one of the best fellows who ever lived, and who admires you, God knows why—"

"Yes, God knows why," said Sally bitterly. "Are you trying to marry me off to Captain Avery? Because I don't intend to spend the rest of my life listening to his version of Pickett's Charge, or what happened the night the Yankees set fire to his mother's cotton gin. He's very handsome, I grant you that; but he's only got two ideas to knock together in his head."

"You might go further and fare worse than Jack Avery."

"Suppose I'm not interested in going any distance at all in the matter of finding a husband?"

"I swear I don't understand you, Sally. When Helen was your age she had a score of beaux, and she enjoyed their admiration like any normal girl."

"And she waited until twenty-seven to get married."

"Because she gave up the best years of her life to trying to make a lady out of you."

"No, Andrew. Helen told me herself, the night before her wedding, that she had made up her mind never to marry until she met her true love. And neither will I. Only it won't be somebody like Charles Cartwright."

"Who, then?"

The candle flames stood up like two spears in the breathless night. Between them Sally's face was tinged with gold, and softened in the contemplation of a dream.

"I don't know yet," she said, and for once there was something like a drawl in her clear voice. "Not—someone very courtly

and formal and . . . rich and . . . important to himself, like
Charles. I think . . . a man of action."

It was so strange to see Sally in this mood, rapt away all
in a moment from her constant concern with practical things,
that Andrew was for a moment without words. But he recovered
himself, and said in his usual scoffing tone:

"Men of action must be a dime a dozen among the bachelors at Carlóta."

"Don't let's go to Carlóta, Andrew . . . dear."

The spell her own words had evoked still lent that unusual
gentleness to her voice, and the young man, with a half-smile,
said:

"Don't worry, Sal. Matthew Maury and I agreed, at the
end of our talk, that I could do better by going straight to
Mexico."

"Oh! Oh, Andy!" She flung herself upon him, seizing his
unresponsive hands. "Oh, I'm so thankful, and so glad! I knew
you couldn't really mean to throw away the wonderful chance
that Uncle Andrew gave you! Think of taking his place at the
School of Medicine, and in the hospitals, and all the new interesting friends you'll be sure to make!"

"I certainly shall," said Andrew. He held her at arm's
length, and looked up at her, still with the little sarcastic smile.

"Mr. Maury is sailing for Europe in a very short time.
Well, you heard that at dinner—he's off to London, to bring
Mrs. Maury and the younger children out here before the end
of May. But he's going to give me letters of introduction to General Magruder at the Land Office, and Mr. Gwin, and other
Southern gentlemen who're trying to relocate all the veterans
who crossed the Rio Grande since last April. He wants me to
spend the three months of his absence in the capital—you staying at Carlóta while I'm gone—and then decide, after giving
Mexico a fair trial, if I want to take the practice he offers me,
or not."

She stared down at him as he lounged on the bed, and all
the softness, all the gaiety and relief went out of her face.

"I'm much obliged for Mr. Maury's plans for my welfare," she said. "I decline them absolutely. I will not be packed off to the Carlóta Colony like a troublesome child while I've a house and land of my own waiting at Cuernavaca. And his plan for you, which you think so fair-minded, is far more dangerous than a simple invitation to join the colony. He means to involve you with men who are not here as planters or farmers. With politicians—men trying to keep the Confederacy alive in Mexico. And you know yourself that General Lee advised them all, and especially Mr. Maury, to give up the colonizing schemes."

Andrew knitted his brows. He knew only too well that Robert E. Lee, his hero, had spoken out strongly and publicly against the Maury plan.

"Don't be melodramatic," he said. "Maury and Magruder aren't plotting to invade Texas, or overthrow the United States government, merely to resettle the veterans; what's wrong with that?"

"But in every one of those groups and settlements they'll tell the old stories and nurse the old enmities, and they'll foster and cherish what Lee and Lincoln—yes, and our own father—prayed would soon die: the hating and the rancor of the war."

She spoke sorrowfully but calmly. If he had been listening to the tone he would have recognized a woman's voice and not a stubborn child's. But Andrew Lorimer was suddenly possessed by rage.

"And *you* hoped it would all be forgotten by this time, didn't you?" he said.

"We can't let hatred poison the rest of our lives. Let go my arm, please. You're hurting me."

"You can forget that your own sister was murdered by these swine? You can forgive them for what they did to Helen and her child?"

"Don't you believe Helen has forgiven them now?"

"*I* have not," said Andrew Lorimer. He sat forward on the bed. He dragged Sally down until her face was on a level with his own.

"I haven't forgotten anything," he said, and the sweat stood out on his brow. The little crowded room, with the shut door and window, seemed to enclose Sally in a prison of heat. She tried to pull her arm away. He held her fast.

"Do you expect me to forget how you welcomed Sherman's raiders to my father's house?" he said.

"You promised me!" She was kneeling by his side, kept there by his hand, and her pale face was of a sudden wet with tears. "Over and over again you promised, at Fayetteville before we left and then at New Orleans, that you would never taunt me with that lie again!"

"Are you sure it was a lie?"

In the gold-flecked depth of her eyes he might have read the truth of that wild night, just a year before, when Sherman's Bummers set fire to defenseless Fayetteville, and rode off with their loot to look for more plunder along the river and in the piney woods. For Sally had watched by her father's sickbed, looking from the dying face on the pillow to the glare in the sky as the resin camps went up in a crackle of golden light. Had watched, trying to calm the hysterical old servant, as separate torches kindled at those flames began dancing in a maudlin procession toward the little Presbyterian manse, and swarthy bearded faces under crazily feathered hats became visible beyond the little picket fence. Had gone out alone between the horses trampling and crowding into the yard.

"I didn't welcome the Bummers," she said. "I met them at the garden gate. I didn't speak one word more than I had to. I asked them to respect the church and cemetery. That was all."

"No, that wasn't all. Maggie swore you received their lieutenant in the parlor, and offered him cake and wine."

"We'd had nothing to bake a cake with for over a year, and the only wine in the house was the bottle of port prescribed for father, and that was in his room. You should know Maggie McClymont too well to believe her fabrications. She was upstairs with father, terrified out of what wits she ever had, when the Yankees came."

"Half the countryside believed in the fabrication, as you

call it. It tallied so well with what everybody knew of Sally Lorimer, who preached Abolition and disloyalty to the South from the time she was a girl at school."

"I only said on weekdays what my father said in the pulpit every Sunday of his life."

She watched for the moment when his grasp would relax, wrenched herself free of him and stumbled to her feet. Her cambric wrap caught and tore on the brass hasp of her little trunk.

"Andrew, this is the last time I'm going to talk about the night the Bummers came. I did ask the lieutenant to come indoors, that's true. I regarded it as a matter of life and death to explain that father was a minister of the Gospel and very—very ill. I wish, now, I had talked to him outside. But I had to make my mind up fast. I was all alone with a dying man and a half-witted servant, and I wasn't quite eighteen. What would you have had me do, Andrew—shoot the lieutenant with his own gun?"

"There were Southern girls of seventeen, and younger," said Andrew, "who met their country's enemies with pistols in their hands."

"Oh, spare me that," said Sally Lorimer contemptuously. "Spare me the Southern heroines with pistols in their pantalettes, who saved the old plantation at the saber's point. Pistols indeed! I don't know how to load a pistol, much less fire it. But you carry a gun, Andrew—why don't you teach me how to use it? It may be needed where I'm going. Because I'm going right on to Cuernavaca, and if need be I'll go there alone. I'll take the train up to Mule Pass tomorrow, and then the coach—"

"Stop it, you little fool," said Andrew, "do you want to rouse the house?" He looked at her, scowling. She was beside herself with fatigue and excitement, but there was a resolution in her face which overmastered him. "All right," he said sullenly, "you win. We'll go to Mexico together, and we'll stay there —until Matthew Maury comes back from Europe at the end of May."

Chapter Two

COLD RIVER

THE GREAT HIGHWAY, drawn across Mexico like a sprawling letter Y, ran from the Gulf of Mexico to the Rio Grande. It began at Merida, in the state of Yucatán which had been loyal to Maximilian ever since his arrival, and went on through Vera Cruz and Mexico City to a little town called Querétaro, where the Esperanza mine had yielded the fire-opals his Empress wore. Beyond Querétaro the highway forked. One branch went northeast through San Luis Potosí to Saltillo and Monterrey, towns held by strong French garrisons; the other northwest to Durango, which since the evacuation of Chihuahua had become the end of the French lines of communication in Mexico.

The key section, from Vera Cruz to the capital, was just short of three hundred miles long. The first lap was easy going. To transport European troops out of the fever belt to healthier regions of the Hot Country, French Army engineers had laid down fifty miles of railroad track from Vera Cruz to Paso del Macho. At the railhead, which Americans called Mule Pass, a coach operated by the Diligencias Generales took travelers on into the subtropical beauty of Tierra Templada and up through the cactus ranges into Tierra Fría, the Cold Country, where the capital stood.

Every morning, while stars still hung low over the railroad shacks and tin-roofed posadas of Mule Pass, six anxious passengers, a Mexican coachman and three armed guards came yawning out to the diligence, where grooms were backing the first team of eight mules between the shafts. The leather portmanteaus and cowhide trunks were painfully hoisted up and strapped to the roof, while sleepy Indian servants brought bread and hot bitter chocolate for the passengers and last night's warmed-over tamales for the crew. At daybreak the Mexican mountains echoed to the French bugles, the Tricolore came up with the sun, and a French patrol rode out to escort the diligence on the first five miles of its journey.

This routine was repeated at the next and cooler daybreak outside the Hotel de France in rose-hung Orizaba, under the white peak which Sally had seen from the sea. The third start was always the worst, in the cold dawn which broke over battle-scarred Puebla, but after that there was a comfortable halt at Río Frío for the midday meal, and an entry by nightfall into Mexico. If all went well, the worst which could happen to travelers was extreme fatigue, for the jolting as the coach rolled down and up the dry gullies called barrancas was hard to endure, and so were the long walks on foot, to spare the mules, as they toiled over mountain passes stretching high above the clouds. Sally Lorimer, at noon on the fifth of March, looked quite exhausted as the diligence lumbered down the last hill on the road to Río Frío.

Andrew, sitting opposite and facing the horses, was smitten with pity at the sight of the small dusty face under a round hat with a black feather, now decidedly out of curl. The four men who were their fellow passengers, and who had traveled the road many times before, had swathed their mouths and nostrils with heavy silk scarves to keep out the dust which settled in the coach with every turn of the wooden wheels. It had got into Sally's eyes and throat and made her cough, but she had not complained —either of the dust or of any other difficulty in their four hard days of traveling. Only an occasional question betrayed her impatience to reach Mexico.

"What time is it, Andrew, please? My watch has stopped."

"It's just gone twelve. We'll be on time at Río Frío."

The four men traveling with them stirred and yawned.

"If we're coming into Río Frío then the patrol is late," snapped one, who spoke with a Prussian accent, and had complained steadily throughout the journey.

"I see troopers at the bridge ahead," said Andrew Lorimer.

"Mexicans?" asked Sally, letting down the window and craning out to see.

"French, I think. They're coming out to meet us, anyhow."

The cluster of French uniforms at a stone bridge several hundred yards ahead resolved itself into a cavalry detachment, riding hard towards the diligence. Sally heard a voice shout an order in Spanish, and drew her head in sharply as a cloud of dust rose all around the coach. She heard the ratchets squeal as the driver applied the brake, and then the diligence began to pull in to the side of the road, with the troopers surrounding it in a double file of sweating horseflesh and saddle leathers. The passengers' view of the road was suddenly cut off by a shifting procession of army boots, the spurs cruelly flecked with blood, thrust deep into European stirrup irons. The coach swayed dangerously.

"What are you doing, you damned fools!" shouted Andrew Lorimer. "You'll have us over!"

"*Oho! un Anglais!* An Englishman!" The answering shout, with a note of laughter in it, came from the middle of the troop. Then the coach came safely to a standstill, two wheels grinding against the stone curb of the village street.

"Mesdames, messieurs, you may get out of the diligence, if you please."

Andrew jumped down first and gave his hand to Sally, the only lady present; the four other travelers followed. The coach had been halted outside a wooden shack with a sign in tipsy lettering: CANTINA EL ESPECIAL. Across the wide empty street, behind a low stone wall, stood their real destination, the posthouse of Río Frío, with two men in French uniforms on guard before the door. Barring the way was a fluid, double line of troopers,

and out in front a man on a tall gelding whose coat, beneath the
dust, had been groomed to bright brown satin.

Sally looked up at the man on horseback. His whimsical
face was tanned and weather-beaten, and there were wrinkles
at the corners of eyes accustomed to the glare of a sun even
stronger than the sun of Mexico. The closely cut hair visible beneath his képi seemed almost white, and alone among the
bearded men around him he was clean-shaven, with a scar seam-
ing the brown skin of his jaw. He was covered from head to
foot in the dust of the highway, but his accouterments, patent-
leather greaves and pipe-clayed gaiters, had plainly been brought,
before his ride began, to the highest pitch of grooming. Between
dark-blue cutaway and red trousers he wore a pale-blue cotton
sash with a pistol butt protruding from the folds. A saber with
a plain, gleaming hilt was run through his stirrup strap to hang
at the pommel of his saddle. He sat his motionless horse like a
Marshal of France taking the salute at a Longchamps review,
and he wore a sergeant's chevrons on his sleeve.

"What is the meaning of this, sergeant?" barked the Prussian passenger, and was stopped by a hand held up for silence.
Horsemen in a variety of uniforms were coming from all points
of the deserted village. The man on the chestnut gelding, who
appeared to be in command, listened to what they had to say
while his narrowed eyes took stock of the five men and one
woman who stood, impatient and at a disadvantage, by the door
of the diligence.

"All right!" he said at last. "*La soupe* for all, then eight
men back to patrol the Black Forest, from the Llano Grande
down to the village, until the carriages arrive. Sentries at the
bridge and the road to the Mine House. Stables for the rest, and
tell Corporal Fournier I'll be with him at once . . . Now,
madame! Now, gentlemen!" His hand flicked to his képi in a
quick salute. "I owe you an apology, I think. I forced your
driver out of his way abruptly, but there's no cause for alarm.
The posada is closed on account of a serious incident: you'll
have to put up with the cooking of the Especial."

"But how about the mules to take us on?" asked Andrew.

"The mules, Lamotte?" the sergeant said, aside.

"We found them in the stable, sergeant. No groom, but—"

"All right. You hear, monsieur? The team is here, you can proceed on your journey after your meal. Lamotte! Give Rataplan a good rubdown."

He swung out of the saddle, patted the chestnut's shoulder, and threw the reins to a trooper before turning back to the travelers for Mexico.

"Will you all have the goodness to go inside the cantina *and stay there?*"

"I object," said the Prussian passenger. "By what authority do you presume to give us orders?"

The sergeant's whimsical face grew stern.

"By the authority of the Supreme Commander in Mexico, Monsieur le Maréchal Bazaine," he said.

There were some men, as Sally had often noticed, who appeared to far greater advantage on horseback than on foot. The French sergeant was not one of them. He was not as tall as the angry Prussian or Andrew Lorimer, but his tough and wiry body had been drilled into such perfect balance that merely by standing still he continued to dominate the situation. The Prussian alone opposed him.

"I refuse to be browbeaten by a noncommissioned officer!" he burst out. "I am the Baron Lensdorf, carrying letters of introduction from His Majesty the King of Prussia to the Emperor Maximilian: I demand to be treated with the proper respect."

"Welcome to Mexico," said the sergeant cheerfully. "If you want to know *my* name, it's Franchet. Franchet Pierre, Jean, Louis; sergeant, First Regiment the Foreign Legion, Colonel Saussier; regularly stationed at Saltillo, if you care to make a complaint in the proper quarter. Good day to you!" And he made to turn away.

"Sergeant," said Andrew Lorimer, the authority in his voice more convincing than the Prussian's bluster, "I think you owe us some sort of explanation. What sort of incident has

taken place here? The place seems quiet enough. Where is the
Mexican force which should have met us? Are we ourselves in
any danger?"

"I don't want to alarm the lady," the Frenchman said.

"I'm not alarmed," said Sally.

He studied the composed, self-willed mouth, and the gloved
hands quietly clasped upon her reticule.

"Very well, madame." He made her a little bow, and looked
at Dr. Lorimer.

"Five members of a diplomatic mission were attacked and
robbed yesterday in the woods we call the Black Forest, on their
way from Mexico to Vera Cruz. Three of them were severely
wounded. They were brought into Río Frío by Mexican troops,
who," he hesitated, "are now in pursuit of the criminals. One
of the victims has since died. The two who escaped with minor
injuries rode back to Xoquiapan and raised the alarm. Does
that answer your questions, monsieur?"

"One more!" said Andrew. "Did you bring any medical aid
for the survivors?"

"The Court Physician is on his way from Mexico."

"The Court Physician!" Andrew's lips pursed in a sound-
less whistle. "Sergeant, I'm a doctor. I'm at your service now."

"Lucky!" said the sergeant laconically. "Follow me."

"Sally, go into the restaurant and get some food. You'll be
all right. There are women there." Andrew's hospital knapsack
was already in his hand. He always carried it in the pocket of
his frock coat—the battered little case he had been issued as a
First Assistant Surgeon, whose duty was to find and tend the
wounded on the field. Sally watched him hurry after the sergeant, his long-limbed lope catching up easily with the Frenchman's more compact stride.

She turned to El Especial. Her fellow passengers were already inside the cantina, arguing about the incident and the bill
of fare; it was not the first such incident, or delay, they had experienced on the great highway. Sally hesitated at the open door.
There were women there, but such women—two old crones bent

over an array of pungent cooking crocks, with their copper-colored faces lit by the flicker of the wood stove, and a painted drab in a pink satin dress and ballroom slippers, setting plates of doubtful cleanliness on a table covered with crumbs and smears of some red sauce. Sally's nerves and appetite rebelled. She looked back thoughtfully at the inn yard, where some of the Frenchmen had started bivouac fires and were slinging their cooking pots from tripods of stacked bayonets. One trooper, who had carried a great sheepskin full of wine on his back, was pouring it into their tin cups.

Deserted, the wide straggling street of Río Frío ran on to-wards the last pass, eleven thousand feet higher than the swamps of Vera Cruz, which guarded the approach to Mexico. Street and impoverished houses lay in a wide plateau, divided into fields in various stages of cultivation, and ringed with mountains thickly forested with evergreens. Down the flank of one of these, where the trees had been cut, a gash of yellowish green shale ran almost from the crest to the brawling torrent from which Cold River took its name. Near the river stood the church, with thick adobe buttresses and slit windows, looking more like a fortress than a place of worship. While Sally watched, one of the French troopers pushed the church door open, and through the hum of the bivouac she heard the creaking of the rusty hinge. Then two more men appeared from the posada. They carried a long trestle board with a shape upon it—a shape so wrapped in blankets that it was hardly human, but with a hand and arm trailing from the woolen folds. The hand struck the church step with a sound quite unlike the blow of living flesh on stone. None of the troopers troubled to look round. They saw death every day. They felt no need to show any respect, or even interest, as the stranger's body was carried past them into the church. Weary after the long hard ride from Mexico, they were far more interested in their food and drink, or in staring speculatively at Sally Lorimer as she suddenly lifted Andrew's heavy surgical bag out of the coach and carried it into the inn.

The sala, or main room of the posada, was long and low,

with heavy rafters and small barred windows which kept the sunlight out. It was cold, although gray wood ash showed that a fire
had burned for hours on the hearth, and smelled strongly of
blood and suffering. A table long enough to seat twenty-four
persons had been pushed against one wall, and chairs for as
many guests piled between the table and door to make space for
a low, broad couch on which a man lay moaning beneath a pile
of blankets and serapes. A French corporal knelt beside him,
holding a glass to his lips. In an armchair pushed close to one of
the windows half sat and half lay another man, of whom Sally
could see almost nothing, for Andrew's tall figure was between
them, and Andrew was bandaging the man's right arm. Sergeant
Franchet, alert as a gun dog after game, was standing beside him
with a roll of adhesive plaster in his hand.

"I—I brought your other bag, Andrew." She got it out in a
whisper, and Pierre Franchet swung around.

"Good girl—I'll need it," said Andrew, without raising his
eyes from his work. "Put it down on a chair—anywhere, that's
right."

Sally put the bag on the nearest of the dining chairs. She
saw a pile of blood-soaked towels and table napkins pushed
underneath the table. She took off her hat, pelisse and gloves,
and laid them aside.

"What are you doing, madame?" snapped the French sergeant. "My orders were that no one was to come in here!"

"I'm going to stay," said Sally quietly, as much to Andrew
as to the truculent figure in the blue cutaway coat. "There must
be something I can do to help."

"Doctor!" said Franchet. "I tell you this is no place for
your wife!"

Andrew ignored him.

"Dr. Herzog," he said in an easy and encouraging tone,
"how does that feel? You've got a beautiful wound, a clean in-
and-out; sure to heal by first intention."

"Thank you, doctor." The man in the armchair sat up
weakly. "Don't waste time on me. Help Monsieur Bompard! I

couldn't . . . my right arm, and then I had no instruments to get the bullet out."

"Never mind about that," said Andrew. "You brought him through the night alive, and we'll take care of him. I've got everything necessary, bullet probes included."

"With a gun and a bullet probe you're well equipped for life in Mexico," said Pierre Franchet.

"Give Dr. Herzog a glass of spirits of ammonia, please," snapped Andrew. "You want to help, do you, Sally? That's very noble of you. Your famous Spanish would come in handy now if you'd go out to the kitchen and ask the cook to prepare some broth, or soup, for Dr. Herzog. Then get her to give you some strong towels, and anything white and clean for bandages, and you start to roll me some, will you? I've used up all I had in the knapsack. Can you do that?"

"Of course I can."

Andrew was already applying his wooden stethoscope to the chest of the man on the couch as she spoke. Neither he nor the French corporal looked up from the patient when she tiptoed past them, going towards the door which, as a jerk of Andrew's thumb indicated, led to the back premises of the posada. Drawing a long breath of relief, she hurried down a short stone corridor, encumbered by huge leather trunks and ornate saddles, into a cooking-place which was a great improvement on the Cantina El Especial. Here a bright fire was burning, and a wooden dresser held colored bowls and a pile of plates ready to be set on the table for a meal. Flitches of bacon and strings of onions and dried peppers were hanging from the rafters, while covered pottery crocks on a brown-tiled stove suggested that an ample dinner was in preparation. But the kitchen was empty. A child's huarache beside an overturned stool and a blue rebozo caught on the handle of the back door were evidence of a hasty flight.

Sally went anxiously through the sculleries, the larders, and stood at the top of the dark wine-cellar stairs. She called "Please!" and *"Por favor!"* outside the doors of silent rooms. There was only one discovery to encourage her: a closet left half-open, in which a glimpse of white led her to the sheets and towels so urgently required by Andrew.

She carried the linen back to the kitchen table, made the first cut with a poultry knife, and began to tear a sheet in strips. Through the window, facing back along the road to Puebla, she saw a new view of Río Frío. It was not deserted after all. Beyond the church, which was separated from the kitchen-wing of the posada only by a rough garden where clumps of blue iris flowered among low shrubs, and across the river, stood a one-story, white-washed building from which the Mexican flag was flying. Outside, with their backs to the wall, with infants in their arms and a few lean chickens scraping in the dust at their feet, sat a silent row of Indian women.

Sergeant Franchet appeared round the corner of the posada, shouting an order to someone out of Sally's line of vision. She saw him stop and shift the heavy leather strap which held his *cartouchière* in place across his breast. He looked unutterably tired. Then, as if driving himself to make the effort, he snapped into a quick marching step, swung across the yard, and made his appearance at the kitchen door.

"Have you come to fetch the soup for Dr. Herzog, sergeant?" Sally asked.

"He says he doesn't want any. He's in a bad way, if you ask *me*," said the sergeant. "But look here! Where have the cook and the maids got to? You oughtn't to be here alone, madame."

He listened scowling to Sally's explanation.

"It beats everything," he said, staring around. "There were five women in the place when we got here, and I never dreamed they'd take to the woods with all the rest. Well, now we'll have to get in the *soldaderas* to clean up the sala, that's all."

"Who are the *soldaderas*?" In all her haste and anxiety, Sally had to pause on the unfamiliar word.

"You see the *cuartel*—across the river there? The barracks, from which our heroic Mexican allies vanished like smoke after yesterday's disturbance? Well, those good ladies waiting patiently outside the door for the heroes to return, are *las soldaderas*."

She looked up at him in some perplexity. In full sunlight, with his képi in his hand, Pierre Franchet looked younger than the thirty-five years Sally had mentally given him. His hair, she saw, was not white but ash blond, sun-bleached at the temples and above the ears. His eyes, when he opened them wide, were a reflective, smoky gray.

"You mean a *soldadera* is a soldier's wife?"

"Well, she follows the troops," said Franchet noncommittally. "And believe me, Maximilian's Irregulars on the march, with the women carrying their brats, and the poultry and the pigs coming along on strings, are a sight to make Bonaparte turn in his grave. However, it's *el costumbre del país,* the custom of the country—you'll get used to it."

Sally did not respond to his smile. Sheltered as her life had been, she had heard of camp followers, and believed the sergeant's explanation verged on the improper. But she had no idea how to snub a man who spoke her own language haltingly, and was giving more than half his attention, as she could guess, to any sound which might come from the sala.

"I thought you said the Mexican troops had gone to pursue the criminals," she said drily, and Pierre Franchet laughed.

"They must have guessed that we'd be coming in, as soon as they knew whom they'd rescued. And—they're not overly fond of being caught in the cross fire."

"Whom *did* they rescue? Someone very important, if a whole troop of cavalry was sent out from Mexico?"

"A half-company . . . Yes, they are important. It was a Belgian party, headed by General Foury, sent by King Leopold II to inform his sister, the Empress Carlóta, that he had succeeded to the throne. They were wined and dined by the Emperor very lavishly for the past three weeks."

Sally started on a new roll of linen. She said:

"It seems odd that such important guests should have been allowed to start for Vera Cruz unguarded, when even coach passengers get some protection along the way. Is that the custom of the country too?"

The Frenchman nodded appreciation of her shrewdness. He had never had an opportunity of meeting a pretty girl who was also intelligent, and this was much more than a pretty girl. Behind Sally, in the kitchen window, a copper bowl was piled high with oranges, lemons and granadillas. Sally's hair seemed to blaze with new color in the light shining through the massed yellows of the fruits, and even her fingers seemed rosy by contrast with the linen sheets. The beauty struggling to be born in her pale face was very clear to Pierre Franchet.

"Apparently they miscalculated the departure of a silver convoy," he said. "Punctuality is not a Mexican virtue. You're sure to find that out during your visit to the capital."

Sally smiled. "We're going to *live* in the capital."

"Really? I supposed you were English tourists, come to see the sights. Only the English travel for pleasure in Mexico nowadays, madame."

"We are Americans, but how could you know that? I don't suppose my brother even told you his name, although we heard yours! He is Dr. Andrew Lorimer, formerly of the Confederate States Army, and I am *Miss* Lorimer, his younger sister."

It was said with a charming smile which should have earned Sergeant Franchet's politest bow. But his humorous, alert face grew suddenly serious. He snapped to attention and stood at point like a gun dog amazed to come across a plaster pheasant.

"Then are you by any chance related to the late Dr. Lorimer of Mexico?"

"He was our uncle. Oh, did you know him?"

Pierre Franchet seemed to choose his words with care.

"I never actually met him. But—I've served in this country for three years, mademoiselle; one couldn't be in the capital for three days without getting to know the Old Doctor by sight. He was here, there, and everywhere—a great character."

Sally sparkled. "And his house, sergeant—our house now —have you seen that too? In the Plaza de Santo Domingo?"

"I know the Plazuelita, yes—quite well. That's what they call it: the Little Square."

"It's a *fashionable* square, we were told."

"It's quite close to the Plaza Mayor, where the National Palace stands."

He saw her wrinkle her brow at the evasive answer and turned thankfully away as Andrew Lorimer came briskly into the kitchen. The doctor had removed his gray frock coat and rolled his shirt sleeves tightly above his elbows. His narrow black tie was loosened and his red hair ruffled, but he looked keener and more invigorated than Sally had seen him look for many months.

"Here's the bullet, sergeant," he said. "What d'you want it for—a souvenir?"

Something passed from his hand to Franchet's, and Andrew wiped the blood from his fingers with a cloth taken from the waiting pile.

"*Merci.*" It was more like a growl than a word of thanks. Sally saw with revulsion that the bullet, so lately taken from a living body, had spread its smear of red into the Frenchman's hard brown palm.

"This bullet was fired from a Springfield rifled musket. You knew that, eh, *docteur?*"

"I ought to. I've seen plenty of them."

"This is the first time," said Franchet, still staring at the bullet, "that we've had any evidence of American weapons in enemy hands farther south than San Luis Potosí. The Brownsville gun runners must be extending their business since their last raid across the border. If you'll pardon me for saying so—"

"Make no excuses," said Andrew curtly. "How Sherman's ruffians break the law is no longer any concern of mine. Sally! Can you make a stump bandage?"

"Yes, I think so," she said with a qualm.

"Get started then. But put all your stuff on the dresser, I want the table clear."

"What are you going to do, monsieur?"

"I'm going to operate. Dr. Herzog is in no danger, although he's weak from loss of blood, but this Mr. Bompard was shot

in the thigh at close range and he's in a bad way. There's a
fracture of the upper third of the femur, with the hip joint im-
plicated, and imminent danger of mortification setting in. I must
operate at once."

Sally tried to speak but could not. It was Sergeant Franchet
who snapped out:

"Not so fast, Dr. Lorimer. An amputation is a serious
matter."

"I'm aware of that," said Andrew testily. "I've considered
excising the injured portions of the femur, but there's been too
much damage done to the great vessels, and in any case far too
much time has been lost. The Surgeon General's rule was absolute in such cases: operate within twenty-four hours. It's twenty-
seven, at a rough count, since this man was shot. I'll work here,
on the deal table; it's a better size than that monstrous thing
in the sala, and there's a better light."

"Does the Belgian doctor agree that amputation is required?" said Sergeant Franchet, frowning.

"Absolutely."

"And Baron Bompard—is he conscious?"

"He was conscious when I extracted the bullet, because I'd
no morphine to give him. Corporal Fournier is giving him brandy
now. That's a capable man, your corporal. He's had more than
a little hospital experience, I should say."

"We don't inquire into a man's past experience, in the Foreign Legion."

"Probably not," said Andrew with a shrug. "Anyway I shall
need both of you to carry in the patient—and I want two of your
tarpaulins, quick as you please. Sally, have you hot water on the
stove?"

"Yes." She started forward, and threw a handful of pine
splinters on the fire.

"You can count on my men for any reasonable help," said
Franchet. "But *mon Dieu!* Even if your colleague agrees, and
the patient consents, *I* can't authorize you to perform an operation of such a serious nature—"

"Of course you can't. That's what comes of sending a sergeant to do a colonel's job, and you can tell the Supreme Commander I said so."

"Juarez sends colonels to do the sergeants' jobs," retorted Franchet. "I don't question your skill or your good judgment, sir. I'm only suggesting that you wait until the Emperor arrives with the Court Physician. You could consult Dr. Semeleder before you cut the man's leg off, couldn't you?"

"You never told us the Emperor was coming too!" cried Sally.

"No, I didn't tell you; our orders are to keep the Emperor's journeys up and down the highway as quiet as possible—or as he lets them be. But we came here as his advance guard, that's the truth of the matter, although he left Mexico before we did—we passed him on the way."

"Will he be here within the next half hour?" persisted Andrew.

The sergeant shrugged. "There's a hospitable hacienda, and a pretty lady, at Ayotla—there are *Mocho* houses all along the road where Don Maximiliano is always welcome. He got the news of this affair at four o'clock this morning—that's when he starts the day's work, or so he says—so he would be quite ready for a second breakfast at Ayotla, where we passed his carriage and the Austrian Hussars. Then he'd stop at Xoquiapan, to hear General Foury's story and eat midday dinner with the commandant. I can't tell you to an hour when he'll arrive, I swear."

"Quite so," said Andrew calmly. "Well, if he and his physician delay much longer, and I delay too, the Emperor Maximilian has an excellent chance of finding two corpses instead of one. If you're willing to take the responsibility of letting this Mr. Bompard die by default, I'm not. If all the crowned heads of Europe were on their way to Río Frío, and this man's life at stake, I tell you I would operate, and that's an end of it. Now then, Sally!"

She had quietly rinsed her hands after mending the fire, and gone to work quickly and deftly at the task he set her. But at the tone of his voice the scissors fell with a clatter on the dresser, and Sally turned apprehensively with the half-made stump bandage in her hand.

"I want you to give the anesthetic, Sally," said Andrew in his gentlest drawl.

"I—couldn't," she said. "I'd be afraid—"

"Don't force her," said Sergeant Franchet roughly. "It's not a job for a lady. I'll give the chloroform, if it must be done—"

"Sergeant Franchet," said Andrew. "I don't doubt you feel equal to performing the whole operation, but I need you to handle the limb, and Miss Lorimer has neat fingers; she'll give the anesthetic very well."

"But if I give the man too much, and kill him?" whispered Sally.

"There's not enough chloroform available to kill a cat," Andrew assured her. "Pull yourself together, Sally! I thought you prided yourself on your cool head in an emergency. Remember that emergency at the manse a year ago? You were telling me about it the other night at Vera Cruz. 'A matter of life and death,' you called it. This is the same sort of thing—life or death for a human being. Are you going to hesitate now?"

THERE WAS a cheap clock on the adobe wall advertising Wilcox and Gibbs sewing machines. In Sally's ears the pendulum sounded alarmingly loud as it ticked off the minutes, while Andrew directed the preparations to save a stranger's life. He was completely at his ease in the Mexican kitchen which offered him better operative conditions than he had ever known at the front. Dr. Lorimer had operated in wet woods where tarpaulin covers slung between the trees kept rain off the army surgeons and their patients; underneath the dripping eaves of farmhouses behind the Confederate lines; in barns where the stretcher loads of wounded occupied so much space that the doctors, with no place to lay down their instruments, held their knives between their teeth as they sutured and ligatured limbs torn by Minié ball and canister. He was actually humming as he watched Sally finish her bandages and cut a length of huckaback toweling to his orders. Trooper Lamotte brought in the tarpaulins, rolled and strapped as they were carried on the saddles, and one was tied down firmly over the kitchen table. Sally covered it with a clean sheet and laid a pillow at one end. The door and window were opened as wide as possible. Andrew took his instruments from their plush cases and rinsed them carefully before laying them out along the dresser: knives, forceps, scalpels, saw, with silk ligatures, needles, sutures and chloroform from the hospital knapsack. There was nothing to fill the Woods endermic syringe.

"No morphine!" he said cheerfully. "I hope Fournier kept the brandy bottle going. Ask Dr. Herzog to step in here."

The Belgian doctor, whose pale face Sally had only glimpsed across her brother's shoulder, came in on Lamotte's arm. He was a small man, inclining to stoutness, with heavy black stubble on his cheeks and chin, and his right arm bandaged and strapped closely to his side.

"This is Dr. Julius Herzog, Sally," said Andrew. "He'll explain the method of giving chloroform to you while I prepare the patient. Herzog, better sit down while you can."

Dr. Herzog smiled weakly. His dark eyes seemed to be asking for their sympathy.

"We are infinitely in your debt, mademoiselle—"

"Please don't try to talk," said Sally. She was shocked by the man's exhaustion. "Just show me—just point out what things I shall need. Or—Andrew said you might have soup—could you drink a little? It would give you strength—"

The sick man shook his head. "It would choke me, mademoiselle. I blame myself for this calamity to Baron Bompard. If I had been able to extract the bullet, his leg might have been saved—"

"Well," put in Sergeant Franchet, "why didn't you? The official physician to the Foury mission might at least have had a bag of instruments. I don't see any sign of yours."

"I was . . . not exactly . . . the official physician," said Dr. Herzog with an effort. "I'm not a surgeon, sergeant. I am a student of the brain."

"I wish you'd kept your wits about you to more purpose, then," said Franchet with a glance at Sally for approval. "What was the sense of letting both the uninjured members of your party go off and leave you in the lurch? What sort of brain study do you call that?"

"Sergeant, you talk too much," said Andrew, reappearing. "Sally, go find some butter while I wash my hands."

"I never saw a *toubib* wash his hands before!" said the irrepressible Franchet.

"I always wash up when I get the chance," said Andrew, with his hands in water. "Always have done, since I was a dresser for Professor Holmes. If you're ready, Herzog, we'll have the patient in."

He slipped off his brocaded vest and pistol holster, and with a grimace for his light gray trousers tied the second tarpaulin firmly round his waist. Dr. Herzog, rising painfully from his chair, directed Sally as she prepared a cone of toweling and plugged the small end with a wad of cotton. Andrew threw her a soft linen cloth.

"Better tie that round your head, unless you want your hair to reek of chloroform."

"No ether, doctor?" said Herzog.

"Devil a drop."

In fact the lack of ether meant little to Dr. Lorimer, who like most army surgeons swore by chloroform, but as he looked at his one professional helper he regretted being without a Lister's horseshoe tourniquet, big enough to control massive bleeding from the thigh. If Herzog collapsed, as seemed more than likely, and he had to fall back on Sergeant Franchet's all too loquacious help, things might go badly for the patient. But the Frenchman seemed calm enough, except that he couldn't take his eyes off Sally in the white coif which so oddly altered the balance of her features and revealed the hollowed cheeks and wide sensitive mouth of a woman wakening to compassion. Lamotte and Fournier brought the patient in, with the rhythmic broken step of men who had carried many stretchers through the desert sand. To spare Sally as much as possible he had been prepared for operation in the sala, and the lower part of his body covered with a sheet. They had plied him with brandy until the brown liquid ran from the corners of his mouth, but he was not insensible to pain. He was a big, fair Fleming, and it was probable that the physical strength which kept him aware of suffering had also helped him to survive his ordeal of the night. But that strength was ebbing fast, although it was still enough to make him shriek with pain as the troopers laid him on the table, and thrash with all the remaining force of arms and shoulders when Dr. Herzog's Laennec stethoscope touched the bare skin of his chest.

"Pinion his wrists, men," said Andrew calmly. "Sally, are you ready?"

"Yes."

Sally's fingers were already dipped in butter. As gently as possible, while the patient's head still jerked from side to side, she greased his nostrils and his upper lip. Andrew passed a one-drachm measure of the precious chloroform across the table. Four men, now, were holding down the screaming patient, and Franchet, with his teeth sunk in his lower lip, looked for a moment from the unfortunate man to the girl in the white coif who stood behind his pillow. Would she fail them now? Faint, or treat them to a disabling bout of hysteria? The small left hand took the cone of toweling and lowered it unwaveringly towards the patient's face. The right hand came up with the drachm measure. The towel was pressed firmly down, the chloroform began to drip into the cotton at the point of the cone. Bompard's voice began to diminish to a meaningless drone. His struggles ceased, and when Andrew touched one eyelid there was no reaction.

He pulled aside the sheet and Sally saw the naked, ruined limb of a grown man, the leg puffy and waxen. She saw the mass of lint and bandages removed from the gunshot wound, and the dexterity with which Dr. Herzog, in spite of his own dis-

ability, grasped the thigh in his left hand and pulled the skin
backward in the direction of the body. Franchet steadied and
straightened the lower leg at a nod from Andrew. The troopers
relaxed but retained their hold on the wrists at another nod; and
Sally for the first time in her life saw Andrew in his element.

"Bless Thy servant Andrew, and touch his hands with Thy
divine power of healing." The words of her father's evening
prayer came back to her as she looked from the unconscious face
on the pillow to the young surgeon. How little they had known,
the father and sisters in their quiet country parlor, of what those
hands had learned and done! The knife, held in those long fingers, slid into the drained and livid flesh. Blood poured out as
Andrew drew it completely around the limb in a circular motion.
Stooping as he began the circle, he slowly drew himself up as it
was completed, his hand, which had been extended and supine,
becoming prone and strongly flexed. As Dr. Herzog relaxed his
pull on the tissues, a flap of skin fell over the raw edges of the
wound.

Andrew used cold water and a sponge to swab the blood
away. The breathing of the three French soldiers was rasping
and loud. Andrew slid the knife round the limb a second time,
nearer to the knee, and shot an anxious look at Sally.

"Give him three drops more, Sal. And keep your head up.
Don't breathe in the fumes . . . Herzog, how is the pulse?"

She heard the voices from a distance. She watched the bright
knife make its red circle for the third time, saw the thigh bone
bared at the apex of the technically perfect, cone-shaped wound.
Andrew took up the saw.

At the first grating sound, when the saw bit into the bone
beneath the great trochantic, Sally was overtaken by a wave of
nausea. She fought it silently, compressing her lips and swallow-
ing down a mouthful of salt water, keeping her eyes fixed on the
patient's face, and trying to think of nothing but the faint breathing which puffed his blackened lips. She heard a shaken *"Mon
Dieu!"* from Pierre Franchet, white beneath the tan and gripping
the nearly severed limb until the marks of his hands showed

purple in the sick flesh he held. Then the sound of the saw stopped, and Franchet laid the severed limb on the waiting towels.

Andrew ligated the vessels, drew the flaps of the wound together in an oblique line of union to promote suppuration and applied sutures one inch apart. Lacking isinglass plasters he laid a wet dressing on the bleeding stump and fastened one of Sally's bandages over all.

"By God, *docteur,* that was quick work!" said Sergeant Franchet, wiping sweat from his sun-bleached hair.

Andrew glanced at the wall clock.

"Not bad!" he said, untying the tarpaulin round his waist and scowling fastidiously at the blood upon his boots. "I'm a little bit out of practice, though. We did four amputations to the hour at Gettysburg, with a pile of arms and legs outside the tent as high as our own heads— Hey, Sally! Sally! where are you going?"

Sally ran with her head down for the open air. Choked with the faint seeping fumes of the anesthetic and nauseated by the sight of raw flesh and bone, her blind instinct was to make for the river which promised cold water for her face and hands. But she was brought up short by the gray adobe buttress of the church so like a fort, and, doubling, found herself at the foot of the steps against which, an hour before, she had heard the sickening impact of a dead man's hand. That recollection sent her headlong into the rough garden, tripping on her long skirt as she stumbled between shrubs and clumps of iris to a crumbling stone seat against the wall. With the cloth snatched from her hair held to her mouth, she fought the recurrent waves of nausea until the physical weakness passed. It was succeeded by a rush of strong emotion which left her equally spent. A curtain had been raised, if only by a fraction, on what the reality of Andrew's life at the front had been, and in her admiration for his skill and resolution Sally for the first time in her life felt the prickings of humility. She laid her head against the sun-warmed stone, and wept.

"Mademoiselle!"

Pierre Franchet, in his heavy boots, must have moved fast

and quietly across the rough grass. Sally was scarcely aware of his approach before he sat down on the stone bench by her side.

"Don't cry, mademoiselle." He actually braced his arm behind her, so that Sally, in drawing away from the wall, could scarcely avoid coming in contact with the strong shoulder in the worn blue serge. "Please don't cry, because you were brave and wonderful, and it's all over now—"

"All over!" She looked with horror at the brown face, nearer her own than a stranger's face had ever been. "You don't mean—he's *dead?*"

"No, no, he came through it splendidly, the doctors say; he'll be all right. Here, drink a little of this."

He produced a battered flask and poured a measure of pale golden liquid into the tin cap. Sally sipped it doubtfully. It tasted like ice and flowers in her mouth, like flowers and fire as it went down.

"It isn't spirits, is it?"

"It's the juice of a cactus plant—the maguey," said Sergeant Franchet reassuringly. "It's the very best tequila from the province of Jalisco—food and drink in one. Don't be afraid of it."

"I'm not afraid of it." She took another sip, and the improvised cup was empty. The delicate aroma of the tequila had driven the fumes of chloroform from her head. Sally felt her fingers warm, her mind lucid and vividly aware of half a dozen small impressions—a neat patch in the sleeve of Franchet's cutaway, a carved date on the church wall beside them, the tight lemon-yellow rosettes of blossom on the shrubs which hid their corner of the yard from view.

"I thought they made pulque from the cactus plant," she said.

"Pulque is for peons," declared Sergeant Franchet. "For soldiers, it's tequila. Cactus pulp for a wound, cactus juice to give you heart—there's nothing like them for troops on the march. If I were a surgeon, I'd back the cactus against the chloroform any day."

She laughed at that, deliciously; with the white cloth that had made her face so oddly withdrawn and austere, thrown away; and the breeze from the pinewoods ruffling the soft hair at her temples. "The cactus and the chloroform!" Sally repeated. It seemed immensely funny. "Why not have it on the Mexican flag? Instead of the Eagle and the Cactus—the Cactus and the Chloroform!" She felt Sergeant Franchet's arm tighten against her shoulder. Mixed with the pungent scent of the yellow blossoms was the masculine odor of tobacco, harness oil and the body of a tired horseman. Sergeant Franchet bent his head towards her own. She felt an instant of complete relaxation, of the muscles as of the mind, and then the Puritan in Sally took command and brought her, blushing scarlet, to her feet. Without a word—with only a diffident, imploring look, she ran back across the yard as fast as she had run away.

Andrew met her at the kitchen door.

"Come on, Florence Nightingale, where have you been? A good nurse doesn't go off and leave the doctor to do her work, you know!"

"I'm very sorry," Sally said. "I *had* to go outside."

"Now you have to stay inside, is that quite clear? Herzog is next to useless, and our man will start throwing up that brandy any time now. Better find a basin, and look sharp."

"Did you have him taken to a bedroom?" she asked, looking at the empty, bloodstained table and the dreadful floor.

"Yes. Don't worry about all this; Fournier is sending in the barracks women to clean up. I thought you were nauseated when you ran out, but obviously not. What a color you have! You look as if you'd been at the brandy bottle too."

"Really, Andrew!" But honesty made her add, "I nearly fainted when you started to—use the saw."

"Never mind," said Andrew, and his hand rested approvingly on Sally's shoulder. "You did better than many a medical student at his first operation. I've seen them fainting right and left in Boston—"

"But not you, Andy!"

"Oh yes, me too, Sally," said Dr. Lorimer. "Once upon a time."

Chapter Three

LA PLAZA DE SANTO DOMINGO

THE EMPEROR OF MEXICO came to Río Frío in the late afternoon, in a procession of three coaches, escorted by a detachment of Austrian Hussars.

Sally watched his arrival through the window of the room where Baron Bompard, under a cradle improvised from two stools to hold the bedclothes off his amputated thigh, had passed from rending bouts of vomiting into the rigors and shivering which threatened the onset of pyemia. Andrew had sat by the bedside during the anxious hours. There was not much more a doctor could do now, and he knew it: nothing but watch the struggle for life on a face which as yet did not show the subtle signs of change believed by surgeons to presage death by asthenia. Bompard was still fighting for life when Franchet's patrol rode in to say that the Emperor Maximilian was within a mile of Río Frío.

"They'll waken Herzog, damn them!" said Andrew, as the troopers led their rested horses out of the inn stables, and orders were shouted and repeated while the French detachment formed a double file along the street and across the yard. He went quickly to the next room, where the Belgian doctor with the wounded arm was lying, and Sally, alone, stood up cautiously by the bedside to watch the Emperor of Mexico descend from the leading carriage.

It was a charming equipage of red, fawn and gold, drawn by six buff-colored mules with zebra-striped hoofs, wearing harness of fawn leather trimmed with scarlet and decked with scarlet plumes in silver sockets. An equipage designed for promenades in the Paseo or the Alameda rather than for an expedition to a desolate mountain village; and there was something incongruous in the sight of the two Hussars with slung carbines who took the place of liveried footmen, and jumped down outside the posada to lower the step for the Emperor.

The four foreign travelers who had come upcountry with the Lorimers, and who had passed the afternoon playing cards in the Cantina El Especial, were at the door to raise their hats to the Emperor, but there was no population to cheer in the village which fear of his mercenaries had emptied. The days were past when the appearance of Maximilian von Hapsburg brought out a dense throng of Indians to cry "Quetzlcoatl! Quetzelcoatl!" —for the humblest of his new subjects, in their simplicity, had at first believed in him as the reincarnation of Mexico's lost blond god of peace. All was silence now, and the ring of mountains echoed only to the voice of Sergeant Franchet shouting a brief order as the sabers of the French troopers flashed upward to their lips. Still the Emperor halted, smiling his set smile, with his tall gray hat in his hand and his black cloak thrown open, as if expecting further homage and applause. Then he walked across the yard and out of Sally's line of vision. The next thing she saw, with a great rush of relief, was three French Sisters of Charity in the habit of St. Vincent de Paul getting out of the small black coach which had followed the Emperor's to Río Frío.

Two of the nuns had relieved her of her duties before Maximilian appeared, and Sally, who had listened anxiously to the muffled sound of a long conversation in Dr. Herzog's room, was in the background behind the Sisters' ample coifs and skirts when he came in at last. Andrew, looking both anxious and arrogant, walked behind him with a stout elderly gentleman in a brown surtout, whom she rightly took to be Dr. Semeleder, the Court Physician. A younger man with a portfolio beneath his arm brought up the rear.

"Poor, poor Bompard! Poor dear fellow!" exclaimed Maximilian, as his eyes took in the tossing, restless head and the maimed body on the bed. "What a terrible calamity!"

He took one of the fluttering hands in his.

"Do you know me, Bompard?" he asked very gently. A jumble of words, in French and Flemish, gave him Baron Bompard's answer.

"He is delirious, Sire," said the Court Physician.

"And I had rather see a man delirious at this point than sinking into hebetude and coma," said Andrew Lorimer.

"Quite so, but he must sleep, my dear colleague, and under drugs if necessary."

Maximilian did not appear to be listening. He laid the patient's hand on the disordered cover, and burst out:

"This will have the worst possible effect in Europe! Eloin" —to the man with the portfolio—"you know my brothers-in-law as well as I do; how am I going to explain this murderous attack to them? King Leopold will demand a huge indemnity—and make this an excuse for recalling the Belgian Corps from Mexico."

"We must hope Baron Bompard will be spared, Sire," said the young man, with a side glance at Andrew.

"To go back to Brussels on one leg?" said Maximilian bitterly. His hand sought his golden beard, divided it with a nervous gesture and twirled at the two points. "Why did this have to happen just when I had assured my brother that we were making immense headway here in Mexico? The Emperor of Austria will say my subjects are no better than barbarians and outlaws, after this affront."

"Come, Sire," said his Court Physician briskly, "there's no need for such a desperate view. Here are four men living out of five—far better than we dared to hope for when we set out—and weeks must pass before the bad news need be known at Brussels. Be persuaded by me to leave both patients to their medical attendants, and do you take some refreshment after this exhausting day."

"My good Semeleder," sighed the Emperor, "I shall go into the church, and pray beside poor Huard's body."

The Emperor's prayers must have been very short. It was only a quarter of an hour before Miss Sally Lorimer, having had just time to tidy her dress and hair, was summoned to the sala, which the camp followers from the Mexican barracks had scrubbed and put in order, and found him talking cheerfully to his equerries.

In the light of a pine-log fire and a profusion of candles the sala now looked a very comfortable place. The bloodstained couch had disappeared and on a small table covered with a fine linen cloth a chocolate service made by the Taxco silversmiths was surrounded by dishes of tempting cakes and sweetmeats.

"Ah, here is Miss Lorimer." Maximilian set down his cup and rose as the girl came shyly into the long room. "Now I can thank you as you deserve for all you have done for our unfortunate guests." He held out his hand, while the six or seven men surrounding him made way, smiling, for Sally to enter the charmed circle of fire and candlelight.

"In Europe, gentlemen are not permitted to kiss an unmarried lady's hand," the Emperor said whimsically. "In Mexico, I may be permitted to salute the nurse! *Fraülein,* my blessings, and my grateful thanks."

The full red lips, the golden beard, clung for a moment to the small cold paw which never before had known such a salute. It was the famous *Küss die Hand* of the Archduke Maximilian, an expression of the charm which had made him so many friends when he first came to Mexico. Sally's fingers did not linger in his clasp.

"You are a great deal too kind, Sir. My brother did it all."

She had heard a purr of *Majestät* from the entourage as she hesitated in the doorway, but "Your Majesty" did not come easily to the American girl, and "Sire" she thought ridiculous. But the Emperor did not take the simpler form of address amiss. He smiled down at her with amused and friendly eyes.

"I know your brother performed the operation, but you gave the anesthetic, didn't you? You see, we've found out all about you! My personal assistant, Monsieur Eloin, heard a long account of your courage from the French sergeant. So you are going to make your home in my capital, Miss Lorimer? I'm glad to be able to welcome you on the very day of your arrival."

The officers around him smiled. Sally said seriously:

"I don't think we shall arrive today, shall we? Andrew will have to stay with his patients, and of course I shall stay too."

The Emperor checked a sigh. His gentle gaze had already and thoroughly explored the possibilities of Miss Sally Lorimer and regretfully dismissed them. She was not his type. The Emperor liked sweet, stupid women with soft eyes and the ambrosial breasts and haunches Rubens loved to paint; his appetite had been well satisfied in Mexico. Clever women, he found, were apt to be like the wife he still called Charlotte, and this one, with her smooth hair and her mourning dress, and her damnable trick of taking each word literally, was definitely the Charlotte type. There was no physical resemblance between the little American and the tall Empress, and yet looking at Sally Lorimer, Maximilian was reminded of the princess—very intelligent, reserved and self-assured—whom he had wooed in a Belgian garden long ago.

"We shall try not to detain you," he said affably. "You must be anxious to reach your new home without more delay. But you will come to see us at Chapultepec as soon as Her Majesty's health has improved. She is always delighted to welcome new members to our rather limited intellectual society. I hope you are interested in the arts, Miss Lorimer? Do you play and sing, or sketch—model in clay—that sort of thing?"

She could have said:

"I like study for its own sake. I want to learn foreign languages so that I can read the great books of other lands, and in all books I like best the stories of missionary journeys, or of soldiers who led forlorn hopes to victory. I can draw maps. I can also grow fruit and vegetables, make my own clothes and raise poultry, but I have no accomplishments likely to give pleasure at an Imperial Court."

She said aloud:

"I don't play very well, Sir, I'm afraid. But I can sing the old Scots songs, which my father taught me when I was a little girl."

"Capital!" said Maximilian, with a twinkle in his eye. "May I present Prince Khevenhüller, who plays 'Auld Lang Syne' upon the clarinet? We shall expect you to favor us with a duet, as soon as the musical Mondays are resumed. Khevenhüller, will you offer our fair guest some chocolate?"

The little audience was thus gracefully concluded. The little court closed again around the Emperor. Prince Khevenhüller did not fluster the only lady in the room with a series of presentations. He introduced only his "comrade in arms, Colonel von Kodolitsch," and soon Sally was almost at her ease, chatting with the two young officers, and marveling at the dainty repast and silver plate which had come to Río Frío in the lockers of the imperial carriage. It was not very long before Andrew entered, with his red head high; Dr. Semeleder pursy and important by his side.

"Sire," said the Court Physician, taking permission to speak for granted, "I am happy to give you an excellent account of both our patients. Dr. Lorimer's intervention was entirely justified, and Baron Bompard's general condition appears to be improved. Good nursing now will pull him through."

Sally watched with sparkling eyes as Andrew, in his turn, was thanked and congratulated. Offered chocolate. Offered wine. Expostulated with, while Dr. Semeleder returned to the sickrooms, on his desire to remain at Río Frío until Monsieur Bompard was "well out of the wood."

"My good sir," said Maximilian, "you say yourself that twelve days must elapse before poor Bompard can be moved. You can't stay at Río Frío for twelve days, can you? This is no longer your responsibility. It's ours. Here is the Court Physician, to take full charge; here are nurses with all the drugs and medicines required; we have no excuse for detaining you further. The diligence is ready to depart—some impatient people, I'm told, have been ready for some time!—and if you start in half an hour you could be in Mexico by midnight. It will be too late to go to your own house; I do beg that you will both put up at the Hotel Iturbide as my honored guests."

"Your Majesty is most kind," said Andrew Lorimer. From her vantage point behind the chocolate table Sally considered the brother to whose lips "Majesty" came so readily. He was holding himself erect as usual, and yet there was deference in his bearing, and his eyes were fixed respectfully on the seated Emperor. Andrew is behaving as if Maximilian were Bonnie Prince Charlie, said Sally to herself.

Once she had made that bold comparison, it occurred to Sally that Maximilian did look more like a king in exile rather than a monarch in the full exercise of his power. It was an absurd fancy, in the face of things: the man was not much more than thirty miles from the capital where palaces and courtiers awaited his return, and he was well protected by his troops. And yet a foreboding, a presentiment of things to come, shook Sally as she looked at the two figures silhouetted against the firelight's glow. The fading of the day made the yellow slide of shale on the mountainside stand out more vividly against the dark trees, and the restless, impermanent sounds of fidgeting horses from the yard began to rasp at her nerves. She listened to the Emperor inviting Andrew to the Court.

"A good American doctor will be a great acquisition," declared Maximilian. "Old Dr. Lorimer has been very much missed. I never knew him well, but I admired his work among the Indians, who adored him. *El Viejo Curandero* was their name for him—'the Old Healer'; and nothing could have been more apt. But our American colony has greatly increased in the past year. Have you any introductions in that quarter?"

Andrew's reply was largely inaudible, but Sally, pouring chocolate for the aides-de-camp, heard with a sinking heart the names of Matthew Maury, General Magruder and Mr. Gwin.

"Ah well, if you've won Mr. Maury's favor, you need no patronage of mine," said Maximilian. "He is more popular with the foreign colonies than all their Ministers together, and of course he is *our* right-hand man in the immigration schemes.

If only the War between the States had ended otherwise, what an American Ambassador to Mexico he would have made!"

Oh, *bah!* said Sally to herself explosively. If only—if only. They never end that refrain! If only Andrew would always be the way he was three hours ago, and not the simpering sheep he looks like now!

And the old wretched feeling of antipathy to so much that Andrew believed in, the sense of being only a spectator at the romantic play perennially presented by the actors of the Lost Cause, rose choking in the heart of the girl who so short a time before had humbled herself in spirit to her brother. From the warm sympathy in the room she felt herself excluded—and knew a physical relief when the door into the hall of the posada was gently opened and a man in uniform inquired,

"Will Your Majesty be pleased to receive Herr Halkett from the silver mine?"

"Don Antonio Mora's manager," Monsieur Eloin prompted his master's memory, and Maximilian's face cleared.

"The Scotchman—I remember him," he said, with an assenting gesture. "Let him come in."

The man who entered brought a breath of cool air and the spice of the woods with him. Grizzled, short of stature, he was as broad as both the dandy officers who stood with Sally at the chocolate table, and his powerful torso was mounted on sturdy legs. He wore a rough frieze suit of some indeterminate heathery color, the trouser ends pushed into Mexican riding boots with silver ornamentation and spurs. His incredible headgear, which he took off as he approached the Emperor, was a blue Scotch bonnet with a red and white check band.

"Your servant, Don Maximiliano," said the newcomer, with a slight and most unservile bow. "I'm John Halkett, the manager of the Mora mine up yonder; I hope you havena forgot your visit to the Mine House?"

"Of course not," said Maximilian charmingly. "We had an interesting day, and excellent sport in the mountains. In what way can I serve you, Mr. Halkett?"

"It's more like to be me that can serve you," the Scotsman said. There was no rudeness in the blunt reply, only a self-confidence as irresistible as a waterfall or any other natural force. Foursquare on his spurred feet, with his blue bonnet in his hand, John Halkett looked the Emperor of Mexico in the eyes and went on,

"We only heard a two-three hours ago about the disturbance in the village. Some poor scared creatures cam' to the Mine House to ask food, and said there had been robbery and murder at the Puerto del Aire. So I loaded the waggon wi' food and wine and medicine and anything I thought might be needed, whistled up a dozen of my own peons for escort and took the road for Río Frío."

"Does your—does Don Antonio know what has happened? Is he at the silver mine now?" interrupted Maximilian.

"What would he be doing at the mine when he has me there to run it for him? He's down at Acapulco this week, for Don Hilarión has had a dose of the fever, and his father was anxious about him. But bide ye yet! When I was half-roads down the hill, I fell in with my boy Tony. He had been on an errand to the woodcutters on the Llano Grande. They had the whole story pat, and had even got word from the Indians that you were on your way. Forbye, it seems the Belgian gentlemen did more execution among the bandits than they thought. The woodcutters saw Perez himself ride by with a corpse across his saddle."

"*What!*"

It was not only Maximilian who exclaimed. The "Two K's," as Sally thought of the officers with the difficult names, spoke up too in their relief and satisfaction, and were not reproved.

"Bandits, sir?"

"You're certain the aggressors were bandits?"

John Halkett looked at the Emperor and his aides with a twinkle in his light blue eyes.

"You were feared it was the Juaristas, were ye? Well, put your minds at rest. There's no guerrillas in the Black Forest, ye can tak' my word for that, but Fernando Perez and his gang o' cutthroats are old acquaintances. No quiet-livin' body hereabouts can be mistaken about *them*."

"Well . . ." Maximilian's shoulders sagged in a long sigh of relief. "That puts a slightly better complexion on this wretched affair . . . doesn't it?"

In the murmur of assent and comment which followed John Halkett turned his head slightly until his eyes rested on Sally Lorimer, and a very pleasant smile came to his grave face. Sally smiled back shyly. She knew who he was—had heard her father speak of him a score of times; could hear, even, in his rougher tone, an echo of the Aberdeenshire accent which lingered in her father's voice.

"John Halkett from Tyrie—a thoroughly reliable fellow," the minister had liked to say. Among the dapper white tunics, in the room which had so recently been filled with blood and pain, he looked a thoroughly reliable fellow still.

"You've brought us good news, Mr. Halkett," said Maximilian. "Good news and prompt assistance, for both of which I'm grateful. The wine and victuals will be appreciated by my men, I know—"

"But what about you, Don Maximiliano?" the Scotsman said persuasively. "Don Antonio would be vexed to think of you and your gentlemen in a place like this, without one servant lass to wait on you, while we have six braw bedrooms standing ready at the Mine House. Would you not do us the honor of coming up there to spend the night? My wife has put a warming pan in every bed, for we'd a touch of snow up the mountain yesterday, and there's a haunch of prime venison started turning on the spit. Then tomorrow morning you might take a turn out with your gun if ye felt that way inclined. It would do you good, Don Maximiliano, to get a day in the fresh air on the hill."

Either the man was as simple and unworldly as any peasant, or else he had a shrewd idea of Maximilian's nature. The Emperor smiled again. He had forgotten, it almost seemed, the tragedy which had summoned him to Río Frío. Already he savored the joys of a night at cards and wine with his intimates, in a mountain retreat far from his Carlóta and his cabinet, and a morning spent in sport. But an uneasy movement from Andrew Lorimer, that unpracticed courtier, recalled him to himself.

"I must make certain that both patients are out of danger before I can leave here, even to go to the Mine House," he declared. "Dr. Lorimer, come with me."

Sally curtsied from behind the tea table, far from certain of what might be court etiquette, when the Emperor of Mexico left the room. As soon as the equerries had gone John Halkett turned towards her with a respect much more marked than the perfunctory bow he had given Maximilian.

"Good day to you, Miss Sally Lorimer," he said with a broad smile. "Did your father ever speak of John Halkett, that he knew back in the old country long ago? I didna need telling you were here, for I would have known you if I had met you in the Plaza of Mexico. The Old Doctor'll never be deid as lang as you are livin', my lassie, and your brother with his red head favors the Lorimers too. Welcome to Mexico!"

"Thank you," Sally said, with simplicity, and let her fingers linger in his clasp. Two men—the foreign Emperor and the Scots mine manager—had bidden Sally welcome within the hour. It was to the hard hand of John Halkett that she clung, as if she felt in him some protective reminder of the father she had lost.

"My father used to tell me stories about you," she said, smiling up at her new friend. "You were only a little boy . . . your father was the tollkeeper on the Fraserburgh turnpike . . . when he knew you first. And then you and your sister—isn't Ann her name?—came out to Mexico together, just like Andrew and me; and you met my uncle—"

"It was your uncle brought us out, ma dear," corrected the Scotsman, delighted to find himself remembered. "He was a good friend to both of us, when poor auld Scotland was in the grip of the Hungry Forties. Aye, he gave us a new chance in life; and I'll be pleased to serve his niece and nephew in any way I can."

"I wish you had been here this morning," sighed Sally.
"You could have done more to help Andrew than all the rest
of us put together."

"You did right well yourself, by all accounts," said Halkett.
"Come now, Miss Sally; you've had a hard day, and there's
plenty room in the wagon to take you both up to the Mine
House. I've a canty English wife, ma dear, and her and Ann—
for my sister never mairried—will be ready to kill you with kindness. They say the house is no' the same since my two oldest
bairns went away to get learnin' . . . and they'll turn out the
best they have in store for the Old Doctor's heirs."

"Quite out of the question," said a cool drawling voice from
the door. "Mr. Halkett"—and here Andrew Lorimer came forward to shake hands—"I believe I know you; a good friend of
my uncle; I hope we shall be better acquainted by and by. But
now, I fear, we must go on to Mexico: His Majesty insists upon
it."

"And you would rather stay with your sick folk, is that
it?" asked Halkett, and Andrew shrugged.

"The case is no longer in my hands," he said.

"Well, then, all the more reason for you to come up to
the Mine House till the morning," urged Halkett. "Dear knows
what like a state you'll find your own house in, if you reach
the city without warning, in the deid silence o' the nicht."

"But we sent a telegraphic message to Uncle Andrew's
housekeeper, from Vera Cruz," said Sally. Everything the kindly
Scots voice said made her realize how tired she was, how
comforting it would be to make that short journey up the mountainside to the place where friendly, house-proud women, speaking her own language, would make her welcome. But the driving
impulse which had brought Sally Lorimer from Fayetteville to
Río Frío was not yet exhausted. "If Lupita Mendez and the
other servants are expecting us tonight, they will be alarmed if
we don't arrive," she felt compelled to say.

John Halkett grunted. "It takes a good lot to alarm Lupita.
Forbye, the woman canna read . . . but if your message reached

the city—and, mind ye, that's a big 'if'—she'll have got one of
the public letter writers in the Plazuelita to read it out to her,
maybe. To tell you the truth I don't know how many servants
are left at Number Four . . . I havena had the heart to go near
the place since the day of your uncle's funeral."

"We'll make no great demands on them tonight," said Andrew impatiently. "Come, Sally, the diligence is waiting."

"There'll be another coach through here tomorrow," said
John Halkett. "Are you *sure* you wouldna rather come up to
the mine with me?"

"His Majesty would think it a great impertinence if we were
to follow him, without his command, to the place where I believe he means to dine and sleep," said Andrew conclusively,
and Sally ran to get her belongings. She reflected, fastening her
pelisse, that Andrew the interpreter of royalty's moods was likely
to be even more trying than Andrew the champion of the Lost
Cause; but Halkett, she saw as soon as she rejoined them in
the yard where only a picket of Hussars was posted, had not
taken offense. He walked beside them to the coach, chatting
amiably, and stood aside when "the Two K's" came up with
courteous farewells and promises to send news of the sick men
to Mexico. The officers had brought Andrew a flask of brandy,
and a foot warmer from the imperial coach for Sally. It was
growing cold at Río Frío, and Sally felt a long shiver as the
wind swept down from the scar of yellow shale on the mountainside. The river sounded louder in the twilight. There was no
sign of Sergeant Franchet or his men.

"A safe journey to you both, then," said John Halkett, his
Scotch bonnet in his hand. "Mind now, Miss Sally, you've promised to come to the Mine House soon. It's a pity my girl Nannie
is away at the school in Edinburgh, but young Tony will let you
see the haunts o' the wild deer, and the silver brought from the
verra heart o' Mexico . . . and I'll tell you stories about the
auld country, and your father and your lady mother when I knew
them first—"

"My mother!" said Sally, her eager face framed in the coach window. "I didn't realize—you knew mamma!"

"Not to speak to," said John Halkett. His own speech had become more staccato, for the diligence was moving, and he had to walk faster to be heard. "But to see. Every Sabbath, when I was a little lad. And she was the bonniest lass ever came into the parish kirk o' Fraserburgh, with her blue eyes sae gentle, and her black curls." He gave Sally's hand a final pat and shouted over the rolling wheels:

"Ye're not one bit like her!"

IT WAS NEARER one o'clock than midnight when the Lorimers, in one of the few cabs plying for hire at that hour, started off across the main streets of Mexico through a darkness so profound that but for the cobbles under their wooden wheels they might have been back again on the road to Río Frío. The feeble light from the side lamps fell upon a causeway which had sunk as the city settled down into its marshy foundations, and on the uneven pavements left wet by an unexpected shower. The low, two-story houses were barred and shuttered. But there was a reflected glow in the dark sky, and the cabman, tapping with his whip on the roof to attract attention, said slowly and sonorously:

"La Plaza Mayor!"

Sally sat up at once.

"Andy, we must be nearly there! Remember, *our* square is quite near the Plaza Mayor!"

"Don't jump about so." She was peering out of each window in turn, trying to read the blurred street names as the cab swayed round a series of short turnings. There was no doubt that they were entering a better quarter, for oil lamps placed here and there on the curb showed handsome houses dating from the Spanish colonial days, and there was a sweetness, as of hidden gardens, on the mild spring air.

"I can smell carnations, Andrew!" Sally said. In her excitement she actually seized his hand and gripped it in her triumph, as the cab lurched round the last corner and pulled up.

"La Plaza de Santo Domingo!" said the hollow voice above their heads.

There was an echo in that plaza which threw the words back from the atrium of a great dark church on the north side of the dusty, ill-lighted square. *La Pla-za-de-San-to-Do-min-go* —it echoed from the frowning walls of two high buildings, one protected by a chained area, facing an arcade of thirty-two portals on the west. Above the arcade a row of narrow, two-story apartments looked down into the plaza. There was enough light to see every detail of their fronts, from which the gamboge, crimson, or pale yellow paint was peeling, and of their broken shutters and rusty balconies. The light came from a few cheap cantinas in the arcade, where pulque and mezcal brandy were on sale; and from stubs of candles stuck in glasses striped with the Mexican green, white and red and placed along the broad steps leading to the church. Each cluster of candles marked the stance of an Indian vendor, selling drinks of pulque from the jug. In the middle of the little square a few lean dogs were asleep near a meanly proportioned fountain, where scraps of food and other refuse had been piled.

"Are you sure this is the right place? *Aquí la Plazuelita?*" asked Andrew Lorimer.

"*Sí, sí, señor.*" The man began to set the baggage on the ground. None of the Mexicans lounging under the portals, near the drink shops, made any move to come to his assistance, although the cowhide trunks were heavy. They were apparently not interested in earning money—or else the night's pulque had fuddled their wits, for they looked with complete apathy at the newcomers to the Plazuelita. There was something of the same stunned look on Sally's face as she took in, slowly, the details of the scene.

"Well, Sally, so much for your fountains and your patio," said Andrew grimly. "We should have stayed at the Iturbide.

Do you want to go back there now and let me look into all this in the morning?"

She turned on him with a flash of tawny eyes.

"Go back, when we're expected here? Can't you see that there are lights burning all over our house? Lupita and her husband must be sitting up for us, just as I thought they would . . . The only thing I don't understand is, why are they flying the French flag?"

"There must be some mistake," said Andrew, but he was counting as he said it, and he knew there was no mistake. Number Four, Plaza de Santo Domingo, was certainly the apartment where Colors that were not green, white and red hung from a flagpole attached to one of the low wrought-iron balconies. It had a wider front than the apartments on either side, from which it was divided by spiked railings on both floors. The stucco, newly painted, was washed a plain dark gray. That much was to the good. So was the respectable double oak door under the portal, between a pulqueria full of quarreling men and an open shop front where a game of faro was in progress. As in a waking nightmare Andrew found himself in front of that door with Sally clinging to his arm, and before his eyes a tarnished brass plate with the words DR. ANDREW LORIMER.

"Sally, ask the cabman what—"

"There's some sort of watchman, Andrew."

An elderly man wrapped in a serape, whom Andrew had taken for an outcast from the pulqueria, was huddled on a reed mat at one corner of the doorstep. Andrew shook him roughly by the shoulder. He started up. He cried in welcome:

"El Señor Güero!"

"No," said Andrew in his halting Spanish. "No el señor Guerro. Dr. Lorimer. *Cómo ésa!*" He pointed to his uncle's name on the brass plate, and the watchman, with an exclamation, crossed himself.

"He thinks you're Uncle Andrew's ghost," Sally whispered. She was trembling.

"Not he. Come on, let's get indoors."

Slowly, reluctantly, the man admitted them into a dark hall, from which a staircase decorated with blue and white Talavera tiles rose sharply to a darker landing.

"Go upstairs, Sally. Can you see your way?" Andrew impatiently lighted a vesta. "You—*hombre*—where is Lupita?"

The darkness of the hallway above gave way to a brilliant light. As Sally halted on the stair, one hand upon the railing, a door was flung open and a girl came out upon the landing.

She held in her hand an old-fashioned Argand lamp, whose singular brilliance rose at shoulder level to touch with gold a skin as fruity as a ripe peach, a mouth as rosy as the peach's heart. Glossy black hair was topped with a wide scarlet bow, and many strings of beads, glittering in the lamplight, filled the golden hollow where a red rebozo was folded over the girl's full breast. The bright necklaces swayed forward as the Mexican girl, her own eyes dazzled by the lamp she carried, bent over the baluster and said eagerly:

"Oh, Pedro, my darling, is that you?"

There was a breath of silence on the stair. Then Sally said:

"I am the señorita—I am Miss Lorimer. The señor doctor has arrived from Vera Cruz. Are you Lupita? . . . Answer me, please."

She had not meant to speak so sharply. But in her weariness and disappointment Sally found something intensely irritating in the beautiful and vivid figure standing with such confidence at Andrew's own front door. She received no answer to her questions. The Mexican girl, still carrying her lamp, gave her one startled look and disappeared as quickly as she had come.

"For God's sake!" said Andrew, finding himself again in darkness, and with the cabman, carrying some of the baggage, breathing heavily at his heels. "Was that the housekeeper? Why did she take the light away?"

The night watchman, carrying the smallest of the bags, wormed his way past them.

"Your pardon, señores," he murmured. "I will tell Lupita that your graces are here."

Andrew ushered Sally into what had been the Old Doc-

tor's house, and was now his own. Before them was a barricade
of furniture. Piled high in an insignificant lobby leading to a
long narrow passage which ended in another flight of stairs, were
heavy mahogany chairs, a tallboy with a smaller table reversed
on top of it, a horsehair sofa, a secretary, a roll of carpet, half
a dozen cheaper bedroom chairs. There seemed to be no end to
the household goods stored in the corridor.

A door on the right side of the lobby opened suddenly,
and a good-looking, flushed young man in the familiar French
uniform came quickly into the hall. Quickly, but not fast enough
to prevent the Lorimers from catching a glimpse of a brightly
lighted room, or hearing the last chord of guitar music stopping
in the middle of a melody. The Mexican girl whom they had
seen upon the landing slid out of the room at his heels and stood
confronting Sally.

"Dr. Lorimer, I believe," said the young man, hooking the
collar of his blue tunic and bowing low to Sally. "Mademoiselle!
Allow me to present myself—Sergeant Michel Ney, Chasseurs
d'Afrique—and also to present my excuses for a welcome which
must seem to be lacking in—in *empressement*."

His English, until he fumbled for the final word, was good;
his manner that of a gentleman. His dismay, all too clearly, was
great.

"Sergeant Ney," said Andrew Lorimer, "what the devil are
you doing here?"

"Please," said Sergeant Ney swiftly. "Please come into the
surgery and sit down. That is *one* room, I assure you, which we
left entirely as it was. In fact it was exempt from the requisition-
ing order. You see, we knew you were expected, but not when—"

"I suppose my dispatch from Vera Cruz was not received?"
said Andrew, and the Frenchman shook his head.

"This way, mademoiselle . . . Marina, would you light the
lamp?"

He showed them, as he spoke, into the room opposite—a
narrow, unaired room with a strong smell of drugs and medicines. It was furnished only with the high wooden desk at which

the Old Doctor had stood to write, a deal table like the one Andrew had used at Río Frío, and a short couch covered in shabby horsehair.

Sally sat down on the couch. A little sigh, which she could not check, brought the Mexican's black eyes quickly to her face. The girl had lighted another of the Argand lamps, and the hissing sound as the current of air was drawn up through the circular wick seemed to fill the musty room.

"Really, monsieur," said the French sergeant earnestly, "I wouldn't have had this happen for the world. If only your telegraphic message had arrived— But the Juaristas cut the lines from time to time, and so— And you know how it is in Mexico. *Mañana, hasta mañana!* Lupita and Jorge allowed us to go on from week to week as if you might never come at all . . . not that they had any say in the matter, of course. You must understand that the late Dr. Lorimer's house was requisitioned by the French Army soon after his death last year. Sixteen non-commissioned officers are billeted here. It's what we call a transit billet for *les isolés*—let me think—for replacements going back to their units; and in fact we were giving a little party tonight for one of our comrades of the Foreign Legion, Sergeant Franchet, who has been posted back to his regiment at Saltillo."

"Sergeant Franchet is at Río Frío," Sally said.

It was the first time she had spoken since they entered the house.

"It needn't be the man we met," said Andrew.

"I think it must be," said Sergeant Ney. "He *did* go to Río Frío early today, I know . . . and when we heard you arriving Marina thought he had come back . . . She—was anxious about him," he concluded apologetically.

Sally straightened her back. The beautiful Mexican girl on the far side of the table, who had understood nothing of what was said but the name of Franchet, seemed to sway and dazzle before her eyes in the white light of the lamp. *"Oh, Pedro, my darling, is that you?"* An emotion, which she could not identify as jealousy, took Sally Lorimer by the throat.

"Is Marina one of the maids?" she asked icily.

Sergeant Ney looked like a man plunging deeper into the mire.

"No, no, mademoiselle. Doña Marina is—an actress. She was to have been Sergeant Franchet's guest tonight. Er—may I present Doña Marina Perez of the Teatro Iturbide, Miss Lorimer? Doctor?"

He made the introduction in Spanish, and the Mexican girl swept her red satin skirts to the floor in a graceful curtsy. Andrew Lorimer gave her a stiff little bow of acknowledgment.

"We need not prolong this—misunderstanding, Sergeant Ney," he said. "I didn't bargain to take over a sergeants' mess, and I shall see your commanding officer in the morning. But Miss Lorimer has had a hard day and is extremely tired. Can not this woman, Lupita, be found—to prepare a room for her?"

"Of course," said the dismayed young man. "At once. There is one vacant room upstairs, I think—a very small one, but perhaps mademoiselle . . . As for you yourself, monsieur, I really don't know what can be arranged . . . unless you sleep here in the surgery."

"Don Miguel," the Mexican girl interrupted, in a voice as melting as the rose and gold of her face and bosom, "do these people know when El Güero will come back from Río Frío? Will he come tonight?"

"I don't see how he can, Malinche dear . . . Miss Lorimer!"

Sally had risen to her feet. The other girl's tone of privilege, her form of words—the casual "these people" instead of *los señores*—acted like a whip on the temper she had vainly tried to curb.

"Sergeant Ney," she said sharply, "I would prefer not to be interviewed in my uncle's surgery and dismissed to an attic bedroom like a newly hired kitchenmaid. There are lights and music in our drawing room, and no doubt the choicest of theatrical company. May we not go in and meet your friends? We already know Sergeant Franchet—though not well."

She swept out of the room with such angry dignity in every

line of her slim body as somehow diminished Marina's sensuous appeal. The others, however unwillingly, followed her across the hall.

Over Sally's shoulder Andrew saw a room thick with the smoke of cigars and pipe tobacco. The only remaining piece of furniture was a dining table covered with plates of half-eaten food, used glasses and bottles of wine. The walls had been lavishly decorated with swags of carnations and tuberoses, nailed to the wallpaper and draped, so as to cover a set of large steel engravings, above dingy army bedding rolls arranged against the walls. The only persons on their feet were three Mexicans in white shirts and loose white trousers, with ribboned guitars slung across their shoulders, who were lounging near an empty fireplace and obviously waiting for the order to strike up a tune. The rest of the company were sprawling rather than sitting on the bedding rolls. The Frenchmen had taken off their heavy tunics, and against their white shirts the copper-colored shoulders of their companions, the little Juanitas and Mariquitas of the bullring and the Alameda, shone with something of the fruity warmth of Doña Marina's skin. They were dressed in imitation of the Paris fashions, with draggled lace berthas and crinolines, in all the violent hues from cerise to viridian green, short enough to reveal bare copper-colored ankles. There was a moment when more than ankles were revealed—when slim naked legs flashed bronze to the thigh as the Mexican girls scrambled quickly to their feet; and that was the moment when their escorts stood to attention for Miss Sally Lorimer.

"Will you introduce your comrades in arms, Sergeant Ney?" she said.

He named them one by one. Sergeant Adolphe, Sergeant Lambert, Corporal Clary—a string of names, to Sally a blur of faces. She was aware that Lupita had burst into the room at last, a stout disheveled woman who kissed Andrew's hand and began to babble about a search for clean sheets and a warming pan for the señorita. But Sally's attention was held by the girl they called Malinche, who had moved across the room to take her place with the other guests at the interrupted party.

There was Spanish blood in La Malinche, for she was taller by a head than any one of them, and as proudly insolent as they were divided between giggles and alarm. Marina Perez, of the ballet at the Teatro Iturbide, achieved at that moment a classical distinction which won Andrew's unwilling admiration.

Once, and once only, in his student days, he had gone to watch cockfighting in a Boston stable. He was reminded of that occasion now as Sally and Marina faced each other in their unexplained but obvious hostility. The small black figure and the glowing scarlet one had focussed in themselves all the trouble in the room.

"And now may I present—er—the young ladies?" asked Ney.

"No, Don Miguel!" said the girl in the red dress. "*Compañeras, La Gringa* has no desire to know you. She is very tired, the señor doctor says, and hardly knows what she is saying. Señorita, you had better go with Lupita now, and let her show you to your room."

It was the indulgent dismissal of an elder to an angry child. Sally felt tears of fury come to her eyes.

"How dare you give me orders in my brother's house?" she said. "Are you the mistress here, or am I?"

Marina's grass-green slipper tapped out a derisive rhythm. She snapped her fan open, and looked over it, away from Sally, at Andrew Lorimer.

"The señor doctor is the master, is he not?" she said.

"He will agree with me, I think," said Sally grandly, "that the sooner this entertainment comes to an end, the better. You and the other young women are free to return to your lodgings, wherever they may be—unless the French Army has requisitioned space for you as well . . ." She looked into Marina's face, shocked, hardly recognizing her own voice, with a bitter echo from Río Frío,

"*Buenas noches, señorita soldadera!*"—and walked out of the sala with her head held high.

Chapter Four

THE CUSTOM OF THE COUNTRY

THE COFFEEPOT was of Georgian silver, stamped with an ornate L, and the table was spread with a cloth which, though much washed and worn, was of the finest Dunfermline linen. A bowl of cut melon and mangoes flanked a silver dish containing eggs served on black beans with a savory sauce of tomatoes and chili peppers, and a basket held a warm assortment of French rolls. The breakfast table was a soothing sight to Andrew Lorimer, weary as only a man can be who has spent half a night composing his six feet for sleep upon a five-foot couch.

Lupita, anxious to please her new master, had hung about the table setting butter and honey within his reach and fiddling with Sally's empty cup and plate until he told her to leave the room. Dr. Lorimer's thoughts were up at Río Frío. A French-language newspaper called *L'Ere Nouvelle,* which he had found folded at his place, gave a garbled account of the shooting and the death of Comte Huard, but—he supposed for security reasons—made no mention of Maximilian's trip into the mountains. Andrew wondered if Baron Bompard had survived the night. He had advised the Court Physician to use a weak solution of perchloride of lime on the wet dressings next time the stump was bandaged, and if that were done, and the "laudable pus" well established in the suppuration he was inclined to give a patient nursed in the pure air of Río Frío rather more than the usual thirty per cent chance of life. And if the man survived the first two days he might well survive the crucial twelve.

He looked up from the newspaper in surprise at the sight of Sally.

"Downstairs already? I thought you'd want to take a rest in bed this morning."

Sally was dressed with her usual neatness. She was shivering a little, for mornings in the Cold Country were sharp, and her eyes were heavy, but her black merino dress was carefully brushed, the white cuffs crisp and fresh. It occurred to Andrew, as he rose to pull out her chair, that in spite of his deep respect for the dead, he would not be sorry when Sally put off her mourning.

"Downstairs?" she said, from the foot of the table. "I went right down the *back* stairs at a quarter to seven o'clock, and not a minute too late to get Lupita started for the day. The dirt and confusion in the kitchen are really terrible. Do you know that the larder and sculleries are right next door to the stables—"

"Where there aren't any horses, of course."

"There wouldn't be room for a Shetland pony. Every stall and loose box is crammed with Lupita and Jorge's relatives from Xochimilco! They moved into the city, group after group, and now they're *living* here and eating their heads off at your expense!"

"But you'll clear them out pronto, won't you, Sally?" said Andrew with a heavy-handed attempt at humor. She was not listening.

"What happened to this room?" she exclaimed. "Why, it's transformed! Don't tell me those shiftless servants laid the carpet, and brought in all the furniture overnight?"

"No, it wasn't the servants. It was Sergeant Ney and the other boys. They started in about four o'clock, just as I was getting to sleep on that penitential couch in the surgery, and they creaked and banged around until six, when I suppose they went on duty. Their kit and bedding are still in the other rooms on this floor, but you must have scared them into leaving the sala in decent shape for us."

Sally was touching one piece of furniture after another.

"The tallboy is just like the one in father's room," she said. "See the thistle design on the brass handles! And look at the engravings—Covenanters Preaching, and John Knox—and this little mahogany console is the mate to the one we had beside the fireplace in the parlor. Only we never had so many silver bowls and candlesticks to put on ours! Oh, Andy, isn't it just like home?"

Her lips were quivering. Andrew was buttering a brioche and took no notice.

"The furniture, the silver, the china and all that sort of thing are first rate," he said. "If you could forget the noise outside and the drunks lying on the pavement, or the tortilla women fighting with one another at the fountain, it would be very like home, indeed. Unfortunately—"

Sally came back to the table, felt the coffeepot, and poured herself a cup of coffee and hot milk.

"—Unfortunately, it hardly measures up to your fairy tale of the patio and the roses, does it?"

"No."

Andrew looked at her more attentively.

"I'll have to prescribe Blaud's pills for you," he said. "You're as white as a ghost. And your eyes are swollen. Have you been crying?"

"Certainly not!"

"Then you're the only female in this house who wasn't shedding tears in the small hours of the morning. Lupita cried because she thought you didn't appreciate her, and all the little Mexican girls squalled like cats except our friend Franchet's inamorata—and she went into screaming hysterics because you called her an insulting name. Isn't it an extraordinary coincidence that this should be his billet too?"

"Quite extraordinary," said Sally shortly. Her lips were drawn to a thin line. There was a foreshadowing in her face of the "New England schoolmarm" which Jonas Wilkinson had feared she might some day become. "You seem to think it was all quite amusing, Andrew. I thought it was a disgraceful scene!

Those men and those painted girls lolling round on the floor like
a—Roman orgy! And as for that bold-faced hussy in red, I'll insult her in the same way with pleasure if she presumes to act the
hostess in this house again."

Andrew laughed: "Women! But you left the battlefield too
soon, Sal. The *soldadera,* or whatever it was you called her, was
all for standing her ground until Franchet turned up—"

"And did he?"

"Not as far as I know. But I locked myself into the surgery
and let them fight it out. Lupita gave me the key to my uncle's
desk—I will say, she had it carefully put by in a sealed envelope—
and I was anxious to know if he had left me any private instructions or advice."

"Oh! Was there anything for me?"

"Only this."

He took a letter from his pocket and handed it across the
table.

Mexico
June the fifteenth, 1865

My dear Nephew [the letter began]

*The state of my health indicates that you will soon succeed
to my practice and take my place in the City of Mexico. That is,
if you accept your legacy. The sad news of your father's death
and the events reported from Appomattox suggest that for both
private and public reasons you will be disposed to do so.*

*Your father and I were good friends in our youth, but we
were two brothers who fell in love with the same woman, and
for many years we have continued friends apart. Remember that
whatever I have been able to leave to you and Sally will come
to you for Lillian Fraser's sake.*

*Perhaps you can remember my visit to Fayetteville in 1845,
when you were a lively lad of seven and Helen a beautiful
child of ten—the image of her mother as I knew her first. I had
intended the sugar hacienda at Cuernavaca for Helen, although
after her advantageous marriage to Mr. Cartwright it would have*

seemed very insignificant by comparison with her husband's estates of Belle Isle and Hampton Oaks. Her death was a sad blow. Now the hacienda goes to little Sally, whom I have never seen. No doubt you will prefer to convert it, when the time comes, into her marriage portion. In this, and all transactions relating to the hacienda, be guided by

Here the letter stopped in the middle of a line. There were a few indecipherable words which might have been "the wisdom of" or "the advice of" which trailed at an angle down the page. Then the writer began again, on a new sheet and in a feebler hand:

Don Antonio Mora, a good friend.

I leave you no advice concerning the practice, for with your Harvard M.D. and your hospital experience your medical knowledge must now be far in advance of mine. One warning, however, I must and will give you.

Steer clear of the Emperor Maximilian. He is an amiable ass married to an hysterical and ambitious woman, and after a year of their socalled reign in Mexico I see nothing ahead of them but ruin.

You will be summoned to court, that is certain. Maximilian, among whose recent achievements is the closing of our University, fancies himself as the patron of educated men. Go to court only when you must, and above all do not identify yourself with their foreign entourage.

When I decided to leave Scotland at the age of twenty-five, I chose to settle in Mexico because I was stirred by the country's great fight for independence from the yoke of Spain. While I was still on the high seas one of the republican "liberators" had established the First Empire—with himself of course as Emperor. He bore the ill-omened name of Agustín Iturbide. Within two years he was overthrown, banished and shot dead, as Benito Juarez, mark my words, will one day put a bullet through Maximilian.

On the third sheet broken words and syntax showed that the Old Doctor was coming to the end of his strength.

I wish you good health and fortune Mexico. You will not be troubled place flowers on my grave, for my cadaver is willed to the School of Medicine, where it may be use to the new generation of anatomists. No lack of subjects however in Mexico.

Yours faithfully,
Andrew Lorimer

"Poor old man," said Sally pitifully. "Poor Uncle Andrew! I never knew he was once in love with mamma—did you?"

"No, I didn't, but never mind that now. You see he means *me* to judge what's best to be done about the hacienda—sell it, obviously; just what I've said all along."

"It's conditional," said Sally. " 'No doubt you will prefer to convert it' and so on. What he said to *you* is positive. 'Steer clear of Maximilian. Go to his court only when you must.' How does that fit in with all the invitations we were offered yesterday at Río Frío?"

"Naturally, you disliked the Emperor at sight?"

"I didn't dislike him," said Sally. "It worried me that he didn't seem to care a fig for the men who had been hurt but only for what his brother and his brothers-in-law were going to think of *him*. But about Cuernavaca: I don't care how many letters of advice Uncle Andrew left you. I stand by the terms of his will, which left the hacienda to me unconditionally; and I intend to keep it."

"Sally, you're impossible!"

There was so much anger in his handsome ruddy face that another quarrel might have broken out between them. But just then Lupita knocked, and came in with a message of which Andrew understood not a word, so that he was forced to ask his sister:

"What does she say?"

"Some people are here to see you. I'm not sure, but I think she means a group from the infirmary."

"Nonsense," said Andrew. "Would doctors be paying calls before nine o'clock in the morning? Go and find out who they are."

It was a group of infirm persons who had come to see the doctor. The news of his arrival had passed rapidly round the Plaza de Santo Domingo and the narrow streets beyond, and already half a dozen Indians had returned thankfully to the house where El Viejo Curandero had always been accessible to the poor. Just outside the sala door, where the furniture had been piled, stood two men in the white shirts and trousers of artisans, with huge sombreros pressed respectfully to their chests. One had a roughly bandaged hand. Four women held infants in their arms, each little mouth and nose covered by the folds of the mother's rebozo.

"*El señor doctor, señorita, por favor. El curandero,*" one of them got out.

Sally held the door wide enough for Andrew to see them all.

"Here are your first patients, Dr. Lorimer," she said, and the wicked sparkle he knew gleamed in her heavy eyes.

Andrew rose.

"All right," he said, "I'll see these people, since they're here. But try to make Jorge understand that the surgery will not open until tomorrow. Tell him to keep the street door closed. The dispensary is as good as empty, and I can't cure all the ills of humanity with a jar of leeches! Besides, I must find the Town Major's office, and get the billeting order revoked at once."

Sally was left alone in the living room. Transformed, she had called it, but the prim domestic drop-scene which had fallen over the soldiers' sala could not shut out the humiliating awareness that between these four walls she had given, before strangers, a wretched display of temper and bad manners. She went quickly to open one of the three long windows which Andrew had closed against the noise of the Plazuelita. It was not difficult to maneuver her hoop skirt out on the balcony, hung with pots of

pink geraniums, which jutted over the arcade. And there, quite
oblivious of the hostile or mocking eyes looking up from several
points at La Gringa, the foreigner, exposing herself like a loose
woman to any passerby, Sally took stock of the Plaza de Santo
Domingo.

She had seen it first in darkness, after rain, and it had
shocked her. Now in the invigorating, balmy sunshine of a March
morning in the Valley of Mexico, Sally had a fairer look at the
square which had pleased the Old Doctor so well that he had
made his home there for forty years.

It was noisy—Andrew was right so far. A procession of
market carts drawn by mules or oxen, which moved slowly
through the chained area in front of what Sally now knew to be
the Customs House, meant the rattle of wooden wheels and the
shouts of men. The tortilla women, mixing dough and baking
the flat cakes on small braziers set round the fountain, were indeed exchanging cheerful insults with one another and with
women coming to the spout for water, and the cab drivers in a
rank along the arcade beneath Sally's window seemed to be involved in a perpetual argument. It was noisy, but it was not
quarrelsome. There was a grace among those humble people
which Sally felt by instinct. There was a gaiety, all the more
enchanting for being subdued, in the voices of the vendors who
along the curb were proclaiming the merits of their shoeshines,
newspapers, love potions, peanuts, lucky charms and rosaries.

"*Refrescos!* Jellies, orangeade! *Refrescos!*"

The voice of nineteenth-century Mexico, pleasure-loving
and condemned to pain, rang through the Plazuelita which Andrew Lorimer had called a slum. It was no more a slum than it
was the "fashionable square" of the Raleigh attorney's imagination. It was simply a backwater from which the tide of fashion
had ebbed since the Spanish colonial days, to be filled with a new
life which, though poor, was not impoverished. It was true that
there were drunken men lying in the shade of the portals, and
too many of the sullen beggars who bore the uninviting name of
léperos lounged naked to the waist against the pillars of the

Customs House; but the mule drivers, the public letter writers, the flower sellers were hard at work and cheerful. The flag-stones where the companions of Cortés had strode in armor now felt the lighter tread of new parents stumbling across the atrium to Santo Domingo's baptistry with a baby stifling beneath white flannel and cheap cotton lace, and the *compadres* solemnly important at their heels. Youths carrying heavy textbooks strolled in and out of the building painted the color of dried blood, which a sobered Jorge had told Sally was the School of Medicine where the Old Doctor taught. Sally leaned out as far as she dared to watch a religious procession, carrying an image decked with jewels and satin, to which the people knelt as it went by. She was absorbed, caught out of herself; the cry which echoed across the plaza took her unawares.

"*Mueran los Franceses!* Death to the French!"

A man in blue uniform, riding a chestnut horse, did no more than turn his head slightly in the direction from which the cry had come. Above the heads of the silenced crowd, he must have seen the scuffle beneath the wall of the School of Medicine, as the student who had screamed defiance was hurried indoors by his friends. Indoors, and away from that wall the color of blood, along which the stone was freshly chipped here and there in an irregular row about the level of a man's heart.

The mounted Frenchman made no sign. But his eyes narrowed into the creases which an Algerian sun had made, and as he raised his chin in a sudden gesture of authority Sally recognized Pierre Franchet.

"*Viva Escobedo! Viva el vencedor de Santa Isabel!*"

More than one voice was taking up the ragged chorus as Sally slipped quickly back inside the sala. Her heart was beating fast. Sergeant Franchet coming back to his billet—expecting to find what, or whom? Herself or—La Malinche? She snatched up the discarded copy of *L'Ere Nouvelle* and carried it to a small settee beneath the steel engraving of John Knox Rebuking Mary, Queen of Scots. If he came in, he should find her reading, calm and absorbed.

"ESCOBEDO CLAIMS VICTORY NEAR SALTILLO," she read. "COLONEL DE BRIANCOURT AMBUSHED AT SANTA ISABEL."

She read the headlines twice over without fully understanding the kind of news she had read so often in the war years, which stupefied by mere repetition. The smudged text told more fully, although always discreetly, that a French colonel and a detachment of the Foreign Legion had been cut to pieces in one of the dry gullies called barrancas of which the diligence had crossed so many on the road from Vera Cruz. Then Lupita's greasy head came round the door and Lupita said, with the first smile Sally had seen on her copper-colored face,

"El Señor Güero to see your graces!"

"Good morning, Sergeant Franchet," said Sally quickly. "Will you come in?"

He came in, képi in hand, wearing his official face, and fumbling in the folds of his blue sash.

"Good morning, mademoiselle. I hope you are well? Not too much fatigued by all your yesterday's—exertions?"

She heard the note of irony, and stiffened to meet it. "I am quite rested now, I thank you."

"I have a letter from the Court Physician for Dr. Lorimer."

"Is it an urgent letter? My brother is seeing patients at the moment."

"Already?" A flash of humor, gone in an instant, sparked the cold gray eyes surveying Sally. "It is not urgent, mademoiselle, so far as I am aware. It conveys the assurance that Baron Bompard continues to do well."

"I'm *very* glad." Sally held out her hand to take the crumpled letter. But Sergeant Franchet laid it carefully upon the table.

"Perhaps you would hand it to the doctor when he is free, mademoiselle. And—if I may charge you with the message—tell him, at the same time, that this house has been taken off the requisitioned list, and will be vacated before six o'clock tonight."

Sally felt her face and neck grow warm. He knew, then—he

had not come directly to the Plazuelita! She answered in a tone as stiff as his own.

"My brother intended to call on the Town Major in the course of the morning."

"Sergeant Ney was so much impressed by your—distress, mademoiselle, that he went to the Town Major's office himself before he reported for duty. My own troop was replaced by Austrians during the night, and ordered back to Mexico. By the time I reached Buena Vista barracks the billeting order had already been revoked."

"That is most satisfactory," she said.

"Army transport will remove our equipment in the course of the day, mademoiselle. A fatigue party has been ordered to clean the requisitioned rooms; after which I hope that Dr. Lorimer—and more particularly Miss Lorimer—will have no further reason to complain of the French Expeditionary Corps."

"I trust not, sergeant. I hope that when the inventory is checked, nothing will be found missing since the house was occupied."

"The inventory?"

"Is that something new in your billeting experience?" Sally looked at the console table. It held a glittering array of silver; snuffboxes, candlesticks, a toddy ladle and an old Scots quaich. "With an army of occupation one can't take honesty for granted, I'm sorry to say."

"Was that your experience of the Confederate States Army, mademoiselle?"

"That was my experience of the Union Army, sergeant."

He muttered something that might have been "I'm sorry" and looked down at his heavy boots. Sally felt the pulses begin to hammer in her wrists. For the second time in her life she was alone with a man—the same man; and between the comradeship of yesterday and this morning a gulf had opened. It pleased her to think that she could check his prepared speeches and put him out of countenance at last.

"Very well," he said. "If an inventory exists, it shall certainly be checked. Though I should like to say that some of my comrades have no need to covet the late doctor's grape scissors or make off with his nutcrackers. Michel Ney, whom you met last night, is in fact the Duc d'Elchingen, a peer of France and the grandson of Bonaparte's marshal. Comte Clary is a cousin of the French Emperor and in high favor at the Tuileries. Such men are noncommissioned officers of their own choice, and can't be classified as rogues and vagabonds."

"Really?" said Sally. "Now are you going to tell me that you're a descendant of the Marquis de Lafayette?"

"It amuses you to be sarcastic, mademoiselle. I am a no-body—a soldier from Provence—with no relatives left but an older brother. A Protestant minister in Nîmes, who washed his pious hands of me many years ago." .

"But you have an alias, haven't you? Why do you call your-self Señor Guerro?"

Pierre looked embarrassed. "Not Guerro," he said. "It's El Güero. Meaning *le blond,* the fair one . . . and it's only a joke. Someone gave me the nickname, and the servants picked it up."

That someone, Sally's newly awakened jealousy told her, was the girl Marina. La Malinche—she had her nickname too; her hands had touched that crisp blond hair. Her husky voice had called her foreign lover "El Güero."

"Nickname or alias?" she said. "Our Confederate soldiers fought under their own names."

Pierre flung his képi down on Andrew's vacant chair. He came across the room to Sally with the quick light tread of the yard at Río Frío.

"I serve His Imperial Majesty Napoleon the Third under *my* own name, as my grandfather Pierre Franchet fought for his uncle at Waterloo," he said, and the white scar stood out on his jaw. "If you can use a word like 'false' to me, things have surely changed between us since you drank tequila from my cup at Río Frío!"

"There was nothing between us to change," she said in a whisper.

"Oh yes, there was. There was a task we shared, and performed well together. And there was the moment beside the church when you let me comfort you . . . and put my arm around you—"

He expected her to protest, or even to cry out as fine ladies did, that the common soldier was impertinent. But Sally denied nothing. She flung back at him,

"Before the task we shared, you had a chance to *tell the truth!* More than one chance! Why didn't you—oh, why didn't you say, quite openly and truthfully, that you were billeted here? When I asked you, in my ignorance, 'Do you know our house in the Plaza de Santo Domingo?' you only had to say, 'I know it well, because I live there!' But you were evasive—yes; you talked about knowing my uncle by sight, and all that—I suppose you thought yourself very diplomatic! I say you lied to me! You left unsaid what was the truth, and you acted out a lie!"

"If I was evasive, as you call it, it was because I hoped to spare you something. I was sure you would spend the night at Río Frío, and I meant to ride back to the city ahead of you and get the house cleared for your arrival. Do you think I wanted a young lady to walk into a sergeants' mess— Yes, Ney told me, that's what the doctor called it, and he was right, of course. I meant to make Lupita put the place in order before you came. Then that Whitecoat—that Austrian colonel sent us up to the Mine House on reconnaissance, before Maximilian risked his precious life in the forest, and when we rode in again, you had two hours' start along the highway. I couldn't stop you from starting your life in Mexico in a French billet, in the Plaza de Santo Domingo of all places, where the whole neighborhood will be only too ready to say you approved of and sheltered *us*."

Sally shrugged. "I gather the French aren't popular in this neighborhood. Or was '*Mueran los Franceses*' meant for you alone?"

"You heard that? I thought you would. I caught a glimpse of you on the balcony as I rode in . . . No, you could have heard 'Death to the French' any day in the Plazuelita since last December."

"Why since last December?"

"Did you ever hear of the Black Flag Decrees, also known as Maximilian's crowning folly? The decrees giving every troop leader in the Imperial Army the right to carry out drumhead courts-martial and summary executions? Yes, I see you have. Well, such an execution was carried out here in the middle of December, with the whole of Santo Domingo parish weeping and shouting, and a full company of Zouaves standing guard with bayonets fixed. You can see the bullet marks on the School of Medicine still."

She looked at the chipped plaster of the dark-red wall and back at Sergeant Franchet's face.

"You mean there has been actual fighting inside the city between the Juaristas and the French?"

"No, there was no fight. The men we executed were caught red-handed in an attempt to assassinate Marshal Bazaine."

He fancied she looked ill, and thought savagely that he had frightened her at last. But Sally only said, in a tone of detachment,

"My brother is an American. No Black Decrees, no summary executions, can possibly affect his position in this city. He was an Army surgeon, he understands billeting regulations, so do I. We—I—could have overlooked everything, every inconvenience, if only you had told the truth at the beginning, Sergeant Franchet!"

Pierre made a little gesture of despair. He was not a man who gesticulated much, his Provençal vivacity had been too firmly compressed into the Army mold for that; but now he shrugged his shoulders, and looked round blankly at the room his comrades had worked hard to make habitable for Miss Sally Lorimer.

Then he said, as if he had arrived at some kind of decision,

"You set great store by truth, mademoiselle? For you, it is one of the highest qualities a human being can possess?"

"Yes."

"Can you bear to hear the truth about yourself? Will you whimper, or scream for your brother, if I tell you that last night you behaved with abominable cruelty to a few poor girls who never meant to do you harm?"

"The girls those men brought here? I hardly spoke to them!"

"You ordered them to leave the house. They didn't understand what you were saying, but when they realized what you meant they were cut to the heart. Mexicans are courteous to their guests, mademoiselle. They say to every one who visits them '*Esta es su casa,* this is your house,' and they mean it! To put a guest to the door as you did was for them a gross violation of hospitality."

"They were not here on my invitation," Sally reminded him. A great aching sob was coming up in her throat, but she kept her eyes wide open, in case tears fell, and fixed on him. "They were here because of the custom of the country. You explained it all to me at Río Frío—*el costumbre del país*—the girls who follow the soldiers . . . only I hardly expected to meet them in Dr. Lorimer's house."

"And so you permitted yourself to call Malinche *la señorita soldadera,* meaning to cause her pain—"

"Why do you call your mistress 'Malinche' like the Indian girl who loved Cortés? Is your Marina's a nickname—or an alias?"

To hear the words "your mistress" on the lips of a girl like Sally stopped Pierre's attack as effectively as a Juarista bullet. He said "Cortés?" in a voice of pure bewilderment.

"Cortés took an Indian girl for a camp follower, who betrayed her own people for his sake. Your Malinche looks as if she could betray the whole French Army, and never turn a hair."

The golden flash of triumph in Sally's eyes drove Pierre to say:

"You are so very well read, mademoiselle; you must forgive me if I failed to understand you. I only wished you to show pity, rather than contempt, for a girl we Frenchmen met among

the ruins of Puebla, when she was as innocent as you. I ask you
to forget my mistake. As I shall forget the mistake I made yesterday, when I saw a lady I took to be all goodness and compassion, and was very nearly ready to worship her—"

"I had no idea there was so much sentimentality in the
Foreign Legion," said Sally. She clenched her hands in the folds
of her skirt to hide their trembling.

"Hadn't you?" Pierre considered. "Let me tell you something. I joined the Legion when I was eighteen—not exactly of
my own free will. Except for a few weeks in '59, when my regiment fought in Italy, I spent six years on active service in Algeria.
Fourteen days in a hill blockhouse, fourteen days on the coast—
with now and then a razzia in the desert, chasing the Kabyle
rebels, or a hunt after terrorists in the Aurès mountains—no, it
wasn't a routine that lent itself to sentiment. But some of the
Légionnaires were tenderhearted, for all that. Sometimes they
spoke of their old homes, even of their parents. Some used to
wonder what it would be like to be in the company of good
women—*ladies*—the kind of women some of us had known as
boys, busy with good deeds and charity. And when MacMahon
came out to Algiers as Commander-in-Chief, he made a great
deal of how the heart of France was with the Army of Africa.
Women remembered us in their prayers, the marshal said. Now
there was a fine sentiment for you! We believed him. The day
came when they told us the Emperor meant to create a new
Algeria in Mexico, with our invaluable help. *Hop-là!* We were
shipped out to Marseilles en route for St. Nazaire and Vera
Cruz. Now we shall see those who pray for us, we said. We did.
The ladies came down to see us at the Gare St. Charles. Real
ladies like Miss Sally Lorimer, with brothers and husbands to
protect them from the wild men. They looked us over as if we
were gorillas in a traveling fair. They threw us fruit and tobacco
—yes, and money; I heard one lovely girl say 'Degraded wretches!'
when the recruits were scrambling for the *sous*. But not one of
them would have touched our hands in friendship, or done what
you did yesterday at Río Frío . . . On bivouac last night, when

I knew you must get here before me, I dared to think that your charity might cover Malinche too . . . and the little street girls . . . and even me. But at heart you're like the virtuous Marseilles ladies, mademoiselle. You throw us your crumbs and draw your skirts aside from contamination—damn your frozen, empty, self-righteous little heart!"

SALLY REMAINED standing in the sala where he had left her for many minutes after the double oak doors on the street level closed upon Pierre Franchet. Only the oily black head of Lupita, poked in inquiringly, roused her to walk into the hall with a mechanical smile for the woman, and limbs that felt like lead. Outside the surgery door, through which Andrew's voice could be heard doing violence to the language of Cervantes, the squatting Indians rose and bowed respectfully as Sally passed. She had no recollection of walking up the long flight of stairs until she found herself in the room where she had spent the night. It was a high, whitewashed cell which the Old Doctor had kept for the use of his infrequent guests, sparsely furnished with a brass bed and a varnished pine bureau holding toilet articles of cheap white crockery. A few of the cold blue and white Talavera tiles used in the staircase made a haphazard decoration on the walls.

Sally flung herself on the bed and gave way to tears.

She thought she was crying for her father, who had petted her and understood her, for she spoke his name aloud, with her quivering mouth muffled in the cheap flock pillow, and her hands clutching the brass bars of the bedstead. But it was the voices of living men which echoed in her head, and struck again and again at the self-confidence which had brought her from war-scarred Fayetteville to the war in Mexico.

"She was the bonniest lass ever came into the parish kirk o' Fraserburgh . . . and ye're not one bit like her . . ."

"Sally, you're impossible . . ."

And then the third voice, the foreign accent stumbling at the English words, the contemptuous aversion all too plain:

"Damn your frozen, empty, self-righteous little heart!"

The storm of angry sobbing left the girl exhausted, deaf alike to the sounds of coming and going in the rooms below and to the incessant noises of the square beneath her window. Then the great bell of the Cathedral, two streets away, began to toll the hour. It was answered, in a mellow harmony, from the belfry of La Profesa. The bells of San Francisco called across the narrow streets to Santa Clara, and from farther west the voices of San Hipólito and San Fernando floated across the tree-tops of the Alameda. She listened, calmed and enchanted, as the bronze mouth of Santo Domingo himself took up the song. From that sweet and broken cadence Sally took new heart. For the first time consciously, for the first time in surrender, she listened to the bells of Mexico.

Chapter Five

LA PALOMA

THE TWO BRONZE BELLS of Santo Domingo chimed away the hours of a whole day while Sally lay weary and defeated in her conventual bedroom. Andrew prepared and made her drink a composing draught, and Lupita, bringing a bowl of bread and milk liberally sprinkled with wood ashes, predicted a bout of *la sorache,* the mountain sickness known to attack gringos who traveled from the tropical zone to the Cold Country without long halts by the way. But a night's rest revived Sally, and while Andrew escaped from domestic warfare to pay the customary calls on his Mexican colleagues, she began a thorough reformation of the household.

The hangers-on in the disused stables were sent packing, and lazy Jorge set to whitewashing the stonework and the stalls. Of the six maidservants, only Conchita and Luz were retained to help Lupita, and even they were made to weep at La Gringa's sharp comments on their slovenly dress and uncombed hair. The bedrooms cleaned by the French fatigue party were cleaned all over again with cactus soap and boiling water, and the doctor's trunks unpacked in the best of the three. Sally announced that she would continue in the guest bedroom—it was "hardly worth while changing," she said, "because I'll soon be going to the hacienda"—but everywhere else moldy feather mattresses were aired or burned, floors scrubbed, and larders cleared of sour and spoiling foodstuffs. "This is a shame and a disgrace!" said Sally, so many times that the maids recognized it as the key phrase of

La Gringa's regime. They had no idea that she was still arguing with El Señor Güero, whose easy rule they all regretted.

Andrew made few demands on his sister's housekeeping in the first week of their life in Mexico. He kept his surgery hours in the morning and evening, and ate the *comida,* or principal meal of the day, at El Tivoli or Maupin's with groups of the Southern gentlemen connected with the Land Office. Not all of these were of Matthew Maury's quality. General Magruder was thoroughly respectable, but an ex-Senator from California, by name Gwin, and his son William, were obviously Southern counterparts of the Northern carpetbaggers swarming over New Orleans, and Andrew could see no possible advantage to Southern veterans in their highly speculative schemes for mining in the provinces of Sonora and Sinaloa. He was careful not to mention his disillusionment to Sally, either at the breakfast table or on the two or three occasions when he escorted her to look at the shop windows in the fashionable streets leading to the Alameda park.

Don Antonio Mora, their uncle's good friend, paid his first call on the Lorimers at the end of the week, on an afternoon when Andrew and Sally were working together in something approaching harmony. The girl, wearing a severe brown holland pinafore, was writing at the high desk in the surgery; the doctor dictating a list of drugs to be ordered from a pharmaceutical house in Philadelphia. All medicines, and particularly narcotics, were in short supply in the Mexican capital.

"It may take three months to get this order filled," Andrew said gloomily. "If I don't get a hospital appointment soon, I'll have to use Perry Davis Pain Killer for an anesthetic . . . and be glad my uncle left a dozen bottles, with the seals intact!"

Sally went on with the list in her boarding school copperplate, not looking up, but noting with a little gleam of pleasure that this was the first time Andrew had shown any interest in a permanent post in Mexico. She was cleaning her pen on her brown holland bib, and Andrew was disgustedly examining some old bottles caked with Rochelle salts and Dover's powder when Jorge announced:

"Don Antonio Mora."

"Don Andrés and Doña Sarita! Welcome to Mexico!"

Sally had barely time to drop a curtsy before the newcomer, dressed in the European fashion introduced by Maximilian, was gently kissing her ink-stained fingers.

"You find us at a disadvantage, sir—" Andrew began.

"Nonsense!" Don Antonio Mora, taller than many of his countrymen, was able to fold the tall American to his heart in the affectionate Mexican abrazo. "I find you *busy,* as your uncle would have wished, and well I hope; but can you forgive the Moras for their neglect of you? I only knew this morning that you had arrived in Mexico. I am so sorry that I was not in town to meet the diligence and take you home at once to Doña Mercedes and our girls."

So much of the rapid Spanish was lost on Andrew Lorimer that he could only look to Sally to reply.

"We knew that you were out of town, señor," said Sally, coloring. "Mr. Halkett told us that your son was lying ill at Acapulco. I hope your return to Mexico means that he is quite recovered?"

"Not *quite* recovered, but on the mend," said Don Antonio. It was a pleasant look that he gave Sally, with a smile that lit up his round olive-skinned face, but there was a quick, appraising gleam in his dark eyes. "I left him yesterday to convalesce at my villa in Cuernavaca. Then I came on to Mexico, read John Halkett's letter about your arrival as soon as I reached home, and—here I am!"

"It's uncommonly kind of you to come to us so soon," said Andrew. "I do appreciate your welcome."

"A welcome can be empty words," said Don Antonio, "but by good fortune this is a fiesta day at the Casa Mora. We have had few celebrations lately, for Hilarión's ill-health has been an anxiety, and then both my second son and my son-in-law are serving in the north with General Márquez, but my youngest daughter is fifteen years old today. We heard a Te Deum for María de la Soledad at La Profesa church this morning, and tonight my wife is giving a tertulia, an evening party, for all her young friends and relatives. Do come! I have three daughters unmarried, so there will be beaux galore for Doña Sarita, and music and dancing until midnight. Everything young ladies like, eh, señorita?"

Five minutes later Sally was running upstairs, eagerly untying her pinafore. She had never attended an evening party other than church "sociables" and the commencement exercises of her school in Connecticut, but she was well aware that her high-necked black merino was not suitable for a *quince años* party in Mexican society. In her small wardrobe there was only one garment even moderately decolleté. It had begun life as a white brocade, made for Helen during her engagement, and Sally, much later, had dyed it black, filling the low neck and elbow sleeves with a lace ruching before adapting it to her own slighter figure. Ripping out the lace, she now slipped the black brocade over her hooped petticoat. There was no need to call for Lupita's help, for Sally's eighteen-inch waist had never required tight lacing, and she realized as she fastened the hooks that she had grown even thinner since the dress was altered. Her face stared back at her from the dimmed mirror. All eyes and wide, narrowed mouth—she looked a fright! Impulsively she pulled the chenille snood from her chignon. The tawny rope of hair fell on her shoulders. She had no curling tongs, but the comb softened the silky sprays at her temples, and her quick fingers twisted a looser and more fashionable knot at the nape of her slender neck. It was becoming! Sally caught up her pelisse and ran downstairs.

THE MORA EQUIPAGE, a handsome landau, was attracting much attention in the always crowded Plazuelita.

"My house in the Calle de los Plateros is only five minutes' walk away," said Don Antonio. "My three lazy girls and their dueña will be able to pay a call on you after Mass on any morning of the week, if you permit it, Doña Sarita. But I want your first visit to be paid in state: we shall take the long way round, through the Plaza Mayor."

The scene which opened before them as the landau entered the great square was beautiful and serene. In the far distance Popocatépetl and Ixtaccíhuatl, the snowcapped volcanoes which stood guard over the valley, seemed to swim in the March blue, while in the foreground the first colors of the sunset fell on the yellow walls of the long two-storied National Palace which occupied all the east side of the square. In the clear rarefied air the scent from booths fashioned of living hedges and festooned with flowers, where sweetmeats and *refrescos* were sold, mingled agreeably with woodsmoke from the braziers round the outer limits of the square where tortillas and tamales were cooking. The inner garden, dominated by the majestic Cathedral and Sagrario, was laid out in tree-shaded walks and lawns, beautified with rose pergolas and fountains, where ladies in crinoline gowns were squired by men in a score of different European uniforms. These strangers, like the Indians who stalked gravely among the braziers and booths, moved with the quiet step and gentle exchange of greetings which seemed so characteristic of Mexico. The only sound which imposed itself upon the golden air of sunset came from a kiosk in the center of the square, where an Austrian military band was playing selections from Donizetti.

"It is a fashionable scene, is it not?"

"Yes—oh yes!" said Sally fervently; and fashionable it was to the girl from the piney woods, who for years had known nothing but the hamlet round her father's church, with its straggling dirt street and one general store with bulging panes of iridescent glass. But Sally's more sensitive perceptions, newly and keenly awakened, saw beyond the veneer of European fashion to the grace and gravity of the Mexico which owed nothing to Europe, unless it was to Spain. There was something in the harmony of those buildings and their setting in the ring of mountains which profoundly appealed to her. "It's *so* beautiful," she said.

"It is the heart of Mexico," said Don Antonio, touched and pleased.

"Mr. Halkett said your silver mine was the heart of Mexico," she replied with a smile.

"Don Juan said that? I never knew the Scotsman had so much poetry in him! At least, this is the heart of our government. Don Maximiliano drives to the National Palace every day from Chapultepec, and many of us wish Their Majesties would live here, surrounded by their people. Alas! when they arrived at the palace, Doña Carlóta found bedbugs in the sleeping rooms and vermin in the kitchens; so in spite of much renovation and decorating here, they moved west to Chapultepec. Perhaps we should follow them. Tacubaya is the fashionable quarter now; and San Angel and Coyoacán are favored by many of our friends. My girls are never tired of telling me that the Calle de los Plateros began to go down when the Iturbide palace was turned into a hotel. *Ay de mí!* Time brings many changes, but the Moras have lived here for over two hundred years, and I hope my boy Hilarión will live here after me."

The house at which the landau stopped in the Street of the Silversmiths was built, like its neighbors, of the warm dark pink tezontle stone and decorated with sculptures in the ornate Churrigueresque style. Two vaqueros in the Mora livery of dark brown and yellow came running out as the footman let down the carriage steps.

"*Esta es su casa,*" said Don Antonio, ushering his guests through the heavy carved wood doors. "Everything in my house is yours . . . My dear Don Andrés, don't you carry a gun?"

The change from polite formality to sharpness was so sudden that Sally nearly laughed. But she saw that the Mexican was in deadly earnest. As soon as his cloak was taken by one vaquero, he had unbuckled an ivory-handled pistol and handed it to another; a third servant, who had bowed in front of Dr. Lorimer, remained emptyhanded.

"I carried a weapon on the highway, sir," said Andrew, discomfited. "There seemed no need to do so in the city."

"*Always* carry a gun in Mexico," said Don Antonio emphatically. "I never cross this threshold without being armed, and there are pistols in the pockets of every vehicle I possess. In about half an hour, when our guests begin arriving for the tertulia, this hall will look like an arsenal, I promise you . . . But let us go and find Doña Mercedes."

They passed from the stone-flagged hall, through another heavy door, into a patio open to the darkening sky. It was such a patio as Sally had dreamed of for their own home in Mexico, for the fountain was there, tinkling deliciously against one wall, and climbing roses wound their way round every pillar of the arches which supported the galleries of the noble house. There was even a grass lawn, mowed to the texture of velvet, and in every corner stood white crape myrtle trees. Over each stone arch hung a brightly blazoned shield with the arms of one of the noble Spanish-Mexican families allied by marriage with the Moras since their ancestor entered the Aztec city at the side of Cortés, and at the fork of the grand stone staircase which rose on the left side of the patio two coats of arms in painted wood displayed the quarterings of Don Antonio and of his wife.

At the far side of the patio, almost opposite the entrance door, a shrine protected by a conch shell of beaten silver contained an image of the Holy Child, cradled in a silver cactus. The figures of Mary and Joseph, supported by the eagle and serpent of Mexico, knelt in the background on a mesa where the sand was powdered silver and the cactus plants had solid silver leaves. The scene was lighted by candles burning behind a mosaic screen of topaz and amethyst. In front of the shrine stood a girl. They saw her face quite clearly by the candles' glow—heart-shaped, ivory-tinted beneath a weight of black hair wreathed with pink camellias, and she wore a rosy stole over a dress that was the violet gray of the twilight creeping through the patio. Her slender arms were curved to the weight of an infant who laughed and stretched his little hands to the Child of the Cactus,

and they could see her lips move in prayer above his small dark
head. She was completely unaware that she and the child were
not alone. Then Don Antonio said tenderly and proudly, "Silvia,
querida!" and the spell was broken.

Silvia Mora was not in the least self-conscious. That was
clear when she came smiling to meet them, her crinoline swaying
gracefully on the smooth grass, and put the baby boy into Don
Antonio's arms.

"Take Pablo, papa!" she commanded, and then without
waiting for a formal introduction kissed Sally on both cheeks.

"Doña Sarita, I'm so glad you're here! Mamma and my
sisters and I have been longing to meet you! And this is Don
Andrés: you are welcome, señor. Your fame has gone ahead of
you in Mexico."

Lamplight was moving behind the glass doors revealed beneath the arches. At Don Antonio's shout these doors flew open
on a band of brightly dressed young people led by the birthday
heroine, Doña Soledad. A nurse-girl leading another little boy
carried the small Pablo away, and the Lorimers were surrounded
by the boys and girls who shook hands and kissed Sally warmly.
Delighted, the American girl allowed herself to be led into the
house between Soledad, whose pretty head was completely turned
by the day's gifts and flatteries, and the next oldest girl, Pilár, who
had a plain, plump face not unlike her father's. Silvia led the
way. Her two young brothers came behind with Don Antonio
and Andrew—handsome, noisy boys of eleven and twelve, in
elaborate charro costumes of gray cloth laced with silver.

On this wave of youth and gay voices, of the perfume and
chatter of which her own youth had been starved, Sally was led
into a drawing room rich in gold embossed furniture from Spain,
with elaborate carved screens, and a portrait by Goya over a
hearth where a small fire of scented logs was burning. And there
sat Don Antonio's wife, a soft-eyed, soft-voiced lady in amber
velvet, who took Sally at once into such a warm, scented embrace as she had never known since Helen left them.

"There, there!" whispered Doña Mercedes, caressing her.

"You poor dear good child. What an experience you have had. What courage, to leave your home behind you and come to Mexico. No wonder you feel you are alone among strangers. But here are all my girls eager to be your friends, and *very* thrilled about what you did for Baron Bompard. He was dancing with Silvia and Pilár, the poor young man, at their uncle's house not fifteen days ago."

Sally sat up very straight on the sofa by Doña Mercedes' side.

"But I don't feel strange in Mexico," she said. "Right from the first day at Vera Cruz I felt at home here, and when you are all so kind to me, I feel as if I'd lived here all my life!"

"No wonder His Majesty is so enthusiastic about Don Andrés and yourself," said Doña Mercedes, tapping Sally's hand playfully with her fan. "You are to be summoned to Court at the first opportunity. As Doña Carlóta is in mourning for her father, Their Majesties have entertained very little since December—except of course for that unlucky Foury mission! But Don Maximiliano likes gaiety. I am sure he will arrange a reception very soon. And now here is my married daughter Vera, Señora Pablo Guzman y Mora . . . you saw her little boys, I think?"

Doña Vera, whose pale blue gauze crinoline elegantly concealed the imminent approach of her third child, nodded and smiled casually at Sally, reserving the warmth of her greeting for Dr. Lorimer. Her manner was at the opposite extreme from her mother's, for Don Antonio's wife, though little more than forty, belonged to a generation of Mexican gentlewomen who were indolent, acquiescent, ill at ease in formal dress and accustomed to spend half the day in lacy, beribboned deshabillé. Doña Vera, married at the beginning of the French Intervention, was febrile, fashionable, impatient of Mexican provincialism and very willing to embark on a married woman's flirtation with the handsome *Norteamericano*. But Andrew was watching her sister Silvia, who had taken a salver from the footman and was carrying glasses of sherry to the guests.

"I beg your pardon, ma'am?" He was embarrassed to find that Doña Mercedes had asked him a question.

"I asked if you had ever attended a court ball in Madrid, Don Andrés?"

"In Madrid? No indeed, Doña Mercedes; I've never been to Europe."

"I spent two years in Madrid as a very young girl," said Doña Mercedes, "visiting my Spanish relatives. Queen Ysabel was only a child then, but I have *never* forgotten the splendor of the court or the distinction of the Queen Regent—poor maligned woman! My husband is fond of saying blood is the only thing that really counts in life. Well, poor Don Maximiliano and Doña Carlóta have certainly their share of royal blood, and yet there is not the same real elegance in their soirées as one finds at the Court of Spain. My dears, I wish nothing better for any of you than a season at Madrid."

"We'll have to rely on Silvia for that," said Doña Vera with her shrill laugh. There was no explanation of the allusion, for the fifteen-year-old debutante, who had been flitting excitedly from window to door, now announced "a crowd of people coming across the patio" and Don Antonio gave his arm to his wife and led her to the door of the sala to receive their guests. In a very short time the room was crowded. Andrew shook twenty hands, and stood up to the impact of as many vigorous abrazos, while the tertulia spread gaily from one ornate apartment to another, and Silvia gracefully offered trays of good things to the guests and never came his way. Don Antonio brought up John Halkett's elder son George, a sturdy broad-shouldered young man, very like his father, who was a student at the School of Mines, and George led out Sally to take part in the cotillion opened by Soledad and a handsome Mexican youth. There was no hope of engaging Silvia for the dance, for Andrew was seized on by an elderly gentleman who wanted to know how the United States government intended to discipline the Brownsville filibusters who had recently invaded Mexican territory near Matamoros.

"Remember, they were Negroes," Andrew said sarcastically. "President Johnson is sure to back them up through thick and thin."

After that a group formed round Dr. Lorimer and the questions were fast and pointed. Why did the United States continue to recognize Juarez as President of Mexico, after even his interrupted term of office had expired? Why did the State Department revile Maximilian for the Black Decrees ordering the summary execution of all prisoners of war? Didn't Mr. Seward know the Juaristas killed and mutilated prisoners? Surgeon Captain Lorimer, C.S.A., found himself—much against his will—defending a government which had just deprived him of his passport. He was thankful when Don Antonio deftly extricated him from the group.

"You've missed a place in the cotillion, Don Andrés," he said solicitously. "Never mind! There will be music and perhaps a round game or two before supper, and as much dancing as you care for later. Just now I'm going to take you to my study, to have a glass of wine in peace."

They went out into the patio. The candles were still burning before the Child of the Cactus, but the moon shed a stronger light on all the painted shields which proved Don Antonio's belief in the importance of blood and noble lineage. It silvered the jet of water which flowed into a stone basin on one side of the courtyard, and Andrew turned aside as they strolled across the turf to examine the sculptured figures above the fountain. They were ancient, moldering and strange. Seated upon a skull was a Siren with a woman's face, a woman's breasts, and the trunk of a mermaid dividing into two heraldic tails. The Siren's face was drowsy with desire. Its long fingers plucked at the strings of a guitar, and it had a pagan, terrible allure.

"That interests you?" said Don Antonio's soft voice at Andrew's elbow. "She has been there since the days of Cortés, who laid the foundation stone of this house. My great-grandfather raised the shrine to the Child of the Cactus, to exorcise her . . . but our Siren has a powerful charm!"

He led the American into a room on the far side of the
grand staircase, where a curtain of silence seemed to fall as Don
Antonio closed the door. The study was not large, but richly
furnished with Oriental screens and tapestries. A fine Chinese
rug lay on the floor. Eighteenth-century chairs were upholstered
in rich yellow tribute silk. Bibelots of jade and ivory were arranged on a large desk and on a side table lighted candles stood
beside an array of crystal glasses and decanters.

"I don't know if you care for Oriental curios," said Don
Antonio deprecatingly, "but some of mine are supposed to be of
value. My ancestors did a good deal to develop the trade between Acapulco and Manila in the days of the old Spanish gal-
leons, before they turned to silver mining. If the value of coined
silver continues to fall, we may have to turn to the Manila trade
again." He poured two glasses of sherry and offered one to Andrew. "And now, I hope you will bear with my very faulty English and let me know what I can do to serve you. First, are you
satisfied with the state of your uncle's practice?"

"Frankly, no," said Andrew. "At least, not with the state it's
in at present. The books—such books as he kept—show a steady
loss for years past. The patients, the pathetic Indian beggars who
come to my door, prove it! I've taken four *reales* in cash fees
in the first seven days. Fifty cents for a week's work! And yet
there's money in the bank, enough for us to live on for a year
if we live carefully; no horses, but good furniture and plate—
how was it done?"

"Your uncle was a great speculator in his day. Not after
Juarez came into power. He always said he could outguess every
other President, but not Juarez. He hoped to leave you a com-
petence, but I think he realized in the last year of his life that to
succeed here, an American doctor would have to establish himself in the foreign community, out in the western suburbs."

"But in a suburban practice it would be difficult to hold a
hospital appointment, surely?"

Don Antonio smiled. "Have you one in view?"

"I may be presuming, señor, but up at Río Frío the Emperor did mention something about the new Maternity House—"

The smile grew broader. "I know he did, and what is more he has remembered it. That's a matter for congratulation, because Max is as difficult to net as one of his own butterflies. But you made a great impression on him, and after the Council meeting this afternoon he told me that you would be offered a consulting post on the Maternity House staff. That would be an excellent beginning for you, and I think I can use my influence in this parish to secure a similar post for you at the Hospital of Jesus the Nazarene. You can't hope to take your uncle's place at the School of Medicine for at least five years, but that will come."

Don Antonio leaned back in his chair and looked with approval at the handsome young man before him, whom his patronage was helping to a start in life. He was surprised by the dismay in Andrew's blue eyes, and by his next words,

"At least five years!"

"That's not very long"—rather stiffly—"at your age, and as time is reckoned in Mexico."

"It's not a question of my age, señor. It's—your generosity deserves complete frankness on my part. Before I make any long commitments in the capital, I must consider a proposal made by Mr. Matthew Maury when we met at Vera Cruz."

"He wants you to set up in practice at his colony, I suppose?"

"Yes. But nothing has been decided yet, nor will be, until Mr. Maury returns from London at the end of May."

"H'm." Don Antonio shifted in his chair, and the candlelight revealed new planes and angles of his plump cheeks and powerful jaw. "I wish you good health, my dear Don Andrés, until Matthew Maury completes his voyage back to Mexico."

"D'you mean he won't come back? But that's impossible! The colony could never survive without him! And every Southerner I've met since I came here swears that the Emperor regards him as indispensable—"

"Indispensable to Maximilian, perhaps. But not to the

Council of Ministers, to which I have the honor of belonging. The Council is growing weary of Maury's fault-finding and over-bearing ways. No!" Don Antonio raised one fat ringed hand to stop the American's shocked expostulation. "We won't discuss it more, and remember I rely on you to keep the hint I've given you to yourself. You've been given unusual opportunities in Mexico. Make the most of them, and don't rely on your country-men to help you."

"Should I even rely on Maximilian's favor, if he can reject a better man than me?" said Andrew bitterly.

"You might prefer to rely on the Empress Carlóta," said Don Antonio. "She has the better head of the two when it comes to politics. I've no love for the lady, but we miss her at the Council since she's been ill."

"Seriously ill?"

"They say she was given poison on her trip to Yucatán. Possibly toloache, or the juice of the palo de leche tree. We have several drugs in Mexico which affect the mind. And there's a persistent rumor among those who see her at the castle that she has grown torpid and dull, given to occasional loss of memory, and painfully altered in appearance. It would be interesting to have your opinion of her," he ended casually.

"Are they popular in Mexico?"

"It's not a question of popularity. It's like some appalling—what's the word—swamp, quicksand that they've led us all into. So that a Mexican like me doesn't know where to put his foot next—or how to drag it out on solid ground. That's the position in Mexico after two years of Carlóta and Maximilian.

"Listen, Don Andrés. I was one of the Assembly of No-tables who voted for the Archduke to be our Emperor. Within my memory—and I can just remember the First Empire—we have had *thirty* presidents of the Mexican Republic. Including Santa Anna, who got us into a war with the United States which lost us half our territory! Including Juarez, who got us into a war with France that isn't over yet! So, I thought, Maximilian is the man. With authority, prestige, experience in government, great alliances in Europe. We bring him here—with his young wife. Then what happens? Elected by the great landowners, these two become the champions of the Indian laborer. Blessed by the Pope, they quarrel violently with the Papal Nuncio. Maximilian dismisses the Finance Minister and mismanages the finances. He lets Bazaine and the French feather their own nests at our expense. He keeps up a running and public quarrel with his brother, the Austrian Emperor, about some wretched family pact he claims to have signed under duress. And Carlóta, in a country where sterility in a woman is a shame and a dishonor, turns out to be a barren wife."

"How long have they been married?"

"Nine years. Incidentally, of Don Maximiliano's virility there can be no doubt—the gardener's wife at Cuernavaca is with child by him. Which, by a calculation everyone has been making, must have been conceived about the time he and Carlóta perpetrated their supreme folly: they adopted a child and made him heir to the throne. And no ordinary child, I assure you. Don Agustín—"prince," we have to call him now—is the grandson of the late General Iturbide, sometime Emperor of Mexico."

" *'The ill-omened name of Agustín Iturbide,'* " said Andrew Lorimer, remembering.

Alertly: "Why do you say that?"

"Because my uncle said it, in a letter he left for me."

"Oh! El Viejo! He died two or three weeks before the adoption, though. His comments would have been worth hearing. 'Ill-omened' is a good word, as Max may find out. He is a fool to keep the people in mind of Iturbide by adopting this boy as his heir . . . Yes, I remember now about your uncle. He always had a grievance against Iturbide . . . I think because he lost money in some speculations when he was a young man. The little sugar estate was all he had left by 1840. And it, of course, has been neglected for years. It would fetch very little today as a going concern."

"I wish you would explain that to my sister," said Andrew keenly. "She has the hacienda very much on her mind."

"Explain the position to Doña Sarita?" said the Mexican in genuine surprise. "But surely you are her guardian and trustee till she marries? How old is she—seventeen?"

"Nineteen. She had a birthday while we were at sea, so it's nearly two years until she comes of age."

"Nineteen, and—forgive my curiosity—you have no marriage arranged for her?"

"American girls choose their own husbands, señor."

"Incredible!" said Don Antonio. "—Yes—who is it?"

Andrew had not heard the light knock, but now the door opened a little way to reveal a woman in a black garment, with a black veil concealing her hair, who said submissively:

"Forgive the interruption, cousin. But you are asked for in the sala: the music has begun, and Señor Lacunza has just arrived."

"The President of the Council!" said Don Antonio, getting up alertly. "Come, Don Andrés; we mustn't keep the great man waiting."

When his voice was heard, the door closed as gently as it had opened on the woman in black.

"I didn't present you to that lady," Don Antonio went on. "She prefers to remain almost invisible at a fiesta. She has taken religious vows, you see, but following the custom of the country, a Beata may be permitted to live in the house of relatives. I must say the Tía Beata has been an invaluable friend to Vera, and an excellent dueña. You will make her acquaintance later."

He slipped his ringed hand through Andrew's arm as they walked back across the lawn.

"Try not to live your life too seriously, my dear young man," he said. "I'll have a word with Doña Sarita later, if you really wish it. But now you must enjoy the music; our Mexican belles are all delightful musicians. And I would like you to hear my daughter Silvia sing."

THE MUSICAL PART of the soirée had already begun
when Sally saw her brother return quietly to the sala and take
his place among the gentlemen standing at the back of the room.
It was the one thing needed to complete her pleasure—that Andrew, who loved music, should be in time to hear the accomplished piano playing of the young ladies who advanced to the
instrument one by one, with much shaking of ringlets and pretense of shyness. There seemed to be a great deal of hair and
gauzy draperies in the room, for the heavy Mexican coiffures
soon fell out of curl, and the crinolines had been allowed to run
riot as to width and color, generally in the favorite combinations
of green and white or white and blue. Doña Mercedes, serene
on her sofa with Vera by her side and a few older ladies around
her in easy chairs, seemed to be sitting in a bright flower bed of
billowing skirts and dark heads dressed with blossoms.

Sally, alone among the young girls, wore no flowers or
jewels. She was unaware of one beauty which brought her many
admiring glances—the flawless, creamy skin which matched her
tawny hair and eyes, and which the low neckline of the dyed
black brocade showed off to great advantage. Some of the French
officers in green and silver, wearied perhaps of the Mexican
charmers, also noted with approval the keen, critical attention
Miss Lorimer gave the amateur musicians, which contrasted
strongly with the indolent passivity of the lovely girls around
her. Sally, in fact, was a success. She could not help but know
it, and it was some balm to her anxieties—some kind of a cushion
which dulled the words still ringing in her ears—*empty, frozen,
self-righteous heart*. It was very pleasant to find herself among
those new, affectionate friends. George Halkett, seated between
herself and Pilár Mora, would be a good friend, she was impulsively certain, and Pilár, the pianist among the Mora sisters,
had already proposed that she and Sally should study duets together. But any musical program began to seem insignificant

when, as the last strains of "Tus Encantos" died away, and a
flushed young soloist returned through applause to her seat,
Silvia Mora stood up to sing.

For Silvia possessed a soprano voice of a range and power
far above any heard that night. Her gift had been developed
by a wise teacher, but only her natural grace had discarded the
tricks of deportment imparted by the singing masters of the day.
She neither gestured nor grimaced. There was no pointing of
toes, no fidgeting with the ends of the rosy stole, and her long
ivory fingers were lightly clasped in front of her. Silvia sang as a
bird sings, without coquetry; and her smile, as she began, was for
her mother:

> *"If a dove should hover*
> *At thy window wide*
> *Give it love, my lover*
> *It is I, thy bride;*
> *When the sunset closes*
> *Whisper words of love*
> *Crown the bird with roses,*
> *It is I, the dove!"*

"La Paloma" was only a popular song, as hackneyed as
"Kathleen Mavourneen" or "Lorena," but it was new to Sally,
and also, as a glance across the room assured her, to her brother.
She wondered what he was making of the words. "La Paloma"
he must know meant "the dove," and as for the rest of it surely
anyone could translate *flores* and *amores?* Thus far Sally, until
the look on Andrew's face told her that he was enthralled by the
singer rather than the song.

She looked away from him at once and back at lovely
Silvia, innocently beginning the second verse. A new idea, opening up a whole new perspective, had occurred to her: that
Andrew and Silvia might fall in love and marry. None of the
obvious objections occurred to Sally in that happy moment. She
only saw the obvious advantages: Andrew in love would be less

harsh in his judgments of his sister, and Andrew's marriage would set that sister free.

No one applauded "La Paloma" more enthusiastically than Sally Lorimer—or, since she had no evening gloves, more loudly. She was equally enthusiastic about the round game proposed next—for no young lady cared to sing after Silvia—and went romping into the patio with the two Mora lads to look for a good "den" for hide and seek. "Sallee! Sallee!" Andrew could hear the boys shouting as he went after them—they had dropped the stately "Doña Sarita" already.

"Where are you going, Sally? Don Antonio wants to speak to you."

She looked back at her brother gleefully, feeling that she had seen past his mask of irritable civility to his real emotions; and then she grasped his meaning and came to him at once.

"About the hacienda? Yes, of course."

Don Antonio was waiting for them in one of the smaller drawing rooms. He took Sally's hand and tucked it paternally through his arm.

"Your brother tells me that you are anxious to hear about the Hacienda de las Flores," he said. "Now, I happened to pass by there only yesterday, and had a few words with Ramón Martínez, your overseer, so I think I can tell you anything you may need to know. Shall we go into my daughters' boudoir? It's more suited to a 'business talk' with a young lady"—he gave a humorous inflection to the words—"than my study."

He ushered the Lorimers into a small sitting room, with a French window which opened on the patio directly under the magnolia tree. By the light of an oil lamp with a crystal shade covered in pleated rose-colored silk, Sally saw a small upright piano with sheet music on the rack and a ribboned guitar standing against the tufted plush piano stool. A round table with a ball-fringed cloth held fancy needlework in various stages, including a satin pillow with a pattern of bobbin lace in progress, French and Spanish fashion magazines and a box of candy—a pleasant confusion which Sally looked at with a half-envious eye. She sat down in the crinoline chair which Don Antonio pulled out for her, and waited composedly for what he had to say.

"I've been explaining to your brother," he began suavely, "that the hacienda near Cuernavaca which your uncle bequeathed to you has been neglected for many years. Even the dwelling house, where he lived occasionally, has fallen into disrepair. It really would be prudent to sell the whole thing now for whatever price can be obtained. In fact, I've advised Don Andrés, as your guardian, to put the property up for sale immediately."

"Did you agree?" Sally turned her head very slightly towards her brother.

"I'm not the owner, am I?"

"Under Mexican law, dear miss, your brother would be the person to *administer* your property—"

"But I didn't inherit it under Mexican law," she said quickly. "My uncle never gave up his British nationality. His will was executed—isn't that the word?—at the British Legation here; and I've been thinking . . . if there were any difficulty . . . I could ask Sir Peter Campbell-Scarlett to explain it all to me."

Don Antonio looked at Andrew, and Andrew shrugged. Sally looked with feigned interest at the dainty tools for needlework arrayed on the round table by her side. There were silver embroidery scissors a fairy might have used, and tiny silver daggers for Richelieu work in green plush cases; there was also a silver thimble engraved with an initial S fitted into an opalescent green glass slipper. She picked it up and tried it on her little finger.

"*Ay de mí!*" Don Antonio broke the silence. "I don't think we need call His Excellency the British Minister into our councils, need we? There's no doubt your title to the property is perfectly clear—that's not in dispute; what I have suggested to your brother is—mightn't it be more profitable to yourself, and only yourself, to dispose of it now, for cash?"

"How can I tell that when I haven't seen it?" retorted Sally, and the Mexican's jaw dropped.

"How could you tell if you did see it?" jeered Andrew. Sally's color rose.

"You may think me very foolish and headstrong, Don Antonio," she said appealingly, "but I do feel that I ought to see the Hacienda de las Flores, and the whole of Cuernavaca, before I agree to sell. Even if the place is in bad repair the land itself must be going up in value since the Emperor took a fancy to spend his leisure at Cuernavaca. You told us about your villa there. Doña Vera says it was only built last year, and you're going to build one for her and her husband soon. Perhaps my land would be a good building site—I can't tell till I've seen it. But I might be smart, don't you think, to hold it for a raise?"

"Sally, upon my word—!"

Don Antonio held up his hand to check Andrew's outburst.

"And there's another thing," said Sally. She slipped Silvia's thimble back inside the green glass slipper and looked up. "You say, señor, the place has been 'neglected.' Does that mean the house only? What about the furnace and the refinery? Is the place working at a total loss?"

"No, not a total loss. But the sugar market, like the silver market, has been hard hit this year."

"On account of the war?"

"Yes."

"But I thought Cuernavaca wasn't in the war zone? The sugar canes can't have been destroyed?"

"No, the plantation is intact. But a sugar hacienda requires a first-rate man to run it. Ramón Martínez, whom your uncle took out of some Indian village and put in as overseer, is quite a reliable fellow, but he's too old for the job now, and he can't get the help he needs in Cuernavaca."

"Perhaps they've all found work in the building trades," said Sally innocently. The first hint of exasperation appeared in Don Antonio's manner.

"You understand that if you were to keep the hacienda in

operation, even for a short time, you would have a considerable
bill in wages and merchandise to meet every month. How would
you propose to do that?"

"I can't say until I've gone through the books with Don
Ramón. You see I got a lot of pamphlets on the sugar industry
from Washington, and they said Mexico hadn't nearly developed
its sugar resources, even for domestic use. And I've been thinking, since I do happen to own a sugar hacienda, if I tried to run
it in a really up-to-date way, perhaps I'd quite soon make a
profit—it's all a matter of marketing, the pamphlets said."

"Pamphlets on the sugar industry!" said Don Antonio.
Across the crochet hooks and macramé work on his daughters'
table he looked at Sally with something like consternation. "Run
the hacienda! Do you seriously mean that you contemplate living
there, and conducting the plantation business singlehanded?"

"A great many Southern women have been running plantations singlehanded for the past five years, as my brother would
be the first to tell you."

"But not coping with the special problems of our peonage—"

"I thought peonage was abolished in Mexico," said Sally
sharply. Don Antonio saw her look of triumph fade, and pressed
home the advantage.

"As long as there are Indian laborers in Mexico, there will
be peonage," he said. "Last year, I agree, the Empress Carlóta
introduced a wild, impractical scheme to give the peons liberty.
But it was never enacted, and while landowners govern this
country it never will be."

"The peons are still slaves, are they?" said Andrew.

"In the sense that they are unable to leave the plantations
where they work, yes. You see, they are all in debt to their—
master—for the food and clothing which he sells them, and in
debt not only on their own account but on their parents' and
grandparents' before them. No other *ranchero* in the province
would employ your men if they tried to cancel their debts by
running away from you. You can send the officers of the law in
pursuit, you can use dogs to track them, you can have them

flogged or thrown into jail without a warrant. You are their owner and they are your slaves, and that's the meaning of Mexican peonage."

"So my sister is a slaveowner, whether she likes it or not?" asked Andrew. Sally saw the amusement and satisfaction in his face. The tables turned on his Abolitionist sister—that was how he saw the future of the Hacienda de las Flores.

"But if I remit their debts, these Indians would be free?"

She hardly recognized her own voice in the low, painful murmur; indeed she hardly knew what she was saying. Sally was only aware that she had come face to face with a great test of principle. How she could meet it she was not yet sure. But the terrible words, *dogs, flogged, jail* were a challenge she could not ignore.

"The remission of such debts won't make you popular with your neighbors," smiled Don Antonio. "Come, my dear young lady, think very carefully over what I have said. Discuss it, if you wish, with any of the gentlemen at the British Legation. And go, by all means, and inspect your property before you make your decision. Only remember that Cuernavaca is forty miles away, and Don Andrés at present has neither mules nor carriage. I suggest that you both come with us as our guests when we go to the villa after Easter. Then," he added with a laugh, "I hope to prove to you that I have no designs on your estate, or plan to add it to my own—"

"Oh, I didn't mean that!" said Sally. "Surely you don't think—"

"*I* think Don Antonio has been remarkably kind and forbearing to you, Sally," her brother interrupted. "You should thank him for even listening to your notions. You enter the sugar trade, indeed! Don Antonio has forgotten more about Mexican business than you're likely to learn in your whole life."

"Miss Sally is a very modern young lady," said Mora pleasantly. "She wants to manage her own affairs and make her own mistakes: she may be right. My eldest daughter was rather like her—'strong-minded,' isn't that the North American word? Dear

Vera! I remember when we betrothed her to her cousin, every word of the contract and the settlement had to be scrutinized, and whole clauses redrafted to please the bride. Silvia, now, has a different nature. She left her marriage contract in papa's hands, and said she knew he would arrange everything for the best."

It was Sally who broke the little silence which followed.

"I didn't know that Doña Silvia was engaged to be married, señor," she said. "Is her future husband among your guests to-night?"

Don Antonio Mora laughed proudly.

"Don Felipe is visiting his Spanish estates at present," he said. "He is putting his house in Madrid in order to receive his bride. But he is expected at his quinta near Orizaba shortly—and the marriage will take place soon after he returns."

Chapter Six

ON GRASSHOPPER HILL

I

THE EMPRESS CARLÓTA was playing the piano. She played Bach and Mozart particularly well, but on this warm afternoon the two Ladies of the Palace on duty at Chapultepec exchanged smiles as they listened to the folk tunes she was playing to please the child leaning shyly against the instrument.

Agustín Iturbide, the adopted son and heir of Carlóta and Maximilian, was a handsome little boy whose large brown eyes were fixed anxiously on the lady he had been taught to call mamma. Seven months was such a large proportion of his three years that Agustín had almost forgotten his father and mother, or any other home than the Alcazar of Chapultepec, but he was not yet quite sure of his new mamma's moods. She was never as amusing as papa, who could make paper boats and remarkable houses built entirely out of cards, nor was listening to music Agustín's favorite way of passing the early afternoon. He preferred dabbling in the pool beside the great green Grasshopper on its miniature Hill, the presiding genius of Chapultepec; but that, the three-year-old philosopher realized, meant listening to a long story, conscientiously recited by mamma, about the Boy Heroes who had died by leaping from that place when the American troops captured the castle many years before. When mamma played the tunes he liked, Agustín knew that she was at least trying to entertain him.

Presently he began to dance to her playing; up and down the drawing room, between the vibrating black piano and the

silent instrument of warm golden wood on which the Emperor
sometimes joined his wife in duets, smiling at his mamma with
all the grave courtesy of his father's race. He was not as dark as
most Mexican children, for he had chestnut hair like his grandfather, the Emperor Agustín I, and a fair complexion inherited
from his American mother, born Alicia Green. If Doña Alicia,
now far away in Paris, could have seen the sturdy little figure in
long white nankeen trousers and loose white-pleated shirt caper-
ing round the formal Buhl furniture, she might have caught him
in her arms and covered the small flushed face with kisses. Carlóta felt no such impulse. But she laughed aloud, and said
"Bravo, Agustín!" so that out on the terrace Señora del Barrio,
the only one among twenty Ladies of the Palace who really
loved Carlóta, breathed a prayer of thankfulness.

O Señor Dio, said the señora's anxious heart, let *him* come
to her in good time today, without stopping at La Teja. She is so
much better and calmer now. Let nothing ruffle her serene mood
—above all not the child, because she hasn't yet made up her
mind to love the child or to be jealous, as she has had cause to
be jealous of so much else.

The Empress came through the open doors of the drawing
room with a smile for the curtsying ladies in the arcade, and
walked down the terrace with Agustín's hand in hers. They were
going to look at the lake, the child's chatter told Señora del
Barrio, and that too was a great improvement. There had been
times when the mere sight of the Chapultepec lake had annoyed
Carlóta, and she would suddenly refuse to join a boating party
or go for a moonlight swim under the cypress trees. She did not
care to know that the woods round the lake had been the favorite
haunt of Moctezuma and the Aztec warriors, or that Cortés
and his Malinche had plunged naked into those same moonlit
waters. Her only standard of comparison had been the Prater
and the Bois, and Chapultepec park, she made her new subjects
understand, was nothing but an insignificant picnic ground in
the heart of a savage country. We haven't heard so much, lately,
about the Empress Eugénie's favorite drive round the lake in the

Bois de Boulogne, thought Señora del Barrio. Perhaps she realizes now that no princess ever lived in a lovelier palace than Chapultepec.

Certainly no royal residence of Europe had a lovelier setting than the castle on the porphyry crag, built by a Spanish viceroy and captured by an American general, where tall cypresses and flowering acacias waved on cliff and woodland in the eternal spring of Mexico. Carlóta with her arm round Agustín as he perched on the stone coping could look across to the city and the snowcapped volcanoes, and in the middle distance, beyond the cypress woods, the boggy meadows surrounding the old haciendas, mills and convents which lay between the city and Chapultepec. Among them there was one—the Hacienda de la Teja—which her husband with his passion for building had remodeled into a little bachelor nest where he enjoyed playing cards or billiards with his Austrian equerries and discussing a bottle of Tokay when the pressures of politics became too intense. He could reach La Teja discreetly on his way back from the National Palace, by driving down the Paseo de Bucareli and taking a short cut through the pastures. Carlóta said the Paseo was in wretched repair, as indeed it was, and she had ordered a new road to be cut, running straight from Chapultepec to the mounted statue of Carlos IV, called "El Caballito," inside the city. When it was finished she would be able to watch from her own windows and see the Emperor's carriage proceeding, without a detour, from his residence to his council room, and back again.

The woman and the child came back along the terrace, and the Mexican ladies began to busy themselves with ice and silver goblets set ready on a low table, for Carlóta liked to dispense with footmen and pages during the lazy hours of early afternoon. She was even dressed informally, like a Mexican woman, and in spite of the court mourning her white silk deshabillé was fastened at neck and waist with ribbons of her favorite color, lilac blue.

"Please, mamma, may I have a *refresco* instead of chocolate?"

"Very well, Agustín. What would you like?"

"Some orangeade—may I?"

"We both like *naranjada,* don't we? I will have orangeade too, Señora de Pacheco."

Fresh oranges, fresh water from the spring that rose on Grasshopper Hill and was carried to the city in the great Belem aqueduct, were ready with ice and sugar to be blended into the Empress Carlóta's favorite drink. Her ladies prepared several *naranjadas* every day, for Carlóta suffered much from thirst, but this afternoon as she stood by the balustrade, sipping at the frosted goblet, the Empress of Mexico looked relaxed and happy, with a new contentment in her face.

The eyes of the two Mexican ladies met in an expressionless glance. Seen in profile, with the spring breeze molding the loose robe about her, Carlóta's figure seemed softer and more ample: the ribbons at her waist were certainly tied in a looser knot. Now could it be—the opaque eyes queried—that, after all, Her Majesty is with child? The Señoras del Barrio and de Pacheco knew of a certainty what was often rumored in the city—that Carlóta and Maximilian had never shared the same bed nor even the same apartments at Chapultepec. But they also knew that three months earlier, at the time of her father's death, Maximilian had been sympathetic and tender with Carlóta. He had taken her away to a small hacienda near Orizaba where they were almost constrained to live on an intimate footing, and she had been conspicuously loving and gentle with him since their return. Could it be that after nine years of marriage Maximilian's wife was to bear a direct heir to the throne of Mexico?

"Mamma, can I go and see the sentries saluting papa?"

"That's just an excuse to see the Grasshopper and go paddling in the pond. Papa won't be here for a long time yet."

"I heard the carriage drive into the patio, mamma."

The Empress looked bewildered.

"I heard nothing." The buzzing in her ears had begun again; it had troubled her intermittently for some time past, shutting out the ordinary sounds of the world around her. But she caught the Emperor's quick step as he came round the buttressed corner and her ladies stood up to curtsy low. Agustín, with a shout of "Papa!" hurled himself at the tall man's knees.

"Have you been a good boy today?" Maximilian stooped to kiss the small flushed cheek. But he resisted Agustín's entreaty to be lifted to his shoulder for the ride round the terrace which the little boy loved.

"Not now, my dear, papa is busy . . . Take Prince Agustín to his aunt, señoras, and be good enough to leave us for a time."

It was a more abrupt order than Maximilian usually gave the Ladies of the Palace, and Carlóta looked at her husband in surprise.

"Is something wrong, Max?" she asked as soon as they were alone.

"Now what should be wrong," he said with forced cheerfulness, "in my wanting to spend a little while alone with my wife?"

He put his arm around her and led her gently back into the drawing room. The awnings had been lowered, and the room, although overfull with its two pianos, the Gobelins tapestries and heavy furniture presented by the Emperor and Empress of the French, was cool and restful. Tall vases held spikes of blue larkspur and delphinium from the roof garden which Maximilian, when he restored the dilapidated castle, had created for Carlóta's pleasure. Maximilian felt her body consenting beneath the thin silk. The face turned to his own was so serene that he cursed his luck in being the bearer of bad news. She had been so reasonable of late, so much less demanding and more hopeful, that he hated to unsettle her on the day of a diplomatic reception. But just on that account he dared not dissimulate. There was always the danger that some malicious tongue would ask the Empress, at her soirée, what she thought of the news from France.

"My dear, I think there *is* something that you ought to know," he began deprecatingly. "Some urgent dispatches came in from Almonte this afternoon."

"Well?" She drew away from him. "What is the latest news from Paris?"

"It's—not good on either count. The Iturbides have been making trouble again. Doña Alicia is pestering Secretary Seward about little Agustín. Asking him to help her as an American citizen—to get back her child."

"We've known all about that since last November."

"Yes, but now she and her husband have taken their troubles to the United States Minister in Paris. Almonte is afraid that Mr. Bigelow may use her complaints to make trouble for us with the Quai d'Orsay."

"If Almonte were an efficient ambassador he would point out to Monsieur Rouher that every member of the Iturbide family received thirty thousand dollars in cash from you before they left here. And that on the fifteenth of February they drew the first half of one hundred and twenty thousand dollars more, in bills on Paris."

"Almonte did better. He gave John Bigelow a full account of the money transactions. Perhaps Seward's sympathy for Doña Alicia will evaporate when he learns that the Iturbides literally sold the child to us."

"Poor Agustín! I think I'd be sorry, now, to give him up."

"We won't have to give him up."

Carlóta looked at him intently.

"You said, not good news on either count. Is there something worse than Doña Alicia's nonsense? . . . Is it—Napoleon?"

"Charlotte, my poor girl—it's what we've been afraid of since the beginning of the year. Napoleon has yielded to pressure from the United States, and, I fear, to pressure from his own legislature. He has promised his ministers that all French troops of the Line shall be withdrawn from Mexico."

Before his eyes, he saw her happiness wither, and the old look of frustrated ambition come back to take its place.

"It isn't possible," she said, trembling. "Napoleon and Eugénie swore to us by all the saints in heaven that they'd not forsake us. And the treaty, Max! The Treaty of Miramar alone binds him to keep twenty-five thousand men in Mexico for the whole of this year, and twenty thousand men through 1867. Too many French troops have gone back already. How dare Napoleon contemplate recalling more?"

"I'm afraid it's more a question of money than of politics."

"It always is with a Bonaparte."

"Yes, well—Napoleon accuses *me* of defaulting on the twenty-five million francs due for maintaining the French Corps in Mexico—"

"Which you didn't know was your liability."

"—and says his second Mexican Loan has been so badly undersubscribed in France that he can't give me more time to pay."

"That's Napoleon's concern. How could you pay for the army when you had to start paying that man Jecker's atrocious claims last year?"

Maximilian groaned. "Bazaine says the Jecker bonds were at the bottom of the French Intervention, and he thought I knew it all along."

"You've seen Bazaine?"

"I sent to Buena Vista for him. He doesn't think the position is quite as bad as it seems. He has been working out a new scheme for Mexican recruitment—to create mixed regiments of Mexicans and French. That might work quite well, you know. Bazaine is sure Napoleon would agree to it. Remember, even if the Line regiments go home, the Foreign Legion remains here unconditionally. We have Napoleon's word for that."

"The word of a Bonaparte?" spat the Empress Carlóta. "The word of a liar and a cheat! Eugénie says he prays for us every night, and she prays for us too—the hypocrites! I hope I may be given the strength, some day, to kill them both!"

THE EMPEROR dined alone in his rooms that afternoon, wearing his favorite blue flannel dressing gown with his chamois slippers, and waited on only by his Italian valet, Grill. Tudos, the Hungarian chef, prepared a menu of his master's favorite dishes to compensate for the trouble which every member of the Household knew had broken out again between Their Majesties. He tore his hair when half of them were sent away untasted. But although Maximilian had been physically shaken by the scene with his wife, what food and wine he swallowed did him good, and so did the cigar he lighted when coffee was brought and he sat down at his desk to write a memorandum to Napoleon III. He worked quite steadily for the first half hour, laying each page on the carpet to dry, for it was one of his minor manias to use no blotting paper. Then Maximilian yielded to the torpid warmth of a room which, perpetually suffering from cold, he kept heated by stoves to the temperature of a Russian bath. Reminding himself that the musical soirée would mean a postponement of his usual bedtime hour—eight o'clock—the Emperor of Mexico lay down on a comfortable sofa, and composed himself for sleep.

But the Empress walked upon the terrace until the early twilight fell, with something so lost and lonely in the sound of her footsteps that the sentry on duty in the outer court where the Boy Heroes had leaped to death and glory crossed himself as he heard her come and go. Sometimes for very weariness she leaned on the stone coping, staring through the early twilight at the lights beginning to shine out in the distant city, and then the restless pacing was resumed until her experienced maid, Mathilde Döblinger, coaxed her indoors at last. Once in the lamplit bedroom, where her plain black tulle crinoline with its trimmings of fine Brussels lace lay ready on the bed, she became more composed. She swallowed a thimbleful of ether, over Mathilde's protests, knelt for a few moments at her prie-dieu, and suffered herself to be made ready for the evening. Then she summoned her anxious Ladies to follow her through the Patio de Honor to the reception rooms, where Maximilian waited to lead her round the diplomatic circle. It was not large. Imperial Brazil was the only country in the hemisphere which recognized the

Empire of Mexico, and the last American Minister, Mr. Thomas Corwin, had been recalled to Washington two years before. The envoys present looked grave and ill at ease. Looked, indeed, as if a posting to Monaco or Montenegro would be preferable to staying on in Mexico.

As soon as Carlóta saw them, she knew that every member of the diplomatic corps had heard the news from France. With a fixed smile she continued to receive the presentations of those outside the official circle, made by her Grand Chamberlain the Conde del Valle. Those favored were not all persons of high rank and title. It was sometimes said by members of the thirty families who could claim descent from Cortés and the Conquistadores, that "the Belgian lady" and "the Austrian gentleman" kept not so much an open house as a free-for-all. Although Maximilian had found time to compile seven volumes of court etiquette since his arrival in Mexico, there was little ceremony at Chapultepec. There was no marshaling of those to be presented by gentlemen ushers and Gold-Sticks-in-Waiting. There were no thrones. Carlóta sat in a large ornate chair, the arms carved to represent the Plumed Serpent, symbol of the god Quetzlcoatl, and the Emperor, wearing the green and red sash of the Mexican Eagle over his dark green tunic, stood by her side. A small orchestra played "La Donna è Mobile" in fandango time as the small procession moved up to the Imperial couple.

Among those presented to the Empress that night was a pretty American girl in a white crinoline, wearing a necklace of seed pearls and a tiny wreath of white tuberoses in her hair, who was brought forward by the wife of Don Antonio Mora. Don Antonio himself presented two young men—one the pretty girl's brother, a doctor lately arrived from one of the Confederate States, and the other a boy named Halkett who had won a gold medal presented by Carlóta to the best student about to graduate from the School of Mines. These caught and held Carlóta's capricious interest: the younger man for his ability in a technical subject of great importance to Mexico, the brother and

sister for their good looks and the air of good breeding which
distinguished them from so many of the Southern exiles who had
lately sought acceptance at the Imperial Court. She looked at
them more than once after they were seated, not too far behind
the government and the *corps diplomatique*. The faces of all
three struck her as not only handsome but refreshingly vivid and
original among the masks she already knew too well. She glanced
at Marshal Bazaine, whose flabby cheeks and leaden eyes betrayed the slackening of physical and moral fiber which had overtaken him since the marriage with a Mexican girl, young enough
to be his daughter, which was steadily ruining his prestige with
his army. Monsieur Dano, the French Minister, was squinting
at her balefully. He was a spy of Napoleon, as General Thun,
commander of the Austrian brigade, was a spy of Franz Josef.
Spies everywhere; an enemy behind every polite, civilized mask.
Even good-natured Colonel van Smissen, commander of the tiny
Belgian corps—what lies had *he* written home to Brussels to set
the new king so violently against them? Why was everyone in
the world turning against Maximilian, who—but for one crime
against herself—was the man selected by God and nature to be
the Lord of the whole world?

Sally Lorimer saw no enemies, but many new friends, in the
long room at Chapultepec that night. No Mexicans could ever
be got to listen to music in strict silence, for music was as much
part of their lives as flowers; and the Europeans present, who
knew the insipid program of Bellini, Donizetti, and Verdi "selections" by heart, were equally ready for whispered greetings and
conversation. So there were smiles and compliments for Sally,
sparkling in her first grand dress, and much more of a challenge
than a foil, if she had known it, to Silvia's passive beauty by her
side.

Many great houses had been opened to the Lorimers since
the night of the tertulia at the Casa Mora, and not only because
they were introduced by Don Antonio and his wife. Dr. Rafael
Lucio, the leading doctor of the capital, had been much im-

pressed by Andrew when they met in consultation at the Maternity House, and many fruitful meetings with his new colleagues proved to the young man that medicine in Mexico had gone several stages further than the leech jar and the bullet probe. Then the British Legation deigned to take notice of the Americans: one of the attachés had been transacting current business, in Sally's absence, with her overseer at Cuernavaca and had accounts and a sum of money to hand over. Invitations followed, notably on Sundays, when Andrew and Sally, as the nearest approach to their own form of worship, went to hear the Church of England service read at the Legation. But in all the comings and goings which filled her days Sally was faithful to her first impression of Silvia Mora.

So, it appeared, was Andrew. On every possible occasion he was seen by her side, ready to fetch and carry, watching for her smile in a way which would have caused scandalized comment in Fayetteville, but which was taken for granted in the easygoing society of Mexico. Every beauty was admired and courted; flattery was as natural as the abrazos and the kissing and the instant use of Christian names between new friends. It shocked no one that the American doctor should pay such obvious court to an engaged girl. Don Felipe Vega might have reason to complain, later, but he was almost unknown in his native land and had nobody's sympathy. To *mañana,* the eternal *mañana,* the problem of Don Felipe's feelings had been postponed.

Doña Mercedes, with her stricter notions of Spanish etiquette, might have kept her betrothed daughter more closely by her side, but Doña Mercedes' chief concern at that time was for Vera. On Easter Sunday, which fell on the first of April, the eldest Mora daughter had given birth, some weeks earlier than was expected, to a puny baby girl, and anxiety for mother and child kept both Doña Mercedes and the Tía Beata in Vera's sickroom for many days. Don Antonio, on the principle of safety in numbers, took the three younger girls without a chaperone to parties where he soon became too much engrossed in politics to notice the flirtations going on beneath his nose.

Soledad was a consummate flirt at fifteen, as Vera had been before her. Pilár, the plain sister who was destined for the convent, had obviously lost her heart to young George Halkett, and Sally listened to many whispered confidences which seemed to promise badly for the happiness of the future nun. Silvia made no confidences of any sort. She had great reserves of secrecy, as Sally soon discovered. She refused to discuss her approaching marriage, and the only comments Sally ever heard her make on the Marqués de Vega were the *"muy elegante"* and *"muy simpático"* which were the least good breeding could require.

There were some grave days to be lived through in March, which brought Sally and Andrew the first anniversary of their father's death, and involved the Mora sisters in the mystery and pageantry of Holy Week. But in the beautiful April weather Sally went nearly every afternoon to the Casa Mora, to sit with the young sisters in the little private garden behind their boudoir, and sew, and chatter in complete freedom from Doña Vera's sarcasms or the Tía Beata's unobtrusive espionage. Sally's sewing was always practical, for Doña Mercedes had persuaded Andrew to let his sister put off mourning entirely when the year was up, and with the assistance of the sewing women constantly employed in the great house, she was making herself a whole new wardrobe—white, pale gray, lilac—of the thin inexpensive tarlatans and muslins which Mexican looms were beginning to turn out. Sometimes Silvia brought out her guitar and sang to them with her lovely head drooping above the strings, and then Sally was uneasily reminded of the Siren of the patio fountain. More often they leafed through the fashion magazines which were their only reading matter—although Pilár sometimes looked at the *Diario del Imperio,* and lamented that all the sisters had been taken from the Colegio de Niñas at the age of twelve.

By Sally's standards they were ignorant creatures. They knew little or nothing of the world outside Mexico. Madrid, of course, was its center. Rome was where the Pope lived, Paris where the pretty dresses came from; Vienna the place where Don Maximiliano's brother ruled over an empire which for all they knew stretched from Lapland to the Cape of Good Hope. But she never criticized the Mora girls, even silently. They were the first friends to accept her for her own sake, without any reference to the quarrel between North and South which had embittered her early girlhood. They had never heard of Gettysburg or Appomattox, but they never could hear enough about life in the pine woods of North Carolina. They laughed gently at Sally's Spanish pronunciation (self-taught from the appendix to her Castilian grammar book) and marveled when in three weeks she had learned to speak their language like a Mexican. And they spread their genuine sweetness over what had threatened to become the acid of Sally's nature. They were so lively and so outgoing in their affection that Sally's powers of loving, checked by a relationship with Andrew which was no better than armed neutrality, grew greater every day. Sometimes when the girls and their schoolboy brothers crowded round her at parting with warm abrazos and many kisses, Sally went back to the Plazuelita feeling certain that none of the Moras would ever say she had an empty, frozen heart.

So Sally was almost happy as she sat beside Silvia at the Chapultepec reception, and blushed and fluttered her eyelids like a Mexican girl when Prince Khevenhüller, standing with a group of officers against the wall, discreetly mimed the duet of "Auld Lang Syne" which the Emperor had threatened them with at Río Frío. But her eyes were caught and held again and again by the central figure of the evening, whom she was now seeing for the first time.

"I wonder why she goes on wearing those dreary opals," whispered Silvia, indicating the Empress with the merest flicker of her fan. The Moras, like all the Mexican ladies, preferred colored jewels to pearls and diamonds, and that night Silvia, in pale blue, was wearing an elaborate necklace of sapphires.

"I wonder why she sits beneath her portrait," Sally whispered back. "When was it painted?"

"Only last year."

The two official portraits of the Emperor and Empress, sent out to Mexico by Graefle of Munich, did indeed make an odd background to the living man and woman. Maximilian, handsome and at ease, with one hand resting on the back of his wife's chair, challenged any comparison with his picture in the imperial robes. But the change in Carlóta's appearance was disquieting. Nearly all her guests had known her as she appeared in her portrait: slender, engaging, jeweled, with pearls embroidered on her white flounced crinoline and her dark hair arranged in a glossy curl on her bare shoulder, under the Imperial crown. Now, still less than twenty-six years old, she sat huddled like an elderly woman in her black dress, her face pale and puffy, her eyes dilated by the drug she had swallowed, wearing no ornaments but her wedding ring and the parure of fire-opals from Querétaro.

"Señorita Concha Mendez, the Cuban Nightingale!" announced the master of ceremonies, to a decorous clapping of hands. In the front row of the audience Marshal Bazaine called out in his coarse voice:

"*Olé, señorita! 'La Paloma'!*"

"*Your* song, Silvia," said Sally jealously, and looking up at Andrew, standing behind Don Antonio's chair, she saw the same thought in his eyes.

"La Mendez sings it better," said Silvia sweetly. But the Cuban Nightingale, tired of the hackneyed number she sang every night at the Teatro Imperial, shook her head at the Marshal of France. With a deep curtsy to the Empress, she began:

"*Vola—o serenata—la mia diletta è sola—*"

A long sigh shook Carlóta. She relaxed in the chair carved with the symbol of the Plumed Serpent, and surrendered herself to the memories evoked by the liquid Italian song. It had been the great favorite of those early married days when she and Maximilian, then Governor General of Lombardy, had escaped from their palace in Milan to a villa on Lake Como where in the moonlit gardens they had listened in each other's arms to that very serenade.

"Vola—o serenata—la mia diletta è sola,
E con la bella testa abbandonata
posa tra gli lenzuoli . . .
O serenata, vola,
O serenata, vola."

With that song, Carlóta's defenses of pride and etiquette were breached. As it died away she turned to Maximilian, and beneath the amused, skeptical, or astounded gaze of three hundred pairs of eyes, she laid her wet cheek against her husband's hand.

II

"I can't imagine such behavior at the Court of Spain."

It was Doña Mercedes' only comment on Carlóta's display of emotion, and it was not made until she had settled her party in an alcove in the supper room and sent the two young men in search of ices. Sally did her best to appear interested.

"You've often told us, ma'am, about the Queen Regent's good—good—"

"The Queen Regent's *perfect* propriety of manner," Doña Mercedes interrupted with unusual energy. But the inevitable account of her stay in Madrid was to be spared the girls that night, for not one but half a dozen *caballeros* came up to take the places vacated by Andrew and George Halkett, and beg respectfully to escort the señoritas on a stroll through the picture galleries.

"You don't want to walk through those crowded rooms, do you, my dears?"

Silvia smiled a soft denial. But when Andrew Lorimer's red head was seen, well above the sleek black heads around him, as he forged his way back from the crowded buffet, her lovely face became at once more animated. She gathered her pale-blue flounces in one hand as if preparing to rise and go anywhere on the arm of the American. But Andrew had lost George Halkett in the crush and found a new companion, who came up to their table with a deep bow which included all the ladies in its homage.

"See whom I've brought you, Sally!" Andrew said. "Doña Mercedes, Doña Silvia, may I present Dr. Julius Herzog, one of the unlucky Foury mission, whom we met at Río Frío?"

"Whom he *saved* at Río Frío, madam," said the Belgian doctor emphatically. "Your very obliged servant, Miss Lorimer! I trust I see you well?"

The man whom Sally had left lying in a heavy sleep at Río Frío still wore his sleeve pinned to his dress coat, but the pallor had given place to a healthy tan, and thick spectacles, which she did not remember, perched almost jauntily on the bridge of an inquiring nose. Dr. Herzog's neat black mustache was trimly clipped and shone with much the same luster as his evening shoes. In the conversation which followed, it appeared that after nearly a month recuperating from his wound at the Mine House, he had just arrived at Chapultepec to be the guest of Their Majesties until the time came for him to return to Europe.

"But is your arm really better?" asked Sally, when she found herself walking through the picture galleries at Dr. Herzog's side. "I see you still wear a sling."

"I'll be able to do without it very soon. I was extremely well nursed at the Mine House, you know. Mrs. Halkett and her sister-in-law were more than kind—and I think just as capable as the Sisters of St. Vincent who nursed poor Monsieur Bompard."

"I'm afraid *he* won't be coming to Mexico, will he? We heard he meant to convalesce in the Warm Country."

"He's going to spend a month at the Emperor's hacienda near Orizaba. His brother is on his way to Vera Cruz to take him home."

"A very sad homecoming for both of them."

There was a lighted chandelier above their heads, and lights streaming in from the fairy lamps in the gardens. In this brilliance Dr. Herzog took a long look at Sally.

"Well," he said, "with all this talk of wounded men and sadness, I needn't ask how *you* got on, Miss Sally! May I tell you that I find you in great beauty, now that we meet again?"

"I wish I could believe you, Dr. Herzog."

She turned aside his compliment simply, and the doctor realized that with the new beauty had come a new sophistication, a patina which covered Sally Lorimer from the little coronet of tuberoses in her hair to the beaded tips of her white satin slippers. There was a delicate color in the face he had only seen pinched with fatigue and anxiety. Her shoulders, revealed by a wide lace bertha, were smoothly, softly round.

"I mean it, mademoiselle. You look very lovely."

"Mexico agrees with me, I think."

"I can see that. And do you agree with Mexico? Do you enjoy living here?"

"Every minute of every day. We've made so many friends—"

"Dr. Lorimer I see has made a particular friend."

Sally followed his discreet glance. Andrew and Silvia, who had accompanied them into the new picture gallery, had paused beside a presentation portrait of the Empress of the French. Neither one appeared to be interested in Eugénie's wistful beauty. Andrew was talking low and earnestly, Silvia fingering the sapphires at her throat. They were quite obviously in a world of their own.

"Doña Silvia is the friend of both of us," said Sally, equally discreet. "Oh! they're going out into the garden. Doña Mercedes won't like that."

"Shall we play propriety, and follow them at a respectful distance?"

The doctor offered Sally his sound arm as they crossed the threshold of the gallery into one of the small bright gardens which were the jewels of Chapultepec. It had been so constructed that the cypresses, the murmuring *ahahuetes* of Moctezuma, sheltered it on two sides from the night breeze, and on the third the stones of the castle wall held all the warmth of the daytime hours. There were loggias covered with purple bougainvillea, in which several silent couples were strolling, and in the flower beds carnations and lilies glistened with the spray flung by the single plume of a tall fountain.

"I hope you'll be able to pay a visit to the Mine House before long, Miss Sally. They're all very eager to have you, and you'd enjoy John Halkett's anecdotes about the late doctor. He must have been a very remarkable man."

"I wish we could have stayed at the Mine House on our way to Mexico. It might have—simplified a lot of things."

"Mr. Halkett spoke more than once of driving in to Mexico to see *you*. But his son apparently told him that you were on the point of going to the Hacienda de las Flores, and he was afraid of missing you."

"On the point!" said Sally angrily. "I wish I were! But what can I do, when we're supposed to wait on Don Antonio's convenience? I couldn't very well urge him, when he was alarmed for Doña Vera, and now he lets day after day slip by, and never mentions leaving for his villa. *Mañana,* always *mañana!—*"

She caught back the emphatic words. Dr. Herzog, intentionally or not, had touched on the sore point which Sally had tried to soothe with the bright affection of the Mora girls. Her hacienda, which she was not allowed to visit—her peons, whom she was unable to set free—her sugar canes, growing tall in the sunshine of the Warm Country—the tantalizing images rose before her in a frustration which, under the fairy lamps of the garden, Dr. Herzog could clearly read upon her face.

"You feel that if they would let you go to Las Flores, you could handle it as well as you did the situation at Río Frío?"

"*Please,* Dr. Herzog!"

She slipped her hand from the Belgian doctor's arm. She moved a few steps away from him, impatiently, as if to indicate that the subject was closed. He followed her through the flowery loggia to the parapet on the fourth side of the garden, which overlooked the Patio de Honor. The pillared entrance to the castle itself was brightly lighted, for the guests were still moving in and out, but the side of the courtyard near the sentry boxes at the main gate was in darkness, and in the darkness could be heard voices and the jingle of harness.

"Who are these men?" said Sally sharply.

"Only the soldiers, the guard on duty—and I presume some of the coachmen," said Dr. Herzog. "You're not nervous?"

"Not at all."

"Here on this little lighted rock in the middle of a hostile country?"

"Not hostile to me, I assure you."

"Miss Sally, I'm afraid I have offended you, by probing into your thoughts. Believe me, it was only my deep interest—"

"And your business?" she cut him short. "Aren't you—what was the description—a mental specialist, a student of the brain?"

"You and Sergeant Franchet despised me for that, didn't you?" said Herzog quietly.

"I and Sergeant Franchet?" with a gasp.

"Oh, yes. You found me singularly ineffectual. When I produced my feeble excuse for having no surgical instruments I saw contempt in Franchet's eyes . . . and he was right. If I had equipped myself properly I might have saved Bompard's leg and even Huard's life. I should have handled my own wound better and been able to give your brother more effective help than I did. But of course you met the crisis like a heroine. It's in your nature, as Franchet himself said yesterday."

"Yester— You were talking to Sergeant Franchet yesterday? In the city? Here?"

"When my coach halted at Buena Vista, where he was on duty."

"I thought he had gone to Saltillo," Sally said.

"He was posted to Saltillo, but his wound opened after the ride to Río Frío—"

"I never knew he had been wounded."

"He received a chest wound in a guerrilla raid near Tampico last December. It was badly handled at the start, and cost him a spell in the hospital, but he's fit for guard duty now. Of course he should have reported sick when they ordered him to Río Frío—"

"Sergeant Franchet is too good a soldier to shirk his duty," Sally said.

"You thought so? From such a brief acquaintance? But that's natural. Franchet and you are two of a kind, you see. Alert, self-assured, reliable in an emergency. And able, when the emergency is over, to go on your way without self-doubt or -questioning. How I envy you!"

"Doña Mercedes will be looking for me," said Sally, trembling. "Will you take me back to her now, please?"

Silvia's mother was not actively looking for Sally. That would have been a betrayal of her graceful indolence. But she was coming through the reception rooms, where the crowd had now thinned out, with an unusually purposeful step, and something very like annoyance in her gentle face. Silvia was walking between her parents, with her violet eyes cast down.

"Now really," said Doña Mercedes, "you are both naughty girls, to wander off into the gardens and stay away so long. Our coach will be one of the last to leave the castle, and I particularly wanted to drive home when we had company on the road."

There was no more delay as the Mora party climbed into the big berline waiting in the courtyard, and the crinolines were settled without being crushed. Silvia hardly spoke. In the darkness of the coach she took Sally's hand, and Sally could feel her fingers trembling in their white *glacé* kid. She returned the pressure silently. There had been a crisis, possibly even a declaration, between Andrew and Silvia in the garden, she was sure. It had left Silvia as shaken as she herself felt by the linking of Sergeant Franchet's personality with her own.

The berline rumbled slowly downhill through the cypress woods. George Halkett had got on the box beside the coachman and the vaquero on duty, to make more room for the ladies, and his always cheerful talk was missed. Don Antonio offered a few criticisms of the food and drink served at Chapultepec, which he

described as suitable only for Austrian half-pay officers, and
his wife made a few fretful comments when they halted at the
two guard posts in the castle grounds, but the three young people
said as little as possible. They were out of the Chapultepec gate
and traversing the flat causeway toward the city barrier before
Andrew spoke at all, and then only to inquire when the highway planned by the Empress was likely to be opened for traffic.

The attack which came upon them out of the darkness was
so swift and sudden that George Halkett and the vaquero beside
him had fired once before those inside the coach had fully realized their danger. They felt the jolt as the horses were dragged
to a halt. They heard the hoarse cry as young Halkett flung
himself down from his high seat on one of the men who had
come out of the woods to surround the great berline. Then Doña
Mercedes shrieked in terror:

"Don't fire, Antonio! Don't fire!"

For more than a minute, which seemed like an hour, Sally
was almost stifled in the folds of Doña Mercedes' gabardine
sortie de bal as the poor lady lurched across the coach and flung
herself upon her husband's pistol arm. With Silvia clinging to
her and crying, Sally pushed the silk-lined folds away, and realized that Andrew, whom she knew to be unarmed, was tugging
furiously at the strap of the carriage door. Then the door was
dragged open from the outside; there was a scuffle in which a
pane of glass was broken, and a man with a black sombrero
pulled low over his eyes was forcing them all, at the pistol's
point, to clamber down to the turf by the side of the causeway.

"Your lives are in no danger, señores," the bandit said.
"We want your jewels and your horses, nothing more . . . Hold
that man!"

Andrew was struggling fiercely in the hands of two of the
bandits. Don Antonio, speedily disarmed, supported his fainting
wife. And Sally flung herself down beside George Halkett, who
was lying on the ground with blood pouring from a knife wound
in his leg.

The only light on the scene was thrown by the carriage

lamps. By their flicker Sally saw the robbers working with practiced speed. They cut the traces and led the two valuable horses
out between the shafts without any opposition from the coachman or the vaquero who had backed up George's efforts to beat
the bandits off.

Sally looked about her in despair. She had no fear for herself, not even when a rough hand tore from her neck the seed-
pearl necklace which Charles Cartwright had presented to
Helen's schoolgirl bridesmaid, her only ornament of any value;
but George's blood was draining away in spite of the pressure of
her hands above the wound. And Silvia was sobbing as the
priceless sapphires were stripped from her throat and wrists and
flung with her mother's rubies into a leather sack held open by
the bandit chief.

Sally could not tell, then or ever, how many men had set
upon them. Eight, perhaps, or ten—the figures moved so rapidly
round coach and passengers, the light was so uncertain, that an
exact count was impossible. More than enough to overpower all
their party, even if three of them had not been women, and one
of the women now inert and helpless in her husband's arms. But
the man most seriously hurt kept his wits about him. George
Halkett, with a great effort, raised himself on one elbow and
whispered:

"Get me—the carriage pistols, Sally!"

The steady voice, with the faint Scots accent which young
George had brought from the Mine House, thrilled and nerved
Sally to obey him. That Doña Mercedes had perhaps chosen the
wiser part in imploring her husband not to open fire, never for a
moment occurred to her. The blood of the Scots lords who for
generations had fought in the battles of their country inspired
their youngest descendant to strike one blow, however imprudent
and however feeble, against the robbers who had so easily mastered the whole party of their victims.

Even so, Sally might not have been able, unnoticed, to
cross the few yards to the carriage if her brother, at that very
moment, had not made a furious attempt to escape from his

captors. The sight of Silvia, weeping and disheveled, drove Andrew to struggle until his dress coat was ripped across the shoulders and under his disordered red hair his cheek and temple were marked with a heavy bruise. Sally, with her dark Paisley shawl wrapped over her white dress, had slipped inside the berline before he was subdued.

As Don Antonio had once boasted, every vehicle of his was supplied with pistols. In the side pocket, close to where he sat, Sally's questing hand encountered two antiquated weapons with long chased double barrels and carved ivory butts. She took it for granted that they were loaded.

There was no hope of carrying them to George Halkett, because George had fainted. She realized that when she looked fearfully out of the window and saw his body spread-eagled on the sodden grass. Sally, and Sally alone, held in her hands the means, if not to defeat the robbers, at least to summon help. Were they close enough to the city barrier for the sound of shots to reach the sentries? Or still near enough to the second guardhouse they had passed? Was there a French patrol anywhere along the causeway? It was the moment of decision, for she could see the robbers massing as if about to ride away, with the Mora horses reined to two of their own mounts. She had no idea how to fire the pistols.

She laid one of the heavy weapons on the seat of the berline, and leveled the other through the window, taking a wavering aim at a point above the mass of men and horses. She lifted the hammers awkwardly, with her left hand. Then Sally set her teeth and pulled the triggers—one, two—while the pistol bucked in her hand with the force of the recoil, and the sound of the shots was deafening in the enclosed space. There was a yell of fury from beneath the trees. But there was also the sound of rapid fire from close at hand, and of French voices shouting the familiar challenge:

"Qui va là? Qui vive?"

Then came the thunder of horses, the stabbing flashes of carbines fired from the saddle, and the mounting, swooning pain in wrist and forearm which crumpled Sally Lorimer on the floor of the Mora coach while a French patrol rode headlong after the robber gang.

"WILL YOU allow me to speak to you, mademoiselle?"

It was said so humbly, and by contrast with the uproar of the past hour, so quietly, that Sally was forced to meet Sergeant Franchet's eyes. She had known from the start that he was among their rescuers: indeed, while one half-section of the patrol pursued the robbers, Franchet had been his most active and efficient self in caring for the robbed. But Sally had found it possible to avoid him as he supervised the harnessing of two army horses to the Mora carriage and the improvising of a litter on which George Halkett was carried the scant half-mile to the city barrier. She was fully occupied with Doña Mercedes and Silvia. The older lady was in a state of collapse, the younger hysterical when a young French captain, greatly concerned, took all three into a warm room at the guardhouse and brought them extra wraps and hot spiced wine.

It was Silvia who answered Sergeant Franchet—Silvia who had done nothing but cry and chafe her mother's icy hands, but who now looked up with a gleam of hope in her wonderful violet eyes.

"The jewels, señor! Have the jewels been found?"

"Not yet, señorita, I'm sorry to say. Our men rounded up your carriage horses, though. Perhaps by morning they'll secure the jewels, too. You can be sure we shall make every effort—"

"Señora Ramirez never got her jewels back."

"Regrettable," said Sergeant Franchet. "Miss Lorimer, may I have the honor of a word with you?"

He was holding the door open. Sally could not refuse to pass through. He ushered her into another small office where belts and equipment hung from wooden hooks along the wall, and chromolithographs of the French and Mexican Emperors hung side by side above the empty grate.

"Did my brother send you to fetch me?" said Sally sharply.

"No, mademoiselle. He's in consultation with one of our army doctors. He doesn't need the services of amateurs like us tonight."

"But poor George Halkett—"

"He's not a candidate for amputation," said the sergeant, and over his grave face came a fleeting grin. "Dr. Lorimer is a quick hand with the knife, I know, but even he can't cut off Monsieur George's leg for a knife wound in the calf, which will leave him with an interesting limp, at worst. Don Antonio has sent for the Sisters of Charity; they'll nurse the lad at the Casa Mora, and he'll do all right. Never mind them. What I want to know is, how are *you?*"

Sally felt her hand taken in a strong clasp. In spite of her resistance she was gently turned towards the lamplight.

"Yes," said Pierre Franchet on a long breath of satisfaction. "That's the girl I remember. When I saw you at the castle tonight in your ringlets and your finery I thought they had turned you into a beautiful doll like Mademoiselle de Mora. But when we came up to you on the causeway, and I saw you with blood on your dress and that great horse pistol in your hand, I knew you were still the girl I met at Río Frío."

"Sergeant Franchet," said Sally, trembling, "what possible interest can you have in me? Do you remember how you spoke to me, last time we met? Please let me go back to Doña Mercedes; she is unwell, and shouldn't be alone—" She tore her aching hand from his.

"She has her daughter with her, hasn't she? *I've* been alone for weeks, mademoiselle. Alone with my shame and anger at the unpardonable things I said to you at the Plaza de Santo Domingo. Then I saw you at the castle tonight and heard what you said to Dr. Herzog—"

"Were you one of the soldiers in the Patio de Honor?"

"Yes; and I was on *duty* there, mademoiselle. I wasn't spying on you."

Sally was silent. In the weeks behind her, she had many times imagined another meeting with Pierre Franchet, in which she would wither him with a look, or a crisp sentence of rejection. In this fantasy she was to be beautifully dressed, surrounded by admirers, in some flowered patio or glittering sala. Certainly not in torn satin shoes and a bloodstained dress, in a room hung with sabers and cartridge belts; when her head was so confused by the alarm on the causeway that she could hardly remember what she might have said, and Franchet overheard, in the garden at Chapultepec. And the words of rejection would not come.

"You needn't boast of being an eavesdropper!" was all she could achieve.

"I am not boasting," said Pierre. "I am begging your pardon. I know you think of me now as an eavesdropper—just as you thought of me before as a liar and cheat. And if it's any comfort, you must know that I've been lower in my own eyes than I can ever be in yours, since that—that morning in the Plazuelita. There wasn't any real excuse for what I said or did. Except perhaps that I was in pain and fevered—not that that should matter—"

"Your wound!" she got out, and managed to raise her head. His own was bent close above her, his gray eyes smoky and dark, and a light sprang into them at her voice.

"You care about my wound? You care? But—if I was wounded, you were tired out that night when you reached Mexico—I should have known—"

"I never meant to be unkind," she said, in tears. "To hurt —those girls."

"You're just a baby, aren't you?" he said wonderingly. "So brave . . . and so reckless . . . and so lovely . . ."

With a great effort she made herself say:

"You should keep your compliments for La Malinche."

"I swear I have never seen her alone since the day I first saw you!"

"How can you expect me to believe that?"

He had taken both her hands now, but it was to put a bracelet of kisses round the wrist swollen from the pistol's kick, and a long kiss into the bruised palm.

"You know you can believe me, as I believe in you. Don't you? Don't you know we are just what Herzog said—two of a kind? Except that you are far above me, Sally—with your great heart, which made you tell that man tonight that I was a good soldier—"

"I've always thought of you as a good *soldier*—"

"Will you help me to be a better man—"

Chapter Seven

A CONSULTATION

THE DOCTORS—
The doctor, the American doctor—
Is here, is here, they are both here to see you now—
Your Majesty.

Carlóta came up slowly from the ocean depth of sleep. The words washed over her, uncomprehended at first and then clearer and more imperative: The American doctor, whom Your Majesty sent for this morning, has reached the castle.

She opened her eyes. She saw Señora del Barrio's good grave face, with tears on the olive cheeks, bending over her. She realized that she was in her own bed at Chapultepec, with the afternoon shadows of the acacias wavering on her lowered blinds.

In the instant of returning awareness the Empress of Mexico gathered herself up in a single frantic movement and grasped the Mexican lady's hands.

"Doña Manuela, is my baby safe? I didn't hurt him when I fell?"

Señora del Barrio checked a movement of surprise. Two years in the Imperial service had given her great self-control. She was able to say reassuringly:

"Thank God, Your Majesty has had no fall. You decided not to accompany Don Maximiliano to the city in the morning, because you felt unwell—"

"As is quite natural," said Carlóta proudly.

"As is natural, of course—and you spent some time quietly writing in the boudoir. You fainted, sitting in your chair; and when we had revived you with Dr. Herzog's help, you sent him into the city to fetch Dr. Lorimer."

She spoke quietly and distinctly, aware that Carlóta was following every word. It was not the first time in the past few months that the Lady of the Palace had acted as Carlóta's memory.

"Who else knows that Dr. Lorimer is here?"

"Only the sentries, Señora. Dr. Herzog brought him in through the postern gate and the arsenal. But—we cannot keep his visit here a secret."

"Not after tonight!" The drawn face, relaxed and even rosy from sleep, softened into such a bright and hopeful look that fresh tears came to Manuela del Barrio's eyes. "The American doctor's visit most certainly need not be a secret—once I have told the good news he will confirm, to my dear husband!"

She looked quickly round the room. Another woman might have asked for a mirror, powder, brush and comb to make herself attractive for a young physician. It was instinctive with Carlóta to make sure, instead, that the bedroom was in impeccable order, with all the furniture mathematically angled, and a fresh white linen cloth on the table which held cooling drinks and fruit.

"Where are the doctors now, Doña Manuela? In the salon?"

They were in the boudoir, a very small room next to Carlóta's bedroom, and Andrew Lorimer was wondering audibly why, with so many fine reception rooms in Chapultepec, the suite set apart for the Empress of Mexico should be cramped to the point of discomfort. The walls of the boudoir were tapestried in old rose silk, matching the thick carpet; the Louis XVI furniture so gracefully fragile that the tall young American had not risked sitting down. Dr. Herzog was seated. His shorter, more compact body fitted easily into the spindling armchair, and over joined finger tips he watched Andrew studying the latest portrait of Carlóta.

It was a head and shoulders painting, showing Carlóta in such a prim, plain, white bodice as a governess might have worn. A small gold cross on a thin chain was her only ornament. In her dark hair, with desperate coquetry, she wore a red rose, and the artist had caught the passion in her smoldering eyes.

"Do you see any contradictions in that picture?" asked Dr. Herzog in a low voice.

Andrew shrugged. He had not looked below the flat oil surface for any symbolism.

"Is this the Iturbide boy?" He picked up a miniature from a small table which held other trinkets of the same sort.

"That is *Prince Agustín*," said the Belgian. "Doctor, pray don't think me officious if I ask you not to discuss the child, or any of the court relationships, until we return to the Plaza de Santo Domingo."

"I promised you that before we started out," said Andrew stiffly.

"Her Majesty will receive you now, señores," said the soft voice of Señora del Barrio. Andrew looked at her with interest as she stood aside to let the two doctors pass. Discreetly dressed in black silk, she wore a diamond monogram brooch, the badge of Carlóta's service, pinned above her heart. He remembered that Silvia had told him how, a few months ago, Carlóta had ordered such brooches from Paris for all her Ladies, in resentful imitation of the Empress Eugénie.

At the threshold of the bedroom Andrew halted and bowed low. The courtier's gesture, which came to him naturally, was acknowledged by Carlóta with a bend of the head.

"I am glad to see you, Doctor. Thank you, Dr. Herzog!"

It was said dismissively, but the little Belgian stood his ground. Señora del Barrio, who understood no English, looked anxiously from one to the other.

"I am sorry to hear Your Majesty is indisposed," said Andrew.

"It is quite a natural indisposition. I have overexerted my-self since we came back from Orizaba; last night at the concert I was very tired. So, having met you then, and having heard your praises sung by many people . . . I decided this morning that you were the right person to consult."

"You have had a deep, refreshing sleep since you sent for me, Madame," said Andrew gently. "I think you're still a little drowsy. Because of course you remember quite well that the musical evening, when I had the honor of being presented to you, took place more than a week ago."

"Did it really?" She put her hand to her forehead and rubbed her temples in perplexity. "I must have been dreaming, I suppose. Yes, you and your pretty sister came with Don Antonio Mora and his family (you see I do remember) and you had that terrible adventure on the outskirts of the city. The young man—the Mining School medalist—was wounded, was he not, and poor Doña Mercedes too?"

Carlóta brought the facts out defensively, in a rush of words.

"Doña Mercedes was not injured in any way, Madame, but the shock was very great, and she has been confined to bed for some days. But now let us come to *your* health, if you please. Will you allow me to raise the blinds?"

He took her silence for consent. The brilliant sunshine lit up a somber room, overfull of furniture, where Carlóta's blue-spread bed with the crucifix above it was jostled by two heavy wardrobes, two marble-topped Buhl tables, a cabinet, a writing desk—the whole divided from the eyes of any persons passing on the terrace only by two tall, frosted-glass doors. It was from their ornamental panes that Andrew pulled the shades away.

"The sunlight is too bright," said Carlóta, forcing a laugh. "How hot I am—and how very thirsty!"

"Shall I pour some water for Your Majesty?" asked Dr. Herzog.

"Or some orangeade?" suggested Señora del Barrio. "Her Majesty prefers the *naranjada,* in the afternoon."

"Give the doctors some orangeade too, Doña Manuela," said the Empress. "And then be good enough to leave us."

A shadow passed over the devoted olive face. Señora del Barrio had grown accustomed in Carlóta's service to many breaches of strict Spanish etiquette, but it had never occurred to her that any lady could consult her doctor without the presence of a dueña. She busied herself with the fresh oranges and iced water, saying firmly:

"I shall remain in the boudoir, please Your Majesty— within call."

"Now I can see my patient properly," said Andrew with a smile. He approached the bed, carrying himself lightly; his tone continued to be low and gentle, very unlike the incisive voice which Dr. Herzog remembered, rapping out orders in the kitchen at Río Frío.

"May I take your pulse, Madame?" His fingers slipped around her lax wrist. His eyes studied her eyes, with the dilated pupils; the dry lips, the thinning hair.

"Did we not meet *before* the concert, Dr. Lorimer?" said Carlóta suddenly. "Was it—in Brussels?"

"I have never been to Europe, Madame."

"You remind me very much of somebody I used to know."

Andrew looked at her compassionately as he released her wrist. All the romance and chivalry in his nature responded to this ailing lady, so far from her friends and home. Already, on the night of the concert, he had been stirred by her response to *Vola, la serenata*—the words, so far as he could understand them, might have been written for herself. *La bella testa abbandonata* —there it was before him now: "the beautiful abandoned head, laid on the sheets." And this head wore a crown! Andrew thought confusedly of Marie Antoinette, and of the guillotine.

"This tastes like bad copper coins," said Carlóta, putting down her glass. Andrew quickly recollected himself. He poured some orangeade from the jug Señora del Barrio had set beside him, and tasted it.

"The oranges are not particularly good this year," he said

easily. "Now, Madame, I would like to ask you about your faint this morning. Was it the first time such a thing has happened?"

"It was nothing of any importance," she said almost pettishly. "I sent for Dr. Herzog—Dr. Semeleder was in the city with my husband. Then I sent for you, sir, because the time has come for physicians not connected with the Court to vouch for—what I know to be my state of health." She paused. "I am expecting a child in the month of September. In a little less than six months from now."

"That would be very happy news for Mexico," said Andrew.

"And for the world!" she said. "I want you, Dr. Lorimer, to sign—you are an American and so they will believe *you*—to sign, sign papers I mean, declaring that I am *enceinte,* for us to send to all our family. To the King my brother in Brussels, and my cousin the Queen of England. To the Empress Eugénie" —she caught her breath—"and to my dear brother-in-law, the Emperor of Austria."

"I'll do so with pleasure, as soon as I am certain of Your Majesty's condition. When did you first suspect that you were pregnant?"

Andrew knitted his brows at her answer. He asked her some further questions, and then gently asked her to lay aside the covers. The beautiful abandoned body, with all its youthful outlines blurred, lay on the silken sheet beneath the doctor's eyes. He took a stethoscope from the pocket of his frock coat and bent over her.

"No! *No!*"

Carlóta rolled on her side, writhing away from him, her knees jerked up and her shoulders hunched defensively over her shaking body.

"I can't possibly have hurt you, Madame!" There was a touch of sternness in Andrew's voice to which Carlóta instantly responded.

"Forgive me, doctor." With an effort at self-command she turned on her back and lay gazing up at him. "I—hate the smell of chloroform. It reminds me of Vienna, and a doctor there who hurt me very much—"

"I ask *your* forgiveness," said Andrew. "I was at the hospital when Dr. Herzog came, and I hurried to the castle without taking time to change my clothing." He hesitated. "Would you, for the sake of your own comfort, allow me to take off my coat?"

He laid his black coat over one of the heavy carved armchairs, and almost automatically removed his cuff links and rolled his white shirt sleeves above his elbows. The light reflected in the wardrobe mirrors caught the reddish hairs above his wrists and turned his powerful forearms to gold.

"I still feel we have met before," said a perplexed voice from the bed. "Was it at Laeken, at my father's house?"

"Please, Your Majesty—"

She allowed him, though her teeth were clenched and she was shuddering, to move the wooden stethoscope along her body. His auscultation was careful and very slow. Carlóta almost ceased to breathe; it seemed as if with all her force she was willing him to hear another heartbeat underneath her own. But Andrew, when he straightened up at last, could only shake his head.

"You may have miscalculated, Madame; such things happen. I shall have to proceed to a complete examination."

"Why won't you sign the document I asked for, and let me rest?"

"Because no doctor could give you a certificate of pregnancy on the evidence produced so far. But the pregnancy may very well be in an earlier stage than you supposed, and in that case, as Dr. Herzog will agree, there is only one way to find out."

"Dr. Herzog!" The Empress, it seemed, had forgotten the unobtrusive witness in the far corner of the room. Now, with one terrified glance in his direction, she raised herself in bed and with surprising strength seized Andrew's white shirt front. The young doctor, taken unawares, put out a hand to steady himself. The bed jarred beneath his weight; his red head came very close to the Empress Carlóta's. He heard her frantic whisper:

"Send that man away! If you must examine me, I won't have him in the room!"

"But—"

"He is one of *them,* I tell you. One of the creatures sent to hunt me down!"

"Try to be calm, Madame." There was something in the American's blue eyes, his fresh-complexioned face and firm mouth which did calm Carlóta, and enable her to lie still, although with her hands nervously clenched, while Dr. Herzog slipped from the room. She told Andrew, rationally enough, that he would find water to wash his hands in the adjacent bathroom. But to his dismay he heard her moving about while he was splashing cold water hastily into the chipped china bowl which was such an odd contrast to the bathtub hollowed from a solid block of marble, and adding to the water a measure of chlorine solution from his bag. He knew well enough that it was not ethically prudent for a physician to be alone at a clinical examination of a hysterical woman, and yet he had not dared to risk opposing her, in her distracted state, when she sent both Herzog and her Lady from the room. Drying his hands quickly, he felt a sharp desire for the assistance of a reliable nurse. One of the grave-faced Sisters of St. Vincent, whose discretion was beyond all praise—

Or even Sally.

He found Carlóta standing in the middle of the bedroom, with her hand in the open drawer of a small cabinet. Her feet were bare, and the thin white silk of her nightgown clung clammily to breast and thigh.

"Will you please return to bed?" Andrew omitted any formal address; she seemed to respond to sharper treatment, and she should have it. But this time he had miscalculated. The Empress stood her ground and even looked affronted.

"I wish you to understand, sir, why you ought to sign the paper I require. A signature—such a little thing to ask! *We* have signed our names time and again without a murmur. Sign the marriage contract, sign the Treaty of Miramar, sign the Family

Compact! We take the quill, we gain the crown, but you argue and hesitate when a child's life is at stake! *My child:* how dare you deny him life? The future Emperor of Central America, the great successor of the great Charles? I know I carry him within my body. I have known it ever since I made a pilgrimage to the shrine of La Guadalupana, and drank the waters of the Little Well—"

"Alas, Madame," said Andrew, "there is no well in all the world which performs the miracle of conception."

"You speak from prejudice!" she said, and her hand came out of the drawer holding a rosary of pale carved stones. "There *was* a miracle at the well of El Pocito, because the Virgin of Guadalupe heard my prayers and answered them. Look! Every bead upon this chain represents a pilgrimage of mine. In two years, I have knelt at every altar from Merida to Taxco where the curse of barrenness has been lifted from Mexican women. I prayed to La Conquistadora, who brought the Spaniards victory. I went into Oaxaca, risking death at the hands of Diaz, to entreat the help of the Virgin of Juquila. I've gone to every church in the capital—veiled, of course, but the people knew me, and some jeered, and sung that hateful song they call 'Mama Carlóta,' to shame me; and still God was not moved. But last December, on the twelfth of December, La Guadalupana's own day, I went back to Tepayac—to the shrine of Guadalupe, where Max and I heard the Te Deum on the day of our joyous entry to our capital. But this time I wore no diadem. I crept to the Virgin humbly, on my knees. She put roses from Tepayac Hill into the poor Indian's cloak three hundred years ago . . . and I knew when I fell upon that filthy floor beside the humblest Indians in the land . . . I *knew* She carried roses in Her hands for me!"

"WE CAN TALK freely now," said Julius Herzog, with a sigh of relief. They were in the old-fashioned parlor in the Plaza

de Santo Domingo, with the door shut on Lupita's retreating
back and the decanters on the table—a world away from the
emotions of Chapultepec. But Andrew Lorimer, who had said
so little on the long drive back to town, seemed reluctant to say
much more now, or even to move away from the window, where
he was feigning an intense interest in the Imperial coach waiting
in the crowded Plazuelita.

"I'm very anxious to know just how you did it," said the
soft, insistent voice behind him.

"Did what?" said Andrew with an awkward laugh. "Forgive me, Herzog: I'm a bad host. What will you take to drink?
Sherry? Madeira? Bourbon?"

"May I have a glass of sherry?"

Dr. Herzog had already dined at Andrew Lorimer's table
together with two doctors from the School of Medicine. He
knew the Old Doctor's admirable sherry, which had traveled
from Spain by way of Cape Horn and Acapulco, and watched
appreciatively as Andrew poured out a brimming glass. The
American splashed bourbon whisky into a tumbler for himself
and lifted it very slightly in a salute to his guest.

"I am really curious to know how you contrived to calm
the Empress," Herzog persisted.

"Are you?"

"But naturally! I could do nothing with her this morning,
try as I might; you handled her superbly from the start of the
consultation. Gentle, patient, yet absolutely firm—I could see you
winning her trust; but I confess I didn't expect such a sequel. To
be recalled to her room and find her sitting up in bed as grave
and dignified as her father meeting a Crown Council, ready to
announce the negative finding of your examination and apologize for all the trouble she had caused—well, after this morning's
hysteria, that was something very like a miracle. How was it
done?"

"How was it done?" Andrew echoed. He flung himself
down on the little horsehair sofa and stared miserably at the
other doctor. "Well, I'll tell you, Herzog—I let her talk."

"Ah!" The Belgian's attentive face relaxed into a smile.

"Don't grin! I listened to a long rigmarole about the well of El Pocito and the Virgin of Guadalupe until she started crying, and then I let her cry till she was tired. After that"—and Andrew himself looked unusually pale and tired—"I appealed to her enlightenment, and her interest in science, and all that, to let us settle the point at issue in the light of biological truth. She gave in, and I was able to examine her, in spite of great tenderness in the pelvic area; and finally to convince her, in her own words to you and Señora del Barrio, that she isn't pregnant at the present time."

"And never will be, eh?"

"I didn't tell her that!" said Andrew quickly.

"Because she's too unstable to be told?"

"Because I'm by no means certain that it's the truth."

"Oh!" said Dr. Herzog, and his eyes gleamed behind his thick spectacles. "Now you do surprise me, Dr. Lorimer!"

Andrew shrugged.

"Did you—er—hold out any hope to your patient?"

"My patient!" said Andrew. "You're confusing me with the Court Physician."

"The Court Physician will soon be relieved of his functions. A Dr. Basch, one of Maximilian's protégés, is on his way from Europe to replace him. But the Empress won't consult Basch any more than she would consult me: for all her liberal opinions, she has no especial love for Jews. I'll wager you'll be asked to go with the court to Cuernavaca when they move down to La Borda."

"I don't consider the Empress equal to a day's driving over bad roads in her present state."

"If Max insists on going, she will go; and if she goes, she will need you."

It was said flatteringly, persuasively, but it acted on the American as an irritant. He got up, towering over Herzog, and said almost menacingly,

"You're trying to push me into something—why? What's

your game—what's your motive in all this? That poor woman whispered today that you were one of the men hunting her down. Yes, that's the word she used: hunting. Who was she talking about? General Foury, and the other members of your famous mission? Or Marshal Bazaine, and the French jackals on his staff?"

The questions, rapped out viciously, brought Dr. Herzog to his feet, ready with an indignant answer. But some ingrained habit of mildness seemed to prevail: he bowed his head before the tall American and said:

"The Empress Carlóta's delusions of men hunting her are on the same level as her delusions of pregnancy—produced by a disordered brain."

"I saw no sign of brain disorder. Hysteria, yes: acute hysteria, but that's not uncommon in women who have been taking drugs. I knew on the night of the concert that she'd taken ether—her eyes gave her away; and by the same token she had had a dram of ether this very morning—"

"She started that at Miramar. There's hardly a fashionable woman in Europe who doesn't 'steady her nerves' with ether before a grand soirée—"

Andrew's face showed his disgust.

"Maybe, but this is Mexico. Where does she get the stuff? It's in short supply in the hospitals, as I've good cause to know. Does Semeleder get it for her? Or—do you?"

"She gets it through one of the younger Ladies—a relative of Madame la Maréchale Bazaine."

"God help her!" said Andrew Lorimer. "So Bazaine *is* a traitor!"

"He knows nothing at all about it"—Dr. Herzog looked faintly amused—"any more than General Foury knows about the sealed orders from Brussels which appointed me a member of his mission. Be sure Bazaine means no harm to Madame Carlóta, nor does the man who sent me here. Because that man—who appointed me his confidential adviser on his sister's health—is Her Majesty's favorite and devoted brother."

"The Belgian King?"

"The Count of Flanders. King Leopold has always been jealous of his sister's talents; Philippe is genuinely fond of her. He has scientific tastes—as an amateur, of course; and there was a good deal of public mention of my work," said Dr. Herzog modestly, "when I first went to Austria as assistant to Dr. Riedel."

"Riedel?"

"The director of the Vienna Lunatic Asylum."

"Well, sir?" said Andrew impatiently. "The Count of Flanders sent you out to Mexico with Foury—"

"Not exactly," said Herzog quickly. "I was already in the United States, studying your systems of detention for the insane. When our ambassador called me to Washington, I was the guest of Dr. Thomas Kirkbride at Philadelphia—"

"All right, I remember now," said Andrew. "You were telling us about Kirkbride at dinner the other night. So you were co-opted to the Foury mission—"

"Without adequate equipment, as Sergeant Franchet was acute enough to see," said Herzog, "and with a special mission of my own: to furnish the Count of Flanders with a confidential report on his sister's mental state."

"When had he seen her last?"

"Two years ago, before they sailed for Vera Cruz."

"He never visited her in Mexico?"

"Never."

"Then how could he know if her mental state was sound, or the reverse?"

Dr. Herzog coughed. "That's what His Highness sent me to find out," he said. "Her letters—and the hallucinations they reveal—are distressing her own family and her husband's relatives."

Andrew considered. Mechanically, he unstoppered the decanters, replenished the sherry which Herzog had barely tasted, and poured another measure of bourbon for himself.

"Herzog, I owe you an apology," he said, and the Belgian bowed. "I've known you were a good fellow since I saw you first at Río Frío. If you were retained by Her Majesty's family to investigate the state of her health, your position is unassailable, and *her* fears of persecution groundless. She was, without a doubt, in an extremely hysterical state today. But tell me this: on your professional oath, do you believe that the Empress of Mexico is mentally deranged?"

"Upon my oath, I do," said Julius Herzog. "She presents some of the classic symptoms of insanity. Amnesia—you saw an example of that this afternoon, when she thought last week's concert had taken place last night. A fantasy of pregnancy—acting out her fondest wish, suppressed under the cold façade of executive ability she shows the world. The delusion of being hunted, or persecuted—the feeling that every man's hand is against her. Yes, she is deranged, poor lady, and who, in the light of her case history, can wonder?"

"What do you mean by her case history?"

"May we sit down, my dear Lorimer, and discuss this rationally?"

Andrew hooked an upright chair towards him with one foot. He sat down, straddled, on the seat, with his arms folded on the chair back, staring at the other man.

"The Princess Charlotte of Belgium," said Dr. Herzog carefully, "was born of a loveless marriage between the first King Leopold and Princess Louise of France. She was given her name, Charlotte, in memory of her father's first wife, whom he mourned so constantly—and so publicly—that Queen Louise died of melancholia before reaching middle age.

"Then Max of Austria came courting Charlotte. For reasons of state, you understand. Charlotte fell in love with him, unluckily, although she was well warned that his heart was buried with the young Portuguese princess who had died of consumption during their betrothal. So Charlotte entered marriage as she entered life—coming a poor second to a ghost.

"With any luck, she could have laid the ghost of Princess Marie Amélie by giving Max a child. But Charlotte, with all her brains, has never had good luck. She had to consent to the adoption of little Agustín, whom Max loves because he's handsome and lively and brave, and just what he wanted his own son to be. So Carlóta retreats into her fantasy of pregnancy and childbirth—her escape from a situation she can neither control nor endure."

He pulled out his silk bandanna and dabbed his forehead. Andrew, who had more than once tried to interrupt him, said contemptuously,

"So that's how you study brain ailments in Vienna. Sweating over the death of your patient's father's first wife, which took place thirty years before that patient was born, as if it had something serious to do with her state of mind! With due respect, Dr. Herzog, if that's the sum and substance of Dr. Riedel's teaching, I imagine the Vienna Lunatic Asylum is full to overflowing."

"It's not Riedel's own teaching," said Herzog patiently. "Riedel began only where Philippe Pinel left off. He is a humane man, and knows that madmen can't be kept in chains, nor cured by bleeding or the ducking stool. But I may say in all humility that the group of young Viennese doctors to whom I now belong has already outdistanced Riedel and the conservative alienists. We have nearly all studied under Charcot at the Salpétrière. We are developing theories of the free association of ideas, which enable patients under our guidance to bring to the surface memories purposely forgotten, or repressed, which have been the hidden cause of their nervous disorders. We—"

"By 'under your guidance' do you mean under hypnotic influence? Can this mumbo-jumbo be called Mesmerism?"

Dr. Herzog sighed.

"Mesmer has had his day," he said. "You mustn't think of us as charlatans. We are pioneers, exploring the relationship between erotic disturbances and mental illness, such as the case of the Empress Carlóta may reveal."

"May reveal!" said Andrew. *"Does* reveal—if you mean the lady has been an innocent victim of her husband's debauchery."

"Did she say so?" asked Herzog sharply.

"After I told her that I knew the nature of her ailment. It's

the old story. Her husband contracted a disease from a loose
woman in Vienna—after they were married—and communicated
it to her. They were both cured by treatment, but the Empress
has suffered agonies from the aftereffects, which she owes to the
ignorance of one of your famous Viennese physicians. This
quack put her through a brutal course of cauterizations by silver
nitrate and calomel, given every day instead of every fifth or
sixth day. He subjected her to astringent injections thrice daily,
over a period of years, and she still follows his prescriptions
of snakeroot and gentian syrup and soapwort leaves, so that
everything she eats tastes vile. No wonder her appetite and general health are ruined! She was a sick woman when she arrived
in Mexico. Now, after two years of overwork and strain, which
she tries to combat by taking ether, the Empress Carlóta's bodily
sickness is real and acute, and has nothing whatever to do with
her suppressed memories!"

"If you took charge of her case, how would you prescribe?"
said the Belgian impassively.

"I'd cut off the supply of ether for a start, if I had to take
the matter up to the Supreme Commander. Then I would order
two Vallet's pills every morning and one of mercury protoiodide
at night. With hot water baths to relax the nervous system and
daily local irrigations per canula to soothe the site of the cauterizations. Then I'd—"

"Enough," said Herzog, holding up one plump hand.
"Can't you realize that you did her more good today than a
year of Vallet's pills? You forced her to confront and destroy her
fantasy of motherhood. In exchange you gave her a new interest—yourself!"

"Myself?"

"Remember, Carlóta asked you twice if you had met before. She associated you at once with her girlhood at Brussels
in her father's palace. When you took your coat off, you reminded her of—you can guess who?"

"Maximilian," said Andrew Lorimer unwillingly.

"Don't be offended," said Herzog. "Max is considered

handsome! You don't wear a beard, but you have the same height and coloring, and the same way of assuming authority over her—yes, it was an easy identification for a woman in her state. Now, if the transference becomes complete, and you win her entire confidence, you may be able to save the Empress from insanity."

Andrew Lorimer, so utterly confounded that all his movements became slow and heavy, put his chair with elaborate care back in its place at the dining table before he spoke.

"What do you mean by a complete transference? You want me to seduce the Empress—is that it?" Then, as Dr. Herzog gave him no answer but a smile and a shake of the head, the American went on:

"Because I tell you there's only one sure way to cure the Empress—permanently. It's to heal her body first, and let the mind look after itself. If I had proper instruments and trained assistants I would risk it—even here. If the Maternity House had any instruments more modern than a Levret's forceps or an old Récamier curette, or if I had even one good intern from the Massachusetts General to help me—damnation, Herzog, if *you* had the hands, and the eyes, or anything to offer but your silly babble about erotic disturbances, I think I could heal the Empress Carlóta."

"You'd risk a curettage? It could be fatal."

"It was dangerous when Récamier performed it first in 1850, it isn't fatal now. No, I'd go further than that. I'd risk an ovariotomy. Why not? Tarnier did it in Paris. Marion Sims did it in New York. I believe the removal of only one ovary would restore the Empress to complete health and strength. It might even restore her hopes of motherhood."

The confident voice, which Herzog remembered so well from Río Frío, rang through the old-fashioned room. Andrew's face wore the same look of dedication, of absorption, as it had worn when he bent over the suffering Empress. Herzog said:

"Was it your plan to become a woman's doctor?"

"Of course it was," said Andrew wearily. "But the War

wrecked the careers of better Southern doctors than myself. It forced Marion Sims out of Woman's Hospital in New York, to give you one example. It forced me to give up my plan to work under Braxton Hicks at Guy's, and then go on to Paris, to the Maternité. A woman's doctor—that was my dream since I was fourteen . . . or even earlier. From the time when I understood that giving birth to Sally killed my mother."

"Your mother died in childbirth?" asked Herzog quietly.

"Of puerperal fever. Killed because some ignorant backwoods sawbones had never heard of Semmelweiss or Oliver Wendell Holmes, but came to her with dirty hands and unwashed linen . . . Yes, she died in childbirth, Julius. Nineteen years ago."

"Is that why you resent your sister Sally?"

The words were hardly audible above the noise of the day's commerce in the Plazuelita. Yet the sibilants of "res-sent your si-sster" hissed in Andrew's ears as if they had been uttered by an adder.

"Resent Sally? How dare you say so?" he blustered, and his high-colored face grew crimson. Herzog raised a hand.

"Forgive me," he said deprecatingly. "It isn't easy, I know, to see oneself as one appears to others. To me the resentment has been quite obvious, even at Río Frío, and whenever I have seen you two together. Oh! don't misunderstand me; you never fail in courtesy toward your sister—consciously. It was the steady, unconscious belittling that struck me: even the other night at dinner, when we were discussing that shocking attack on your way back from the castle. It seemed as if you were almost jealous of her courage and quick thinking—"

"Oh, Sally and Sergeant Franchet were the heroes of that affair," said Andrew. "George Halkett, too. He got a knife in his leg, while I stood tamely by, doing nothing to help my friends—"

"Now you know how I felt at Río Frío," said Herzog with a wry smile. "We can't all be heroes, Lorimer! But is that any

reason why you should feel bound to prove Miss Sally always
in the wrong?"

"Are you one of those who think with Sally herself that
she's always in the right?"

"Not always, no. But you must realize that she is excep-
tionally capable—in some ways really talented—and so enchant-
ingly vivacious and aware of things compared to those vapid
Mexican belles."

"Sally's talents!" said Andrew. "If you had lived with them
as long as I have—! If you'd lived through the phase when she
wanted to attend the female seminary at Mount Holyoke, or the
doctor phase, when she wanted to follow in Miss Blackwell's
footsteps, and worst of all the Abolitionist phase—well, I needn't
go into that. Sally is as smart as a cartload of Yankees, I've
never denied it, but her pursuit of learning is a little tedious,
that's all."

"Exactly what Princess Charlotte's brothers used to say
about their sister," said Herzog drily. "Don't you realize that
you can't judge Miss Sally by your own rule of thumb? She's one
of the new women, new since your war and perhaps new in
Europe since the Crimea, who will always be happier thinking
and doing than leading the sheltered lives their mothers lived."

"Then that's another grievous consequence of the War,"
said Andrew grimly.

"You mustn't blame the War for everything. Your Dr.
Marion Sims was a fool when he left New York for political
reasons, and you are worse than a fool to let yourself be side-
tracked here to Mexico, where midwifery is still at the level of
the witch doctor and the shamán. Why don't you cut your losses,
sell up, and get out before Maximilian loses his gamble here?
Send your sister to her college—let her talents have full scope—
and come to us in Vienna— No! No! Not as a student of the
brain. Come to *our* maternity houses, work with *our* great ob-
stetricians, and leave the Mexican women to the sweatbath and
the hands of the *partera*."

"Too late," said Andrew wearily. "Sooner or later, I shall

fit into my small place here. In a few years it'll be my turn to be the Old Doctor in the Plazuelita, whom foreign ladies call in for their confinements because he's always willing to give a whiff of chloroform. That, and tying up an occasional knife wound, should keep me in bread and cheese."

"Don't talk as if old age were round the corner," said Herzog. "If you could only forget the War, you would realize how very young you are. With any luck you have a lifetime of peace ahead of you. Don't look back to eighteen sixty-five! Think what you will be in the year nineteen hundred!"

The door opened and Sally Lorimer came in.

Chapter Eight

FIRST LOVE

"I HEARD raised voices," said Sally with a mischievous glance from one to the other. "It's a poor lookout for patients when doctors disagree!"

"But you're obviously not a patient, mademoiselle," said Herzog, bowing low.

She laughed and came forward, laying her parasol and a small package on the table before giving him her hand in the frank American way still a little disconcerting to the doctor from Vienna. He thought her not only the picture of health but prettier than ever in her plain white muslin dress, tied with a black silk sash which matched the streamers of her wide Italian straw hat. Sally's cheeks were glowing and her lips a lovely vivid red. There was more assurance in her manner; and Dr. Herzog could have sworn that she wore a dusting of pearl powder as well as slippers with high heels. He was too sophisticated to be deceived by the Quaker simplicity of her dress. It was unusually elegant for an afternoon toilette in Mexico, where ladies in their own homes lounged uncorseted and uncurled until the hour of the merienda.

"I'm sure I'm not interrupting a medical discussion, monsieur," she said demurely, "for I distinctly heard you saying something about the year nineteen hundred."

"Ah! I was asking your brother what he expects to be when the new century begins," said Herzog.

"A name on a gravestone," Andrew said.

"Oh, nonsense, Andy! You'll only be—what?—sixty-two in

nineteen hundred. Rich and famous in two continents! I'll be
fifty-three. Well, yes, that *is* old." Sally looked pensive for a moment. "But did Lupita look after you properly? I was upstairs
—I had no idea we had a guest!"

"You were prinking in your room, I suppose," grumbled
Andrew. "Are you going to visit Doña Silvia? You spent the
morning with her."

Sally shook her head. "I don't expect to see Silvia," she
said. "She and her sisters have gone to visit their aunt at
Tacubaya. I only want to inquire for Doña Mercedes, she wasn't
quite so well this morning, and leave a book for George. Do
stay for the merienda, Dr. Herzog! I'll be back in good time to
pour out for you."

"You're very kind, mademoiselle," said Herzog with a
quick look at Andrew. "But I mustn't keep the horses standing
—and at Chapultepec the Household dines unusually early."

"Tell the man to put his horses in my stable, God knows
there's room for them," said Andrew. "Stay on and dine with us
at seven. I don't imagine there will be much of a formal dinner
at Chapultepec tonight."

"Why not?" asked Sally. "Is anything wrong at the castle?
Were *you* there today, Andrew?"

Cursing her quick wits: "The Empress is a little out of sorts,
that's all," he said. "Don't mention it to Doña Mercedes—or
Doña Vera."

"I may not even see them," Sally said carelessly. "I want
to be sure George Halkett has something to read, because he'll
be alone all evening, and now he's so much better he gets restless and bored with nothing to do."

"His leg is mending quickly, then?" asked Dr. Herzog.

"Oh, yes—they can hardly make him stay in bed. Pilár reads
aloud to him as often as her mother will let her, and George
loves the sound of Pilár's voice, but he whispered to me this
morning that he was terribly tired of *Don Quixote*. I think that's
the only book the Mora girls possess, apart from their missals."

"And have you found something more suited to Mr. Hal-kett's tastes?"

"I think so. I hunted in vain through every bookstore in the arcades for something he wanted about a detective called Gaboriau. The book I did find has the right kind of title," said Sally, taking up her parasol and package, "so I hope it pleases him."

"What's the title?" Andrew asked.

"The Murders in the Rue Morgue."

"Really, Sally!"

But Sally escaped on a peal of laughter, stopping only at the door for a quick promise "to be back in half an hour," and then all the men heard of her was high heels tapping down the hall and an imperious voice calling for "Jorge!" and "Con-chita!" The front door closed.

"Well, there she goes," said Andrew. "My intellectual sister. I wonder if they've heard of Gaboriau at Mount Holyoke?"

"Your very kind and perceptive sister," said Herzog. ". . . You don't object to her walking in the streets alone?"

Andrew shrugged. "She has two servants with her, and it's broad daylight," he said. "Besides, it's only five minutes' walk to the Mora house, straight there and back; she goes there all the time."

But when Sally left the Plazuelita with shuffling Jorge and shiftless Conchita at her heels, she turned aside from the straight street which led to the Casa Mora, walking left on the Calle de Medinas and into the Plaza Mayor at a pace which made the public letter writers waiting for business in the shade under the portals wonder at La Gringa's energy.

There had been a shower in the middle of the afternoon, a forewarning of the rainy season now not far off, and the gardens in the center of the square were refreshed and sparkling. The Palace flagstaff, empty above a bell bearing the date 1530 which had been sent out from Europe when Maximilian's ancestor, Emperor Charles V, ruled all the lands and colonies of Spain, indicated to Sally that the descendant of the great Charles had

ended official business for the day and gone home to dine at
Chapultepec. She knew as soon as she saw it that a certain sergeant of the Foreign Legion, who had been on palace duty since
six o'clock that morning, would now be free to join the promenaders moving slowly round and round the bandstand where
the band was playing a selection from *La Sonnambula*.

Sally drew a deep breath and crossed to join the slowly
moving throng. She knew Pierre Franchet was not far away, but
walking Rataplan up and down on two sides of the square only,
along the tanbark spread for those who took the air on horseback. She knew his narrowed eyes would be watching the few
streets down one of which she must come, if she came at all;
and she had come to meet him now four times, without a word
said to Andrew, or any planning more clandestine than a slight
adjustment of her visits at the Casa Mora or the excuse of buying some forgotten trifle at the Merced market, which was open
until sundown. Nobody had warned her, as Doña Vera would
have enjoyed doing, that no lady went alone to the afternoon
promenade in the great plaza, although it often happened in
those unsettled days that a married woman muffled in her mantilla would slip out of her patio to join her foreign lover in the
wooded alleys where Carlóta's planning of the gardens had un-
intentionally given such lovers shelter. But Sally knew nothing of
this; so far from hiding her face La Gringa tilted the little black
lace parasol farther back over her shoulder, the better to watch
in the gay procession of riders for the one horseman whom she
hoped to see.

The plaza which Don Antonio Mora called the heart of
Mexico was not quite so crowded now as when Sally saw it in
his company a few weeks earlier. The news that the French Emperor intended to withdraw his troops had been responsible for
a quiet exodus as various families, foreign and Mexican, decided
that the time had come for a prolonged vacation in Havana.
But the Austrian band played cheerfully in the perpetual sunshine, and the jugglers and guitarists performing at all the corners
of the square slowed down the promenaders so effectively that

several minutes passed before Sally saw the tall chestnut and his rider coming down the tanbark from the direction of the palace.

There were always handsomer men than Pierre Franchet to be seen in the Plaza Mayor. Most of the Austrian officers, glittering with medals, seemed to have been hand-picked for their blond good looks, and the Mexican caballeros in their short jackets and trousers laced with silver were equally handsome in their own way. But the face Sally looked for was the bold, keen face of the Frenchman, which so far from softening at sight of her into the quivering tenderness which was the accepted expression among the Mora girls' admirers seemed to grow even sharper with the anticipation of the matching of their wits.

Pierre met Sally not as a suitor, nor even as a man in love. One less perceptive might have been tempted, at those meetings which were no less private for being completely public, to press his courtship further. Pierre did not. He had summed up Sally's nature so accurately that from the moment they met again after the holdup in the forest he made sure that the wry smile, the ironical and authoritative manner of Río Frío should be the mask he used to hide the lover's face. All he asked, in that week of their meetings in the Plaza Mayor, was to see the golden sparkle in her eyes when he met her, and hear the soft note in the voice which said, *"Bonjour!"*

"Bonjour, mademoiselle." He pulled Rataplan up and saluted from the saddle. Then he was off the horse's back in a moment and throwing the reins to an Indian boy who came running up.

"You look like a May morning," he said. "How do you manage it on an April afternoon?"

"It's May the day after tomorrow," Sally reminded him.

"And you'll be gone to Cuernavaca before the start of the rainy season. Too bad—I was looking forward to carrying you over the gutters, once they start running two feet high. Nothing like the rains to bring out the highest in Mexican chivalry."

"Would you be able to lift me over the gutters today, dry as they are?" demanded Sally, and the Frenchman laughed. In his parade uniform he was even smarter than in campaign kit. The white neckcloth was replaced by a green band worn round the képi with the gilt One of the First Regiment of the Foreign Legion, and his dark-green epaulets were fringed with heavy gilt bullion. His gauntlet gloves were pipe-clayed to the elbow. There was nothing in his bearing to betray that beneath the shabby, well-fitting tunic was a tightly wound linen bandage, holding a lint dressing in place above a recent lancet cut.

"I could lift you—*con su permiso,* as the caballeros say— with one hand tied behind my back," he said.

"You know what I mean," she said with a frown. "I want to know how you are! What did the surgeons say this morning? Did you go before the Board at Buena Vista?"

She saw the muscles tighten round his mouth. She was learning all the moods of that expressive face, and she knew at once that the Medical Board's decision had gone against Sergeant Franchet.

"I'd like to tell you about that," said Pierre. "But let me get you some flowers first. No lady strolls in the Plaza Mayor without flowers and a fan—where's your fan? I'll buy you violets. That would sound very well in Paris; here it's almost an insult to offer a lady flowers, they cost so little and grow everywhere. Imperial violets for the señorita!"

He threw a quartilla into the lap of an old Indian woman who was tying her flowers into large soft bunches in one of the little leafy booths which stood here and there along the bridle path. The wrinkled, coppery face looked up incuriously at the fair-haired foreign soldier and the pretty Gringa, and from them, without a flicker of expression, at the two servants of her own race who had settled down lazily, preferring to sit than to stand, in the shadow of a tree.

"*Chico!*" Pierre raised his voice. "Keep the horse moving! Walk him up and down!"

"I know Rataplan is the apple of your eye," said Sally, putting the violets in her sash, "but do you realize that I asked you a question about the Board? Don't put me off, Pierre. I want to know."

"I did," said Sergeant Franchet. "'Seconded from guard duty between the hours of ten A.M. and twelve noon for the purpose of a medical examination'—just when I had the best cards at écarté that I've held since we took Monterrey. Yes, Rata and I jogged off to Buena Vista, and there they found that the wound hadn't quite completely healed, required more treatment and so on, and that—according to them—I couldn't be passed fit for active service. Whereupon I said that trotting up and down to Chapultepec behind Max's carriage was as strenuous as chasing Escobedo—"

"Or being chased by him," said Sally.

"You're thinking about Santa Isabel? So was I."

"You want to go north again, don't you?" the girl said slowly. "You want to march with Saussier when he takes his revenge for Santa Isabel. You'd like to be in the barrancas shouting '*Marchez ou crevez! Marchez ou crevez!*' as you shouted till your throat was raw on the march to Monterrey. Ninety miles in thirty-two hours, and straight into action at the end of it—wasn't that the way it went?"

"Yes, that's the way it went, Sally," said Pierre. "And that's the way it's got to go again, if we're to keep Juarez on the far side of the Rio Grande."

"So what happens now? Did they take you off guard duty? Andrew says you never ought to have been sent on that long ride to Río Frío. If he'd been in the north when you were wounded he would have done a rib resection immediately."

"I'm sure he would," said Pierre drily. "Well, our own *toubib* had his hands full after that action, and I tried a poultice of cobweb and cactus pulp—the one Diaz taught me when we had him prisoner in Puebla. It usually works wonders on a bullet wound."

"Just because you think Diaz is a good soldier it doesn't follow that he knows anything about medicine," said Sally argumentatively.

"He's the only soldier Juarez has got. And I hope you don't intend to remind me again of Escobedo."

"Shall we walk on?" said Sally.

"Please, Sally—please forgive me." Pierre leaned across the living hedge of the little flower stall with contrition in his smoky eyes. "I didn't mean to speak abruptly. I was—I've been torn in two today, thinking about you, and the boys up at Saltillo, where I ought to be—"

"You feel you're missing something, don't you?"

"I feel there should be other work for me than drilling the Mexican recruits Bazaine is going to take into the Foreign Legion. *Los Cazadores,* he means to call them—*chasseurs à pied* we say; and by any name a liability. However, that's my posting," said Pierre bitterly. "Back to the barrack square, teaching native troops to know their right foot from their left. I thought I'd left all that behind me in Algeria."

"And where will you drill them? At Buena Vista?"

"No, the depots are to be outside the city. One down at Puebla. One at Cuernavaca. I think I can arrange to be posted to either one."

"At Cuernavaca!"

There was something more revealing than amazement in her face. The old Indian woman, who had been watching them without understanding a word they said, smiled a cracked and toothless smile as she began to arrange a sheaf of gladioli. But the great cathedral bell called "Doña Maria," tolling the half-hour after four and answered by all the bells of Mexico, gave Sally an opportunity to collect herself. She turned away in the direction of the Casa Mora, saying carelessly:

"I wish I were as certain as you of getting to Cuernavaca. We were going to drive down with the Mora family, but since Doña Mercedes took to her bed of course they can't leave Mexico. Sometimes I think I'll hire a carriage and go down by myself—"

Pierre halted her with a touch on her gloved hand. The maid Conchita, who had risen languidly from the curb to follow her young mistress, looked wonderingly at El Señor Güero, grimmer and more serious than she had ever seen him when he lived in the Old Doctor's house.

"I'll only go to Cuernavaca if you say so, mademoiselle. You know I want to be near you all the time. Not only to see you and talk to you sometimes, when you permit me, but to protect you if the Chinacos—the Juarista gang—move into Michoacán while you're there. But I can't ask you to say yes or no until I've told you something about myself. You accused me once of having been untruthful. I want you to know the truth about me now."

Pierre hesitated. He felt tired and feverish. The hardship of a service in which every French soldier had to do the work of three weighed on him like a physical pain, as real as the throbbing in the wound a surgeon had lanced and drained only a few hours before. He felt unequal to the confession he dared delay no longer. He longed, instead, to kiss Sally's stubborn young face into softness, and feel her soft hands on his scarred and burning breast.

But Sally twirled the lace parasol on her shoulder and looked away from him, across the rose beds and the flowering hedges of the Plaza Mayor. That scene had known the first phase of her first love, which was ending inexorably with every word he spoke. She was looking, almost in bereavement, at the kiosk where the musicians were folding their music sheets and wrapping their instruments in green baize, when she heard him say quickly:

"When I was eighteen I was condemned to death for murder."

That brought her clear eyes back to his, with such a look of horror that he could only plunge ahead, with no choice of words or appeal to pity.

"It was in my first session at the university. At Montpellier. I got into a fight in a wineshop, over a girl. I hit the other man too hard, and he died of it, and so it was to be—the guillotine."

Sally tried to say something. He could only distinguish the words "mean to do it."

"God knows I didn't mean to do it!" said Pierre Franchet. "But the court wouldn't listen to my plea, and the Prefect wouldn't listen to my father. There was no hope of a commuted sentence. And when I thought of Cayenne, and the *travaux forcés,* I almost believed the guillotine was the better end."

"But you were pardoned?" Sally whispered.

Pierre straightened his weary shoulders. The worst was told, and she hadn't screamed or run away from him. And now he was at that part of it which, in spite of all, he cherished, which had been his inspiration in half a hundred desert battles, his support in many hours of pain and thirst. *L'Impératrice des Français,* he thought, and spoke the proud syllables aloud.

"The Empress of the French—herself—obtained my pardon. She came to Montpellier with the Emperor, on one of their progresses through the South, when I was lying in the condemned cell. Yes! She came, without fear, into the courtyard of the prison, with all of us wretches staring out at her; dressed in white and looking like an angel, with a great bouquet of violets in her hand."

"Is she so very beautiful?" asked Sally.

"The most beautiful woman in the world. *He* thought so— Napoleon thought so—she had given him a son not long before, and he could deny her nothing. *'Louis, he is only a boy!'*—I can hear her say it now. So he talked awhile with the governor, and then I was brought out to the courtyard—so near, I could have touched her dress if my hands had not been shackled. And Napoleon said, 'Young man, you must give France a life for the life you took. France needs soldiers in Algeria. Go and join the Foreign Legion . . . and thank Her Majesty for her compassion.' "

It was all said now. There was no need to tell Sally of the brutal night journey to Marseilles, under police guard, nor his enlistment, nor the equally brutal voyage to Algiers which followed it. All he had to say was:

"You don't hate me for it, Sally? You don't despise me for

something that happened more than eight years ago, when I was a boy?"

At that direct appeal some of the shocked look left her pale face.

"I—don't hate you, of course. It was an accident—it was very, very sad. And they were right to pardon you—if the pardon had been free."

"It was free, Sally."

"Then why did you re-enlist in the Foreign Legion, when your first five years were out? Or are you condemned still—to go on soldiering until you give the Emperor a life for a life?"

"I re-enlisted freely," he repeated. "Where else was I to go? I'd been promoted. I'd been decorated, after the campaign in Italy. They marched us through Paris with *Magenta* on our flags. You can't imagine—"

"I ought to be able to imagine; I've been told about enough battles in the past five years," said Sally Lorimer. Her dark lashes blinked. He thought there were tears in her eyes, but her voice was still quite steady.

"You must have been responsible for a good many deaths since you joined the Foreign Legion. In Algeria, in Italy, and now in Mexico—haven't you?"

He nodded in reply, his lips compressed.

"Why is it punishable to kill one man in hot blood, and praiseworthy to kill a hundred men in Algeria?"

"Sally, for God's sake don't torment yourself and me with talk like that!"

"But I must," she cried, and there was no doubt about the tears now. "Can't you see that I'm trying to understand you? You ask *me* to decide if we shall meet again. You put all the burden of our friendship upon me; you tell me a dreadful story of injustice—that's what it really was, injustice; and when I try to find out what value you put on it, you tell me I'm tormenting you—now is that fair?"

"I can only ask you to forgive me once again, mademoiselle."

He called the boy who was holding Rataplan, gave him a media, and took the bridle in his own hand. In silence, leading the chestnut, with the Mexican servants dawdling behind them, he accompanied Sally across the plaza to the Street of the Silversmiths. She snapped her parasol shut as they entered the shelter of the arcades, where the fashionable Mexican shops and French boutiques were doing a brisk trade. She said in her normal voice:

"Don Antonio Mora appears to have visitors."

A handsome traveling carriage, covered with dust, was in fact drawn up outside the Mora door, where all the charro vaqueros were helping strange servants in a blue livery to empty the vehicle, and the fourgon which followed it, of a pile of baggage and heavily corded bales.

"They've gone to Tacubaya," Sally said, and then stopped short. Carriage and fourgon were blazoned with a crest she had seen once, and remembered, on a white vellum prayer book sent to Silvia Mora from Madrid. It was the crest which Don Antonio, that lover of ancient blood, proclaimed exultantly to be the noblest in all Mexico: quartered with the arms of Vega, Galvez, Revillagigedo and Cortés del Valle—the family crest of Silvia's betrothed.

"Oh, Pierre!" she said, hardly above a whisper. "Don Felipe —Silvia's future husband—must have arrived before he was expected! That's his carriage, I feel sure."

"We can soon find out," said Pierre. "Shall I ask them to announce you? Or would you rather I left you here?"

"I am not going in," she said, shrinking. "Please ask the footman to give this book to Don Jorge—and let us go."

He nodded, and took the small parcel containing *The Murders in the Rue Morgue* from her hand.

The afternoon tide of life in the Street of the Silversmiths flowed all around them. Sally took a step nearer the tezontle wall and looked from the strange man's carriage to the alert figure of the Légionnaire. Her head ached with the weight of his confession. An accident, a sentence too severe, a life mortgaged at its very start—yes, she believed all that, but the truth was blurred by the images her jealousy called up. A brawl in a wineshop over a girl—the blind worship of the beautiful empress—these now contended with Sally's anger, never quite allayed, at the thought of La Malinche's place in Franchet's life. For a moment she was tempted to hurry away from him, back to the shelter of her brother's house.

Then Pierre turned back from the Mora door, with a laugh and a wave of the hand for the vaquero on duty, and she saw the swing of his broad shoulders, and the supple movement of a body instinct with energy and sexual promise. The elderly servants, busy round the strange coach, looked up and smiled as if they too felt some outgiving from his gay and challenging spirit. Sally thought of all she had learned, from expressive looks and sentences left unfinished, of the rich widower who had come to claim Silvia Mora, and shivered in the sun.

"It's true," said Pierre beside her. "Don Felipe Vega arrived about an hour ago. They've sent to Tacubaya to bring Doña Silvia home."

Sally hardly seemed to listen to him.

"Pierre," she said, "I've made up my mind. I want you to go to Cuernavaca—if you can."

Chapter Nine

THE CATHEDRAL

ON THE EVENING after Don Felipe Vega arrived in
Mexico, Sally made his acquaintance at a grand tertulia at the
home of his betrothed.

In appearance he was a short, slightly built man of about
fifty-five, with jet-black hair receding from a high forehead and
a wide, clean-shaven upper lip. The studied elegance of his deportment was set off by London tailoring which made the Mexican caballeros in their tight trousers and ruffled shirts look garish
and theatrical, and Don Antonio, by his side, absurdly over-
dressed.

Don Antonio, in his satisfaction with events, was not aware
of being absurd. Silvia's future husband had the distinction, rare
in 1866, of being a *Gachupino,* descended from the Bonnet-
wearers of the Conquest, the last of a line whose marriages had
always been contracted with persons of European birth. Silvia
would be the first bride born in Mexico to enter the proud family
which claimed kinship with Cortés, and with two of the most
famous of the Spanish Viceroys. Her father's cup, as he pondered
the new blazon to be added to the shields in the patio, was full
to overflowing.

Don Felipe Vega had been a childless widower for more
than ten years. During the lifetime of his first wife, related to the
princely house of Bourbon-Parma, he had preferred to make his
home in Madrid, and even since her death had not been often
seen in Mexico, where his chief occupation was growing garde-

nias at his quinta near Orizaba. His interest in public affairs was exclusively Spanish. The campaigns of General O'Donnell to put down rebellion in Cuba and Peru were far more absorbing to him than the campaign against Juarez, and Maximilian's problems took second place, in his conversation, to Queen Ysabel's disagreements with the Spanish government. It was a viewpoint likely to please Doña Mercedes, but the poor lady, who had not recovered health and spirits since her adventure in the forest, seemed pale and extinguished as she stood by the future bridegroom's side in a spreading gown of garnet velvet.

Silvia was pale too, but so lovely in blush pink, with a spray bouquet of stephanotis in her hand, that Sally was reminded against her will of the statue of the Virgén del Rosario in Santo Domingo, Silvia's own Patroness and the especial treasure of the ancient church. That Virgin was represented as a beautiful Spanish doll, crowned, with her crowned Son on Her arm, and robed, on the one occasion when Sally stood silent before Her altar, in a pale pink crinoline embroidered with pearls and silver thread. Silvia's beautiful face, which her fiancé's cold black eyes often studied, had some of the statue's own expression of wistful sweetness. She did not kiss Sally, nor single her out in any way from the line of friends now advancing with unaccustomed formality through the usually lively sala to wish her well. It was left to Doña Vera, restored to society with her thin face sharper and more alert than ever, to name Sally to Don Felipe as "our dear little American friend, Miss Lorimer, so brave on the fearful occasion you have heard about"—a recommendation which won from the gentleman nothing more than a very low bow. Don Felipe's silences and distant manners soon cast a chill over the company. The younger Mora children, always petted and noisy at a tertulia, crept away to the nurseries of their own accord, and even the hired musicians, strumming the eternal *Paloma* and *Sonnambula,* began to play false notes on their muted strings. The Mora cousins from Tacubaya, as a rule so easily persuaded to stay overnight, left early and drove Sally home to the Plazuelita. Andrew, who had flatly refused to attend the reception, was nowhere to be seen, and his sister went upstairs with a heavy heart.

She had barely time to fold her Paisley shawl, however, before she heard him calling, and hurried back to the sala. She heard the chink of decanter on glass as she ran along the corridor, and when she went in she found him with a tumbler of his favorite bourbon in his hand. He was flushed and unsteady. It was the first time she had seen him drunk since they left Vera Cruz.

"Did you have a pleasant evening?" he said with exaggerated courtesy. "I didn't expect you back so soon."

"It was very dull. Is there anything I can do for you, Andrew?"

"You can listen to me. Got something to tell you. Something you'll be mighty glad to hear."

"What is it?"

"The State Council threw Matthew Maury out of Mexico."

"Threw him *out?*"

Andrew shook his red head, like a dog climbing out of a pond, and said more coherently:

"It's not as bad as that. Maury is in London, as you know. I mean it's public, what Mora told me privately when we came here. The Council dismissed him today from the Immigration post, and they mean to close the Southern Land Office."

"In spite of all the Emperor had promised? Can it be true?"

"The Council overrode the Emperor. It *is* true, Sally. I was dining with Bill Gwin at the Eliseo when Masseras of the *Ere Nouvelle* came in. He'd just had orders from the Council to print the story in tomorrow's paper."

"Then what will happen to the Carlóta Colony?"

The smile on Andrew's flushed face was not pleasant.

"That's what I wanted to hear you ask, my dear. I knew you couldn't resist it. The colony will collapse, of course, without Mr. Maury. Even Dick can't take his place as the leader of the group. Now go ahead and preach to me, why don't you? Tell me how right you were when you refused to have anything to do

with Carlóta Colony! Tell me what a fool I was to believe in
Matthew Maury—"

The naked trouble and confusion in his face checked Sally's
sharp rejoinder. She said, "I'm sorry you feel so bitter, Andrew,"
and went quietly from the room.

From that night on, the old happy intercourse between Sally
and the Mora sisters was at an end. Silvia's marriage of course
could not take place in May, the Virgin's month, but Don Felipe
was pressing for the first of June, and his betrothed was already
in the hands of the dressmakers, modistes and jewelers, who
saw in the Mora marriage their greatest opportunity since Doña
Josefa de la Peña's grand wedding to Marshal Bazaine in the
previous year. Silvia proposed to have Sally among her bridesmaids, but in her docile way yielded to Vera's objections that
the inclusion of a Protestant would give offense in many quarters,
not least to the bridegroom. So Sally was excluded from the
gatherings where the bridal retinue endlessly discussed Silvia's
trousseau, and fingered the heirloom linens and laces which servants were packing into antique chests to send to her future home.
Few callers came to the Plazuelita, for the rainy season began
punctually, and from two o'clock every afternoon the streets of
Mexico were lashed into a sea of brown mud, so that Sally, looking down on the deserted booths and the ugly fountain in the
square, was disconsolate until the day when Andrew came back
from Chapultepec and told her she might start her own packing,
because they were going down with the Court to Cuernavaca.

"The Empress wants me near her," he said with an affecta-
tion of carelessness, "and as by good fortune we have the hacienda, it will be more convenient to be there than lodged somewhere in the town. La Borda is quite a small house, and I'm
told it will be full to overflowing."

"I'm glad you see some advantage in the hacienda at last!"
But Sally was too delighted to be sarcastic. It was the first time
she had seen Andrew in good spirits since Maury's dismissal.
She danced a galop round the heavy old furniture, with her skirts
caught up above her ankles, while Andrew watched with a stiff

smile. He was glad to give Sally pleasure. Dr. Herzog, now on his way back to Europe, had planted several barbs in his self-satisfaction where his sister was concerned.

"And the best of it is," cried Sally, twirling to a standstill, "we don't have to wait any longer on Don Antonio's whims. Horrible old man, always grinning and bowing and putting me off! Going down with the Court—that'll teach him a lesson; and to think you've done it all yourself in less than a couple of months!"

"Done what, girl?"

"Become the Court Physician, of course."

"Don't be ridiculous. Dr. Samuel Basch is the new Court Physician; he'll be here in a matter of weeks."

"But *you* cured the Empress. You're the one she trusts."

Andrew shook his head. Sally knew only that the Empress had been in poor health since her return from Yucatán; she supposed that Andrew had prescribed successfully for some digestive upset. But she was quite correct in her second statement. Carlóta, though far from cured, showed more trust in her new doctor with every visit he paid to the castle.

"Andy!"

"What now?"

The gaiety had gone from Sally's face.

"I'm sorry," she said. "There's something I forgot for a few minutes. Perhaps you know it already, though? I only heard today—that the Mora wedding is likely to be held at Cuernavaca."

"Have you seen Silvia?"—eagerly.

Sally shook her head. "The carriage called here this morning —Pilár was taking George for his first airing and wanted an extra chaperone. The dueña was there, of course, and Soledad, and the two boys, but it was very much George and Pilár's day. She told me about the wedding then."

"You went driving with them?"

"Once round the Alameda—that was all."

Andrew considered. There was no more elation in his face, and only bitterness in his voice when he said:

"Pilár and George Halkett, eh? I can imagine how Don Antonio will treat that youth's aspirations, if he ever puts them into words—! Well, if Pilár says the wedding will be in the country, it probably will, provided the Emperor and Empress stay there. Our friend Mora may have his doubts about Maximilian, but as long as Imperial favor is worth having, he'll be eager to bask in it."

"Have you ever spoken to Don Antonio about *your* aspirations?"

It was gently said. The look he turned on Sally was revealing and harsh.

"Have you spoken to Silvia, Andrew?"

"She never told you—"

"No."

Andrew looked bleakly out of the long window at the Customs House across the plaza. He had kept Sally at arm's length for so long that it was hard to make a confidante of her now. But an irresistible desire for sympathy made him say:

"I told her that I loved her that night at Chapultepec. In the garden, before we ran into the bandits. And she said she loved me. Next day—no, it was the day after, when he'd got over his fright about Doña Mercedes, I asked her father to break off the engagement with Don Felipe, and let her be my wife."

"Was he angry, Andy?"

"No, that's not Don Antonio's way. He was kindly, amused, sorry for my disappointment, but he pointed out that I had nothing to offer his daughter compared with Don Felipe's riches, and that I was a heretic into the bargain. I said I would put *that* right—"

"Put it *right!*" said Sally, firing up. "You don't mean you'd go over to Rome?"

"Why not? Do you think a difference in the form of Christian worship means anything to me? At least I forced Don Antonio to change his tune. He began to boast of Don Felipe's ancestors and noble blood. I told him my mother's father was the tenth Baron Sandhaven in the peerage of Scotland, and that we were on excellent terms with the cousin who succeeded him."

Sally successfully checked a smile. The present Lord S., a crusty old gentleman who seldom left his crumbling Aberdeenshire tower, kept his American cousins at a distance crossed only by curt notes of condolence on their recent bereavements, and his heir, an attaché at the British Embassy in Paris, was no more expansive. But she knew how highly Andrew valued the connection, and some stubborn Scottish pride in her own heart made her feel that a Mexican Mora might well be impressed by the once-great name of Fraser of Sandhaven. She said with real feeling,

"I only wish there had been a Lord S. among the Conquistadores!" And then, with her hand on her brother's arm:

"Oh, Andy, don't be too disappointed, dear! We know the way Don Antonio's mind works well enough. But what about Silvia herself?"

"She hasn't said anything to you?"—wistfully.

"Not to me, no. But I think she may have told her sister Vera."

"Why?"

"Because now I come to think of it, I never was alone with Silvia after Vera came downstairs. She or that slinking Tía Beata was always there. But if Silvia really loves you, wouldn't she stand up to her father for your sake? She can't care for that old man they want to make her marry. He looks like a sick monkey, and I'm sure his hair is dyed. How dare Don Antonio think he has the right to dispose of his daughters as *he* sees fit! Look at poor Pilár, being forced to enter a convent, just because she's not as pretty as the others, and Don Antonio wants to get her out of the way before he makes a match for Soledad. Can't Silvia see it? Has she no spirit? Shall I speak to her, and see what I can do?" asked Sally, with her fists clenched in the pockets of her holland apron, and her face flushed with eager sympathy.

"No, for God's sake, don't you say anything, Sally, you'd spoil it all," said Andrew. "Can't you realize that this is *why* I love Silvia—because she's not a fighter and a rebel, but the sweetest, the most gentle girl who ever lived? She says she must do what her father wishes. All right, I have to accept that, and you must promise me not to disturb her with any of your wild schemes, either here or at Cuernavaca. Do you understand me?"

"I understand you're both too ready to accept defeat," said Sally.

She gave him her promise not to seek out Silvia, and she kept it to the letter. But three days after that, when half their trunks were already packed for Cuernavaca, a message came from Silvia to her.

It was a dark, rainy afternoon, and Sally had already lighted her bedroom candles to dress for the evening when Lupita came lumbering upstairs with a little note folded in the familiar cocked-hat shape. Before Don Felipe's coming, the servants had carried half a dozen such notes between the two girls each day.

"*Sally*"—the spiked handwriting ran—"*I am on my way to the Cathedral. Please come to me in the Capilla de San Miguel. I beg you—Silvia.*"

She read it twice, hastily, and looked up at Lupita.

"A vaquero from the Casa Mora brought it, not five minutes back," said Lupita defensively. "By all the Saints, señorita, I have not delayed in bringing it to you."

"Then get your rebozo, Lupe. I need you to come out with me," her mistress said. "Has the señor doctor come in yet?"

The señor doctor, by good fortune, was still out. Sally consulted her watch and looked at the sky darkening above the Plazuelita. She had never been out at night with only a servant for protection, and although Lupita was by far the strongest and most aggressive of the domestics, and the Cathedral less than five minutes' walk away, the girl trembled a little as they let themselves out at the door between the pulque shops and picked their way between the little braziers beginning to flicker in the Plazuelita. There were always half-drunk, half-clad *léperos* demanding alms at this hour, between light and dark, when it was not too difficult to imagine the Plaza Mayor in the days of Moctezuma, when a temple of sacrifice, reeking with the blood of ten thousand victims, stood on the spot where Cortés had first held on high that image of the Virgin still worshiped in Mexico as La Conquistadora. The smoke from the woodfires in the little booths curled above the treetops, the music throbbed, the Indians paced the causeway with the same quiet step as their Aztec ancestors, and three hundred years of Conquest and Intervention were as if they had never been. Sally went quickly across the atrium towards the main door of the Cathedral. She had taken the precaution to wear a black lace mantilla, Silvia's own gift, and to draw it well over her tawny hair and the white pagoda sleeves of her gray dress. Still, she knew that no one who looked twice would take her for a Mexican woman, and felt herself an interloper.

Delicacy of feeling as well as religious conviction had kept the Presbyterian minister's daughter from visiting many of the famous churches of the capital. To Sally, who in her secret heart considered even the Church of England prayers which she heard read at the Legation "too ritualistic," there could be no spiritual ease in the rich imagery of a Catholic church, and she hesitated to offend the devout Mexicans by entering their places of worship as a mere sightseer. She had already visited the Cathedral, although only once. Nothing in the great church had then horrified her like the statue of the Savior in Santo Domingo—a statue kept inside a glass case, in which the wax figure, wearing a crown of thorns, was dressed in the crimson velvet knee breeches and gold-braided cape of a matador. The all too realistic blood of His wounds streamed from the naked breast. That sight had sent Sally, trembling with revulsion, into the open air of the Plazuelita. There was only beauty before her eyes at the entry to the Cathedral, where the great white Churrigueresque altar to the Virgin of Forgiveness blazed with flowers and candles. A hundred worshipers knelt or lay prone before it in attitudes of contrition. Yet the little Calvinist instinctively braced herself, as Lupita, by her side, made the sign of the Cross, and bent her knee. The noble altar meant as little to Sally as the Aztec Calendar Stone leaning against the outside wall of the Cathedral.

"Have you come to pray for El Güero, Señorita Gringa?"

The insolent words, spoken in a loud whisper, caused several of the worshipers to raise their heads. Sally, taken by surprise, stepped back at the sight of La Malinche, who with two handsome youths for escort appeared to be on the point of leaving the Cathedral. Her red rebozo was drawn modestly over her head, hiding the ribbon bow, but the strings of beads swung defiantly at her golden throat, and her bright skirts glowed in the lights from the altar. Sally knew now that what Malinche wore was the China Poblana dress, the nearest approach to a national costume any Mexican woman could wear: it had precisely the same irritant effect upon herself as the red rags fluttered in the bullring, to which she never went. "Let me pass at once, señorita," she said sharply.

"You think I'm not good enough to speak to you?" said Marina. "Look at her, señores! See the Gringa who stole my lover, and shows herself off with him in the Plaza Mayor, like the *hija de putana* as she is!"

"Are these fit words for a house of God?" said Sally. But Lupita came between them then, edging Marina away as a priest approached with his finger to his lips, and hustling Sally towards the gilded grilles of the Chapel of St. Michael and All Angels.

"It is much better not to speak to La Malinche," she whispered, with more friendship in her voice than she usually showed to Sally. "She is a bad woman. Think, señorita, you are here to meet with the Señorita Mora—who kneels in prayer yonder, like one of the angels of God."

There were many people pressed against the grilles but so few inside the chapel that Sally at once distinguished Silvia. On the altar steps were bunched three crinolines: one of lavender gauze, which Sally identified as belonging to Pilár Mora, one of black bombazine, which plainly belonged to the Tía Beata, and a drapery of white lace beneath the hooded black burnous which hid Silvia's slenderness. Silvia's hands were joined in prayer. Her perfect profile was lifted reverently to St. Michael Archangel, and to all the winged Company of Heaven starting out of the golden reredos behind him. Her lips moved. She looked like a woman taking a victorious decision, and to Sally, who knew that Silvia Mora was engaged on the pathway of defeat, there came a verse from her favorite Browning:

> *Only they see not God, I know,*
> *Nor all that chivalry of His,*
> *The soldier-saints who, row on row,*
> *Burn upward each to his point of bliss—*

She shrank back, humbled and ashamed, as the great organ pealed out, filling the nave with sound. Somewhere a bell tinkled. Silvia rose and came straight through the gold gates to Sally.

"Sally, *querida,* you came to me! I mustn't stay—I ought not to be here. But I had to know . . . what Andrés thinks of me."

The violet eyes implored Sally to reply. But the American girl looked about her first—at the veiled shape of Pilár, halted a yard behind her sister's shoulder, and the bundle of the Beata's shawls.

"Are you unhappy, Silvia? Are you being forced into this marriage against your will? You know quite well what Andrew thinks of you; he adores you. Haven't you the courage to give up Don Felipe for him?"

Sally saw young Pilár edge the dueña back into the crowd round the Altar of Forgiveness, and come closer with her own hooded burnous outspread, as if to screen them into a corner of quiet.

"I dare not," whispered Silvia. "There's no escape, Sally. You don't know my father. There's no way out."

"There's always a way out," said Sally. The clear voice, the bright strands of hair escaping from under her black mantilla caused heads to turn in the crowd around the chapel gates. "Silvia, if you love my brother, if you're brave enough, you could soon outdistance Don Antonio. Horses to Cuernavaca— a stop to rest at Taxco and then on to Acapulco, and the first boat sailing for a Californian port. You could marry in Mexico or in the United States—"

She stopped. She had just remembered the oath sworn by Andrew at New Orleans. As long as it was binding, he could go ashore nowhere in California, nor anywhere else in United States territory.

"It's no use," said Silvia, crying. "I don't want to run away and be despised by everyone. Don Felipe is very kind to me. I only wanted to be sure Andrés wouldn't be unhappy—and to ask you to give this back to him."

The hot, thin fingers slipped something into Sally's hand. She looked down at a little keepsake ring of purple enamel viola flowers, each with a tiny pearl at the center, which she knew had belonged to her mother as a girl.

"Come to my wedding," said Silvia on a despairing breath, and was gone behind the white lilies and the candles on the Altar of Forgiveness.

Chapter Ten

THE WARM COUNTRY

THE EMPEROR OF MEXICO had a new traveling carriage
with the motto EQUITY AND JUSTICE painted below the blazon
on the doors. To do it honor, he had replaced his fawn-colored
team by twelve snow-white mules wearing blue velvet harness
ornamented with plumes of gray and scarlet feathers. Preceded
by the inevitable escort, and by outriders wearing silver gal-
looned livery, this stylish equipage appeared to great effect one
day in May when it rolled rapidly down the old Tlalpan highway, carrying the Emperor and Empress of Mexico to their villa
in the Warm Country.

They were followed by a long procession of other vehicles
from the Imperial coach houses, from private homes and even
from hackney stables, increased by carriages waiting in the cool
wet morning at the crossroads which led to San Angel and
Tacubaya. The white bellies of the new mules were splashed
and stained long before the procession began the slow ascent of
the cobbled highway laid over three hundred years earlier by
Cortés, when he first discovered the beauty spot his men called
Cuernavaca, and the straw of Sally Lorimer's bonnet was soon
wilting as she leaned from the carriage window to look back on
the city they were leaving behind. She was traveling with three
of the younger Ladies of the Palace, in the rear, while Andrew
was close behind the Imperial carriage, in a britska driven with
spirit by Colonel von Kodolitsch.

The wet mist clotted into a freezing rain in the pass of La

Cima, and at ten thousand feet the long procession seemed to ride above the clouds. After that began the comforting drop down into Tierra Templada, and the dark-haired, disheveled beauties of the court began to take heart and preen themselves for the traditional halt at the posthouse of Las Tres Marias, beneath the three peaks which stood guard over the valley of Cuernavaca. Before them as the carriages rolled to a stop were rich sunlit meadows and pastures, groves of fruit, prosperous white haciendas set among brilliantly flowering trees. A murmur of satisfaction, soft as the singing waters of the Warm Country, arose as the Mexican ladies emerged from the cocoons of their wraps and shawls, and fluttered down from the high vehicles like a bevy of brightly colored butterflies.

An alfresco picnic was Maximilian's favorite form of entertainment. It was on a picnic at Las Tres Marias that he first looked down on Cuernavaca and was seized with one of his recurrent impulses to remodel an old dwelling and build a new one, and since then every halt at the posthouse had been celebrated with a picnic, even when the whole Court was on the move. Servants had gone ahead of them to lay cloths on the well-trimmed meadow grass and set out dishes of chicken in aspic, thinly sliced ham with papaya, and thick avocado sauce. Corks were being drawn from bottles of Rhine wine, cooled in a mountain stream, as one by one the butterfly crinolines dropped gracefully to the turf. The men in bright uniforms solicitously bent above them, adjusted rugs, opened the fringed silk parasols. The high-pitched Spanish chatter began to rise above the sound of the guitars.

The Empress Carlóta did not join in the gaiety but, complaining of headache, went inside the posthouse attended by Dr. Lorimer. Her husband did not seem unduly concerned. Soon after the meal was over Sally saw him on horseback competing with the Mexican caballeros in an impromptu game of tent-pegging. His spirited bay, Orispelo, had been brought up from Cuernavaca for his master to ride into the town, and in the saddle the Emperor looked magnificent in his charro dress of dark blue, with a gray silk neckerchief matching his huge gray sombrero, and a brilliant Saltillo serape flung across his shoulder. He was at his best then—a man among men, yet gaily aware of the line of laughing ladies watching him from the bank where the highway ran beside the Tres Marias meadow. Sally was among them, completely absorbed in the virtuoso display of horsemanship—too absorbed to be aware of a light touch on her elbow, or respond until the voice of Silvia's elder sister spoke her name.

"Good day, Doña Vera," she said then composedly, although the surprise of the meeting brought the color to her cheeks. "I had no idea you were traveling to Cuernavaca."

"Nor I you, until I saw Don Andrés in attendance on the Empress. Then I looked for his devoted sister, and found her presently. Would you like to see my baby?"

"Very much . . . Are any other members of the family with you?"

"Only my little boys, and one of the Tacubaya aunts for chaperone. I've been deputed to open up the villa. Poor mamma isn't well enough to travel yet, and besides, she has to stay in town with Silvia."

"Of course." The two girls walked away together, Sally's soft gray skirts eclipsed in size and color by the magnificent peacock blue shot silk which Doña Vera had thought appropriate for a day's travel in the crowded Mora family berline. It was empty when they reached it, for the small boys had been taken off to play with Prince Agustín Iturbide, and the Tacubaya aunt, a flirt at sixty, was watching the horseback riding. The Indian nurses were sitting in the baggage cart, one with baby Catalina on her lap.

"She's sweet!" Sally, who had no experience of babies, bent cautiously over the sleeping infant. "She's grown, hasn't she?"

"She's only six weeks old."

"But I haven't seen her for two of them."

"I know," said Vera, looking slightly disconcerted. "I—you

206

must come and visit me at Cuernavaca. I shall be almost alone
until the family comes down in the middle of June."

"I thought the wedding was fixed for the second?"

"It's been put off," said Doña Vera, "for two weeks, until
the seventeenth."

"Put off!" Sally echoed, with sudden hope in her heart.
"*Silvia* has put it off?"

"Silvia wouldn't dare, and our ardent young bridegroom is
very angry. But papa is adamant that this must be a gathering
of the whole family, with my brothers and my Pablo present,
and there has been some trouble about getting leave for them.
General Miramón is having difficulties in the north, it seems.
Those vile Juaristas!" said Doña Vera, moving into the shadow
cast by the berline and snapping her parasol shut decisively.

"Don Pablo will be so happy to see you—and the new
baby," Sally said.

"Yes, well, provided he doesn't leave me with a successor
to her. His last visits were a great deal too fruitful for my comfort," said Doña Vera flippantly, and laughed at Sally's expression. "Don't look so shocked, my dear! You must have a very
good idea of what marriage is, an eager little matchmaker like
you!"

"Not a very successful matchmaker, I'm afraid," said Sally.
She knows, she thought. Her spy the dueña told her that I met
Silvia in the Cathedral.

"That's what I wanted to talk to you about, Sally," Vera
said good-naturedly. She looked round; there was no sign of the
aunt approaching, or anyone within earshot but Indians.

"I know you met Silvia at church two nights ago, and pled
your brother's cause for him. Silvia came home in tears, Pilár
too; they couldn't hide what had happened from me. Ridiculous
behavior—all sobbing like a pack of hysterical schoolgirls—"

"I didn't cry, Doña Vera."

"No, you wouldn't. But you may make Silvia cry again, if
I let you; and I won't do that. Silvia has got to be kept calm
and contented until she is *la señora marquesa,* one month from

now, and takes such a position as most girls would give their ears for—"

"With that old man? Who was another woman's husband for twenty years?"

"Oh, you *Norteamericanos!*" said Vera. "What a pack of romantic children you all are! First Don Andrés with his naïve proposal, then you with your headstrong plans for an elopement! Don Felipe Vega's age is no disadvantage. My sister may find it adds greatly to her enjoyment of married life. He gives her rank, jewels, establishments such as no other man in Mexico can offer; why should she object to his years, and widowed state? Upon my word," said Vera forcibly, "my father has managed the whole thing very badly! Instead of foisting me off on Cousin Pablo, he should have married *me* to the marqués! I could have put up with a good deal, I tell you, to get out of this barbarous country and be off to Madrid! Then Silvia could have entered the convent, instead of poor clumsy Pilár—it would have been the perfect outlet for all her sentimental vaporings—"

"For shame, Doña Vera!" said Sally with such indignation that the other woman stopped short. "Have you no respect for your sister's feelings? She loves my brother—she told him so; and he loves her—"

"But of course!" said Vera with provoking calm. "But naturally! And since marriage between them is impossible—don't you see, you silly girl, they only have to wait? Once Silvia has done her duty to the house of Vega, and given the marqués a son and heir, what objection can there possibly be to a discreet affair with her—physician?"

"You insult both your sister and my brother when you even hint at such a thing"—furiously. "Doña Vera, I shall always be grateful to your parents for the kindness they showed me when I was a stranger to Mexico. But since you have taken it upon yourself to tell me what I am to say and not say, do and not do, I must decline your polite invitation to visit you at your father's villa. Andrew himself says he never wants to hear me speak

of Silvia again. Perhaps it would be better for both families if
our acquaintance were to end now."

"As you please," said Doña Vera with provoking good
humor. "So Don Andrés doesn't want to hear *you* speak of Silvia
—that I can well understand. But are you quite sure that he
never wants to speak to Silvia herself?"

IN SPITE of his prancings and curvettings on Orispelo,
the arrival of Maximilian in Cuernavaca was quiet and informal.
The long hilly main street took an awkward turn at the very
gates of La Borda, the Imperial summer residence, which left
little room for mounting a guard of honor, and the royal party
got out of the carriages with no delay.

"Look sharp, Sal," said Dr. Lorimer, putting his red head
in at the window of Sally's coach. "Von Kodolitsch is lending
us his britska to go down to the hacienda."

"You don't have to stay with the Empress?"

"No, she stood up to the journey very well. Quick now!"

The light carriage belonging to Sally's favorite of "the Two
K's" was stopping the way at the awkward turn. Sally felt herself swung up high, was joined by Andrew, and they rattled
downhill into the plaza through a warm wind which blew dust
into Sally's eyes.

"Hold on to your headgear," Andrew counseled her. "This
thing jolts unmercifully. I've had eight hours of it, and I should
know."

"We haven't far to go," she reminded him. "Only two
miles."

"Two miles to the famous hacienda! Are you glad?"

She nodded without speaking, and Andrew was actually
moved to pat his sister's hand. But the two miles seemed as long
as twenty, for the road running southwest of Cuernavaca speedily
became a cart track, then a mere cow path, and Colonel von
Kodolitsch's soldier driver swallowed an oath as he edged the

britska into a cluster of prickly pears to let pass a string of
donkeys laden with vanilla, which came scrambling wildly out of
a deep barranca which apparently circled all that side of the
town. Then it was their turn to descend into the ravine, and up
on the other side to half a mile of main road in fair condition,
near a white adobe barracks with a red-tiled roof and bales of
fodder piled against the end wall. The French flag flew over this
building and at the gate of a military corral beside it, a sight
which caused Sally's heart to leap and Andrew to say, as he
acknowledged the half-salute sketched by two sentries on duty,

"You won't fume or fuss, will you, Sally, if your hacienda
turns out to be requisitioned property?"

"It won't be," she said confidently, as the britska swung
through a grove of banana trees, and over the stone bridge span-
ning an arroyo. A few more turns of the wheels, and they came
within sight of a tall white chimney towering above the treetops
and the stone cross on a little country church.

"That must be the refinery chimney," Sally said. Excitement
had brought a warm color to her cheeks; she tried in vain to
appear indifferent. At last they were driving between thatched
adobe dwellings—some the merest hovels—towards which men
were slowly sauntering from fields of young sugar canes.

"Do you suppose these are *my* fields, Andrew?"

"Very likely. Your own peons too, don't forget."

It was a much humbler village than Río Frío, Sally's only
standard of comparison, and yet there was a sense of tranquillity
about the place. Children and lean black pigs sprawled together
contentedly beneath the mud walls, and the women grinding corn
in stone querns to make the evening tortillas did not shrink away
in panic as the britska passed. Sally sat up straighter. In an up-
surge of pride and confidence she saw, at the far end of the village, a square of umbered stone walls, two stories high and
pierced by deep, round windows, which enclosed the Hacienda
de las Flores.

"It's a regular fortress, Sally!"

A crumbling fortress, with half the iron window bars

rusted and moldering in their sockets, and creeping plants blossoming in the gaps of the unpointed stone. But almost before Andrew had lifted Sally down, two Indian lads in clean shirts and leather trousers came through the open gate, with smiles and bows, to take the baggage, and on their heels an older man and woman, also dressed in spotless white, came forward respectfully to greet the señor doctor and the señorita.

They were Ramón Martínez, the overseer, and his wife, and Sally went to meet them with outstretched hand, calling them "Don Ramón" and "Doña Juanita" with a grave courtesy which matched their own. She had a pleasant word, too, for the yard *mozos,* and for Mariquita, the plump young woman in agonies of shyness who was to be her cook. Andrew stood aside from the little scene of welcome. Sally was managing very well, he thought. This was a more gracious beginning by far than their stormy arrival at the Plazuelita and he looked about him with curiosity. He saw some sort of office on the left of the gateway, what appeared to be a shop or store on the right; a stable beyond the office and next to the shop a low veranda on which lounged a half-grown boy, very dark of skin, whose black hair urgently wanted cutting.

"My son, Tomásito," said Don Ramón, following the young doctor's eyes. "He is very timid. He will pay his respects to your graces presently. That is the overseer's house, señor; and there, just opposite the entrance gate, is the Casa Grande."

It was an imposing title for a little house, and this was the first and last time that Don Ramón was permitted to employ it. From then on, and in Sally's heart forever, it was La Casita, the little house whose gables were the two end walls of the main enclosure and whose front lay engagingly open to a wide garden and a vista of blue mountain ranges, turning to violet in the dusk of the Warm Country. .

"Oh, Andy! Oh, how wonderful!"

The door from the courtyard opened directly into a square room, or patio, with a well-polished red-tiled floor and steps leading down to the garden under a wide archway draped in

white casahuate, the tree morning glory, among the branches of
which hung cages of singing birds. Beyond, on a well-kept lawn,
two white flamingos stood pensively beside the stone coping of a
little fountain, and parrots on a swinging perch chattered beneath a cypress tree. The flower beds were brilliant with scent
and color. The rich crimson petals of the Aztec lily blossomed
under crape myrtles which reminded Andrew of their old home;
the star lily, *flor de Pedregal,* was planted among tuberoses and
tobacco plant. In the middle of the lawn, where the evening
shadow of the garden wall met the last of the sunlight, a striped
kitten was frantically chasing its tail.

"Well, Sally, there you are," said Andrew. "You've got
your fountain and your patio at last; congratulations."

"I hope the señorita will be satisfied," said Martínez' wife
anxiously. "We have cleaned and polished everything, every day
since we knew the señores had arrived in Mexico."

"It's beautiful," said Sally from her heart.

The little house was beautiful in its simplicity. The arched
patio served as a dining room and general living place, and was
furnished with a plain oak table and a variety of chairs. A small
parlor on one side contained a comfortable sofa and a fireplace
filled with purple and white gloxinias in pots, a whatnot holding some books and curios, and a little escritoire. On the other
side of the patio was the kitchen, where Mariquita was hanging
anxiously over a long charcoal stove faced with the familiar blue
and white tiles. An unusual feature was the two separate stair-
cases, very steep and narrow, which led from the patio to two
bedrooms on the upper story, with a dressing room and ample
closets in between. And that was all of Sally's house, lacking in
silver, fine linen, solid furniture, pictures or ornaments of any
sort; thoroughly delightful to her eyes and ears.

If she stood by the round window in the gable end of her
room above the kitchen, she could see the Indians quietly seated
at supper round the little braziers burning at the doors of their
lean-to huts. If she looked out of the casement window above
the garden, she could see the evening star rising above the glim-

mering flowers. The soft voices of the Indians blended with the chatter of the parrots and toucans being shut up for the night, and from somewhere close at hand Sally heard the high notes of a French bugle.

"Come along, Sally, supper's getting cold!" called an impatient voice from the patio.

"I'm sorry!" She ran downstairs smiling, as eager to please as Mariquita, who had not waited for their orders to serve the simple meal. It consisted of an excellent vegetable soup, eggs poached in a purée of tomatoes and peppers, and a deep dish of tortillas baked with grated cheese and cream. Mariquita had expressed her welcome by weaving chains of flowers over and round the fruit piled in a straw basket, and a bottle of Baja California wine stood by Andrew's place.

"Do you suppose the Emperor and the Empress are having anything half as good as this at La Borda, Andrew?"

"You wouldn't suppose if you had ever eaten a meal at their table, my child. Talk about starvation diet!"

Sally laughed, and Mariquita came in to clear the table.

"Is there anything more I can do to serve your graces?"

"Nothing, thank you, Mariquita. Sleep well."

"I will prepare the coffee at six o'clock tomorrow morning, señorita. Or earlier, if the señor doctor wishes."

"Six is quite early enough . . . Doesn't she sleep in the hacienda?" he inquired, as the maid curtsied herself out.

"She's married, Doña Juanita said. She goes home to her husband and three children in the village. Anyway, I don't know where she *would* sleep, in this house."

"True; it's compact enough, in all conscience. I can hardly stand upright in the bedroom."

"But we've a patio and a garden here!" she said quickly. "It isn't really as cramped as the Plazuelita."

"That's so. You've got your lawn and your roses—small scale—Sally-size," he said teasingly, "with a few birds and beasts thrown in." For the striped kitten was snugly established on Sally's lap, licking cream from fragments of tortilla.

Andrew finished his wine and asked Sally's leave to smoke. It was one of the outward ways in which he was invariably courteous to his sister; she usually answered with an offhand "Yes." Tonight he was touched, in spite of himself, when she smiled, and said prettily,

"Esta es su casa, señor."

"You're very generous, Sally." It was not his house, of course, it was her house—and welcome to it, a tumble-down liability at the edge of nowhere; if he had any sense he would improve the occasion by reminding her that she mustn't fall in love with the place or make great plans for it, since their visit must end when the Court went back to Mexico. But when he bent over the little oil lamp to light his cigarillo, and the flame sprang up, the destructive impulse died at the sight of Sally's face, half-smiling and withdrawn, as with one finger she traced the velvety black line running between the kitten's little ears. She had changed her traveling dress for an old, washed-out pink cotton which he remembered from the War years, which showed her rounded forearms and a triangle of white skin at the base of her throat. A lock of hair, escaping from its pins, fell over Sally's eyes without her lifting a hand to put it in place. In the warm lassitude of Tierra Templada she seemed lost in some intimate and drowsy dream. Andrew felt his taut nerves beginning to relax. For weeks past he had been harried by his desire for Silvia and his knowledge that he would never possess her, and by the bitter certainty that he would never work with Matthew Maury for the Southern colonists in Mexico. Yet in Sally's silent companionship and the beauty of the starlit garden, he felt himself coming to the threshold of a hard-won peace. He finished his cigarillo in that comfortable silence, and presently lighted Sally's candle for her, and watched her climb her wooden staircase with the purring kitten in her arms.

AT NOON next day Sally returned from her first survey of the sugar fields, the deserted refinery, the empty storerooms on the upper floor of the hacienda and the straggling village where the peons lived. It had taken her the better part of five hours, and cut her city shoes to ribbons. The overseer, himself exhausted by the pace set by his new mistress, went to the tienda and brought her a pair of the thonged leather sandals called huaraches before going to his own house for the midday meal.

Andrew was at La Borda, and Mariquita had spread a small table for Sally in the garden. A true Mexican in her love of beauty, the maid had chosen an enchanting spot, where the white floripondio hung its scented wedding bells above the lawn, and tame white cockatoos with yellow crests chattered and strutted in the branches of a tall cypress. Between the cypress and a flowering camarón tree Tomásito, the overseer's boy, had slung a hammock newly woven out of cactus fiber for Sally's siesta.

But Sally, as soon as her simple meal was eaten, went back through the little house and across the silent courtyard to the office beside the gate which Don Ramón said he had always placed at the Old Doctor's disposal when *el patron* visited Las Flores. It was at Sally's entire disposal now. Airless, lighted by a small window and through the open door, the hacienda office contained records of the plantation which went back twenty years to the tally sticks of the eighteen forties—cut by Ramón Martínez in the days before the first Dr. Lorimer taught his protégé to read and write. The dusty calf-bound volumes on the shelves carried on the story through Santa Anna's wars to the days of Maximilian, and on the bare desk, furnished with nothing but a standish and a homemade quill pen, a new daybook and ledger waited for the clear, determined writing of a girl.

Sally pulled the heavy leather chair up squarely to the desk and rolled her cotton sleeves above her elbows in Andrew's own shipshape manner. It was the hottest hour of the whole day, and Atlacomulco parish slept in its hammocks, on its serapes, or with its sombreros over its collective face in the shade of the banana trees. Sally slipped one bare foot out of the new huarache and thoughtfully rubbed it on the other. It was the first time she had known the freedom of stockingless feet since her early childhood by the Cape Fear River.

Looking to her right across the courtyard, she could see the locked tienda. They had left its inspection until a later hour, partly because the bell had to be rung for the noon break, and partly because of Sally's unconfessed reluctance to grapple with the problem of the shop which would be open to the peons and their families as soon as the day's work was done. The famous Washington pamphlets had not warned her that the owner of a sugar plantation, or any other type of ranch in Mexico, was automatically a storekeeper, retailing food and clothing to his own laborers, chalking up their purchases against their earnings, and making what profit he could from his own bulk buying. It was this system which, as Don Antonio Mora had warned Sally, put not only the peons employed at Las Flores in debt to the hacienda, but their fathers before them from the time the Old Doctor started the plantation in 1841.

The sum involved at Las Flores was not large. It was less than one thousand U. S. dollars. It was, by precisely that sum, less than the hacienda could afford to remit and remain solvent. For three years past the cut canes had been sold on contract, direct from the plantation. This year the planting had been begun on the third of May, because Holy Cross day was considered "the blessed day for planting," which meant there would be no new crop until November. This too, Martínez had advised Sally, should be sold in cane, to obtain the small but certain margin of profit which paid the running expenses of the hacienda.

There had been no attempt to refine sugar at Las Flores for some years past. Where all else was neat and tidy, the empty refinery was conspicuously run-down and out of order; the furnace grate broken, the molasses tanks full of scum, the pans, kettles, defecators, clarifiers, evaporators all rusted beyond repair.

The profit on refined sugar would—on paper—be enough to wipe out the accumulated debts of the laborers to the hacienda, and free them, so far as it was in Sally's power to do, from the heaviest shackle of their peonage.

To make that profit, new equipment for the refinery would have to be bought before November, and, very probably, a sugar master hired for the season. This was quite beyond the slender means at Sally Lorimer's disposal.

It was characteristic of Sally that she gave only a brief consideration to borrowing money for the re-equipment of the refinery. Raising a loan in Cuernavaca or Mexico would require the consent of Andrew during her minority, and any Mexican willing to take a bond on a woman's property would almost certainly require her brother's house and practice to be called in as collateral security. To involve Andrew to that extent was out of the question.

Less than two thousand dollars would clear up the whole thing. Five hundred for machinery, one thousand to clear the tienda slate and start afresh. So little, by comparison with all that had been spent in the war which had wrecked the Confederacy, or on the two palaces, the summer villa, the three haciendas restored or built in Mexico by Carlóta and Maximilian.

"You're looking very fierce," said Sergeant Franchet. "May I come in?"

Across his dark-blue shoulder she saw the bright blue sky, a trail of wall geranium, a fantail pigeon on a broken coping. And the Hacienda de las Flores, her dear possession, painfully reached and tenaciously held, was suddenly of no account compared with the man for whom Sally had been waiting all day long.

Her face was radiant as she gave him her hand.

"Where have you come from? I didn't hear a horse!"

Pierre kissed her fingers lightly. He was deeply tanned as always, but now there was a healthy color beneath the desert brown, and the taut lines round his eyes and mouth had relaxed.

"You've got a nice little sweet-grass corral, a few hundred meters down the arroyo. I turned Rataplan in there, *con su permiso, señorita.*"

"I've got four cows and a calf in that corral," said Sally composedly. "If your charger won't disturb them, he's quite welcome to stay there."

"Overlooked your stock already, have you?" said Pierre with appreciation. "I shan't leave Rata with the cows long. This is a highly irregular visit, unless you're prepared to rouse Doña Juanita from her hammock and talk to me in the presence of your dueña."

"You know the Martínez' as well as the corral? You seem to know your way around Las Flores."

"Of course"—unruffled. "I've done a reconnaissance, horse and foot, round Las Flores every day for three weeks past. I've reconnoitered every possible way the Chinacos could raid your place, up through the canyon or across the barranca, including through the gate at the foot of the garden which doesn't lock because nobody can find the key. Know the Martínez! I'm the best friend they ever dreamed of making in the French Expeditionary Corps. They won't expect to see me now because evening is my usual time for dropping by Las Flores. You keep a pretty good wineshop, Sally, I'll allow; it isn't every *hacendado* who sells such a fine brand of aguardiente."

"What are you talking about!" Sally jumped up, a small fury, with gold sparks in her eyes.

"Why—like every prudent employer, you sell liquor to your peons when they buy beef or shoes at your tienda," said Pierre equably. "Only yours is honest rum. It must be fermented from the best of your sugar canes. It's not as good as the tequila you drank at Río Frío, but better than the pulque they sell in the Plazuelita; many a glass Don Ramón has sold me over the counter while we waited for the Señorita to reach Cuernavaca."

He was laughing at her, as usual, and Sally cried out furiously,

"Do you mean to say *spirits* are sold to the Indians—under my roof?"

"Why not? It's done on all the haciendas, especially where there's sugar grown. How can you help it?"

"'The custom of the country,'" quoted Sally bitterly. "No wonder the peons are in debt."

He read her mind so well, looked so quickly from her downcast face to the *Report on the Peonage Commission,* which she had laid open on the desk, that the whole thing was clear to Franchet in a moment.

"In debt to the hacienda? Yes, of course, they would be," he said. "Poor Sally! As the Emperor Napoleon likes to say, you're 'face to face with your responsibilities now'—aren't you?"

The tone, the words were flippant; if there was tenderness in the gray eyes Sally did not see it. Her stubborn jaw had set at the word *responsibilities*.

"You oughtn't to be indoors worrying over ledgers on your first day here," he said persuasively. "You ought to be out and about. On horseback, riding in to Cuernavaca to see the sights. It's only two miles away—"

"Considering that I've never ridden two yards in my life—"

"I know you haven't. But I've got your brother's authority to teach you, if you care to learn."

Sally's eyes grew wide.

"You talked to Andrew? When? This morning?"

"Yes, mademoiselle. I was at the gate, fired with zeal to inspect the sentries from the moment I saw the mule cart coming out from the banana trees. Greetings, conversation, good fellowship all round."

"But wasn't he amazed to see you? I didn't tell him you were here."

"Quite right," said Pierre, with his wry smile. "It was better this way. Now I have the doctor's gracious permission to call upon you regularly and take you riding, to provide a mount for you from our stables, and generally to put you in the way of visiting his exalted friends at La Borda whenever you wish. Is this agreeable to you, mademoiselle?"

"But are you equal to it?" said Sally seriously, and Pierre flung back his head with a shout of laughter.

"Equal to teaching one young lady to ride, after drilling the Cazadores? I should hope so!"

"I was thinking of your wound, Pierre," she said gently. He was lounging against the big desk, very close to her, and they were alone in the hot room, without a sound but the plash of water in the horse trough outside, and for the length of an embrace they stared at each other without touching, while Sally's mouth grew dry.

"Thank you," he said at last. "My wound is healed. The next Board will pass me fit for active service. It won't be long now. Sally, do this for me. Let me take you riding. Let's be together while we can and let me know, above everything else"— urgently—"that you won't be helpless here if the Chinacos come, but able to get away on a good horse, into the town and safety."

She was going to tell him that she feared no danger. But her mood altered to match his own earnestness, and she only said:

"I won't have to ride Rataplan, will I?"

Pierre laughed again in his relief.

"No, Rata isn't broke to skirts. But I've a quiet beast picked out for you, and a lady's saddle, too. I'll come tomorrow, as soon as Mexico's Boy Heroes of 1866 have settled down for their siesta. It'll be hot, but I won't work you hard at first."

"You work *them* hard enough," said Sally. "I've been hearing your bugles blowing all day long."

"All day?"

"When I was in the fields with Don Ramón, and even at noon in the garden."

"You didn't hear our bugles," Sergeant Franchet said. "You heard *el clarín*. How do you say in English, *l'oiseau moqueur?*"

"The mockingbird?"

"That's it. The woods round Cuernavaca are full of them. And those crazy little mockingbirds, they imitate the French bugles all day long."

Chapter Eleven

LA BARRANCA

SERGEANT FRANCHET was the first of many visitors to the Hacienda de las Flores. Colonel de Beauvilain, the officer commanding at the replacement depot, paid his courtesy call on Dr. Lorimer and assured him of mademoiselle's perfect safety in a countryside so constantly policed by the Imperial troops. The neighboring rancheros brought their wives and daughters on a two or three hours' drive in jolting oxcarts with hanging leather shades instead of windows to pay their respects to the Señorita of Las Flores and were equally certain of the safety of the province. Even the little parish priest came once, scenting a heretic influence among his flock, and was so charmed by Sally that he took her to see his dark impoverished church, where a gaudy reproduction of the miraculous picture of La Guadalupana was lighted by the stubs of a few votive candles. Sally made them all welcome. She was very happy in those days.

For the first time in her life she felt that her powers were being used to the full. Her old haphazard ambitions, to study medicine or languages, or to teach, had crystallized into a marked capacity for business, and she looked forward as eagerly to the afternoons spent with Don Ramón in the office or the tienda as to the early morning hours spent working among her uncle's flowers. Then the casita and everything in it delighted and satisfied Sally. She was undisputed mistress in the small kitchen with the red-tiled floor, where her own pottery ollas and cazuelas simmered for hours on the charcoal stove, as she had never been

in the gloomy den in the Plazuelita where Lupita grumbled at La
Gringa's interference. At least once a day she begged the overseer's wife to come in from her own house, to show Mariquita
and herself how to make some special dish—wild turkey fricas-
see, or a tasty pozole of meat and maize, and Doña Juanita was
delighted to be called upon. Sally was well aware that she was
fortunate in the Martínez. They were both *mestizos,* of mixed
Indian and Spanish blood, but where that mixture had turned
to poison in the veins of La Malinche it had given to Doña
Juanita the grave courtesy, the courage and the fatalism of both
her races. She had a faithful heart, and Sally realized that the
uncle who had made her his heiress would never be forgotten
at the Hacienda de las Flores.

"You are so like the Old Doctor, Doña Sarita," said the
overseer's wife when Sally had spent two days at the hacienda.
"In your looks, and the quick way you talk and move; as like
as a lovely señorita can be to an old gentleman!"

"Pity there's no daguerreotype of the old boy in existence,"
said Andrew, when this opinion was reported to him. "How can
I tell whether you look like him or not? I was only seven when
he came to Fayetteville. He was a dogmatic little man with ginger hair and whiskers, as far as I recall. You'd better keep your
hat on in the garden, or you'll finish up with ginger hair too, my
girl."

"I don't care," said Sally. "Up to now I've always been
told whom I *didn't* resemble. Not a beauty like mamma, not a
patch on Helen, not like any of the Sandhaven family. Now I
know I look like somebody—barring the ginger whiskers; and
d'you know, I think I enjoy it?"

She came to have a deep sense of identification with the
Old Doctor. She pictured him distilling the remedies from herbs
and flowers which Doña Juanita said were better than anything
the local shamán brewed. She read the few books he had left on
the whatnot in the room with the fireplace, which included *The
Three Musketeers, The Heart of Midlothian,* and some manuals
of first aid and military surgery dating from Santa Anna's wars.

And she sometimes wondered what their uncle, who had left a written injunction to Andrew to keep away from Carlóta and Maximilian, would have said if he knew that his nephew spent his mornings at La Borda with the Empress, and the afternoons at the new chalet which the Emperor was building in the Pompeian style out at Acapantzingo.

Sally no longer questioned her brother's proceedings. She saw that his attraction to Maximilian was strong, and had come about inevitably. She knew, too, that the continuation of their life in Mexico depended upon money, and that Monsieur Eloin, on behalf of the Emperor, handed Dr. Lorimer a weekly fee for his attendance on Carlóta which a New York specialist might have envied. Maximilian himself, as a token of his gratitude, had presented to the young man a copy of his last book published before leaving Miramar, *My Travels in Brazil*.

There was only one thing lacking to make Sally perfectly happy at the hacienda. She had expected—she would hardly admit what, even to herself. Something different, from Pierre Franchet. Something that belonged to the violence of their first quarrel and the romance of their stolen meetings in the Plaza Mayor. At Las Flores after the first day, Franchet had met her without any show of emotion, or said a word unsuited to the most correct of riding instructors. Really, said Sally to herself, that hussy with the hair and the beads might not have flared up so, that night in the Cathedral, if she knew all I should hear from Pierre would be the curb, the snaffle, and keep your heels down, please, mademoiselle.

It was especially galling to Sally that when the riding lessons began she should fail in everything asked of her, like one of her instructor's Mexican recruits. She had never had anything to do with horses, and even to be near Rataplan had secretly unnerved her in the days of the walks in the Plaza Mayor. He was so tall, and had such an alarming way of nuzzling her shoulder with his hairy lower lip, that she could never be persuaded to offer the bits of sugar cane which young Tomás Martínez selected for the Fair One's horse. Sally, who danced so lightly, whose father had always praised her neat, workmanlike hands, grew nervous and clumsy as soon as she was up on Nelly, the patient black mare whom Franchet had broken to skirts by riding her through every siesta hour for a fortnight with a horse blanket belted round his waist. On the first evening, sitting on the heavy European side saddle, she hardly took in a word of Pierre's instructions as he walked her round the courtyard with his hand on Nelly's bridle. On the second, when he tried to make her move in a circle on the leading rein, she was so terrified that the mare felt her panic and began dancing sideways, while Rataplan neighed alarmingly from the stable door. Sally lost both her stirrups; her scream, and the dropped reins, and the convulsive twining of her hands in Nelly's mane, brought smiles even to the grave faces of half a dozen peons watching critically outside the tienda. There was no doing anything with her at that time; Franchet lifted her down, and she stood in the courtyard trembling, with one hand on his arm.

"Sally, you're as good as a circus," said Andrew, lounging at the door of the casita. "I don't see you riding to La Borda yet awhile."

"I'm sorry," she said with chattering teeth. Then, with what every man present could see was an effort, she took Nelly by the bridle, led the mare to the horseblock, mounted without assistance and tried again.

Damned if I could do that, thought Andrew, with all the Indios grinning at me. He was not acute enough to notice that after that night Sally, who had never been "the Foreigner" at Las Flores, ceased even to be *La Señorita*. From then on, she was called, like every Mexican mistress of a household, *La Niña*—the beloved and petted Little Girl.

Three weeks from that time, she was teasing Pierre to let her gallop.

"On the hill today—on that wonderful short turf—I'm sure I could, Pierre."

"If we go on the hill today I shall make you canter until

you've learned to keep your back straight. Last time you
slouched like a sack of potatoes."

"I couldn't help it, I felt so lopsided, somehow. Do you
think I'd do better on a Mexican saddle?"

"Why don't you ask me for a rocking chair?" said Pierre
contemptuously. "You wear Mexican boots and clothes to ride
in—I don't mind that; but what sort of figure would you cut in
the Bois de Boulogne on a Mexican saddle?"

"I'll never come within a thousand miles of the Bois de
Boulogne." Sally tucked her feet beneath her chair at the mention
of her riding boots. She hadn't put them on yet; and remembered
too late that her feet were bare in the thonged leather huaraches.

They were sitting in the garden, under a camarón tree in
full blossom, and the thick flowers, of every shade from shrimp
to rosy gold, threw a warm reflected light on Sally's eager face.
Her hair, unpinned, was tied at the nape of her neck with a
dark-blue ribbon. As Andrew had said (and Pierre had silently
observed) the Mexican sunlight had turned the tawny lights in
the brown to reddish gold, framing a face as delicately sun-
touched as the skin of a ripe apricot. Sally wore a plain white
cotton camisa, tucked inside a dark-blue skirt patterned with
the white crosswise strip of the Otomí Indians—the local dress,
which Doña Juanita had suggested as suitable for riding. It was
a costume much worn by the European ladies at Cuernavaca,
and Sally now wore some variant of it all day long.

"Would you like another drink, or shall we start?" she
said with a touch of impatience, as her instructor showed no
signs of moving. It was a lazy afternoon, in spite of the brilliantly clear air, and Doña Juanita, at her post as dueña, was
frankly sound asleep. Franchet, arriving half an hour earlier,
had said it was too hot for the horses to go out.

"I'd like another drink, thanks." His hands moved expertly
between the jug of fresh pineapple juice, the cut limes, and the
bottle of sugar-cane rum—now sold at the tienda, by Sally's
orders, only on Saturday nights. "I had a pretty heavy morning
today. Your friends, Prince Khevenhüller and Colonel von

Kodolitsch, came out from Cuernavaca to inspect our new intake. The *patron* wanted a full dress parade, so Rataplan and I were run ragged keeping the stragglers in good order."

"Patient Nelly too?"

"The stable sergeant was riding patient Nelly, and he rides at ninety kilos. You'll find her nicely quietened down this afternoon."

"So the Two K's came out to the training depot," said Sally thoughtfully. "What do you suppose that means? Are they going to incorporate the Cazadores with the Austrian Legion after all?"

"The Whitecoats can have the lot, and welcome," said Pierre indifferently. "But thanks to our heavy morning, Captain Clapier gave me an hour's extra leave this afternoon."

"Really, Pierre, I sometimes think you haven't very much ambition," Sally said, and at her tone the cloudy gray eyes opened wide.

"No?"

"I don't like to hear you sounding so humble, and so grateful, for an hour's leave of absence from barracks," said Sally crossly.

"No need for humility when it's Clapier," said Pierre. "We know each other pretty well. I served under him in Algeria."

"Served under him!" said Sally scornfully. She felt suddenly wretched, but quite unable to keep from baiting him. Anything—to goad him out of his courteous impersonality! "Did you never want to be an officer yourself, and have men under *you?*"

Sergeant Franchet refused to be goaded. "I can't say I've thought much of promotion, or not for a few years now," he said reasonably. "For one thing, I've never been able to purchase a commission."

"Does it cost so much? You've saved your pay, Pierre. You bought land when you were up at Tampico. Couldn't you have bought a step in the army, after eight years with the Colors?"

"Maybe," said Pierre, "but once I'd bought my step, I couldn't have lived as the Emperor Napoleon expects his officers to live—with horses, servants, sporting guns, and all the rest of it. As for the land at Tampico, five hundred acres of it were going for a song, and who knows? If trade ever picks up at the port, it may turn out to be a good investment. Surely the Lady of Las Flores won't grudge me my modest stake in the country?"

Sally bit her lip. She felt herself worsted in that exchange, but twenty minutes later, when they were on the hillside over-looking the barranca and the town, the crystal air and the ex-hilaration of the ride had ended her spurt of bad temper.

"That was better, wasn't it?" she called over her shoulder to Pierre, watchfully riding a full length behind.

"Much better today. Now put on your hat, mademoiselle, there's no reason at all to lose your hat in a canter. And keep your hands clear of the pommel, if you please."

"Can we gallop now?"

"Not yet. Now, begin again. Walk—and sit up straighter. Trot. Heels down, remember. Heels *down*."

They moved into a canter. Rataplan flung his head up to tell his master how weary he was of this exercise, and how fast his stablemate would follow if he were allowed to gallop. But his master's hands, which could be so gentle, held the chestnut in an iron grip. Gracefully, quietly, Sally and Pierre cantered down the hillside meadow to the barranca beyond which Cuernavaca lay. Sally wheeled her horse.

"There's the waterfall, Pierre—it feeds the arroyo, you know, that provides power for the refinery."

"But we can't see your tall chimney, high as we are."

"It's on the other side of the canyon. We can see nearly everything else, though."

From the little plateau of turf where they stood, a bright prospect stretched before them. To the north lay Cuernavaca, with the spires and domes of many churches making one honey-comb of ocherous pink and gold; to the southwest, banana and orange trees hid the village and Sally's hacienda. Between lay the red-roofed barracks where the flags of France and Mexico drooped in the crystal air. Above the town rose the sheltering

peaks of the Tres Marias. Far away, dominating the blue mountain ranges, the Popocatépetl volcano was etched in snow
against the blue.

"*Mia tierra y patria chica,*" said Sally softly.

"Where did you learn *that?*"

"I've heard the Indians say it, haven't you?"

"They say it, Sally, but can you mean it? 'My little world
and motherland'—in three weeks' time?"

"Three weeks? Three months, you mean. Since the day I
came ashore at Vera Cruz. Now, more than ever."

Pierre Franchet looked at the girl on the black mare, and
the passion he had fought for many days leaped to his lips and
eyes and threatened to betray him. From the straw sombrero
perched on her shining hair to the sweep of dark-blue skirt falling to the toes of her soft leather riding boots she looked what
she had just declared herself to be: at one with the land she
had chosen for her own.

Pierre urged his horse up close to hers. He reached out,
and took one of the small hands in the fringed doeskin gloves
into his own stiff gauntleted clasp.

"Sally, there's no one like you—"

"Hush!" she said peremptorily. "I hear a child crying."

The three months' cannonading at the siege of Puebla had
left Pierre's hearing less acute than Sally's.

"You hear the water," he said. "We are too close to the
falls; turn back."

"It *is* a child, I tell you, some Indian child must be lost
in the barranca," Sally said excitedly, and now they could both
hear the crying. Not an infant's feeble wail, but the loud, jerky
bawling of a terrified child.

Sally, dismounting without assistance, ran in the direction
of the sound. Pierre, with an oath he took no trouble to suppress,
caught at Nelly's reins, and spurred forward to hitch both horses
to the scrub cottonwoods which made a little patch of shade in
the wide expanse of turf.

"Never leave your horse unhitched if you want to ride away

again." That was what he meant to say to her, but the words remained unsaid. For Sally was out of earshot. She was down in the barranca, among the dust and the boulders, with her riding skirt gathered up in one hand and the other outstretched to help not a child but a woman—a woman struggling to free herself from the spikes and tendrils of the thicket that held her dress, and caught at her disordered loops of black hair, and shook the red petals of the Corona de Cristo flower over the torn clothing of the heavy child she carried in her arms. Blood oozed from a long scratch running from her temple to her throat, and along another running the length of her left arm, from which the sleeve had been torn completely away.

"Don't move!" cried Sally. "Pierre, your knife!"

He had his heavy knife out of its sheath on his hip already, and was hacking clear the spiked branches which caged the woman and the child.

"Give your child to me, you poor lost creature," Sally begged. "You're quite safe now, and we'll take care of you—"

The woman stepped clear of the last ropelike tendril and said to Pierre:

"*Je suis la princesse Charlotte de Belgique: qui êtes-vous?*"

Pierre scrambled up from the ground and stood stiffly at the salute.

"*Le sergent Franchet à vos ordres, Altesse!*"

Sally gasped. Then, as the woman's green eyes flashed, conviction came. She had seen those eyes before, as she bent in a curtsy in the music room at Chapultepec; and the poor lost creature in the bloodstained, ragged dress, clutching a filthy child, was the Empress of Mexico.

"You are a French soldier?" the hoarse voice said.

"*Pour vous servir, Altesse.*"

"Did Napoleon send you here to hunt me down?"

"Help her to the trees, Sally," said Pierre. "I'll take the boy."

The child almost flung himself out of Carlóta's arms and into Pierre's. He had stopped screaming, but his small body was shaken with convulsive sobs. Sally saw the well-shaped little head and the chestnut hair as bright as her own, and knew that Pierre was holding the adopted heir to Maximilian's throne.

They stumbled together over the edge of the barranca to the meadow.

"Come to the shade, Madame, and let me see those ugly scratches," Sally coaxed. Carlóta pulled away from her.

"I am taking the child to Ixtaccíhuatl. We missed the road," she said. "We have a long way to go before nightfall. I cannot allow you to detain me."

"You couldn't possibly reach the volcanoes tonight, Madame. They look so near, but they're many miles away. You must come back with us to La Borda now and rest until tomorrow."

"Rest? Rest at La Borda? Oh, my God!" cried Carlóta. Only Sally's arm kept her from falling as she sank down against one of the scrub cottonwoods and covered her face with her hands.

Sally soothed her in the shadow of a voice. She barely touched her hand to Carlóta's temples and her wrist. The message she received, of hammering blood and mounting fever, filled her with alarm.

"A touch of sunstroke, would you say?" she heard Pierre whisper. "All the way across the barranca bareheaded in this heat—I wonder they didn't founder at the bottom. The sentries at La Borda should be shot for this."

Sally took off her sombrero and put it gently on Carlóta's bent head. "Get them some water, Pierre," she said. "Haven't you a water bottle on your saddle?"

He ran up the little grove of cottonwoods to the place where he had tethered the horses, thankful for a chance to make certain that his quick hitch of the reins had been secure.

Sally turned towards the child, standing where Pierre had set him down, and put her arms round him.

"What is your name, *niño?*"

"Agustín—Iturbide—señorita." He was rigid in her arms, leaning away from her with all his small weight. Two hours earlier Agustín had been carefully dressed by his aunt, Princess

Josefa Iturbide, for the alarming privilege of taking luncheon alone with his mamma. He had been immaculate in a white charro suit, exactly copied from papa's, when he trotted across the patio of La Borda and entered Carlóta's boudoir with his best court bow. Ten minutes after that, he had been tiptoeing out of a little door at the bottom of the garden wall, where no sentry was ever posted, with his hand tightly clasped in mamma's, at the start of what she told him would be a wonderful adventure. But soon mamma had lost her way, had talked to herself and not to him, and one of his shoes came off, the briars scratched his face and tore his charro jacket, and worst of all his alarm at being dragged painfully through cactus scrub and bushes had caused his self-control to fail him, so that his wet white trousers clung abominably to his legs. "Nobody loves a dirty boy," mamma had always said, even when only the faintest film of chocolate showed on his upper lip; and now, to his shame, he was far too dirty a boy to let the pretty señorita touch him. He tried to wriggle out of her clasp.

"Oh, you poor baby, don't be so scared of me!" said Sally, and she kissed him.

Without thinking, she had spoken in English. It was not likely that the child understood her. But something in the sound of her voice, something in her warm kiss must have brought back to Agustín the image of the other American girl, whose baby he had been not so very long before. With a sob more poignant than any of the wild shrieks they had heard from the ravine he flung himself on Sally's breast and whispered his only words of English,

"Oh, mother, mother!"

"Here's the water," said Pierre gruffly. He watched the Empress and the child as they drank; nonplused, baffled for once by an emergency beyond his skill to handle.

"Can you rip off your neckcloth?" Sally asked. She took the fold of white linen from his hands and twisted it deftly into a cap for the bareheaded child.

"Look, Agustín," she said, twirling the four corners into

jaunty knots, "you've got six ears now. Poor us, we've only got two each!"

A smile at last broke over Agustín's tearstained face, and he put up his hand to touch his linen ears. It was the kind of simple joke at which his new papa excelled. It helped him to feel secure with Sally.

"Poor you had better wear my képi," Pierre said to Sally. "I'm accustomed to the sun. But how the devil are we going to get them home? Take them straight down to the depot and send to La Borda for an escort, eh?"

"So that all Cuernavaca can have the story by sunset? Don't be silly! We'll take them to the hacienda, of course, and send for Andrew. I'm sorry—did you ask me a question then, Madame?"

"I asked how you would feel, what you would do, if you learned that this man, this soldier, your husband, was about to become a father by your gardener's wife?"

In one glance at Franchet, Sally realized that what Carlóta had revealed by implication was something he had heard many times before—common talk of the army stables and posadas of the capital.

"I'm not married, Madame," she said very gently. "I'm Dr. Lorimer's sister. He will be disappointed to hear of the hot, tiresome walk you had this afternoon."

"He'll be very *angry*," breathed Carlóta, as if there was pleasure in the prospect. "But I shall tell him it's his own fault, for leaving me. He goes away every day to the Emperor at Acapantzingo—*I* have never been invited there—"

"You've never been to the doctor's new house either, have you?" Sally achieved a smile. "Do come home with me now, and tell me what you think of it. Could you ride there with us—it isn't very far?"

"I haven't ridden since I was in Yucatán." It was the first rational answer she had given them, and Sally plucked up courage as the Empress rose stiffly, holding to her arm and to the tree. But Agustín, breaking away from Sally's clasp, ran to the Légionnaire and grasped his tunic.

"Can you ride behind me on Rataplan?" Pierre asked Sally.

"Won't he shy at my skirts?"

"Not if I can help it . . . Let me go, *mon petit,*" he said to Agustín. "I'm going to get a horse for you to ride."

He brought up the animals, Nelly plodding along, Rataplan tossing his head and dancing a little as he came.

"The chestnut is much the better beast," pronounced Carlóta.

"Nevertheless," said Pierre firmly, "Your Majesty will ride the black and hold Prince Agustín in front of you."

Carlóta flashed up to the saddle, one foot resting for an instant on Pierre's clasped hands. It was a very different mounting from Sally's cautious approach by way of the horseblock. It was a woman who had ridden since earliest childhood who leaned forward confidently to pat the black mare's neck.

"Is your horse gaited, soldier?" she called out. "All Napoleon's hacks are gaited, aren't they? Look—I'll show you how my brothers and I were taught to ride at Laeken long ago. Only we have no music. You must sing 'La Brabançonne'!"

"Check your horse, Madame!" cried Sergeant Franchet. "Nelly, stand!"

But the black mare was off, goaded by a sharp kick from Carlóta's ragged shoe, jerked out of her patience by the unaccustomed signals as Carlóta expertly shifted the reins upon her neck. Sally saw her usually quiet mount checked to a sudden halt, urged to step out in a new rhythm; and then the mare reared on her haunches in fury, bucking in a vain attempt to rid herself of the woman on her back. Carlóta laughed; and at the sound Rataplan began to plunge where Franchet had tethered him for the second time, striking the branches of the sheltering cottonwood with his forefeet to the sound of splintering twigs. The child screamed aloud in terror. He ran away from the trees and the horses, straight towards the waterfall. Sally ran headlong in pursuit. Behind her she heard the drumming of the black mare's hoofs. She flung herself down upon the child, feeling a sharp pain in one shoulder, and seeing, as they rolled on the turf together, a terrifying vision of Carlóta's bloodstained face falling backward as if her throat were offered to the guillotine. The black mare reared again and pawed the air.

Then Franchet had the beast by the bridle, and with his head lowered and his back and shoulders straining, dragged her by main force to a halt. Carlóta slipped her feet from the stirrups and jumped clear. Pierre struck her a heavy blow on the cheek with his clenched fist. She fell in a heap close to his feet. He ran to Sally and the child. The black mare stood trembling with the reins trailing on the ground.

"My darling, are you hurt?" Pierre, on his knees beside Sally, gathered her into his arms.

"No; I'm all right—is Agustín?"

"He's making noise enough."

"No wonder." Sally let Pierre help her to her feet. Her head and shoulder, and all one side, were throbbing painfully. She looked beyond him at the prostrate body of the Empress.

"Oh God, Pierre, you've killed her!"

"No such luck," he said.

Chapter Twelve

FLOR DE CORAZÓN

THE PEONS in the sugar fields ended the siesta they took every afternoon in the shadow of the growing canes, and were languidly wielding their hoes when Pierre's sorry cavalcade came down the track to the hacienda. They looked incuriously from under their broad-brimmed hats at La Niña going by at a walking pace, wearing a soldier's képi and with a Mexican child riding pillion behind her. Her horse was attached by a leading rein to the handsome chestnut ridden by La Niña's *novio* (the whole village knew that the Fair One was La Niña's sweetheart) and he too was riding double, with a woman in front of him half-sitting and half-lying against his shoulder. The peons shrugged. To those Indians of pure Otomí blood all strangers were of one race, and the Belgian lady, the American girl, the child who was half American and the Frenchman were to them merely *los mexicanos,* the city folk, whose doings were incalculable, and not worthy of comment by serious men.

Doña Juanita, for a different reason, was equally discreet. She had seen too many waifs and strays brought home in the Old Doctor's time to be dismayed by the arrival of a half-fainting lady and a weeping child, and while Franchet dispatched her boy Tomásito, riding Nelly, to fetch Don Andrés home immediately, she quietly carried out Sally's clear directions. The strange señora was taken into the living room and laid on the sofa, while the shade was drawn and a small fire lighted. Sally brought down an Indian blanket from her own bed and wrapped it round

Carlóta, who had passed from fever to chills and lay shuddering under the cool lotions which Doña Juanita used to clean the terrible scratches on her cheeks and arms.

"Let Mariquita bring the hot milk and sugar immediately," Sally said, and climbed painfully to her own room. If the Emperor came back with Andrew, as was most likely, they must not find her as dirty and bedraggled as her mirror showed. She poured out water, knotted up her hair, laid a linen handkerchief smeared with one of the Old Doctor's salves on her bruised shoulder, and was downstairs again wearing a dark-blue shirt that hid the dressing before the Indian girl carried her tray in from the kitchen. Sergeant Franchet followed Mariquita to the living-room door.

"Is she all right?" he asked.

"I don't know," said Sally desperately. "Oh, Pierre, why did you strike her?"

"Do you think I liked doing it? I had to, Sally. She meant to ride you down, or go over the falls herself."

"Nonsense—it was an accident. But what if she tells the Emperor? They could punish you for it, Pierre."

"They could flog me for it, I daresay. But before that happens Don Maximiliano would have to listen to a few home truths from me."

"The lady's cheek is very badly swollen." Doña Juanita's voice, low-pitched, came to them from the parlor.

"She fell climbing up the barranca," said Sally, and her eyes met Pierre's as she mixed the frothing milk and coarse sugar in a china cup. There was French brandy on the tray, and glasses. Brandy might make the Empress sleep: but then, it was a stimulant, and Andrew might disapprove of stimulants for a patient so dreadfully disturbed by the knowledge of her husband's—wrongdoing. It was the only explanation that came to Sally's mind.

"There's no tequila, Pierre," she said, trying to smile. "Will you have some cognac?"

"If you will too."

She poured a little into half a cup of milk and drank it at a gulp before she went to sit on a low stool beside Carlóta. The sick woman's eyes were open. They had a clean-washed, innocent look above the pad of lint which had been laid on her bruised cheek.

"Will you try to drink a little milk, Madame?"

"Thank you. Do I know you? Are we at Chapultepec?"

"No, in the country, Madame. I'm Sally Lorimer. My brother, Dr. Lorimer, is on his way to you. Dr. Lorimer will be here any minute now."

The soft, deliberate repetition of his name seemed to soothe Carlóta.

"Have I been ill? I feel very stiff and sore."

"You tried to walk too far in the hot sun, you see. Your little boy was quite frightened about you."

"Is Agustín here?"

"My servant has taken charge of him, Madame. He is quite happy with her."

"I would like to see him." The Empress stirred restlessly.

"Please try to finish the milk first."

Sally got up with a warning look to Doña Juanita. She realized her mistake in mentioning Agustín's name. If the child began to scream again, as well he might; if he refused to go to the woman who, on the hillside, had plainly terrified him, what might not be the effect on Carlóta?

"Is there no sign of Andrew?" she said to Pierre, who was standing at the courtyard door.

"Not yet. Don Ramón has taken the mule team and gone off to Cuernavaca, in case Tomásito doesn't find the doctor with Maximilian."

"He *must* be with the Emperor!" said Sally. "Pierre, why don't you ride Rataplan into town? The mules take three times as long as a man on horseback—"

"I'm not going to leave you alone with a crazy woman," Franchet said. Sally brushed past him and hurried into the kitchen.

The grandson of the Emperor Agustín was sitting at the kitchen table, ensconced on Mariquita's ample lap. The husks of two tamales lay on a plate liberally spread with chiles, chick peas, chopped tomatoes and refried beans, among which Agustín, with a third tamale in his hand, was dabbling with the air of a connoisseur.

"Hallo, Agustín," said Sally. The little boy laughed, and echoed "Hallo!"

"Has he had enough to eat, Mariquita?"

"Now by the blessed favor of the Saints in heaven," said Mariquita enthusiastically, "this boy has the appetite of a caballero. The milk and the light cake of sponge you said, he finished at one mouthful. Now he devours my supper, slowly and with savor. *Ay de mí!* This is the hungriest boy that ever came to our village."

"I had no comida," said Agustín pointedly.

"No luncheon, and then you went for a long walk; of course you're hungry," said Sally easily. "But mamma wants to see you now."

"A wet cloth for the face and hands," said Mariquita. She had already bathed the child from top to toe and dressed him in a clean white shirt belonging to one of the children the Martínez' had lost in infancy. He looked more of a baby in it than in the miniature charro dress, with his chubby brown legs and feet bare, and his damp chestnut hair falling into soft curls. He faced Sally courageously, standing squarely on the red-tiled floor, but his eyelids were flickering nervously, and his lip trembled at the mention of "mamma."

"Can I see the little tiger first?" he said.

"He means the little cat," translated Mariquita. "It ran out and in while I was bathing him."

"Let's go and look for it," said Sally. She felt strung up to concert pitch, concentrating with all her power on making just this one thing go off well—keeping the child calm, and Carlóta in her more tranquil mood, until Andrew came. By good luck the striped kitten was not far away. It sat on the steps of the

patio, its paws curled in imitation of an adult cat, with its
covetous eyes fixed on the caged birds.

"Stroke him, Agustín, he loves to be stroked. And scratch
him very gently, just beneath his little chin—"

The little creature, accustomed to Sally's petting, gave itself
with supine enjoyment to the small eager hands. Then it raced
off down the garden, stiff-legged, slanting, with Agustín in pursuit; let itself be caught and rolled over with miniature growls
and waving starfish paws; chased its tail, and sat down with
sudden withdrawn dignity to lick the tip.

For five minutes the garden had rung with the delicious
sound of the child's laughter.

"What is the small cat's name, please, señorita?"

"We sometimes call it Tim, and sometimes Little Honey.
What would you like to call it, Agustín?"

"El Tigre," he said promptly.

"El Tigre—what a good name; we should have thought of
that. Well, Agustín, why don't you pick up El Tigre (look, behind
his neck, and your other hand *so*) and carry him in to see
mamma?"

It was a bribe, openly offered, and as such accepted.

"Do you mean El Tigre is my very own, to keep?"

"Ask mamma nicely if she'll let you have him, and then
we'll see."

Sally was anxious to return to the house. She had been away
from the Empress for a quarter of an hour, and dreaded the confidences which might have been made to Doña Juanita in that
time. But all was peaceful in the shaded parlor. Carlóta lay on
her side, with her unhurt cheek pillowed on her hand, and the
overseer's wife was slowly brushing out the burrs and tangles
from her long black hair.

Sally gave the child a very gentle push. He took two steps
towards the couch, and stopped, clutching El Tigre to his breast.

"What have you got there, Agustín?" the weary voice
inquired.

"A little cat, mamma, the lady gave me for my own. El Tigre is his name."

"I'm sure you can find room for a kitten at La Borda," Sally said. "This one is a well-mannered little creature, and Agustín would enjoy having it for a playmate."

"Would he really?" murmured Carlóta. "I didn't know. Papa never allowed us to have pet animals at Laeken. But—if he would like it—" her voice trailed off. Sally saw that she was growing drowsy.

"Kiss mamma, and say thank you," she whispered to the child. It had come to seem of extraordinary importance that Agustín should conquer at once whatever fears had entered his small heart on that nightmare journey across the barranca.

Agustín put his lips quickly to Carlóta's hand and backed away. Sally took him in her arms and sat down on a low chair opposite the couch. El Tigre slipped from his new owner's hold and made for the rug before the fire.

There was no sound but the crackle of the newly kindled logs and the rhythmic sweep of the brush through Carlóta's hair. Agustín's dark eyes closed. He put an arm round Sally's neck and whispered:

"Now sing to me."

She smiled and shook her head. But she held the warm, relaxed little body closer, gripping him with arms that had never comforted a child before; and hummed a song without words to him, inexpressibly soothing, a thread of sound.

"What is that tune?" Carlóta spoke out of her own drowsiness, and Sally softly said:

"An old Scotch air my father used to sing to me."

"I like it," Carlóta said. "We had a nurse once, who sang such songs at Laeken. She was a kind, simple creature. Sing it again."

When the Emperor of Mexico hurried into the little house with Andrew Lorimer, he found Franchet standing guard at the door of the parlor, where with two silent women and a drowsy child beside her, his wife lay sleeping with a smile upon her lips.

LATER ON the same night, when Andrew had been for many hours at La Borda, Sally stood in her darkened bedroom and watched lights flickering in the hovels of the Indians.

It was the first time that her brother had left her alone in the little house after dark, and Sally to her shame was nervous. There was uneasiness in the very air. Mariquita, usually so eager to wait for the señor doctor, had gone home as soon as she had served a supper Sally could hardly touch. One glance from Carlóta's green eyes as they were helping her into the carriage had quenched the Indian maid's good will; she had sniffed and muttered about evil spirits and *ojos garzos* all the time she was putting the parlor and the patio to rights. And Mariquita's malaise had spread through the village, even to the presbytery, where Fray Diego—who usually went to bed with the birds—had lighted a solitary candle. In front of the peons' huts, raveled ends of cactus fiber had been dipped in saucers of grease and kindled, and children had been carried out to lie secure in the ring of light in their parents' arms.

It had rained earlier in the evening, a short, sharp, tropical downpour, and Sally as she applied fresh salve to her bruised arm heard the last drops still trickling through the thick banana leaves beneath her window. The water, sliding down the clusters of purplish-green fruit, struck the flower bed below her window with almost percussive force. But the steady, drenching rain which might have released the tensions of the night and sent the watchers in the Indian village to their rest did not break over the Warm Country.

Sally went downstairs. From the back door of the patio she could see lamplight in both rooms of the overseer's house, and the stable mozo lounging under a lantern set for Andrew's benefit in a socket by the entrance gate. After all, it was only ten o'clock, and Sally was not alone in her vigil—even though, all through the familiar patio, there was a creeping strangeness, as if the poor lost creature caught in the thorns of the barranca were still there in the darkness begging for her help.

"I am taking the child to Ixtaccíhuatl." Sally had told her brother what the Empress' first distracted words had been, at the very beginning of the rapid interrogation of Sergeant Franchet and herself which followed the departure of the Imperial coach. Andrew only shook his head. He was impatient to be off to La Borda and see Carlóta settled in her own bed, and Franchet had laughed and said:

"Her Majesty has been corrupted by the Mexicans, they never get anything right. Popocatépetl is the only volcano you can see from La Borda." Instinctively, Sally felt that this was the wrong interpretation. In the journey to Ixtaccíhuatl, *with the child,* lay some clue to Carlóta which even Andrew had not so far found.

The two young men were deep in talk in the courtyard before mounting to ride off, and Sally guessed that the Légionnaire was repeating to Andrew those bitter words about the Emperor's infidelity which obviously could not be repeated in her own presence. That would explain everything to Andrew—probably to anyone who heard the story of Carlóta's flight. In the shock and anger of betrayal the Empress had fled from the summer palace—that was all.

But then why handicap her flight with Agustín?

Sally lighted a little colza oil lamp left on the patio table and carried it into the parlor. There was still a faint smell of woodsmoke from the fire lighted for Carlóta, and underneath it, impregnating the Indian blanket neatly folded on the couch, the scent of some lemon cologne which had survived the sweat and stress of Carlóta's journey. In the lamplight the titles of the Old Doctor's little library glinted gold. Military surgery, romantic fiction, a battered atlas—there was nothing at all between those octavo covers to tell his niece why the Empress of Mexico should make Ixtaccíhuatl the goal of her distracted journey.

For all Sally had read about Mexico since the Spanish Conquest, she knew little or nothing about its ancient inhabitants,
or the legends which still lingered round every mountain peak
and in every hidden valley of the land. She knew that the Indians
had believed Maximilian to be a reincarnation of Quetzlcoatl,
the Plumed Serpent, god of the morning star. She knew that
Ixtaccíhuatl meant "the Sleeping Woman." Whether there was
any connection between the two she could only guess.

The song birds cheeped under the patio arch. Sally went to
draw the thin dark curtains round their cages and breathe in
the sweetness rising from the damp garden. It was the hour when
the blossoms which the Indians called "Xochitl's flowers," from
a beloved little Aztec princess of the past, gave up their fragrance
to the night; and the scent of lilies and tuberoses mingled with
the bitter almond of the red oleanders growing along the walls.
Sally stepped from the stone flags in front of the patio to the
lawn, and felt the springing grass wet on her bare feet in the
thonged huaraches. There was relief in the cool moist touch.

It might have been that the time bareheaded on the hill,
until Pierre forced his képi on her, had left her with a slight
touch of the sun. Or else her bruised shoulder was a focus of
heat and pain which had somehow spread to her head and her
breasts and all the places where her pulses beat. Slowly, with
a light fever burning in her veins, Sally crossed the wide lawn
and buried her face in the rain-cooled flowers.

There was a little adobe hut at the foot of the garden, where
Tomásito's spades and rakes were stored, and where at night
the parrots, toucans, fantails, and even the flamingos of the Old
Doctor's aviary roosted after dark. Sally paused beside the door.
Through the wooden grille she heard the small murmurings and
rustling of the birds at night.

She heard the sound of her own name.

She started; she turned towards the gate deeply embedded
in flowering creepers, of which the key had for so long been lost,
and a wild excitement took possession of her. She could see
nothing but the heavy iron bars, and the branches of a white

magnolia hanging low above them, but she knew that Pierre Franchet was there, so near that he need only whisper "Sally!" and she heard.

"Pierre, where are you?" she said in the same low tone.

"I'm here, my darling." She saw the iron gate move, as if a powerful shoulder were pressed against it, and she ran, letting her dark-blue skirt drag in the wet grass, out at the narrow opening into Franchet's arms.

There was no hesitation, no questioning of his presence; she knew, as she felt herself drawn into his embrace, that the simple need of him was the reason for all the unease and tension of the night. Then he began to kiss her; not on the lips at first, but where the bright tendrils of hair brushed her temples, and on her eyelids and eyebrows, setting a score of tiny kisses, quick and soft, along her throat and the lobes of her ears, so that when his mouth fastened on hers she was on fire for him, and with her body pressed close to his experienced like an act of love that first burning, searching, rocking kiss.

She found with amazement that her feet were still upon the ground. She thought he had lifted her as high as the magnolia flowers.

"Pierre"—she was somehow able to murmur—"did you break out of barracks to come here?"

Instantly she was pressed even closer to his body, and his lips just touched her ear.

"Whisper, or someone will hear—"

"All the village must have heard you, riding through—not that I care."

"I walked, my darling. I always walk. I make a detour by the fields and come up the canyon without going near the village, and nobody has heard me yet."

"You mean you've done this before?"

"Every night since you came home."

Sally leaned back on his arm and stared at him. Her eyes were growing accustomed to the shadows under the magnolia tree, and she could see the flash of Pierre's smile and the glint

THE CACTUS AND THE CROWN

of his fair cropped hair. She realized that he was wearing the long dark-green campaign cloak which the Foreign Legion never used in Tierra Templada, except on bivouac. It enfolded him now like a cloak of darkness.

"*Every* night? Just to be—near me?"

"Just to be sure that you were safe."

Pierre slipped his right hand inside the wide neck of her dark camisa and laid it gently on her bandaged shoulder.

"Does this hurt very much?"

"Hardly at all."

When his mouth fastened on hers again she was aware of his fingers on her bare flesh. She gave herself up to his lips and hands until her body's furious response betrayed her, and she pulled away from him to lean choking for breath against the tree.

"Sally, have I been wrong to come? It's been my only comfort; to feel that I was near you. Nearer than I could ever be by day, when you were the Lady of Las Flores, and I a poor devil of a Légionnaire worth a thousand francs a year to His Majesty, and not even wearing a lieutenant's frock coat for gentility. Sally! I knew as soon as I saw Las Flores that you were rich, and might be powerful, and I had nothing to offer you except my love. So I took what I dared; I was your riding master, nothing more, until today. I was going to tell you how much I loved you, up there on the hill. And tonight, when I knew André had left you all alone, I wasn't able to endure it. If you hadn't come into the garden, I meant to throw myself on the Martínez' mercy. Persuade them to let me talk to you in their house, if you would. Anything—I don't know what I didn't plan in the past half-hour, after I saw the lamplight in the patio. But this is better, isn't it?"

It was better. Nothing had ever been half so good as this sensation of floating in Pierre Franchet's arms. Sally sighed, and shifted a little against his breast so that the mouth so close to her ear might come closer to her lips.

"You smell of roses, Sally. Do you know that?"

"It's the salve on my arm—"

"It's you, darling. It's in your hair, and on your breath. I wish I could see you better. You're pale tonight, as white as the *flor de corazón*. Did you know that's what the Mexicans call a magnolia? *Petite fleur de mon coeur,* when will you make up your mind to love me?"

"But I *am* loving you, Pierre!" She felt his breath catch on a laugh as he wrapped his heavy cloak about them both.

"You're trembling, my darling; don't be afraid."

But she was afraid of love; there was a fear in her mind, deep-hidden, which fought against him, even while her body strove towards its triumph.

"I adore you, Sally. I've loved you since that first hour at Río Frío, and I *will* love you, body and soul, until death—"

"Oh, don't say it! Don't say it!"

"S-sh, Sally! *Flor de mi corazón, niña de mi alma,* hush!"

"Don't say—'until death us do part'."

Chapter Thirteen

THE OPAL BROOCH

TO A PERSONALITY as stubborn as Andrew Lorimer's, there was all the charm of contrast in the extreme flexibility of the Emperor Maximilian. Since the Empress became his patient, the young doctor had had many chances to note the extent of Maximilian's influence over her; he never saw it used to better advantage than in the days immediately following her adventure in the barranca. The guilty husband was penitent, cajoling, flattering by turns: the outraged wife soon yielded to his charm. At the same time Maximilian took quick and secret measures. The gardener's wife, Concepción, who was soon to bear his child, was given money and sent out of the town. The lady-in-waiting, a relative of Madame Bazaine, who had revealed the story to the Empress was dismissed quietly from La Borda. Finally, it was announced that the relaxing air of Cuernavaca did not agree with Prince Agustín, and the little boy and his cat were sent back to the nursery at Chapultepec in the care of his Aunt Josefa.

"Thank God!" said Sally when her brother told her this news. She refused to give him any explanation. But she was readily communicative about her own visits to La Borda, which began as soon as Carlóta recovered from the ill effects of her escapade. The Empress, her doctor noted, had amazing powers of recuperation.

Sally reported that she still talked a great deal about her childhood at Laeken, and at the royal palace in the center of Brussels. Andrew wrote some account of this to Dr. Herzog at

Vienna, adding that Carlóta's mental state was extremely satisfactory. Inspired by Sally's description of her problems at Las
Flores, Carlóta had plunged heart and soul into a new attack
on the abuses of the peonage system, and the American girl, far
from singing Scots songs to an invalid, was soon occupied for
several hours each day in compiling statistics and writing letters
to the dictation of an alert and extremely able woman. Andrew
blessed the circumstance. An interest outside herself and her
wrongs was the best possible thing for the Empress; some check
to the daily rides with Sergeant Franchet might be an excellent
thing for Sally.

Dr. Lorimer had pictured, when he gave his approval to
the riding lessons, some gentle hacking along the road between
the depot and the hacienda, with Tomásito Martinez mounted
on a mule, as groom—not those helter-skelter expeditions to the
high meadows, however providential one of them had been. He
looked up at the plateau above the waterfall as he rode home
to Las Flores one afternoon about ten days after the rescue of
Carlóta—the silver streak of water against the green made it easily identifiable—and estimated that the riding lesson of that day
had taken his sister at least three miles from home.

Andrew sighed. He felt weary and dissatisfied. He had
drunk too much of the Tokay which Maximilian loved, and
pressed on the men who were invited every afternoon to the
new chalet he had built at Acapantzingo, between a marshy hollow and a grove of mango trees. They were nearly always the
same group. Monsieur Eloin, now a councillor of state. Father
Fischer, a priest of dubious reputation. "Charlie" Bombelles,
the Emperor's intimate friend since his Vienna days. Herr Kuhacsevich, called "Kuhacs" for short, the imperial treasurer. These
were the cronies who, with Andrew Lorimer now added to their
number, sat enjoying the Emperor's racy talk through every siesta period, and sometimes into the late afternoon.

Politics were seldom discussed at Acapantzingo. Andrew
knew that a courier arrived from Mexico about noon each day,
and another rode back at first light every morning, but these

were the only contacts Maximilian had with his cabinet. At Cuernavaca the court seemed to live in a vast golden bubble of complacency, a sunlit idleness which was beginning to prey on the young doctor's nerves. Andrew had not, by nature, the same drive and tenacity as his sister Sally, and he had too easily allowed the defeat of the South to turn him from his early purpose in medicine, but he had his fair share of ambition, and as the weeks slipped by in the Warm Country he began to experience some feelings of guilt. Was it, after all, a fit use of his professional training to be in attendance on one woman only, even if she were an empress, when two hospitals in Mexico were full of others needing help and care? He still believed that an ovariotomy would restore Carlóta to full health, if the Emperor could be persuaded to allow it. But Andrew's mind, as he jogged home past the army depot and down the vanilla-scented track to the hacienda, was less with Carlóta's future than with the present of the young Englishwoman, the wife of one of the Legation staff, on whom he had recently performed the difficult operation at the Maternity House. Even with poor equipment and inadequate help, the ovariotomy had been an entire success. But had Mrs. Dixon not a right to her surgeon's care in the postoperative weeks during which he had left her to his Mexican colleagues, while he went off to attend the Empress at La Borda?

There was a frown on Andrew's face when he rode into the home courtyard—a frown which deepened when he saw Rataplan's noble head regarding him over the lower half of the stable door.

"Sergeant Franchet here?" he threw at the yard boy, who ran up to take his bridle.

"He went to the upper fields with La Niña, señor doctor."

A spurt of ill temper sent Andrew to the sugar fields in search of them. He nodded curtly to one or two peons who took off their sombreros as he passed along the stony track leading uphill from the canyon. The afternoon was intensely hot. He was perspiring in his formal clothes, when he heard Sally's eager voice, and some laughing reply from Franchet.

They were side by side on their knees in the dirt—that was how he thought of it—patting earth round the roots of a sapling which Tomásito was holding upright in its new hole. Here and there, neatly staked, a few similar saplings with silvery green leaves were evidence of an industrious afternoon.

"What are you doing?" said Andrew sourly, "making mud pies?"

"*Salud, amigo*," said Pierre easily, looking over his shoulder. "This is the new olive grove of Las Flores: what d'you think of it?"

"Isn't it splendid, Andrew?" cried Sally. "Pierre had the olive bushes sent down from Mexico. He says the roots will help hold the soil together above the sugar canes, when the rains come, and by and by we'll have our own olive oil."

She sat back on her heels and smiled up at her brother confidently, shading her eyes with her hand. Although there was little shade where they were working, neither she nor Franchet wore a sombrero, and beside the hats they had flung aside lay Franchet's dark-blue tunic. Franchet's shirt, washed in the arroyo, was as spotlessly white as cactus soap and a Mexican washerwoman could make it, but it offended Andrew that the man should appear in shirtsleeves before his sister—almost as much as that offhand greeting, *salud amigo!* was distasteful to himself. He had to admit that Sally's own dress did not encourage formality. She was wearing one of her Otomí skirts, of bright yellow linen, sadly streaked with earth, and a square-necked, sleeveless huipil of white cotton stitched with yellow thread. She looked superbly well. Sally would never be plump, but the outdoor life of the Warm Country and the good Mexican food had rounded her throat and breast into curves revealed by the soft blouse, beneath which she all too clearly wore no stays. The sun had brought out a powdering of freckles on the bridge of her nose.

"You'd better put on a jacket, Sally, unless you want to look like a field hand," said Andrew crossly. "Can't you get one of your peons to do your tree-planting for you? And where did the olives come from, anyway? I didn't think there was an olive tree in the whole of Mexico."

"Ah, but that's where Pierre was so clever," said Sally, sparkling. "He *remembered* that the Archbishop had planted olives in his garden at Tacubaya, so he asked one of his friends to get us some, and they arrived this morning."

"To steal you some, you mean. The Archbishop's gardens have been locked and barred since before you and I came to Mexico—"

"Well, bless you, what's the harm?" said Franchet, tying the last stake in place. "His Reverence Monseigneur Labastide y Davalos isn't here to count his precious olive trees. He's with the other *Mochos* in Havana, waiting for better times; meanwhile, you'll have a nice little crop of olives at Las Flores a few years from now. Don't look so disapproving, doctor. Did the Confederate States Army never descend from its pedestal of glory to live on the country?"

Sally suppressed a laugh as Pierre helped her to her feet.

"I never thought of you as an authority on olive trees," said Andrew sourly.

"I grew up among them," said Pierre, "on a bare, stony farm among the crags above Aix-en-Provence. It didn't grow much of anything except olives, but they gave the old man a decent living—while it lasted."

"Is your father dead, Franchet?"

"He died seven years ago."

"Pierre's only brother is a Protestant minister, like *our* father," put in Sally. "He has a charge at Nîmes."

"So kind friends tell me," said Pierre, shrugging into his heavy tunic. "I've never been there to see."

"Don't you want to visit your home country? I thought Frenchmen came out strong for *la patrie*."

"Not me," said Pierre, "*la mia tierra y patria chica* lies elsewhere." He smiled deep into Sally's eyes. Andrew saw her answering smile, as he followed them down the path.

The track was so narrow that two people could hardly walk

abreast. Sally and Pierre went on ahead, their shoulders touching, chattering like magpies, Andrew thought, about some irrigation scheme which Franchet was working out for the sugar fields. He heard something about "springs" and "sluice boxes"; saw the emphatic nods of Sally, and turned to curse Tomásito for walking so close behind him that the boy's spade was banging at his heels. Ahead of him the shining tawny head and the fair one bent to listen were very close together. For the first time Andrew wondered if, as an ultimate folly, his sister were becoming too fond of Sergeant Franchet. She had spoken of him almost possessively—certainly proudly—she had been very quick to produce the Protestant pastor of Nîmes as a link with their own family background. Their family! Was it possible that the granddaughter of Lord S. could think seriously of a sergeant in the Foreign Legion, of all refuse-heaps of ruffians and outlaws! The thought came to Andrew, as he watched their all too casual good-bys, that if Franchet remained at Cuernavaca the sooner Sally was back in Mexico the better.

"You'd better tell Mariquita to bring you some hot water," he said gruffly to his sister, before the yard gate had closed on Franchet and Rataplan. "Take a bath, and change your dress —you need it."

But Sally dipped her hands in the horse trough, which was kept fresh by a pipe of running water, and passed them rapidly over her hot face.

"Why don't you use your hair for a towel, as the Indios do?" said Andrew with mounting annoyance. She looked so happy, and so healthy, and so sure of herself, as she leaned backwards on the stone trough, and lifted her wet face to the sun of afternoon.

"I'm going to work in the office until the merienda," said Sally reasonably. "I didn't expect you home so soon."

"So I gathered."

Sally raised her eyebrows at his tone. She walked away, without further comment, to the office, and Andrew followed her.

"Why do you bother your head with all this stuff?" he said, and pointed at the neatly docketed bundles of correspondence, tied up with red tape, which had replaced the ancient tally sticks. "Don't you know by now that there's no point in holding on to Las Flores? You know you'll have to leave here in a few days, when the court goes back to Mexico."

"I've no idea when they intend to leave Cuernavaca."

"Her Majesty doesn't take you into her confidence to that extent, eh?"

"Certainly not." Sally pulled her chair out from behind the old-fashioned desk. But Andrew stopped her with a gesture.

"Has she told you about the—entertainment—they're planning for next week?"

To his annoyance he saw compassion in Sally's eyes.

"You mean—the plan for Silvia Mora's wedding? You've heard about it, then?"

"The Emperor mentioned it today. Didn't they—didn't the Moras—try to get in touch with *you*, at least?"

Sally nodded without speaking. She pulled open one of the desk drawers. She handed her brother the pasteboard card on which "Don Antonio Jaime Juan, Conde de Mora, and Mercedes his wife, invited Don Andrés and Doña Sarita Lorimer to the marriage of their daughter María del Rosario Silvia Aña, at the palace of La Borda—"

"This arrived yesterday," she said. "I haven't answered it. You said you never wanted to hear me speak of Silvia again—"

"Why are they holding her wedding at La Borda?" he interrupted. "Why not at the Mora villa, on the hill?"

"Because Doña Mercedes is still very unwell. And the Empress thinks it will spare her fatigue if the wedding breakfast is given at La Borda. But I won't go, Andy," said Sally earnestly. "I told the Empress yesterday that I had rather not be present—"

"You wanted to make me conspicuous, did you?" Andrew's brows knotted in the familiar scowl. "No wonder Her Majesty didn't mention her plans to me this morning."

"I don't think she has any idea about you and Silvia,

Andy," said Sally timidly. "She did seem to think you'd feel that presiding at such a big reception would be too much of an effort for herself."

"So it is, of course."

"I think she rather hopes you'll scold her for it."

"I?" said Andrew violently. "I—mention Silvia's marriage, to Her Majesty or anyone? . . . You needn't have hidden the invitation. I've got over that . . . as long as I stay away from her. But you go, Sally. Go, and see if Silvia can bear to have my sister beside her, when she dresses for her wedding."

LA BORDA was not a palace, although Don Antonio's pretentious invitation called it so. It was a simple country residence built by Jean de la Borde, exploiter of the great silver mines of Taxco, and like all his enterprises intended to pay its own way. In the previous century de la Borde had planted mango trees around the quinta, and they were there still, the thick branches keeping the garden cool and gloomy, and the over-ripe fruit falling pulpily upon the paths. Beneath the trees there was always the faintly depressing sound of water trickling through the long narrow gutters which fed four dark, still pools at different levels of the grounds, and the lake in which Carlóta, under Andrew's advice, had lately resumed her old pastime of swimming.

It was the only place in Mexico which Sally found depressing. Not even the School of Medicine in the Plazuelita, with its memories of the Inquisition of past times and the summary executions of the present, repelled her like the little quinta over-shadowed by the dome of the church of Nuestra Señora de Guadalupe, where hammocks hung in the nine-arched patio, and Carlóta's execrable choice of Viennese cane furniture and English chintzes clashed with the simple stonework of the Mexican house. Not even the crowd of guests assembling for Silvia Mora's wedding could make the place look gay.

The wedding bells were already ringing when Sally, who knew her way about La Borda now, made her way to the suite of rooms which had been made over to the bridal retinue. Silvia, of course, was in the inner room, sitting before a hideous cheval glass set in a nest of brass-handled drawers, marble shelves, marble hands with spread fingers intended to hold rings, bottles of smelling salts, hair-tidies and pincushions—everything, in fact, which Carlóta's maids had been able to pile on the massive dressing table. Silvia seemed quite unaware of the atrocious altar to her young beauty. Sally saw her reflection in the mirror as she maneuvered between the white tarlatan crinolines of half a dozen bridesmaids: the lovely face was withdrawn and blank. Then Pilár Mora called out "Sally's here!" and the bride rose up, and put her arms round Sally's neck, and kissed her.

"Darling Silvia, how well you look," said Sally gently. "What a beautiful dress! Let me see you properly."

Silvia turned round mechanically. Her wedding dress of white Windsor satin had an overskirt of net embroidered with posies of white flowers. Its simplicity was the only possible background to the magnificent diamonds with which her neck and arms were loaded.

"Paris, of course," breathed Sally, and Silvia seemed to gain a little animation.

"Oh yes," she said, with a side glance for her reflection in the glass. "It came from Worth. Mamma ordered it months ago, but we were so nervous until it actually got here. Do you think the blond lace is right with it?"

"Absolutely; and the veil to match—it's beautiful."

"She has a coronet," screamed Soledad Mora above the high chattering voices of the girls crowding round the dressing table. "A diamond coronet, Don Felipe gave her. She's going to take her wreath off and wear it at the wedding breakfast. Diamonds in flower clusters to match her necklace. And imagine, Sally! Don Felipe says it's vulgar for girls to wear colored jewels, so we've all had to borrow our mothers' pearls or diamonds for the wedding. He gave all the bridesmaids pearl bracelets except

me and Pilár, and he gave us pearl necklaces because we're
Silvia's sisters. Pilár is going to give me hers when she enters,
aren't you, Pilár?"

"Enter the convent?" Sally drew Pilár a step apart and
lowered her voice. "Is it settled, then?"

"Yes, it's settled," Pilár whispered. "In August—papa wants
it to be in August; if mamma is well enough by then—"

"Oh, Pilár dear, don't let them! What does George Halkett
have to say?"

But Pilár, with a sudden wave of color in her round honest
face, put her finger to her lips for silence. Doña Vera, elegant
in rose taffeta, with the Tía Beata as usual at her heels, had swept
into the room.

"Their Majesties are about to walk to church," she said,
and the chattering of the bridesmaids was stilled by her incisive
voice. "Silvia, are you ready?"

"Is it time?" said Silvia. "My flowers—my gloves—where
are they?"

Doña Vera spoke sharply to the Indian maids. With her
own quick fingers she pinned the tiny wreath of myrtle blossom
above the blond lace veil, and put the bouquet of orchids and
gardenias, stiff in its white paper frill and filagree holder, into
Silvia's hand. Then, while the bridesmaids shook out their curls
and crinolines and prepared for the procession to the church,
Doña Vera gave a small jewel case to Silvia.

"Her Majesty has sent you one more present," she said.
"I imagine you had better wear it."

The leather lid snapped up. On a bed of crimson velvet
lay the fire-opal brooch which formed part of the set of jewels
from the Esperanza mine at Querétaro, given to Carlóta on the
day her husband took the crown.

"Dearest Silvia"—Vera read the little note aloud—"These
opals were my first gift from Mexico. May they be worn today
by the loveliest bride in our land, and bring her happiness.
—Carlóta."

"Opals!" said Silvia, shrinking. "How can I wear an opal

brooch along with Don Felipe's diamonds? He'd never understand!"

"Don Felipe can be made to understand," retorted Vera.
"How can you *not* wear it, you silly girl? A gift from Her Majesty, who has given you so much already? Look, pin it here, in
the lace; it won't be so noticeable, but she'll be pleased—"

"Don't you think opals bring misfortune, Doña Vera?" said
Sally Lorimer.

So far, Silvia's sister had acknowledged Sally's presence
only by a quick sharp glance. Now she turned on the American
girl and said:

"Is that one of your North Carolina superstitions, Sally?"

"I think it's believed all over the world," persisted Sally,
"that opals bring bad fortune. And Silvia may need good luck
in this marriage you've helped to make for her."

Silvia Mora, with the Querétaro opals half-hidden by the
fall of lace above her heart, burst into tears.

"Vera, suppose Sally is right?" said Pilár boldly. "You
know what mamma thinks about wearing opals. Don't force
Silvia against her will!"

"Will you hold your tongue?" It was said so viciously that
Pilár stepped closer to the watchful Soledad. "All right, Sally,"
Vera went on, "you've done what you came to do. You've upset Silvia and started her crying, but that's *all* . . . Get sal volatile
for Doña Silvia," she snapped at one of the Indian maids, "get
her some smelling salts! Señoritas, the bridesmaids are to walk
to church two by two! The bells have stopped ringing—and thank
God, here comes papa."

THE ONE wish which Silvia had expressed concerning her
wedding was that it might take place, not in the vast, forbidding
Cathedral of San Francisco, but in the beautiful Chapel of the
Third Order in the cathedral garden. It was only a short walk
from La Borda to the chapel door, the steep street had been

cleared, and the solemn Indians herded on one side of the road
smiled to see so much youth and beauty passing by. Silvia, on
her father's arm, was followed by her sisters, by her two girl
cousins from Tacubaya, and by four young ladies whose names
read to Sally, following with a group of other girls, like a roster
of the Council of State. She acknowledged that Don Antonio
had contrived to make of his daughter's marriage not only a
family reunion but an imperial and political occasion as well.

The domed roof of the Franciscan chapel rose gracefully
above rounded doors and cupolas which the sunshine of three
centuries had flaked into a harmony of cream and gold. Inside
all was white—plain white walls without statuary, with only the
Stations of the Cross in plain wood frames, and the light coming
in through clear glass windows set high up in the walls. The
reredos was entirely covered with gold leaf. There were golden
vessels on the altar, where a Virgin and Child of Spanish aspect
stood dressed in white and gold. Sally, far back in the church,
clasped her hands in her lap and prayed for Silvia.

Silvia's bridegroom was waiting at the altar, exchanging a
few quiet words with the Emperor and the Empress. His kinsman,
the Conde del Valle de Orizaba, a descendant like Vega himself
of Cortés, stood impassively by his side. They were the only two
men of middle age—of more than middle age—in a church filled
with handsome and high-spirited young people, whose hum of
conversation drowned the sacred music, and was scarcely subdued by the appearance of the priests.

Don Felipe's hair was dyed a deeper jet, his wedding gar-
ments more perfectly London-tailored than even on his first appearance as Silvia's betrothed. Don Antonio was beaming with
satisfaction as he brought Silvia to the altar rail. But Silvia looked
like a sleepwalker, the Sonnambula of whom the Mexican bands
and singers never ceased to warble, as she gave her flowers to
Pilár and knelt down at the white prie-dieu.

They had decorated the white church with white gladioli,
great springing spikes of blossom tied with gold ribbon, and
set jars of arum lilies round the altar. The scent was overpower-

ing. It mixed badly with the strong perfumes worn by nearly all the women, and the incense with which the church was saturated. Sally watched Doña Mercedes borrow Vera's fan, and guessed that the poor lady was feeling faint. The two handsome young men beside her, whom Sally took to be the soldier sons, looked anxiously at each other over her bowed head.

The marriage rites began. The guests pressed forward, whispering, to see all they could of the dresses and the jewels. Sally sat or stood with those around her—kneel she would not —confused by the mumbled Latin of which she understood not a word. It was quite unlike Helen's war wedding at the little Presbyterian church in the piney woods. How well she remembered Andrew in Confederate gray, giving his sister in marriage, and their father's voice breaking as he read the charges! The Scots-born minister had always conducted the marriage service with especial clarity and simplicity. *"Our Lord's gracious presence and first miracle at the wedding in Cana of Galilee."* —Sally could hear the reverent voice still, through the whispering of the guests at Silvia's wedding. Sometimes, in the home church, she had daydreamed of her own bridal, standing at that plain Communion Table with the hero, the man of action, who would one day claim her as his own. If she permitted the dream to invade her thoughts today, the bridegroom would wear French blue, and smile at her with the wry smile of Pierre Franchet. . . . But reality held her close; she might not understand the rubric, but she could see the rings exchanged, hear the responses made. María del Rosario Silvia Aña and Felipe Hernán Jaime were man and wife.

Outside the nail-studded, worm-eaten doors of the Chapel of the Third Order was so large a crowd of guests who, like true Mexicans, had arrived too late to find places within, that Sally had no difficulty in slipping away behind the bridal procession. She waited in the little San José chapel, just opposite, until the cathedral gardens emptied and all the fashionable crowd was on its way back to La Borda. It was quite beyond her to attend the wedding breakfast, and see the newly made Marquesa de Vega exchange her maiden wreath for a coronet. Disappointment in Silvia competed in Sally's mind with a fierce satisfaction in having spoken out, to the very end, against the marriage: she was not such a hypocrite, she told herself, as to simper through the reception, and congratulate the bridal pair. It was even painful to Sally to think of seeing the Empress—the poor, generous, capricious Empress, whose gift of opals had so fluttered the plumage of Andrew's dove. She picked up the skirts of her white muslin dress and almost ran, past a few astonished groups of Indians, down the hilly street of Cuernavaca.

The mule cart which had brought her to town was waiting, as she expected, near the flower market at the foot of the hill. Both the Martínez' got down from it at once and began to rearrange the purchases made that morning so that La Niña could be seated comfortably. La Niña's face was stormy under the white lace mantilla, and she was less grateful than usual for their kind attentions.

"Drive a little faster, Don Ramón, if you please."

"The mules prefer to take their own pace, as La Niña knows."

"I do know it, and you spoil them," said Sally irritably. "Give them a touch of the whip."

She was suddenly impatient to be out of Cuernavaca and on the way home. The overseer looked at her reproachfully and gave the slightest touch of his lash to his petted beasts, while Doña Juanita rearranged the white fringed shade to give Sally more protection from the sun. It was noon, the hour when in the Tierra Templada food and sleep in a shadowed place became desirable, and when the plaza of Cuernavaca was usually empty of all but the beggars asleep under the red oleander trees. Today they had withdrawn to the arcades with their stock-in-trade—the sickly infants, the few whittled pegs or feather charms —and were staring dully at the great gathering of men and horses outside the Cortés barracks, which brought the Las Flores mules to an abrupt standstill.

"Drive *on*, please, Don Ramón," said Sally. They went on,

but slowly, through piles of baggage and stacked arms, earning a few black looks, but nothing more, from busy men who had to move aside to let the mule cart pass. Sally twisted round to stare at the commotion.

"Are they changing the town garrison?" she asked the overseer.

"Who knows, señorita?"

There was no appeal beyond that placid *Quién sabe?* Sally held her peace. The mules quickened their pace as they headed into Atlacomulco parish. She saw the red roofs of the Cazadores depot on the far side of the barranca, and the warmth of Pierre's protective love began to creep back into the heart chilled by the empty pageantry of Silvia's wedding. In not much more than an hour, she thought, I shall be in his arms beneath the magnolia tree, while Doña Juanita is dozing in the shade.

As soon as the track led them up out of the ravine, they all saw the approaching column. It came upon them fast, the Mexican ranks marching quickly and in step, the French officers riding ahead and the baggage wagons bringing up the rear. Martínez, with a shout of *"Hombre!"* was able to turn the mules off the narrow road into a clearing in the banana grove.

"Los Cazadores!" gasped his wife. "Is there a battle, then, in Michoacán?"

Sally said nothing. She could scarcely believe in what she saw. A battle—no; Michoacán province was Imperialist to the core. But those were the newly trained troops, mustered and complete, leaving the depot as, she now realized, the French troops in Cuernavaca were evacuating the Cortés barracks; Colonel de Beauvilain was abreast of the mule cart already and giving her a smile and a salute. She looked beyond him, down the ranks. She saw Pierre on Rataplan, riding in the middle of the column.

"Don't get down, señorita! Don't get down in the road!"

It was Doña Juanita's first and only command as Sally's dueña, and it was utterly ignored. The girl jumped down from the mule cart, and the passing hoofs threw the dust of the dirt road over her crushed muslin dress.

Pierre was off his horse and kissing her hands.

"Sally, thank God," he said. "Our orders came at ten o'clock. I sent one of the *soldaderas* to fetch young Martínez, and gave him a message for you. I couldn't hope to see you before we went away."

"But what has happened?" was all that she could say.

"There's been a big battle up north at Camargo. Our boys were cut to pieces, and they're sending up reinforcements from Durango."

"Where is Camargo?" she said stupidly.

"South of Chihuahua. You remember we cleared out of Chihuahua in January?"

She remembered the distant shoreline of Vera Cruz, and the cheering of the troops aboard the *Impératrice Eugénie,* escaping alive from the Frenchman's Graveyard.

"Are you going to Durango, Pierre?"

"What, with this lot?" He spoke roughly. Her dark eyes were imploring beneath the white lace of her mantilla. And the marching files went past.

"We're only taking them up to Mexico. I'll see you there as soon as André brings you back to town. They won't move us north for a week or two—"

"Pierre, is it as bad a defeat as Santa Isabel?"

"It's worse, *chérie*. This is the big attack beginning. It's a concerted Juarista action right through to the Gulf. Escobedo is moving on Matamoros, and General Mejía may not be reinforced in time. And on the Rio Grande—"

He stopped. But Sally had already guessed.

"Juarez is back in Mexico!"

"He crossed the border yesterday."

The baggage carts were rattling past them now, and Rataplan danced in Pierre's restraining hand. There were not a few of the Mexican *soldaderas* huddled on top of the baggage, with their infants in their arms, and the inevitable poultry strug-

gling at the end of strings. And a French noncommissioned officer, bringing up the rear, leant out of the saddle with a bold
look of admiration for Sally and shouted to Pierre,

"*Allez, sergent! Marchez ou crevez!*"

"I must go, Sally. I'll come to the Plazuelita every day until
you get there. But don't delay—don't linger here—good-by!"

He pressed her hands to his lips again, mounted,
touched Rataplan with the spur, and rode hard past the marching files to his place in the middle of the column. And Sally was
left in the banana clearing, covered in dust from head to foot,
while the column dipped out of sight in the ravine, and the Mex-
can mockingbirds echoed the French bugles until they died
away.

Chapter Fourteen

MARCHING ORDERS

I

WHEN JUAREZ crossed the border, the golden bubble of Cuernavaca burst.

It was shattered for Maximilian and Carlóta first. Within an hour after Silvia and her bridegroom left on their wedding journey, a messenger from the Council of State—more tardy by far than Bazaine's army couriers—brought them the news of the battle at Camargo. It was shattered for all their courtiers, who knew that if Benito Juarez returned to power their property and lands would be confiscated by the republic. It fell in ruins round Sally Lorimer, whose brother told her that if she refused to return to Mexico he would put her in a carriage and take her there by force.

She said good-by to Las Flores very early on the next morning but one, when the lovely crystal light was flooding over the mountains and the Old Doctor's birds were pouring out their hearts in song. She saw the Indian village stirring, an hour before the yard bell would call the peons to work in her fields, as they drove away from the gate where the Martínez family and the three house servants stood looking after them with distress in every broad brown face. And all day long, as they drove in the convoy of carriages hurrying back to Mexico, Sally felt like a coward and a deserter.

There was no consolation to be found at the Plazuelita, where the sala was unwelcoming in dust sheets, with the last raindrops of a wet afternoon rolling down the panes. Andrew left at once to see his surgical patient, Mrs. Dixon, and she was free to read the letter Conchita brought her, which had been left by "El Señor Güero"—the girl said—on the previous day.

Mademoiselle
    On reporting at Buena Vista barracks with my contingent of the Cazadores, I was ordered to proceed to Puebla on a special mission. I expect to return in time for the Supreme Commander's review of troops leaving for the front, and shall come to you as soon as I am free. Please accept this expression of my entire devotion.
                                                    P. J. L. Franchet.

Sally stood by the window with her rain-spattered cloak still on her shoulders, biting her lips as she read her first letter from Pierre Franchet. By no stretch of the imagination could she call it a love letter. The writing was that of an educated man, the terse style that of a soldier: what chilled Sally was the stiff French homage of his *"entier dévouement."* It was to her a sentence from a phrasebook, quite unlike the words of love which had taken her heart by storm at Cuernavaca.

Pierre is in trouble, her instinct told her. Something has gone wrong at Puebla, and they have sent for him. To use him or to blame him—which?

Like every literate person in the capital, Sally fell upon the next day's papers. Nowhere—not in the *Diario* or the *Ere Nouvelle* or even in a well-informed satirical sheet like *La Cucuracha* —could she find any mention of troop movements at or near Puebla. Nor, apart from this special interest, was she much enlightened on the two burning topics of the defeat at Camargo and the reappearance of Benito Juarez. That Marshal Bazaine's new son and heir was to be christened with the Emperor and Empress as godparents took up a good deal of space; but that either the Emperor or Bazaine intended to lead an army north was not suggested.

"You might as well have left me at the hacienda!" she raged

at Andrew on the third day after they returned to Mexico. "I had everything to do there and nothing here! And there's no news, no news, no news!"

Then all at once there was news which shook the capital.

Along the great highway, the French had been compelled by Escobedo's strategy to send reinforcements to two points at once. Durango was threatened by the defeat at Camargo; Matamoros, the third and least important of Maximilian's three Gulf ports, was in deadly danger. The French reinforcements from Monterrey marched on Matamoros at their usual killing pace, but arrived too late to raise the siege. The Juarista general, Escobedo, repeated the tactics successful at Santa Isabel. He ambushed General Tomás Mejía, leading a division of thirteen hundred Mexican and three hundred Austrian troops, and seized control of the mouth of the Rio Bravo river, known north of the border as the Rio Grande.

On the day when the news reached Mexico that Mejía was defeated—and not shot by the victor, according to custom, but set free—the Emperor Maximilian for the first time contemplated abdication.

He had been out at San Angel to inaugurate a very short railroad track linking that fashionable suburb with the capital. It had been looked forward to as a progressive development, meaning among other things a blow to banditry. When the day came he cut the ribbons and waved on the locomotive with the sick knowledge that the first use made of the Chalco Railroad would be to start the foreign residents of San Angel on the way to that other railhead at Mule Pass which opened the way to Vera Cruz and Cuba. He cut the ceremonies short and rode across the fields to Carlóta.

She was waiting in her boudoir—the room which Andrew Lorimer had thought too small and cramped for an empress. It was too small, now, for two people and their burden of emotion, one of whom was a man making a confession of total failure.

"*Abdicate?*" said Carlóta, starting up, "you dare pronounce that word to me?"

In his despair Maximilian was still able to admire her objectively. She could play *Phèdre,* he thought, and play it up to the hilt if she had the full stage of the Comédie Française to move in. We are trapped here between our Buhl chairs and our Sèvres vases; we dare not even raise our voices in case they can be heard out on the terrace.

"Charlotte, my dear," he said, "my poor girl, listen to me. You've always had such a wonderful head for figures. Far, far better than mine. Well, this is a matter of simple arithmetic. We haven't got enough troops, and we haven't got enough money, to remain the rulers of Mexico."

"We have raised nine battalions of Cazadores in the past three months—"

"Three thousand six hundred effectives—not even a complete army corps. I hoped to consolidate them to corps strength with the Austrian and Belgian contingents, but it's no use. The Austrians will fight only under their own officers and the Belgians have finished their two years' engagement—they want to go home. We must face it, dear: we can't look for any more reinforcements from Europe."

"Because your brother is a coward," she flashed. "Because Franz Josef knuckled under to the American bullies who forbade him to send another contingent to Mexico."

"*Your* brother hasn't done much to help us. But the truth is this: we have an army of less than forty thousand men—including the Foreign Legion and the remainder of the French Line. They're asked to control a country of nine million people, at least half of whom never wanted us here, or even knew that we existed, and who if it came to a vote now, would vote for Juarez."

"How you can be so mild about it!" she jeered. "You remind me of my grandfather when he used to make excuses for his abdication from the throne of France. I can just remember him in his English exile. He had his story pat: the democratic process, the will of parliament—bah! I was only a baby, but I

knew he was an idiot—abdication *is* the resource of idiots—and
old men. You will be thirty-four next week—"

"Yes," said Maximilian, "an old man of thirty-four. Perhaps I'm an idiot, too; but—leaving your late lamented grandfather out of it—I'm not so big a fool that I shall go on raising
troops when I can't afford to pay them. Do you realize that the
French are asking me for three hundred and thirty million
francs—sixty million dollars—for their efforts to conquer Mexico
before I became Emperor? Plus one thousand francs a year
for every French soldier serving in this country since my arrival?
Plus, of course, eighty-five million francs to settle Monsieur
Jecker's claims, including a good rake-off for the Emperor's
bastard brother? Listen to common sense, Charlotte! We've spent
nearly all my personal fortune and nearly all of yours. My allowance from Franz Josef is mortgaged for years ahead. We've nothing to expect from Leopold, and nothing left to us in Europe but
our home at Miramar—"

"Have you forgotten the Family Compact?" she said. "You
can't go home to Miramar! Mexico is our home now, our all!
How can you think of deserting Mexico before you've ever led
an army in the field?"

"Don't call me a deserter, Charlotte!" The Emperor's hand
divided his golden beard. With the old nervous gesture he twisted
at the points. "I would ride north tomorrow, if Bazaine would
but agree. He puts me off—he promises a decision after the review,
but he means to delay, I'll swear it, until Napoleon orders a
complete withdrawal. And if that happens, there's no more to be
done—"

"Yes, there is one thing more," declared Carlóta.

"What?"

"I can go myself to Paris, and make a direct appeal to Napoleon."

"Appeal to *him?* To do what, pray?"

"To withdraw his claims for the Jecker money, and the
customs dues, and float another loan for Mexico. To send us
another contingent of French troops. To recall that lecher, that

time-serving Marshal Bazaine, and put General Douay in the supreme command. Max, I implore you, let me go! Our voices are never heard in Europe. Our families have cast us off. Our Ministers—the very men who offered us the crown—have no idea how to describe our needs in the capitals where they represent us. But I can do it, Max! I can make Napoleon *see* how we have fought his battles for him here, without aid or comfort from the princes of Catholic Europe. . . . I can make Pope Pius realize all that we have done for liberal Christianity in Mexico . . . I will talk to my cousin Victoria . . . to Leopold . . . to Franz Josef . . ."

She was clutching at the lapels of his green uniform in the way he knew meant ruination to the set of any coat. It was on the tip of his tongue to say to her:

"Much good your talking to Franz Josef did the last time! Precious little difference it made to his infernal Family Compact!" But the plan she had sketched, with all her former boldness, had something seductive in it too. He let himself be seduced, he forced himself to kiss her tortured mouth and murmur praise of her courage, her self-sacrifice. . . .

At the best, her personal appeal to Napoleon III might stop the French withdrawal.

At the worst, she would be out of Mexico if total disaster came.

Two DAYS after obtaining her husband's permission to go back to Europe, the Empress Carlóta sent for Andrew Lorimer. He had attended her on several mornings since her return to the city, but this was an afternoon call, which lasted until the hour of the castle dinner. Andrew went home without stopping at the hospital, found his sister sewing, and asked her the point-blank question,

"How would you like to visit Europe with the Empress?"

Sally's dark eyes grew round with amazement, and Andrew laughed uncomfortably.

"Don't look so startled! It's a surprising idea, I'll allow," he admitted. "I was surprised myself when she said the Emperor suggested it. You see—now this is strictly confidential, no announcement is to be made until the Emperor's birthday—Doña Carlóta has made up her mind to go to Paris. I don't know all the reasons for it, but I suppose it has to do with the situation here, and the French withdrawal—"

"She is going to ask for money," Sally said.

Andrew waved aside the interruption. "She will travel in state," he said, "with a large retinue; leaving in July, returning in October; and she wishes you to join the party."

"Well!" Sally said. She got up impatiently and walked across the room, aimlessly straightening the antimacassar slipping off the little horsehair sofa. "I'm—I'm thunderstruck, Andrew." She turned to face him. "It would be such an extraordinary thing for me to come so far to live in Mexico, and then to turn right about, and go to France!"

"You're not going to live there. Six weeks at sea, all told; six weeks in Europe—that's what it amounts to."

"But why me? Why the doctor's sister, and not the doctor himself?"

"I shall travel with the party as far as Vera Cruz. The Emperor insists on that."

"No farther? Do you think she's equal to a trip to Europe?"

"If you had seen her today, you'd believe she could go round the world," said Andrew confidently. "The sea voyage will do her good; it's exactly what I should have prescribed for her, and of course she'll be well cared for when she gets to France. Look, Sally, the Empress seems to have taken a fancy to you. She's only going to have two Ladies in attendance, Frau "Kuhacs"—"

"Who's fat and lazy—"

"And Señora del Barrio."

"Who doesn't speak a word of anything but Spanish."

"Well, there you are! That's just why she says she needs a younger lady to talk French, write her notes, make arrangements for her audiences—"

"That should be done by the Mexican Ambassador," said Sally. "I don't think I should shine as an extra *dame de compagnie*."

"Well, you must make up your own mind about it," said Andrew. "Only I do remember the days when it was the *great dream* of your life and *absolute ambition* to visit Paris." He mimicked the enthusiastic schoolgirl of fourteen.

Sally did not rise to the bait. She stood playing with the ball fringe of the antimacassar, her bright head bent, and the reflection of the first night lights of the Plazuelita falling on her white dress.

"You know—I was very disappointed at leaving Cuernavaca," she got out. "I feel as if there were people there depending upon me. Have I the right to leave them, to go as far away as Europe?"

"You'll be in Paris and back again before it's time to cut your precious sugar canes."

Sally looked up at her brother. He had aged, she saw, in their four months in Mexico. The lines of repression round his mouth were clearly marked, and there was something dulled, yet eager, in the blue eyes watching her so closely.

"Do you want me to leave *you*, Andrew? Leave you to Lupita's tender mercies for the next twelve weeks?"

"Lupita doesn't do too badly now. You've trained her very well."

"But Conchita and Luz are so slipshod. They'll soon slip back into their idle ways if I'm not here."

"Oh," said Andrew, "I was thinking, coming along, that I might let the maids go and close up part of the house while you're in Paris. Lupita and Jorge and I will do all right on our own. The fact is, Sally, that without the palace fees coming in I'm going to be rather strapped for money, unless the practice picks up a little."

"I see you have it all thought out," she said. "Do you regard my going to Europe as an economy measure? I don't. Even if I travel as one of the suite, how could I possibly afford the right sort of clothes, the pocket money, the sort of expenses that are bound to occur on shipboard, just as they did aboard the *Jupiter?* I've barely got a thousand dollars to my name."

"As far as that goes," Andrew said reluctantly. "The Emperor has made a very generous offer. I told him you would certainly wish to decline it, because I don't see what you'll spend money on in Paris—God knows you've *made* enough dresses for half a dozen girls—but, well, the Emperor did suggest offering a fee for your services . . ."

"How much?" asked Sally.

"How—? I think he mentioned thirty gold onzas, but of course we couldn't possibly agree—"

"Thirty onzas!" said Sally, and her eyes flashed. "Four hundred and eighty U. S. dollars! Tell him to pay me five hundred in dollars, and I'll accept!"

"Why, you damned little Yankee!" Andrew swore. "You mean that's all you care about—the money?"

"They pay your fees, don't they?"

"That's absolutely different, and you know it!"

"I don't know it," retorted Sally. "You've been trained as a doctor: I taught myself two foreign languages, so let's both be paid for the services those people need. I've no illusions about this trip to Europe. I shall have to work, and work hard at a lot of little thankless jobs. I shall probably be pressed into service as Carlóta's maid—"

"Don't be ridiculous; she's taking Döblinger, and a Spanish woman goes to wait on the Ladies."

"That only means I'll have to translate for Döblinger and the Spanish woman, whenever they want a can of hot water from the French servants. You say there will be two Ladies in attendance and two maids—and the Empress. I'll be at the beck and call of five women, not one, which is well worth five hundred dollars for a twelve weeks' trip."

"I wish my father could hear his spoiled pet now," said Andrew. "You place an excessive value on the pleasure of your company."

"It isn't pleasure they expect from me. It's usefulness. Oh, Andrew, can't you see? For the first time in my life I have a chance to earn money—"

"What about the famous hacienda?"

"Up to now, *my uncle's* money has worked there for me. From now on, what *I* earn will all be for the hacienda. Tell the Emperor—or tell Monsieur Eloin, if you don't want to tell Maximilian that your sister isn't ashamed to work for pay—tell them I'll do the work they want for five hundred U. S. dollars—*not gold onzas*—payable—when does the party leave?"

"July the ninth, from Mexico."

"Payable not later than July the sixth."

"There's something so crude, so crass about payment in advance."

"There's something much more crude about being stranded in Cuba, or even at St. Nazaire," said Sally. "Have you forgotten what happened to Matthew Maury? *He* left Mexico basking in Imperial favor. He was rejected before he crossed the ocean. I shouldn't like that to happen to me."

She saw that she had won the point. Her face, upturned to his, was still rose-tanned by the Cuernavaca sun. Her lips were quivering.

"I *need* five hundred dollars, Andrew dear," she said. "I need it for the hacienda. To help buy new equipment for the refinery. It's the only way to make the sugar crop pay. And the new machinery will have to be bought in the United States, that's why I need the dollars. It may even have to be shipped out via Havana, I don't know. But the steamer will call there, and I can see Mr. Wilkinson and ask for his advice."

"You're prepared to spend more money on that two-bit plantation of yours?" he said. "Don't you realize that you're throwing it away? Why the devil are you so obstinate about hang-

ing on to a place you can never hope to run yourself and killing
yourself to make it pay?"

"Because it's *mine*," she said.

II

SALLY REGRETTED her impulsive words many times in
the solitary hours which followed. It had been fun, when
her blood was up, to tell Andrew a few home truths about
a man's earnings and a woman's; it was less amusing to
think that she had as good as committed herself to a three
months' absence from Mexico in the suite of someone whom
she feared at least as much as she admired. If Sergeant Franchet
could have come back to the Plaza de Santo Domingo on that
day, or the next, to take Sally in his arms and call her the flower
of his heart, she might have given up any idea of accepting the
Imperial offer. But nothing had been heard of Franchet since he
went to Puebla, and her last image of him was of the soldier
spurring away to his duty while his sweetheart stood drooping
in the highway dust.

It was the sentimental image of war on which all the Southern girls of her generation had been nourished, and Sally Lorimer had rejected. It helped to harden her resolution during the
two days which followed. On the third morning, the day of Marshal Bazaine's review, Sally rose early, and sent Jorge with a
written message to an elderly English lady who lived with two
servants in the Calle de Santo Espíritu, whom she had met
at several soirées at the British Legation.

Miss Margery Keane, who gave instruction in literature,
botany, sketching and geography to young ladies of the diplomatic families, was waiting when Miss Lorimer arrived in a hired
victoria, and very willing to provide the chaperonage which had
been asked so prettily. They went first to the Legation, where
Sally had a long talk with the commercial attaché, and then paid
a short visit to the office of the National City Bank of New York.
I wonder what that Confederate brother would say, thought the

Englishwoman, if he knew that Miss had transactions with a Yankee bank; but she was too experienced and discreet to make any comment, or show any surprise when Sally expressed a wish to see the French review.

"I thought it would be an interesting sight," said Sally carefully. "Particularly now. I mean, one hears so much about Marshal Bazaine and his intentions, but he keeps so very much in the background, one hardly knows—"

"Profoundly interesting, my dear."

Miss Keane was too well-bred to reveal her private opinion that not the Supreme Commander, but some young French subaltern was the real attraction for Miss Sally Lorimer at the grand review. She chatted agreeably, but impersonally, as the victoria skirted the Alameda and drove out the Tacuba highway, past the palace of Buena Vista with which Maximilian had rewarded Marshal Bazaine for his earlier victories, past the barracks of the same name, and on to the dusty parade ground, where a number of carriages were already drawn up in the scanty shade afforded by a line of scrub cypress and poplar.

"It's a great pity," pronounced Miss Keane, "that more Mexican *gentlewomen* do not grace such an important occasion as a review of the Imperial troops. I see Madame Bazaine arriving, to be sure, but one could wish for some representation from the Court. I did hear that Madame Bazaine's cousin had fallen into disfavor and was sent away quite abruptly from La Borda; do you know anything of that?"

"I'm afraid not, ma'am. She's pretty, isn't she, Madame Bazaine? Who is the Mexican officer riding so very close to her carriage?"

Madame Bazaine, whom the French troops called Madame Dictator, came up the parade ground in a showy equipage. Triumphant in her eighteen years, her brilliant marriage and her infant son, the Supreme Commander's wife was attended by a dozen officers, both French and Mexican. The man whom Sally indicated was conspicuous among them for his great good looks and fair hair.

"Another of her innumerable cousins," said Miss Keane with a sniff. "Colonel Miguel Lopez. A Mexican born and bred in spite of the blond hair, and *not* a very popular person, I hear." She lowered her voice, "They say the whole family has rather a close connection with Benito Juarez."

The last words were muffled as the band began to play the French National Anthem, "Partant pour la Syrie," and Marshal Bazaine, with his staff behind him, came riding up to the stand where the two flags hung limply in the clear warm air.

He was a heavy man with a coarse face, clay-colored, adorned with waxed mustachios and a short imperial. In uniform, slouching a little in the saddle, he was remarkably like his master the Emperor of the French. Fifty-four years old, a soldier for thirty-six of them, Bazaine bore on his lined face and in the pouches beneath his eyes every mark of the hard-fought, well-planned, dangerous, turbulent career which had brought Achille Bazaine from private soldier to Marshal of France. He held the Marshal's baton stiffly in his hand, moving it very slightly in salute as the Foreign Legion took the lead in the march past.

Only their officers were mounted. On this day the Legion marched as infantry, as they had marched for thirty years, through the Carlist wars in Spain, through Algeria, through Lombardy with today's Supreme Commander at their head. Sally had looked for Rataplan; she could not distinguish Pierre on foot, among the quick-moving, blue-coated files as the Legion dipped its Colors to the Marshal. In the sunshine gold letters glinted upon crimson silk,

MAGENTA
SOLFERINO

"Not very tactful of the Foreign Legion," said Miss Keane, "here to fight for Maximilian, and flaunting the name of the Austrian defeats!"

The next flag dipped. Very new and very precious, it read,

CAMERONE

"Was that one of their Italian victories?" puzzled the governess.

"Oh, Miss Keane!" Sally's flushed face, framed in the soft black lace of her mantilla, looked almost accusing. "Camerone was where three officers and sixty Légionnaires held off two thousand Juaristas, when they were trying to clear a road for convoys during the siege of Puebla. Only three years ago—and only three of them were left alive, after they fought the whole day long. It was the third company of the First Battalion," she added precisely, "and now they have a saying in the Legion, 'at Camerone were none but good soldiers'."

"I see, my dear," Miss Keane said diplomatically, and patted the small clenched hand nearest to her. I see that the sweetheart is in the Legion, she thought; one of those rather operatic officers, no doubt. Dr. Lorimer will *not* be pleased.

The Mexican troops marched past Bazaine. They were sixteen hundred strong, four battalions of Cazadores having been mustered for the review, and Sally heard a knowledgeable spectator, standing just below the victoria, remark that they were to garrison Mexico when the foreign troops went north. Their drill instructors had taught them a number of evolutions which looked well on a relatively small space like the Buena Vista grounds, and they marched and countermarched with a fair display of military precision. There was no review of artillery, and the only arms carried by the Cazadores were the French "snuffbox" muskets fitted with the immensely long Mexican bayonets of Santa Anna's wars.

Bazaine and his Chief of Staff trotted down the ranks of white-trousered Cazadores. The military band played softly. Swords flashed in salute, horses pranced. To Sally it was like a scene from a play, completely divorced from reality. She had come to the review not to see Pierre but to know him, to penetrate the military *mystique* by which he appeared to live; and instead she found herself watching a circus from the far side of the ring.

Except at Río Frío, and on the last day at Cuernavaca, Pierre in his meetings with Sally had been quite alone, with nothing about him but his uniform to remind her that he was a unit of the French Expeditionary Corps. True, he had talked incessantly of the war and the politics behind it; but so did everyone in Mexico. He had told her stories of the prowess of the Foreign Legion, until the storming of Fort Loreto and the hollow square at Camerone passed with the march from Tampico to Monterrey into the place in her heart reserved for her father's Scottish stories of Wallace and Robert the Bruce; but he had never boasted of his own exploits. He had come to her in the Plaza Mayor, or at the hacienda, as a man apparently free to plan his own comings and goings. Abruptly, as soon as Juarez crossed the border, she was forced to realize that Sergeant Franchet was not free. He was a soldier, and although it had been thrust upon him his profession pleased him. A soldier; and able to admire a courageous and skillful enemy. How often had Sally heard him say of the Juaristas: "Porfirio Diaz is the only *soldier* of the lot!" or "Diaz is smart; he escaped from prison twice when we thought we'd cornered him. I hope we play a third match with Don Porfirio!" Now he stood somewhere within her range of vision, unidentifiable. A blue coat and a képi among hundreds of others, with all his keen personality willingly submerged in theirs.

Bazaine came cantering down the parade ground towards the Foreign Legion. There was a sharp "About—face!"; the stamp of heavy boots on beaten earth; a sharper "Present—arms!" and the French troops were face to face with the Supreme Commander.

"*Légionnaires!*"

At the first word he spoke, the *Légionnaires!* instead of the conventional *Soldats!* there was a stir of emotion through the bearded ranks before him. Bazaine's popularity had steadily diminished among the French since his marriage to "Madame Dic-

tator"; the spectacle of the old man lounging on his carriage
cushions beside his girl-bride they found disgusting, and they
saw his energy declining before their eyes. But *Légionnaires!*—
that was the key word, the reminder that he was one of themselves, the living legend who had been with the Legion from the
beginning of its thirty tempestuous years.

"*Légionnaires,* the enemy we hunted from this country has
dared to challenge us again. I have taken up his challenge. I
leave tonight to establish Supreme Headquarters at San Luis
Potosí."

There was a growl of approval all through the ranks.

"You, my old comrades of the desert and the plains of
Lombardy—you who took Puebla and followed me to Querétaro,
Guanajuato, Guadalajara—you will win other and greater victories in the days ahead. Remember, the generals now against
us in the field have already been our prisoners. Ortega, Escobedo,
Diaz, have been beaten more than once. This time they can be
utterly destroyed."

A soldier shouted in the front rank:

"*Allez-y, patron!*"

"A very undisciplined body of men, I fear," said Miss Margery Keane.

"Oh please, do let us listen!" said Sally, trembling. That
contingent of the Foreign Legion, eight hundred strong, was like
no body of men she had ever seen. The first Fayetteville volunteers to the Confederate States Army, whom she had watched
marching out of town on a spring afternoon in 1861, bore no
resemblance to the scarred veterans before her. But the Fayetteville boys had gone wild when the band played "Dixie," and the
gaunt, fever-ridden men in French uniform were cheering a string
of names which meant old victories, and she was nearer than
she had ever been to understanding the dreadful excitement that
sent men to war.

"*Légionnaires!*" The gloved hand relaxed, the Marshal's
baton came gently to rest on the pommel of Bazaine's saddle,
"Your comrades—those who are left of them—await you along

the road to the Bravo river. Follow me, to death or glory! *Vive l'Empereur! Vive la France!"*

. . . Sally had expected Pierre to come to her at the hour of the Cuernavaca riding lessons—the siesta, when the barracks everywhere were quiet. But the Frenchman must have got his horse as soon as the Foreign Legion marched off the parade ground and ridden across the city faster than the ancient victoria ambled round the Alameda. Sally had barely left Miss Keane and returned home when Pierre was announced by Lupita.

He came in with delight written on his face. He took Sally in his arms as soon as the door was closed, kissing her on the lips, the eyes, kissing the bronze hair escaping from the black mantilla; covering her face with kisses until from acceptance she turned to him with a fierce response and buried her head on his shoulder.

"Darling!" he said, when he released her at last, "I saw you at Buena Vista. With your dueña and your carriage, like a little princess—*you* should have taken the salute instead of old Bazaine. But *chérie,* why in black again? You looked very grand . . . but I like you better in your hacienda dress."

Smiling, he gently detached the tortoise-shell combs which held the black lace web in place on Sally's high-piled hair.

"I miss the white shirt and the golden arms," he said. "My little Scottish wild rose!"

"Your little Scottish thistle," she said, and turned away from him to fold the lace mantilla, very carefully and very small. Pierre followed her across the room.

"Don't make me feed on thistles, *chérie,*" he said. "That's dry food for a man on his way back to the desert."

"You're really leaving for the front?"

"Yes, we have our marching orders. Could you hear the *patron's* speech?"

"Every word of it," said Sally. "I heard him promise you new victories, and I heard you all cheering at the mere names of the battles where you were victors in the past. I heard him say he would lead you to San Luis Potosí—"

"We'll go farther than San Luis. San Luis Potosí is the right place for supreme headquarters, but—you'll see—Saussier will take us up to Monterrey. The 2nd Zouaves are going northwest to Durango, confound them. They claim the honor of stopping Juarez, if he ever puts his dog's face outside Chihuahua."

"I've heard men talk about stopping Sherman," said Sally. "But he came right on through."

"Sherman was a soldier. This Juarez is only a conniving Indian lawyer, like Monsieur Favre and the Radicals at home, who're always sniping at the Emperor for sending us to Mexico. They need Juarez for a figurehead, because he was president when Mexico was a republic, but Escobedo is worth half a dozen of him, and Porfirio Diaz is worth twenty."

He was exaggerating now, in the overdramatized Provençal way which Sally knew was his cloak for weariness and strain. She let him take her in his arms again and felt his cheek against her cheek, and his heartbeats shaking the blue stuff of his coat.

"Oh, Pierre, I wish you hadn't had to go down to Puebla!"

He raised his face from hers and said uncomfortably,

"Why, Sally?"

"Because I was so—miserable here. Leaving the hacienda . . . and not knowing what was going to happen next. And I may have to make a big decision soon, and—*why* did you have to go?"

"I want to tell you about that sometime, but not now." He held her strongly, feeling the conflict of resentment and desire in the slim taut body in his arms. "I can't argue over the orders given to me. We're here because the Emperor—*the* Emperor, Napoleon—sent us out to support Maximilian, and our duty is to obey him—"

"You always say 'the Emperor.' Never 'France'!"

"The Emperor *is* France, Sally!"

His kisses weakened her; the hands she had clenched against his shoulders stole round his neck, and with a sigh Sally drew the cropped fair head closer to her own. Soul and body struggled in that imperious desire towards a complete union, and when he lifted his lips from hers Pierre said:

"Marry me, Sally. Marry me tomorrow, before I go away."

"If I do, would you take me with you?"

"Into danger? Never. You must stay here until we've chased Juarez across the border, and then I'll come back to you—"

It was the old refrain to which her early girlhood had been set. When the war is over, we shall be together always. Charles Cartwright had said that to her father, when he asked for Helen Lorimer's hand in marriage. Touched on an acute nerve, Sally cried:

"And while you're chasing Juarez, I'm to be left as my sister was left to die in Vicksburg?"

She had no idea how she came to say such a thing. It was as if some fear, always latent beneath the surface of her mind, had found its expression at last. She knew that a tide of crimson stained her face, and hid her hot cheeks in her hands.

"Sally!"—he had his arms around her—"What do you mean? How was your sister 'left to die'?"

"When . . . her little boy . . . was born."

She ventured to look up at him. She saw in his face pity and—could it be? the faintest hint of a smile. Then he said very gently:

"I won't leave you—to die, Sally; trust me for that. I want your love, *chère*, not your child. Not yet."

"What a very romantic scene," said Dr. Lorimer.

They had not heard him enter. They turned to face him now. He was pale with anger, his gloved hand clenched on a roll of newspaper, his light gray coat flung open.

Pierre kept his arm round Sally. He said:

"Monsieur, I have just had the great honor of asking mademoiselle your sister to become my wife."

Andrew stared at Sally. He had never seen her wearing such a look—tearful, tender, happy; and as she moved a little closer to the protecting shoulder in the worn army blue he thought of Silvia's weakness, and contrasted it with Sally's proud acceptance of the Frenchman's love.

"I *thought* there was some sort of flirtation going on," he said coldly. "I didn't imagine it would go this far. Sally, what answer have you given your suitor?"

"Pierre knows," said Sally confidently—and the look of confidence she exchanged with the Frenchman intensified Andrew's desire to hurt them both—"he knows that I would like . . . not now, but some day . . . to be married to him."

" 'Not now but some day'," her brother mimicked. "How very prudent! I'm surprised you aren't eager to be off to the barracks gate with the *soldaderas*—"

"Don't speak to her like that," said Franchet.

"I am my sister's guardian, and I'll speak as I think fit for her own good. Marry *you*, indeed! A killer from the Foreign Legion to raise his eyes to Lord Sandhaven's granddaughter! I forbid the marriage absolutely; and the association between you ends today."

"Oh, don't be a fool," said Sally. "Who cares for Lord S. in Mexico? Did Don Antonio Mora? And how do you propose to enforce your guardianship of me? We're not in Fayetteville now, you know. We're on foreign soil, and I doubt if the American Consul will back up *your* authority—" She paused expressively. Sally's moment of tenderness was past. She stood erect, with one hand fast in Franchet's; her face, like her words, defying her angry brother.

"You call me a killer," said Pierre Franchet. "What were *your* comrades? You were a noncombatant, but how about the men you served with? Did they only fire blanks in the Confederate States Army?"

"They were fighting for a just cause," said Andrew. "The manhood of the South fought *for* the South, but you mercenaries fight anywhere you can make a profit from your dirty trade. Don't think I don't know how the French have lined their pockets here in Mexico, from Bazaine in his palace to the supply sergeant who sells army victuals at the very gates of Buena Vista! I know all about the graft that goes on, and the falsified payrolls, and the silly women who let themselves be fooled into petting and keeping, yes, and *marrying* the men who plan to leave them flat

as soon as they get their marching orders. And you think you've
found a silly *girl* to keep you, do you? You've seen Las Flores,
you think it may be worth something, at least to a man without
two sous in his patched pockets—"

He saw Pierre take a step forward, with his fist clenched,
and perversely hoped the fellow meant to strike him. Then they
could fight—and then, the animosity he had felt to this man when
they met at Río Frío, and afterward suppressed, could be lanced
like a boil, and relieved along with all the pent-up anxieties and
frustrations of his life in Mexico. His own fist clenched round
the newspapers he still held, and with that he remembered another and a better way to hurt them . . .

"Do you take me for a fortune hunter?" said Pierre furiously. "I want no part or share of the Hacienda de las Flores. I
am not penniless. I've worked, and saved my pay, without selling
Army supplies or cheating the Mexicans—"

"How dare you be so insulting, Andrew!" Sally cried.
"Patched pockets indeed! You and I wore patched clothes, only
a year ago. Pierre owns land at Tampico; I'm proud of that,
and proud of him—"

"Are you indeed?" said Andrew. "Has he told you why he
went to Puebla?"

She saw Pierre flinch. She said:

"No. Why?"

"Here, read it," he said, "it's in all the official papers today.
Franchet Pierre, Jean, Louis—that's you, isn't it?"

"I'll tell her myself," said Pierre. "I— You have to know this,
Sally. I was ordered to Puebla as one of the witnesses at a court-
martial. To give evidence on my—knowledge of Marina Perez."

"Of La Malinche!"

Andrew had wished to wound his sister. He had succeeded
amply. She stood before him pale, dumfounded, looking in her
black dress like the small figure of mourning who had first come
to the Plaza de Santo Domingo.

To Sally it seemed as if there was another presence in the
room. As if the brilliant flaunting creature in her red beads and

ribbons were standing there again with her contemptuous smile
—between them.

"Was *she* at Puebla?" she got out.

"God knows where she is," said Pierre. "The man . . . the
French lieutenant . . . they court-martialed at Puebla was accused of giving away military secrets to her while she was dancing
here at the Iturbide. He was also charged with telling her the
plans for the Foury Mission's journey to Vera Cruz, which she
passed on to Perez the Plateado leader . . . he turns out to be a
relative of hers—"

"Did you know that?"

"Never. But then I didn't know about the lieutenant, either."

There was an irony, which was part of him, in his way of
presenting the story which took some of the sting out of it for
Sally. "You mean he was your unknown—rival?"

"Not unknown now," said Andrew. "Anyone who buys the
Diario today will know what company Sergeant Franchet kept
while he was billeted here in my house. The National Palace was
full of it when I saw Monsieur Eloin there this noon. Agreeable
for me, I must say—"

"Did Monsieur Eloin ask you to visit him?" said Sally
sharply.

"He did, my dear. To inform me that the Emperor had
agreed to your remarkable demand. The money will be paid in
dollars on July the sixth, three days before we leave for Vera
Cruz."

"What money?" said Franchet.

"You and my sister seem to be adepts at keeping your own
counsel. She is going to Europe, in the suite of the Empress
Carlóta; although, as you have just gathered, for a fee."

"You can't do it!" Franchet cried. "Sally—I won't let you
go off with that crazy woman. You—*docteur*—you called me a
killer five minutes ago. I say *you* are the killer if you consent to
such a scheme. You may have your sister's death upon your
hands! Carlóta is insane—I saw that, the day we met her with
the boy, when she tried to kill him, and Sally too—"

"Pierre, you promised!" Sally cried.

"Promised what? To say nothing about it? But he has to know; Sally, he's *got* to know now! Look," he appealed to Andrew, "I wouldn't trust Sally as far as the Plaza Mayor with that woman—"

"How do you mean, she tried to kill them?"

"She tried to ride them down at the waterfall."

"She only lost control of her horse. Wasn't that it, Sally?"

"I don't know!" cried Sally. "I don't know what to believe about anybody any more!"

"And it's not only Carlóta!" the Légionnaire's voice rose to match her own. "There may be war in Europe, any day now. Prussia has started a row with Austria: we—France—may be dragged in if fighting begins this summer; you don't know what you're sending Sally into. Hell and damnation," cried Pierre, "you don't know how good she's been, and how patient, waiting on you, and tolerating your neglect of her at Cuernavaca while you sat boozing with Max and she was all alone with the Indios; and now you only want to get rid of her, to get her away from me, and send her to Paris, where she'll be absolutely friendless—"

"Friendless in a suite of twenty members of the Court?" jeered Andrew. "Besides, she has other friends in Europe. I've kept in touch with Dr. Herzog; he will certainly wait upon the Empress; and our cousin, the Honourable Gilbert Fraser, is at the British Embassy in Paris. Miss Lorimer has kinsmen in Europe—"

"Oh stop!" Sally's voice rang out. "Stop, both of you and don't fight over me."

She silenced them both. She seemed to have grown not only older but actually taller since the dispute began. Her face wore the stubborn, mulish expression Andrew knew so well, and yet there was a kind of grandeur in the poise of her head and the proud flash of her eyes.

"Pierre," she began, "oh, Pierre! I know you mean to protect me, and keep me away from danger. But I'm not afraid of war in Europe, even if war comes. Why should I be? War at home, war in Mexico, war in Europe— There doesn't seem to be any place in the world where people aren't fighting, so what's the difference?"

"But you're afraid of Carlóta, aren't you?" Pierre challenged.

"I say I'm not. And I say you have no right to try to prevent me from going with her, and earning money for the hacienda, as long as you are free to come and go without questioning from me. When you got your marching orders you left me by the roadside in Cuernavaca, just as," her voice shook, "you'll leave in a few days for the northern front. When you were *ordered,* you had to go to Puebla to admit your association with a dancing girl turned spy—as I told you, here in this very room, that she *could be!*—I could do nothing to stop you. Then Andrew, you ordered me to leave the hacienda, where I was very busy and very happy, and come back here . . . as if I couldn't have gone on living there with Mariquita and the Martínez! So now I have a chance to act independently, just as you both do, and I mean to take it. I wasn't decided an hour ago. I am now. I'm going to Paris with the Empress."

"For how long?" said Franchet hoarsely.

Sally was able to laugh.

"It's only for three months," she said. "Not an eternity."

"Will you promise to come back to me?"

She considered. "I can promise that. Only—I'm tired of being the one who does the waiting. Will *you* wait for me?"

Chapter Fifteen

THE GARDENIA POOL

I

ONE OF Sergeant Franchet's predictions came true before Pierre himself, riding in Bazaine's columns, had gone further than the first bivouac on the road to San Luis Potosí. The rumors of trouble in Europe, already current in the French Expeditionary Corps, were due to be sensationally confirmed. On July sixth, dispatches brought by sea to Vera Cruz and telegraphed to Mexico announced that twenty-one days earlier war had broken out between Prussia and Austria, with the Emperor Franz Josef leading the Austrians in the field.

July sixth was Maximilian's thirty-fourth birthday. The effect of the news upon his plans and hopes could only be surmised, but a murmur ran among the Mexican notables at the National Palace when the Empress arrived alone to receive their birthday greetings. Carlóta was robed and crowned, completely mistress of herself and of the situation, and Andrew Lorimer, present with some of his medical colleagues, felt justifiably proud of his patient. She was proving to the world, he thought, that she was fully equal to the trip to Paris.

He was proud of her three days later, when she said good-by to her husband in the rain at Ayotla, the first military post on the road to Vera Cruz. He thought, and he was not alone in thinking, that the two of them had never appeared to better advantage than on that wet roadside, when the tall, golden-haired Emperor stooped to kiss the cheek and hand of the wife who seemed to have recaptured some of her old imperious beauty at this be-

ginning of her desperate attempt to save an empire. The farewells were calmly and quickly said. To the sound of French brass
and Mexican drums the Empress was played away from Ayotla,
and the Austrian Hussars closed in ahead of and behind her
carriage as it began the long slow climb to the passes above Río
Frío.

Dr. Lorimer had himself insisted that the journey south
be made by easy stages. He had no opportunity of talking to his
sister until the first night halt, at one of the great *Mocho* haciendas of the province, for she had evaded him at the daytime
stops as she had evaded him—easily—in the busy preparations
which filled her last days in Mexico. Herr and Frau "Kuhacs"
were pleasant traveling companions, she said briefly. The Empress had had no need of a secretary's help that day.

Next morning Andrew himself was invited into Carlóta's
coach, and rode with her all the way until they were within sight
of Puebla. Giant thunderclouds were piling up in the east above
the twin forts where the Juaristas had hurled back the French
assault on the famous Fifth of May in 1862. The brick turrets
and rounded casemates of Fort Loreto were clearly visible two
miles away, above scrub pine and poplar etched on the plateau
leading to Fort Guadalupe. Then the rain came down, hard, in
long slanting rods which drenched the escort and the grooms,
and water rushed down the arroyos as Carlóta drove into Puebla,
Town of the Angels, where the most carefully selected route between the two-story dwellings, painted in crude vivid shades of
yellow, blue and pink, could not disguise the aftermath of the
battles which had carried Maximilian to his precarious throne.
Churches and convents, used by the besieged as barracks and
military stores, had crumbled under the fire of Bazaine's attack
and Diaz' hard-fought defense in 1863. Andrew saw Carlóta's
nervous hand go to her lips, and the long shudder that shook
her body.

"Your Majesty must retire early tonight," he said gently.
"The bad roads have tired you."

Carlóta sighed.

"We are to be the Prefect's guests," she said. "The Marqués de Guadalupe is sure to offer us a lengthy and elaborate dinner. But tomorrow we shall have the pleasure of supping in one of the most beautiful gardens in the country. We are to stay at a quinta near La Fortaleza, with Don Felipe Vega and his bride."

Only the awareness of Doña Manuela's dark eyes fixed speculatively upon him gave Andrew Lorimer the power to answer naturally,

"I understood the Marqués and Marquesa de Vega were on their way to Europe, Madame."

"Their departure was postponed, I really don't know why," said the Empress vaguely.

"But Your Majesty of course remembers," prompted Doña Manuela, "that the happy couple will be among Señor de Guadalupe's guests tonight."

. . . Sally, who had no warning of Silvia's nearness, was almost speechless when the bride accompanied her to her room.

"But *querida,* I don't understand," she said when the maids had left them. "Haven't you been to the Quinta Vega at all, yet?"

"Oh yes, we went straight there," said Silvia. "The house is really beautiful. I think you'll like it . . . The conservatories are the finest I've ever seen. Gardenias, you know. Don Felipe grows gardenias."

"Yes, you told me," said Sally in bewilderment. This was a new Silvia. The unhappy girl of the Cathedral, the reluctant bride, had turned into this burnished beauty, nervous and smiling, who fidgeted with the trinkets on Sally's dressing table and was unwilling to meet Sally's eyes. "We're to stay with you?" she asked. "Silvia, how can you possibly be here in Puebla tonight and receive the Empress at your house tomorrow?"

"Oh, Don Felipe has a regiment of servants," said Silvia indifferently. "They know exactly what to do. We've been here for a week, paying visits and going to the theater . . . Sally, how extraordinary it seems that you should go to Europe before me, after all!"

"I thought you would have sailed for Spain by now."

"Don Felipe thinks we should stay in Mexico for the present. Queen Ysabel is involved in some political quarrel, I don't quite know with whom—"

"With General Prim and Señor Serrano, isn't it?"

Silvia sighed. "You always understood politics. I never did. I only know that Don Felipe doesn't want to get mixed up in any trouble in Madrid. And he thinks, even with Juarez back in the north, we'll be well out of any fighting at La Fortaleza."

"I hope he's right."

Silvia laid down the small glove buttonhook she had been examining. For the first time she spoke naturally and urgently.

"Sally—did you hear any gossip about my family before you left Mexico?"

"Oh, *querida,* nobody talks about anything these days but Juarez, and the war in Europe; and I'd so much to do to get ready for this trip—what has happened?"

"My sister Pilár has eloped with George Halkett."

"Oh, Silvia!" Even before the bitterness in Silvia's face, Sally could not hide her exultation.

"I thought you would be pleased," said Silvia. "After all, you gave her the idea!"

"You don't believe that, Silvia. I knew she was very fond of George, and I didn't think she had a true religious vocation, but I never suggested an elopement—"

"Oh yes, you did. Have you forgotten that night we met in the Cathedral?"

"When I told *you*—"

"Exactly," said Silvia with a harsh little laugh. "Pilár carried out your plan to the letter. George Halkett hired post horses at Cuernavaca. She slipped away to meet him and they were married in Santa Prisca church at Taxco. Then they posted on to Acapulco and took ship for the United States. Papa got to Acapulco nearly two days too late to stop them."

"I hadn't heard a word of it," said Sally. "I'm sure no one with the Empress knows, because it would be talked about. Oh, Silvia, I can't help being very glad!"

"Remember, no one *must* know—at least for the present. Don Felipe will be furious with me when he finds out. But nothing must upset him while the Empress is our guest. Promise me, Sally, not to mention it?"

"You know you can trust me, Silvia."

"You won't even tell—your brother?"

"No."

Silvia's lovely violet eyes held Sally's at last. The bare arms caught her in a sudden, close embrace.

"Sally, is Don Andrés going all the way to Europe with the Empress?"

"Only to Vera Cruz."

"To Vera Cruz—I see."

They were both whispering. But Silvia heard the faint tap and the gentle opening of the door behind them, and went on in a slightly raised voice,

"You're shivering, you silly girl. Did you get wet, standing about waiting for all the bows and curtsies to be over? Make them light the fire before you dress . . . Yes, Tía Beata, what is it?"

The dueña, whom Sally had last seen in the background as Silvia was decked for her wedding, advanced with her quiet insinuating step.

"I beg Doña Sarita's pardon for entering her room," she said. "The señor Marqués is asking for the Marquesa's presence."

"Good evening, señorita," said Sally coldly. "I hardly expected to see *you* in Puebla!"

"The family was good enough to spare me for a time," said the dueña smoothly. "Doña Vera thought our bride should have someone from her home beside her. At any rate while she remains in Mexico."

BY MIDNIGHT all the lights were extinguished on the ground floor of the Prefect's residence. Andrew Lorimer had spent more than an hour, after the gentlemen left the smoking room, in the company of Captain Léonce Detroyat, the agreeable French officer who had been naval attaché at Mexico and was eager to explain his reasons for going home for good; but even Captain Detroyat's eloquence ran dry in face of the early start and hard day's traveling ahead of them. Andrew escaped at last to his room and his thoughts of Silvia.

Silvia. He had supposed—had hoped—that they would never meet again. Now they had met, if the touch of his lips to a gloved hand and a perfunctory murmur could be called a meeting. And nobody was a penny the worse, least of all the husband who stood silent and attentive at her elbow, the lawful possessor of her youth and beauty.

The only consequence was that which affected Andrew Lorimer: the knowledge that weeks of self-discipline, of willing himself to forget the grace of Silvia Mora had all been in vain. Tonight, they were under the same roof. Somewhere in this rambling house she was lying in her husband's arms.

For nearly an hour, with his red head down on his clenched hands, Andrew wrestled with dreadful fantasies of lust and death. He had drunk wine at table, and brandy later, but the liquor gave him no hope of sleep: he was still awake, in a chair by the dead fire, when he heard the whisper of Carlóta's maid:

"Herr Doktor! Bitte, Herr Doktor!"

He flung the door open on Mathilde Döblinger. She had not undressed, although her cap was crooked and her lace apron awry as if she had been asleep in her chair. Her English, never good, had deserted her. She could only point and whisper.

"Die Kaiserin!"

The Empress was walking in her sleep. Rounding a corner of the dimly lighted landing, Andrew saw her tall figure, with black hair streaming unbound over a white lace shawl, going slowly and uncertainly downstairs.

He pictured her falling headlong down those marble stairs to the stone flags of the patio. Then he was after her, quick and quiet in his stocking soles, thankful that he had taken his shoes off when he removed his dress coat on coming upstairs after dinner. Carlóta walked on steadily. He went down each step by her side, careful not to touch or jar her, until they reached a wide turn of the stair, set out with pots of arum lilies. Then he took her hand gently, tucked it through his arm and said in the softest tone he could produce,

"Will you come back to your room now, Madame?"

She started back, half awake, all terrified.

"Where am I?"

"You are with your doctor, and you are *absolutely safe*."

The reassurance in the familiar voice reached the dark corners of Carlóta's mind. Before her, supporting her, was the familiar image: Dr. Lorimer in his white shirt (her hand was resting on the cool starched cuff) with his straight blue gaze and broad dependable shoulders—she sighed with pleasure. She said, uncertainly:

"Are we at a ball?"

"The flowers look like it, don't they?" he agreed. "But the band isn't playing any more, Madame. May I escort you to your room?"

Gravely, like two partners leaving a ballroom floor, they paced upstairs. Somewhere, Andrew thought he heard a door creak. But when they reached the landing all was silent, all doors fast, except where Mathilde had left Carlóta's door open to guide him back. The maid had put her dress straight, and poked the fire to a comforting blaze. She had even set a little pot of milk to heat on the charcoal stove which was part of Carlóta's traveling equipment. But Andrew made a negative sign and whispered:

"Get my bag."

In the room beyond, the bed had been freshly made up. The sheets and pillows were smooth and inviting. Carlóta, without any bidding, slipped off her shawl and lay down with a long sigh.

"I have had dreadful dreams," she said.

"Hush, Your Majesty; don't talk now; you shall tell me all about it in the morning."

"But I must tell you now!" She raised herself upon one elbow. "I dreamed that Maximilian was the captain of a posse of assassins—and I the captainess!"

The strange words, strangely uttered, arrested him. He brought a fine linen towel, dipped in cold water, and wiped the sweat from her forehead and throat before she spoke again:

"I dreamed of two hands, crossed upon a dead man's breast. They were beautiful hands—hands that *spoke* . . . Doctor, were they yours?"

"My hands are touching your forehead now, alive and warm. And you are going to drink something to please me, and go back to sleep . . . very quietly . . . aren't you?"

"If I sleep, shall I dream again of the three headless men?"

Mathilde had laid his bag on a convenient table, with the water, the spoon, the glass. He mixed a very small dose of the mild sedative with which he had calmed Carlóta's hysterical outbursts in the past. With her history of ether addiction he had never thought it wise to give her a strong narcotic.

"Three headless men . . . lying in the sun . . . upon a hillside," she said again.

"It was only a dream, Your Majesty. Drink this now, and sleep."

He raised her on her pillows. Carlóta turned to him trustfully, and drank from the glass he held to her lips.

"Good night, Max," she said.

Andrew looked sharply round for Mathilde Döblinger. But the discreet maid was no longer at her place beside the bed. She was murmuring to someone in the other room.

Andrew snuffed out the bedside candles and crossed on his stockinged feet to the half-open door.

"Is that Señora de Guadalupe?" he said in a low tone. His first thought was that the incident on the staircase had been seen by one of the guards, who had taken it upon himself to rouse the mistress of the house.

"It is the Marquesa de Vega, sir," said Mathilde without expression.

"Go and sit by your mistress." He managed to say it coolly. He went into the sitting room to Silvia.

He had been so used to seeing her in her girlish finery, with her ringlets falling round her lovely face, that it was almost jarring to see her in traveling clothes. Silvia wore a straight cloak of fawn-colored gaberdine, a little hat with a veil of the same color rolled tightly round the brim, and carried her gloves and reticule in one hand. She asked:

"Is the Empress ill?"

"Madam," he said, "you ought not to be here."

"I saw you on the staircase. She was walking in her sleep, wasn't she?"

"Yes. But say nothing of it to anyone. She had a disturbing day, and will be well tomorrow. Are you setting out so early—or so late?"

"I must, if you are all to be received becomingly at the Quinta Vega in the afternoon."

"I had much rather not accept Don Felipe's hospitality, marquesa."

"There is a good inn at La Fortaleza," she said in tones as indifferent as his own. "But ought you to be at half a mile's distance from Her Majesty? She may walk in her sleep again."

The force of her argument, and the falseness of his situation, face to face with Don Felipe's wife in the sleeping house, kept Andrew silent.

"Is she in love with you?"

"Silvia!"

"I saw her through the door just now—with your arm around her . . ."

"She is in love with her husband. And I—God help me!—I'm in love with you."

The rigid figure in the formal traveling dress relaxed, was in his arms, was taking his kisses with a passion, a tortured erotic awareness which Silvia Mora had never known. And the face lifted to his was the Siren's face, avid and terrible.

"Your husband, Silvia—"

"He is *not* my husband! He is not capable of being any woman's husband! Now—do you understand?"

CARLÓTA'S PROCESSION of outriders and carriages followed by little more than five hours the early start made by the Marqués and Marquesa de Vega. Down from the high altitude of Puebla to the spa of Tehuacán, up the pass through cactus scrub to Acultzingo, the carriages lumbered to the very summit of the Cordillera; swung with the sickening lurch of ships in a storm down to the lush, steaming valley of the Río Blanco and at last reached Orizaba, a stronghold of Imperialist Mexico.

Three miles north lay La Fortaleza, the township nearest to the Quinta Vega and the first place on their route to be decorated for Carlóta's arrival. Swags of blossom in clashing shades of carmine, orange and blue had been strung from window to window, and children strewed rose petals beneath her wheels. There was even a loyal address from the alcalde of La Fortaleza, which the Empress graciously acknowledged, and a band of musicians with guitars and castanets played her carriage to the entrance gates of the Quinta Vega.

Don Felipe and Silvia, with their household grouped behind them, were waiting there to receive the Empress. The sun was setting behind the Quinta, and in the golden light the low white building, with its four exquisitely proportioned Moorish arches, seemed to shelter in the whiter glory of the Peak of Orizaba. All round the house were noble trees. Behind the red-tiled roof rose palms; in front, a grove of lemons heavy with fruit, and lining the broad avenue to the gate more palm trees, in the scaly trunks of which nests of moss and earth had been inserted to hold white and purple orchids in every stage from bud to exquisite flower. A carpet of golden blossoms covered the ground beneath the trees.

"My dear Don Felipe, what a picture!" they heard the Empress say, and her host reply, all gratified politeness.

"Esta es su casa, Doña Carlóta."

"My house!" she said charmingly. "None of my houses has such trees, or such lawns, or such a setting! Your ancestors' connoisseurship was at least equal to your own, señor!"

She laid her hand on his and let Don Felipe lead her up the avenue, pausing more than once to admire the East India laurel, said to be two hundred years old, the Brazilian erocario, the traveler palm of India; the towering beauty of the Peak as it turned to smoky rose in the sunset light.

"You make me dissatisfied with Chapultepec," Carlóta said as they entered the casa grande. "I'm ashamed to think you ever saw the gardens of La Borda!"

With an exquisite shrug Don Felipe dismissed the falling mangoes and leaking gutters of the Borda.

"I have many more beautiful things to show you, Señora, after we have dined," he said, and bowed low as his wife, with a charming shy grace, led the Empress away. Had Queen Ysabel of Spain honored him with a visit, Don Felipe would have walked backward before her to her rooms; it was not necessary to escort Carlóta himself to her apartments. These had been worthy of the Good Viceroys; he had no fear of their being inadequate for the daughter of an upstart Belgian King.

The main house of the Quinta Vega, and the several little streets of lesser buildings where bachelors and personal domestics were accommodated, were full to overflowing for Carlóta's visit, for guests had been invited to meet her from as far away as Córdoba. Even the splendid dining hall was too small for the hundred and more persons who sat down to dinner, and the tables, as the Empress had predicted, were spread in the conservatory, with its glass roof opened to the sky, and all round the wide stone terrace behind the house. From this terrace steps led to a long pool, fed by fountains and covered with white flowers which glimmered in the light of fairy lamps swung underneath the trees.

"How beautiful! Magnificent!" exclaimed Carlóta, when

her host led her out upon the terrace. "Don Felipe, what magic have your people been working here?"

"They have merely added gardenias to the water, Señora; forty thousand blossoms were cut tonight to make the pool worthy of an empress. I hear that you took pleasure in swimming at La Borda. If, in a little while, you and your ladies would care to swim among the flowers, like Venus surrounded by the Loves and Graces, I can assure you of the strictest privacy. The night is hot and humid, and the water is refreshing—"

But Carlóta declared that no human body should break that fairylike skein of white.

"Forty thousand gardenias; you are extravagant, sir!" she said. "The simple water lily is all we can boast of at La Borda. But we are to have nightingales there before long—there and at Chapultepec. The Emperor has grown weary of the mocking-birds. He has sent to Austria for a thousand nightingales to sing the wonderful natural melodies he remembers from his youth."

Don Felipe looked at the Empress shrewdly. To his intricate Spanish mind there was a double meaning in her words.

"A charming idea, and one well worthy of Don Maximiliano," he said. "But for the present—if the gardenia pool does not attract you, may I beg your favor for a short performance of some local songs and dances?"

"May it be prefaced by your bride's singing of 'La Paloma'?" asked Carlóta.

"The Marquesa de Vega does not perform in public," Señora," said Silvia's husband. "But we have found a gipsy singer who will please you, I believe."

. . . Gipsy singer, guitarists, acrobats and clown followed one another across the small wooden platform erected on the terrace, and Sally, in the back row of the spectators, felt her head beginning to grow heavy. They were near the border of the Hot Country, and the scent from the gardenia pool was over-powering in its sweetness. She reminded herself that she was for the time being a member of the Court, and must imitate Carlóta's courteous attention to what was after all a hackneyed entertainment; but the drowsiness, after three hard days of travel, was hard to fight. Then Sally was jerked back to wakefulness as a single dancer appeared upon the stage; and once again, in the dim glow from the fairy lamps, she saw the flaunting crimson headdress and the sensuous olive-skinned face of the girl who had been Pierre Franchet's mistress.

La Malinche—if it *was* Malinche—glowed in her proper setting like a dusky jewel. Her green and red dress became the focal point of all the soft hues of orchid and camellia with which the little platform had been decked. Dark red of bougainvillea, salmon-pink of the climbing geraniums—all the dissonances of color that spelt *Mexico* were resolved by the clear scarlets of the China Poblana dress. A deep curtsy to the Empress, and then, at a chord from the guitars, the dancer stamped her satin slippers and broke into the fandango.

She might have been dancing the tragedy of Mexico. For Malinche's Spanish blood so far dominated the Indian in her veins that even in this incomparably Mexican setting she was driving herself to dance like a Spaniard to the rhythms of Spain. It was not a tempo which suited her or her musicians, and yet she danced well—so well that it was easy to imagine how much better she would dance the jarabe, barefoot, by the light of a village fire. Sally felt a fierce stab of jealousy of the wild girl Pierre Franchet had first seen dancing in the ruins of Puebla.

A handsome boy in a charro suit dramatized by soutache braid of salmon-pink and silver leaped up on the platform to join Malinche in her second number. They danced the Bottle Dance: entirely Mexican, and provocative in each high kick of the man's strong, muscled leg and the woman's slim bare brown one. *"Olé! Olé!"* Applause began to ring across the gardens. The green glass bottle was intact as the ritual dance entered its final movement, engrossing the dancers in each other. The male dancer leaped to the ground as the cachuca whirled to its frenzied end.

"What a magnificent animal! Who is she?" A man stand-

ing behind Sally's table put the question, hardly troubling to
lower his voice.

"They call her Juanita, Señor Conde. They say she took
Córdoba by storm last week."

"I can well believe it."

Sally went indoors with the crowd. She was reasonably sure
that the gipsy dancer known as Juanita was the Marina Perez
of Mexico and of a recent court-martial at Puebla, but how to
prove it? I'd know those beads and that red ribbon anywhere
in the world, she told herself. If Andrew recognized her too,
we ought to tell the captain of the guard. But Andrew was nowhere to be seen, and as the last hour of the reception passed
with offerings of champagne and toasts to the Empress' mission,
some of Sally's conviction ebbed away. She shrank from putting
herself forward in the Quinta Vega, or doing anything which
might embarrass Silvia. All she could do—and she resolved to
do it—was to make certain by her own presence that the Empress
was in no danger from the gipsy band.

Andrew had watched the performance from a point even
further from the terrace than his sister's, and without identifying
any member of the company. He had been aware only of the
intense sexuality of the Bottle Dance, as if the leaping, spinning
figures had turned to flame the smoldering fire which Silvia had
kindled overnight. All day long he had lived in the memory of
her arms. All day, he had heard in his ears the frantic words
which had told him the wretched story of Don Felipe's impotence
and the perversions and cruelties with which the old man had
kindled and left unsatisfied the instincts of his bride. Not for a
fortune would Andrew have broken bread or tasted wine at that
man's table. He had absented himself from the dinner, only to
be lured out by the sound of music, and the desire to look again
on Silvia's beloved face. To be there in case—he hardly dared
to think it—there might be one more opportunity to be alone
with her.

He went back to his room. The white bachelor wing, draped
in climbing roses, was quite deserted: Captain Detroyat and all

the other young men who had only politics on their minds were
still inside the casa grande. He was sitting in the light of a single
candle when an Indian servant in a white livery summoned him
to Carlóta's rooms.

"The young lady asks your grace to hurry—"

"What young lady, can you say?"

"The North American señorita, please your grace—"

Sally. He put his hospital knapsack unobtrusively in his tail
pocket, and followed the man through the courts and pathways
of the vast hacienda. A few people were still walking about, and
guests departing, but the lamps had been put out round the pool,
and in the semidarkness he was hardly aware of the Tía Beata
in her black robe until she halted him with a light touch on the
arm.

"Don Andrés, I was coming to look for you—"

"Señorita!"

"The señora marquesa wished to be sure that you found
your room comfortable."

"The marquesa is too kind to concern herself with me." His
voice was not as even as he could have wished.

"I hope you have had an opportunity of visiting the pool,
señor. The display of gardenias is much admired."

"Is it?" There had been a woman like this once, at Richmond, who had played the part of a go-between in an intrigue
of his first year with the army. But at Richmond he had never
felt this choking, stifling excitement—

"You advise me to look at the gardenias, señorita? At
what time would you suggest? Night . . . or early morning?"

"Eleven o'clock might be a suitable time, señor."

There were people coming in their direction. Andrew bowed
and left her.

There was a sentry posted, he noted with some surprise, at
the door of the principal guest rooms of the Quinta Vega. His
sister, in her white evening dress, was earnestly talking to the
man.

"What's the matter, Sally? Where is Señora del Barrio?"

"I don't know. Gone to bed, I think. The Empress is very restless, Andy. I thought you ought to—"

"Ought to what?"

"I don't know," the girl repeated. They were alone in Carlóta's sitting room, which was filled with flowers. "Sit with her, talk to her for a while . . . You know best how to soothe her."

"Has she been asleep? Dreaming?"

"Oh, no; Mathilde has only just undressed her. She was quite cheerful as we came upstairs; it was when we came in here that she grew distressed. She said her enemies had put their flowers in this room to torment her . . ."

"What flowers, for God's sake?"

"The violets, of course. The Bonaparte violets."

"What infernal nonsense will she think of next?" Andrew checked the impatient words on his lips. Headless men last night, and now a silly fantasy about a flower! "I'd better see her," he briefly said.

"Andrew." Sally barred the way to the inner room. She looked very young and defenseless in the candlelight. "You do think she's *all right,* don't you?"

There was a world of meaning in the two simple words. Sally's brother chose to ignore it. The gilt clock under its glass dome said half past ten; it was time to bring Carlóta's nonsense to an end.

"Another bad night, Madame?" he said as he bent over the restless woman. "Hm—we can't have that, you know! Not with a start at four o'clock ahead of us!"

He opened the little knapsack and took out his endermic syringe.

"Please talk to me," the Empress begged. "Please tell me who *you* think put the violets in my room—"

"The servants, Madame, who else would it be?" It was the calm, reasonable voice she loved. "Violets grow like grass here, as you know very well. But I'll tell you what I'll do. I'll have them take the violets away. I'll get them to bring you some roses, some—"

"Bourbon lilies," prompted Sally. She was watching him charge the syringe.

"Bourbon lilies, that's it. Now this will scratch you for a minute, and then, I promise, you'll have five hours good sound sleep. There, that didn't hurt, did it? Sleep well, Your Majesty. No dreams tonight!"

He put the morphine and the syringe back in place. He nodded to Sally and the maid, and left the room. And all the way through the darkening house, through the now deserted garden, he saw the surprise, the disbelief, hardening to contempt in Sally's eyes.

It was the least possible dosage, he defended himself in thought. It was the only way to give her the sleep she needs so much. It must be two months since she touched a drug of any sort.

—This one time can't do her any harm.

—She might have gone walking in her sleep, or roused the house, without it.

—I am a qualified physician, and what I have done was justifiable—

—I am a man in love, who *will not* risk interruption for the next hour by a . . . fanciful woman—

It was quite dark at the far end of the pool. He could just see the outline of a little summerhouse, or bathhouse—impossible to tell which—beneath the heavily fruited orange trees. It was hotter than in the first part of the night.

The orange groves, and the coffee plantations beyond, were absolutely still. At the Quinta Vega there were none of the friendly sounds of the little Indian village round Las Flores, and he was too far from the house to hear the sentries' tread. He heard only the faint lapping of the water as it sucked against the stonework where he stood.

He stooped, and gathered one of the forty thousand gardenias which the prodigality of Don Felipe had thrown away to give an empress pleasure. He could see the pale color in the palm of his hand, to which the warm petals seemed to cling. The scent was the same which, since his boyhood, had always been associated in his mind with village funerals.

When Silvia came upon him out of the darkness he was drying his wet hands on his handkerchief. They met, they clung together in a frenzy which the long day had whipped to the highest point of anticipation. The door of the bathhouse, where she had waited for him, stood open for them both. But Andrew took her beside the gardenia pool, on the soft turf beneath the orange trees, assuaging his desire and healing Silvia's abused body, until her faint sobs of gratitude echoed each other like the murmur of a mourning dove.

Chapter Sixteen

LA NARANJADA

ON THE HOT August morning when the Empress of
Mexico arrived in France, the war between Prussia and Austria
was already over. The decisive battle, at Sadowa near Königgrätz, had actually been fought on the third of July, three days
before Maximilian knew that his brother had gone to war, and
the victorious Prussians had already clinched their triumph by
a savage treaty of peace.

They told Carlóta the news at St. Nazaire as soon as she
stepped ashore, in a room set aside for her at the Customs House.
It had been an office an hour before her arrival, and although a
sofa and some flimsy gilt chairs had been brought in from a
quayside restaurant, the clerks' desks and high stools were still
standing round the walls. In this setting Señor Almonte, the
Mexican Ambassador, who had come from Paris to receive her,
broke as gently as he could the further news that the Emperor
of the French was ailing—regretted he could not receive her at
his palace of the Tuileries—had not sent a single official to bid
the Empress of Mexico welcome to France.

It was only two years and four months since Almonte and
his friends had gone to Miramar with a Crown for Maximilian
and a gift of opals from Querétaro for his wife. It was to Miramar
that he advised her to withdraw now—"to your own beautiful
home, Señora"—until by diplomatic means some pressure could
be brought to bear upon Napoleon III.

Sally, alone of the ladies in her suite, was with Carlóta

when this advice was given. She saw the Empress shiver as she said:

"I won't go back to the hermitage we left . . . with such high hopes. I won't go into my brother-in-law's dominions, especially at a time like this. If I have understood correctly, gentlemen, there may be revolution any day in Hungary."

"Then go to Brussels, Madame," urged Count Bombelles. "What more appropriate than to make a short stay at your brother's Court? Then we, your servants, can arrange a meeting with the French Emperor in a week, say, or two weeks from now."

"I will not go to Belgium!" said Carlóta violently. "Go back to Laeken, and listen to Leopold's jeers? He will be delighted to know that Eugénie has refused to receive me—as delighted as he is to think the Austrians have been defeated, and Bismarck in Vienna dictating the terms of peace. Leopold is against me, I tell you! He is jealous, he always has been jealous of me and of Maximilian. They are all against me; every one; everywhere I turn, I see my enemies!" She looked up at Sally. "You know we are not welcome at the Tuileries, do you not?"

"I know the Emperor Napoleon has been taken ill, Madame, and is at St. Cloud," said Sally uncertainly.

Carlóta looked at the single sheet of paper in her hand.

" 'My husband's illness . . . impossible to receive you in audience . . . regret you have made such a long journey in vain . . .' " She skimmed again through the letter of rejection from the Empress of the French. "Oh! When I remember how we were petted and fêted on our last visit to Paris—how they urged us both to go to Mexico—" Her voice caught on a sob of anger.

"He isn't dying, is he?" said Sally bluntly.

"Dying? Napoleon? Of course not. Why?" Carlóta looked directly at the American girl. "Oh—I see! You think I should go straight to Paris, and insist on seeing him?"

"Affairs of state are quite outside Miss Lorimer's capacity to advise," said the Mexican Ambassador.

"I advise nothing," said Sally, stung. "I—we can't stay here, that's obvious; I only thought of Paris because the Emperor Maximilian expects Her Majesty to be there. And in a very few days—as we have said so often—the transatlantic cable will be working. A message will go to Mexico in a day instead of three weeks, and a reply come back in another day. Ought not Doña Carlóta to keep in the closest touch with Mexico?"

"The cable!" sighed Carlóta. "Poor Matthew Maury's dream. How wrong I was to let them force his dismissal . . . but I was ill then, and weak—" She stood up. "I shall not be weak now. I shall go to Paris and confront those treacherous Bonapartes, whether they will or no. Bombelles! Tell Captain Detroyat to arrange for carriages, to take us to the train at Nantes. And telegraph to the Quai d'Orsay that I expect to be received with the proper honors when I arrive in Paris tonight."

It was one of the moments when in spite of her weariness and pallor Carlóta looked most truly royal, and the Austrian, without further protest, bowed and left the room. Sally quietly picked up Carlóta's shawl and gloves, and a reticule stuffed with papers which had never left her on the trip.

"Mathilde should be doing that," said Carlóta. "Where is Mathilde?"

"I will send her to you at once, Madame. I know exactly where she is."

"Crying in her cabin over the Austrian defeat, no doubt."

"She had a brother in an artillery regiment. She thinks it very likely he was at the front."

"I had a brother-in-law," said Carlóta with a curious note of satisfaction in her voice. "He rode off the field of Sadowa, they tell me, along with his defeated soldiers—the great Austrian army defeated in a few summer weeks—whereas in Mexico we have fought for years with nothing but half-trained levies and wretched mercenaries. Oh! How I would have liked to see the Emperor Franz Josef's face when he rode into Königgrätz!"

"They say the losses on both sides were atrocious, Madame."

"Oh yes, the losses; that was inevitable." Carlóta took Sally's arm, and moved towards the door. "I hope the carriages are ready. I want to get away from this horrible dock. This room —I never saw such a room. I shall dream about it for nights to come: the place where I was told of the Austrian defeat." She paused and Sally halted with her, trying to study Carlóta's face. The Empress had lowered her veil, but the gleam of the strange green eyes could still be seen beneath her rapidly fluttering lids. "News of a defeat, as soon as I set foot in Europe. Do you know that on the day we landed in Mexico we were told of your General Grant's victory in the Wilderness, which ended our dream of an America controlled by the South, and favorable to our cause? Do you think it is an evil omen, to hear now of the defeat of Austria?"

"He was not 'our' General Grant, Madame," said Sally quietly. "My brother was engaged, as you may remember, on the losing side. But neither he nor I believes in evil omens."

Sally came near it, though, at the end of the long day in the train, when in spite of the telegraphed instructions not a single representative of the French Emperor was present at the Gare Montparnasse. A repetition of the embarrassing scene of St. Nazaire was only avoided by the promptitude of Captain Detroyat, who once again brought up a convoy of vehicles to take the whole party to the Grand Hotel. And there, to turn the tragedies of the day into farce, they found the missing diplomats, who had gone in error to the Gare d'Orleans and realized their mistake in time to reach the hotel ahead of the Empress and her suite.

It was as good as a play to the American tourists sitting in the handsome lobby of the new hotel. To hear the cries, and the apologies—best of all to see the Empress of Mexico in all her fatigue and dishevelment sailing through the newcomers without a flicker of recognition—was well worth the considerable sum they had paid for their night's lodging. Carlóta went up the grand staircase so quickly that the hotel manager had hardly time to slip ahead of her, carrying the lighted candelabra with

which he meant to precede her to the royal suite. Her Ladies
scurried at her heels. Her Chamberlain, del Valle, was only just
in time to follow her, at the prescribed distance, into a salon
where soft lights fell on satin and damask and three marble-
topped consoles bore ornate vases filled with the Bourbon
fleurs-de-lis and dark red roses of Provence.

"I trust Her Majesty will find everything to her satisfaction—"

"I am sure of it," Carlóta cut the obsequious manager
short. "—Señor del Valle, you may tell the French delegation that
they come too late to be received, and must wait upon me at
eight o'clock tomorrow morning. Ladies, I shall require nothing more tonight."

Within minutes of this summary dismissal, a maid and a
valet de chambre had installed Sally and her baggage in a bedroom decorated in pink toile de Jouy, on which two little
shepherdesses guarded, in dainty repetition, a stylized flock of
sheep. And Sally was alone again, as on the first night at Vera
Cruz: free at last to think of Pierre Franchet.

He seemed to be beside her immediately, in the too-bright,
scented room. The fair head and the expressive brown face, the
shabby uniform, the pipe-clay and the polish, came before her
eyes as vividly as if the Légionnaire stood there by the window,
looking down into the Paris street as she had seen him look down
at the Plazuelita.

The louvred shutters, gray-painted, opened easily, and Sally
leaned out. On their drive from the Gare Montparnasse she had
been too disturbed by the tension and argument among the Mexicans to catch more than glimpses of Paris. By a broad river,
a majestic square, a succession of lighted boulevards they had
come to what, she guessed, was the center of entertainment and
fashion in the great city.

Although it was the middle of August, there was no summer slackening in the tempo of that city's life. Rich, avid for
pleasure, reckless and proud, Paris had abandoned herself to
the gaieties of the night. A brilliant restaurant, a café with chairs

set to the very edge of the pavement, a gay little box of a theater, were all attracting crowds of patrons under Sally's eyes. To her nostrils rose the heady scent of Paris, compounded of the perfumes worn by many women, fresh-ground coffee, horse manure, summer dust on the plane trees, spilt wine and the rough caporal which the troopers smoked at Río Frío. Oh, how far away now was Río Frío, how palely the curbside oil lamps of Mexico would shine beneath the endless gas globes of the Paris boulevards!

And this was the city Pierre had known, for a few days only out of one Frenchman's life. The fatal days when the Army of Italy, after its brief and victorious campaign, had paraded through Paris under a rain of flowers, to a storm of cheering, towards the medals and the festivities which persuaded an emotional boy, not long escaped from the shadow of the guillotine, that the soldier's was the path to glory. There was no cheering in those streets tonight. The endless roll of carriage wheels over wood blocks, the shouts of newsboys, the voices of the boulevardiers, brought the faux-bourdon of Paris to ears attuned to the bells of Mexico.

There was a gentle tap at the bedroom door.

"Excuse me, mademoiselle, I have brought a little supper."

An elderly waiter, with gray muttonchop whiskers, set out the dainty meal. Jellied eggs *au porto,* a bowl of fresh raspberries, a crisp roll, and butter in a nest of parsley.

"It looks delicious," Sally said.

"Her Imperial Majesty ordered it especially for the young lady. There are also letters for mademoiselle. Will the lady take some wine?"

"No, thank you."

"White wine with seltzer water is refreshing."

"Very well then," said Sally, to get rid of the man. "But fill the glass right up with seltzer, please." She was eager to read her letters, both addressed to Miss Lorimer at the Palace of the Tuileries—"*Tuileries*" stroked out and "*Grand Hotel*" substituted in a clerkly hand.

So the Empress Eugénie, who had failed to send any greeting to Carlóta, had given her servants precise instructions on forwarding mail!

With a frown, Sally opened the letter with a French stamp, which was written in a lady's pointed hand. It contained a few chilly, polite lines from her kinsman's wife in which Lady Laura Fraser "much regretted" that the family was on holiday at Houlgate during the month of August. They hoped to make Miss Lorimer's acquaintance in September, if she were still in Paris.

Sally laid the little note aside. Unlike Andrew she expected nothing from their relations with Lord S., and the second letter, postmarked in Vienna seven days earlier, was the one which interested her.

My dear Madam [she read]

Today I received from your brother the surprising news that you are about to visit Europe, in circumstances which I cannot but view with much anxiety. My first impulse was to leave for Paris, but my position in regard to a certain lady is delicate, and I have thought it better to write to her brother (the Count of F——) and urge him to join her without delay. Should you need my help in any way, pray summon me by telegraph. All the medical men in Vienna have been recruited to the military hospitals since the disaster of Königgrätz, but I can and will leave the city, if required, to pay the debt I owe to my kind nurse of Río Frío. I shall not prolong this letter, as I must write to Dr. Lorimer before the post goes, but beg you to believe me,

With the deepest respect,
Julius Herzog, M.D.

The frown deepened on Sally's forehead as she read this letter a second time. It echoed, in its guarded way, so exactly what Pierre had said more vehemently about her journey with the Empress, that it struck a jarring note against the evidence of Carlóta's kind thought for her. The poor distracted Empress, in her hour of rejection, wanting "nothing more" for herself that night, had considerately remembered that the healthy appetite of nineteen might hardly have been satisfied by the scanty dinner basket provided on the train. She had ordered the little supper specially. She could be, when she remembered, very kind. And yet the wine and soda brought no refreshment to Sally Lorimer.

All day, as the train carried them deeper into Pierre's native land, a feeling of resentment had been gnawing in Sally's heart. Carlóta's dreadful callousness to the killed and wounded of the Austrian defeat was only less shocking than the words she had used for the French troops fighting in her own cause. *The wretched mercenaries*—that was what she called the soldiers to whom her husband owed his crown.

There might be fighting at that very hour in Mexico. The wretched mercenaries and the levies they had trained might be giving their lives for Carlóta in a pitched battle as terrible as the field of Königgrätz. Sally got up from the supper table. In the pretty room where three Sallys were reflected in as many plate glass mirrors, under the bright light of a gaselier with pink glass globes, she felt trapped and helpless. She extinguished the gas and went back to her old place by the window. The noise and traffic of the boulevard were unabated. Presently she slipped to her knees by the window sill, and with tears on the hands pressed tightly to her face, she prayed with all her heart for Pierre. The words came very easily, because so well remembered. For a brother—for a lover—Sally Lorimer had learned to pray from childhood for a man in the firing line.

For FORTY-EIGHT hours all that Sally saw of Paris was the view from the windows of the Grand Hotel. Those of her suite who were capable of working, Carlóta drove without mercy, and the task allotted to Sally was one which had been totally neglected at the Mexican Embassy—the reading and clipping of European press opinion on the prolonged crisis in Mexico. While M. Eloin wrote letters at Carlóta's dictation in one cor-

ner of the salon, Sally worked on the French and English newspapers in another, and Count Bombelles plowed his way through
the German-language press. When Carlóta was not dictating letters, she was rearranging and collating the mass of statistics
about Mexico which she already had at her finger ends. The
Jecker bonds, the Treaty of Miramar. The dwindling port reve-
nues, the silver slump, the sacrifices Maximilian had already
made to equip the Cazadores. She went through it again and
again with the Mexican Ambassador and his aides until her voice
cracked and her pale face was burning. The Bourbon lilies were
carried from the room and the marble consoles were piled high
with papers, newspaper digests, telegrams, financial reports. The
Empress received the French Foreign Minister and M. Randon
from the Ministry of War. She urged on them her three impossible demands. Bazaine to be recalled, and replaced as Supreme
Commander by General Felix Douay. A French subsidy of half
a million francs monthly for the new Mexican levies. A new
French expeditionary force to replace the Line regiments already
evacuated. Each Minister, and several of the leading men of the
Bourse, was received privately by Carlóta in a small room ad-
joining the grand salon, but sometimes those in attendance heard
the voice of the Empress raised in passionate argument, and the
stern negations of the male voices which replied. The Frenchmen,
after all, held the trump card. They could make no promises to
Carlóta without the assent of their Imperial Master—and their
Imperial Master, so far, had refused to see her.

It was not until the third day, when Carlóta was visibly
shattered by hours of overwork and frustration, that the faithful Bombelles prevailed on her to go for a short carriage drive.
She was very unwilling to leave her apartments, though not, as
they all thought, because she was afraid of missing a summons
to Napoleon: it turned out that she was nervous of once again
running the gauntlet of strangers in the hall. While the maids
were dressing her, she whispered to Sally that the lady guests
who watched the passing pageant in the lobby of the Grand Hotel

had stared at herself with especial meaning, because "they were the widows of murdered men."

It was the first sick fancy she had had for many days, and Sally, following nervously to the marble baluster of the mezzanine floor, saw with thanksgiving that Carlóta seemed to have conquered it before starting to walk downstairs on Bombelles' arm, with the Mexican Ladies at her back. She looked ill, but calm and dignified, and on this hot afternoon there were, after all, few guests idling in the lobby to nudge and stare.

A group of ladies, who had just entered, seemed to be engaging the whole attention of the hotel staff. The obsequious manager was bending almost double; behind him a solid wall of reception clerks and chasseurs half hid the new arrivals from Sally's sight. Then a servant indicated Carlóta on the staircase, the living wall parted, and a tall woman moved gracefully forward alone. Sally had no need to hear a gasp of recognition from Eloin, who had come out on the landing by her side. She knew that lady's fabled face from a hundred prints and drawings: they were looking, at last, at Napoleon's messenger—Eugénie, Empress of the French.

Carlóta stood riveted, clutching Bombelles' sleeve; then with her head high she went down the last steps to meet the woman who, more than any other human being, was responsible for her presence in Mexico; and in the absolute quiet of the hall even the watchers above could hear her say, in the iciest greeting known to protocol,

"Madame and my good Sister . . . it is strange to meet you thus . . . on a public staircase, in a public inn!"

"Madame and my dear Sister," said Eugénie sweetly, "it is a happiness to meet you anywhere; I regret our meeting has been so long delayed."

There were little curtsies. There was the approach of the fragrant cheek to the faded, a murmur in a lower tone, and more curtsies as the ladies in attendance were presented. Then Sally, drawing aside among the potted palms of the mezzanine landing, saw the two Empresses return upstairs together.

Carlóta plodded, head bent and lips close set: Eugénie seemed to float. In the eight years since she appeared to Pierre Franchet in all the triumph of her happiness and her new motherhood, her loveliness had matured, not dimmed, and with beauty's self Eugénie wore like a mantle the assurance of her beauty. Her draped blue-green walking dress flowed behind her like a wave of the Mediterranean seas she loved. A tiny hat, with a drooping ostrich feather of the same color, was set on her chestnut hair. Her perfect profile, showing lips curved by the tenderest sympathy and interest, was turned towards the sullen, exhausted face of the Empress of Mexico. Sally could hear her say as they went towards Carlóta's apartments,

". . . do *so* apologize for any seeming lack of attention! But for several days now I have been positively *tied* to my husband's sickroom . . ."

They paused at the door of the royal suite.

"Enter, madame," said the Empress Carlóta. "As we say in Mexico, *esta es su casa,* this is your house. I am sorry I cannot welcome you to Chapultepec."

NAPOLEON III was prepared to give an audience to the Empress of Mexico. This was the message which Eugénie came to bring, and which was repeated in every Paris newspaper on the following morning. Most of the papers of such mild liberal tendencies as were permitted under the régime of Napoleon III added editorial comment warning Carlóta to expect no concessions from the Emperor. Too many Frenchmen, said the newspapers, had already died in vain for Mexico.

"I dread this day more than any other of my life," said Señora del Barrio emotionally to Sally. "I dread it for *her;* I dread it for ourselves. Those ladies yesterday paralyzed me. I forgot all the French I ever knew, and if Doña Eugenia had not most graciously addressed us in Castilian, Señora Almonte and I would have been as much help to dear Doña Carlóta as a couple of kitchen maids. She knew it too, she revealed it later, when she told us we were to *talk more* when we went to St. Cloud. Talk more! What is there to say, but that our hearts are breaking for news of Mexico, where our sons and nephews are fighting for our lives? Will that be a popular topic in the salons of St. Cloud?"

"If only Her Majesty would allow Frau Kuhacsevich to go instead of me!" said Sally.

"*Madre de Dios,* Doña Sarita! Don't oppose her wishes to-day of all days! Señora Almonte and I depend upon you, *querida*—for at least you understand what they are saying! You couldn't, I suppose, come to the milliner's with me? It's such a responsibility to buy a hat for Doña Carlóta! We are all to wear hats, did you realize that? And the poor Empress looks so very well in a mantilla!"

She looked far from well in the broad-brimmed white hat of Doña Manuela's wild selection, when they set out from the Grand Hotel at two o'clock that afternoon. To Sally's eyes it looked uncomfortably like a sombrero, but then Sally had been studying the Parisiennes as they passed beneath her window, and knew already that what was high fashion in Mexico would appear comical at the Court of Napoleon and Eugénie. Carlóta looked out at the boulevards with indifferent eyes, rousing herself only to bow mechanically when once or twice some bystander raised a cheer for the Imperial carriage and the Sovereign's Escort which Napoleon had sent to bring her in state to St. Cloud.

The Empress Eugénie was waiting to greet them in a salon where ten or a dozen of her Ladies and maids of honor were assembled to sweep their accomplished curtsies to Carlóta, and surround her three attendants with pretty, stylized attentions. For this solemn meeting Eugénie had put on black—the black of a clouded pearl, cut by Worth into the narrower skirt and draped back which was the advance guard of a new fashion. It made Carlóta's wide crinoline and deep mourning look like bulky widow's weeds. Her violet eyes rested compassionately on Carlóta's hat.

Carlóta knew, as soon as the Emperor of the French rose from his padded armchair to greet her, that his illness, at least, was no diplomatic fiction. It was plainly written in the clay-colored face, lined with pain, and the awkward movements of the man. Since their last meeting, two and a half years before, his mustachios and imperial had turned white.

Eugénie, with fluent gestures, installed Carlóta in an arm-chair opposite Napoleon's, and sat down on a broad stool at her husband's side.

"I very much regret, Madame," the Emperor began suavely, "that circumstances have prevented me from receiving you sooner, or more suitably. You gave me, however, so little warn-ing of your visit that if ill-health had not kept me in the neighbor-hood of Paris, you would have found me absent when you reached the capital. This is the first year since I ascended the throne that I have not attended the August maneuvers at the Châlons camp."

Carlóta's grip tightened nervously on her reticule, and the documents it contained crackled slightly. Painfully direct herself, she was not accustomed to an oblique insult, clothed in polite words. She answered sharply,

"What! Would the French Army maneuvers have meant more to Your Majesty than the fate of Mexico?"

"Nothing means more to me than the French Army, Mad-ame. And the fate of Mexico, alas, is already sealed."

Pat on her cue: "Alas, yes!" sighed Eugénie.

"Your Majesty mistakes yourself for your uncle," flashed Carlóta. " 'The man of destiny'! And yet you may find that the fate of Mexico does not depend on you."

"I think it depends on Juarez," said the Emperor, with a half-smile.

"Really, Madame," said Eugénie plaintively, "if you truly believe that the future of Mexico does not depend upon my hus-band, then I confess I do *not* understand the claims, I may say the appeals, with which you have bombarded us for six months past, nor this—this forcing yourself upon him when his physicians have forbidden all other visitors."

Carlóta swallowed. Already, in their first exchanges, to have let her temper master her!

"Our appeals for help are surely justified," she began more calmly. "Maximilian and I went to Mexico as your protégés. You urged us to accept the Crown. You promised us troops and money—"

"You still owe the money, and the troops have done more than their share," said Napoleon. "My government and people are sick of the Intervention. They want the men brought home."

"French troops have been fighting in Algeria for thirty years," said Carlóta. "Are you sick of that Intervention too?"

"Algeria is different," said Napoleon shortly. "Algeria *is* French. Besides, the pacification of the Kabyle rebels will be completed in a matter of months. Whereas—" He leaned sideways and whispered something to Eugénie. She rose at once and brought a small dispatch-box from his desk.

"Have you had any news from Mexico since you saw my wife yesterday?" he asked Carlóta.

"How could I, Sire?"

"You are not aware that the transatlantic cable service has been in operation for some hours?"

Carlóta raised her hand to her head. The buzzing in her ears had started again, and Napoleon's corpselike face wavered before her eyes.

"Today?" she said uncertainly. "I lose count of the days—" Then the meaning of his words came through to her, and she gasped, *"You* have had news? Oh! Is my husband well?"

"Very well, apparently." The Emperor's short thick fingers took a folded paper from the box. It carried the first cabled message sent from Mexico to Paris, via Havana and New York —a message from Maximilian to Napoleon III, offering his best wishes for the fifteenth of August, an important day in the Bonaparte calendar.

He read it aloud expressionlessly.

"Very charming, but not very informative, eh?" commented Napoleon. "Marshal Bazaine's dispatch was a good deal more factual. And since the facts are hard and most unpalatable —I think I'll let you read his message for yourself."

Carlóta read the Supreme Commander's cable with an ashen face.

In terse military language, Bazaine announced his utter failure to stem the advance of the Juaristas. He had ordered the evacuation of Monterrey and Saltillo and the ports of Guaymas and Mazatlán. North of Mazatlán the enemy was advancing on Sonora and Sinaloa. Juarez himself was moving down the western arm of the Y formed by the great highway towards Durango. Tampico had fallen, and north of San Luis Potosí, the cause of Maximilian had been completely lost.

There was something in Carlóta's look of anguish which stirred real pity in Eugénie's shallow soul.

"Is there anything I can get for you, *ma pauvre Charlotte?*" she said. "A glass of brandy? Some eau de cologne?"

She was answered with a babble of words. The cabled sheets fell unheeded to the floor. The old reproaches, the old entreaties—for reinforcements, artillery, a naval squadron to patrol the Gulf of Mexico, a new loan—poured unchecked from Carlóta's lips. The two figures before her might have been made of marble. She sprang to her feet and reviled them in a wild torrent of abuse.

"I should have known what you are," she panted, with her disfigured face close to Napoleon's own. "I should have remembered who I am! I have dishonored the blood of the Bourbons in humbling myself before a Bonaparte! I shall tell Maximilian— tell him you have betrayed us, abandoned us and thousands of our loyal subjects—used him in Mexico for your own vile ends. Why should he suffer and struggle more on your behalf? He will abdicate, I tell you—abdicate, and leave the country."

"The very best thing he could do." The Emperor's cold voice cut like a lash across Carlóta's frenzy. "Sit down, Eugénie" (to his wife, who had herself risen in anger). "Madame Carlóta, be good enough to hear me out. Upon my word, there's nothing stupider than a clever woman! And you used to be very clever, especially in the field of finance. Now I doubt if you could add up two and two and make it four. I can't give you more help in Mexico because I can't afford it. I'm facing an explosive situation in Europe and in case you've missed something as plain as the nose on your face, I mean the Prussian victories over Denmark and Austria. I dare not antagonize my government and country. They're sick—I can't repeat it too often—sick of the war in Mexico. Further, except for the Army of Africa, I must concentrate all my troops in Europe. I shall need every unit at present in Mexico if Bismarck's strategy includes a war with France."

Napoleon spoke less to Carlóta than as if he were reviewing a situation in his own mind. Any one of his Ministers would have recognized the mood, supple and evocative, of the aging plotter who had seduced France fifteen years before, and still, by his mastery of words and situation, held her in thrall. What he went on to say was spoken so dreamily, hypnotically, that his wife smiled and bent her lovely head to listen.

"Women are great gamblers, *chère* Madame. They love the game, they love to win. They never have any idea of how to cut their losses. That goes for the cheapest little tramp in a seaside casino, and for the woman in society who enjoys a flutter on the Bourse. It also goes for the Empress of Mexico."

"You insult me, Sire!"

"I *instruct* you, Madame—for your own good. Cut your losses in Mexico, as I shall have to cut mine. You and Max never seem to realize that I am down, and France is down, millions of francs and thousands of lives, on this particular gamble. And I am much too experienced a gambler not to know when to stop throwing good money after bad—"

"You gambled for the throne of France, and won," said Carlóta, with dry lips. "Throw your dice again for the throne of Mexico."

"I lost two throws for France, and spent years in prison after one of them," said the Emperor of the French. "But then I was good for a third try, and I won. Your worthy husband was only good for one try at greatness, and it's time he realized the game is up."

THE WALLS of the palace of St. Cloud were far thicker than those of the Grand Hotel. It was not possible for the ladies in the salon to hear anything of what was being said in the Empress' study, which made it all the more pitiable that Señora del Barrio and Señora Almonte should have taken up such tense, listening attitudes, like two small black spaniels ready to spring at their mistress' command. The Duchesse de Bassano and the Princesse d'Essling, who had already met the Mexicans at the hotel, made courteous attempts at conversation. They were answered only by mumbles, and anguished looks from the soft black eyes. Sally saw that Carlóta's two Ladies were almost literally paralyzed by circumstances and surroundings so different from their own way of life. She also saw that one or two of the French maids of honor were exchanging covert smiles.

A passion of loyalty to her Mexican friends rose in Sally's heart. They looked odd, and old, and out of place: what of it? I look like a sewing maid myself, she reflected grimly. The gray dress with the white pagoda sleeves bore no comparison with the silks and satins in subtle shades of prune and amber and mignonette worn by the beautiful blonde girls of Eugénie's court. They crowded round Sally with a too-effusive friendliness which reminded her of her first night at boarding school and the teasing of her Northern classmates. And just as on that long-ago, homesick night in Connecticut, Sally reacted energetically. Carlóta had ordered her little suite to talk, and Sally talked—answering their brittle barbed questions with dash and spirit. She was aware that her French was less fluent than when she walked under the trees of the Plaza Mayor with Pierre Franchet, that mistakes in gender were following mistakes in tense, but Sally talked on with her head high, and her white-gloved hands lying composedly in her lap.

It was an immense relief when the Duchesse de Bassano gave up the unequal struggle with Señora del Barrio's silence, and pleasantly said to the room at large:

"Will someone ring for the footman, please? It is rather early, but I believe our guests would enjoy some refreshments." She looked appealingly at Sally. "What would they like, mademoiselle? Tea, coffee . . . or a glass of wine?"

"We take chocolate at the merienda, madame," Sally said. "But please don't order it especially—the hour for the merienda is five o'clock."

Señora del Barrio, who had understood most of Sally's answer, whispered something about *la naranjada*.

"What does she say, mademoiselle?"

"The Empress Carlóta likes orangeade, madame—fresh orange juice with very cold water and some sugar . . . But dear Doña Manuela," said Sally, "I don't think Her Majesty will want anything to drink in the middle of such an important conference."

"*Sí, sí*, Doña Sarita! I make *naranjada* for her even when she meets the Council. At any hour of the day! You know she suffers terribly from thirst—"

Sally moved until she stood between Doña Manuela and the watchful, faintly hostile faces. She bent down, and as Jonas Wilkinson had once said to herself, she whispered:

"Don't let them see you cry!"

. . . If Doña Manuela had expected oranges and ice water to be brought to her for the accustomed ritual, she was disappointed. Following the footmen who carried in the tea and chocolate pots and silver baskets of petits fours, a page brought the orangeade ready mixed, in a crystal goblet.

"Do you suppose this is what Her Majesty will like?" asked Madame de Bassano.

"Yes—oh yes," said Sally. "If *you* think it right to interrupt the conference—"

The French lady gave her an anxious look.

"Certainly the page ought not to go in," she said decidedly. "One of the maids of honor might—or better still, Madame Carette. *Chère,* would you please—"

A pretty, fair-haired young woman came forward with a confident smile. Madame Carette, who held the post of Reader, was a great favorite with Eugénie, and almost certain never to be rebuked. She took up the gilt salver which held the goblet and crossed the room to the door of Eugénie's study. In the sudden silence which fell upon the grand salon they saw her tap on the oak panel and turn the knob.

The door was locked on the inside.

Madame Carette looked round in consternation, and stepped back. The door was opened very slightly. Sally saw Eugénie's face, surprised and vexed, heard the Reader's apologetic murmur of explanation. Then Eugénie took the little tray and closed the door.

"I don't think she was angry," said Madame Carette, returning to the group.

"Let's hope *he* isn't, dear," said someone, and there was a laugh, instantly suppressed by the Princesse d'Essling, which revealed the nervous tension in the room.

"Well," said Madame de Bassano, turning towards the Mexican guests. "May I offer you a cup of chocolate, made I fear in the French way? In this country—" She stopped, appalled.

There were sounds at last from the room next door. The crash of broken glass was followed by a long, ringing cry of terror, which brought every woman in the salon to her feet. Then came a noise that was scarcely human, as if some heavy animal, felled in an abattoir, had crashed moaning to the ground.

"Call the Emperor's physicians!" said the Duchesse de Bassano with heroic calm. "There has been an accident—His Majesty has had a relapse, perhaps a stroke—"

The study door was flung open by Eugénie, shaking and pale.

"The doctors, quickly! And help me, ladies—help! The Empress Carlóta has had a terrible attack—"

Sally pushed someone aside—the stately Princesse d'Essling, she thought, and cared not at all—she was the first of all the hysterical company to get inside the study. She saw the sick Emperor, gripping the arms of his chair and trying to lever himself to his feet. She saw Carlóta writhing on the floor.

Sally knelt down beside her. There was a yellowish trickle on Carlóta's chin and the bodice of her dress was wet and smelled of oranges.

"Tell me where the pain is, dear Madame—" She tried to keep her voice soft and reassuring, like Andrew's when he calmed Carlóta, and through the hubbub in the room it reached the Empress. She raised her head a little way from the floor and laid it on Sally's protecting arm.

"There was poison in the glass," she gasped. "Napoleon meant to murder me!"

Chapter Seventeen

A DOCUMENT IN MADNESS

IT WAS early evening before Carlóta appeared to be completely recovered from what the Court Physicians agreed to call a seizure. She was partly undressed, and made to lie down for a few hours in one of the state bedrooms, but no will on earth could have persuaded her to pass the night under the roof of Napoleon III. Eugénie let her go, declaring that the wretched misunderstanding about the orangeade would quickly be forgotten. Poor dear Doña Carlóta was "not herself" because of the bad news from Mexico. And that bad news kept the whole Mexican entourage out of bed until the small hours, so that Sally Lorimer fell asleep only when the Paris sparrows were beginning to chirp beneath her window.

When the faint scratching at her door began, she woke expecting to hear that the Empress was seriously ill. But it was Carlóta herself who stood there, fully dressed, with a long dark veil over her black hat, bracing herself against the frame of the door.

"You ought to be in bed, Madame!"

"Let me come in. And bolt the door." Carlóta slipped into the room with the desperate speed of the hunted. She hurried to the open window. She looked down into the street. She said:

"Napoleon's spies are on this side of the hotel too. We must close the shutters while we talk."

"There are no spies, dear Doña Carlóta." Sally spoke as gently as she could. In her nightdress, with her feet bare and her head heavy with sleep, she felt physically unequal to coping with the distracted woman. She now had some idea of what Andrew felt at the Quinta Vega when he drove the endermic syringe into Carlóta's arm.

"Look," she went on encouragingly, "there's nobody there but street cleaners and an old woman setting out her stand of flowers. The most ordinary people; I see them every day. But *you*—ought you to be up and worrying about such things, after feeling so unwell only yesterday?"

"I feel quite well now," said Carlóta. Sally saw that it was true. The Empress had reacted in just the same way after her flight across the barranca with little Agustín, as if the plunge into frenzy offered a release to be followed automatically by a soothing of mind and body. The clammy, almost bluish look which her skin sometimes had was gone, and there was even a little color in her face. Only the restless, darting eyes revealed the hidden confusion of her mind.

"I want you to come out with me," Carlóta hurried on. "Now. It is six o'clock. The shops will soon be opening, and we can buy some food."

"*Buy* food—? But mayn't I ring and order you some coffee?"

"No, no, no! As long as we remain in France, I must prepare, or see prepared, everything I eat or drink. I may be safe in Rome, I should be safe in Brussels; I know now that I am never safe in the country of that perjured murderer."

"Doña Carlóta." Sally took her hands, forgetting what little she knew of Imperial etiquette, remembering only that here was a woman little older than herself, and in dire trouble. "You *must* remember, you *must* hold on to this, because every one of us has told you again and again: there was no poison in the orange drink. The French Emperor couldn't possibly have known it would be brought to you. That was Señora del Barrio's idea—"

"Ah," said Carlóta cunningly, "but if his poisoners had orders to put a deadly drug in *anything* that was offered me?"

"Oh come now, you know he doesn't employ poisoners—"

"How silly you are. Naïve and credulous, like all Americans.

But hurry and dress now, there isn't any time to lose; we must be back before my Ministers have time to miss me."

"Does no one know that you intend to leave the hotel? They'll be frantic with anxiety—"

"Mathilde knows. Mathilde will keep the door locked and say I am asleep. She will cook the food we buy, too. I can trust Mathilde. Now get your clothes on—quickly!"

Sally passed into her little dressing alcove and drew the curtain. The washstand mirror, as she splashed water into a flowered china basin, showed her a face as pale and tense as Carlóta's. If only she could believe that Mathilde Döblinger was really privy to this morning expedition! If Carlóta were lying, there might be a hue and cry after them which would do further damage to her nerves and lead perhaps to a public scandal. Sally would have given much for the chance to scribble a note for the chambermaid to give to Señora del Barrio, but Carlóta—she could see through the two edges of the curtain—had seated herself at the writing table, and was using the inkstand and letter paper for some of her endless memoranda. Sally decided that the risk had to be taken. She would humor the sick woman, at all costs.

They left the Grand Hotel by the service stairs and a warren of kitchen premises where scrubwomen and laundresses were coming on duty, and emerged in a side street near the new Opéra house. Carlóta seemed to know where she was, and catching at Sally's hand doubled back across the Boulevard des Capucines into the growing crowd of Parisians on their way to work.

"There must be little shops in the rue Daunou," she said breathlessly, "a dairy—a creamery—where we can buy fresh milk. If *I* choose the place, there should be no fear of poison, should there?"

"There is no fear of poison *anywhere*," said Sally firmly. She stepped aside, put herself between the Empress and a stand where newspapers were being taken from their bundles and hung up. "The Empress of Mexico at St. Cloud"—that might be a headline to distress Carlóta, but how much more ominous was

that other, in taller capitals, splashed over all the front pages of
the Paris press—

GREAT FRENCH VICTORY AT NORIA DE CUSTODIO
HEAVY CASUALTIES REPORTED FROM MEXICO

They found a clean little dairy where the shopkeeper, busy
with early deliveries, had no curiosity to spare for chance cus-
tomers after setting a jug of foaming, still warm milk before
them, with a basket of fresh crescent rolls. Carlóta, who had
eaten nothing since noon the day before, ate and drank raven-
ously. Sally fingered her *croissant* into crumbs. The wheels of
the morning carts rolled down the rue Daunou to the rhythm of
Noria de Custodio. Noria—de—Cus—tod—io. Heavy—Casualties
—in—Mexico.

"I shall not feel really safe until we arrive in Rome."

Startled: "Do you intend to go to Rome, Madame?"

"Certainly I do. I shall ask the Holy Father for his help.
We have done our best for the Church in Mexico; now Pope
Pius must do his best for us. He knows that a victory for Juarez
would be a defeat for Christianity. The Vatican is rich; the Pope
could preach a crusade which would rally thousands of European
troops to aid my husband. Yes; I mean to telegraph today and
obtain the Emperor's approval, as a matter of form, and then
we shall all leave Paris."

She spoke with much of her old confidence, and Sally listened with her eyes lowered. To wander across Europe with
Carlóta while Maximilian's cause crashed to ruin in Mexico was
more than she had bargained for when she made her impulsive
decision in the Plaza de Santo Domingo. The Plazuelita! How
its sights and sounds and smells came back to her as they crossed
the Place Vendôme, majestic and empty, where no women were
baking tortillas, nor leather-trousered Indians setting out the colored jars of pulque! The Marché St. Honoré, to which the dairy-
woman directed them, reminded her a little of Mexico, though
it lacked the color of the papier-mâché *Piñatas* shaped like ani-

mals and clowns which hung with feathered toys above the
booths of Lagunilla and Merced. Carlóta hurried from stall to
stall, peering through her veil at the stallkeepers' faces, rejecting
the idea of dealing with some of them because of a fancied resemblance to Napoleon or Eugénie. Her choice, too, was limited:
only items into which poison could hardly be injected were to
be purchased; so Carlóta bought and Sally paid for ten fresh
eggs, some oranges and apples, and Belgian wafer cakes, of a
kind the Empress remembered from her childhood, which were
sold in a box secured with sealing wax.

"If we bought some of those fowls we could cut their heads
off ourselves," Carlóta said, as they walked down an alley where
live rabbits and poultry were on sale. "Then Mathilde could
pluck their feathers, and boil the flesh to make me broth."

"I don't think the Grand Hotel people would like us to
keep chickens in the rooms," said Sally, controlling her repulsion
with an effort.

"Why? We could tie them up with string to the table leg.
Haven't you seen the *soldaderas* in Mexico, sitting beside the
country barracks with hens and turkeys on string leads?"

"Many times, Madame."

"We need a knife to peel the fruit." Carlóta's uneasy mind
had jumped to another problem; Sally thankfully saw the poultry
cages passed.

"We can use the hotel silver, Doña Carlóta."

"I want a knife of my own."

She paused at a display of kitchen cutlery: butcher knives,
vegetable knives, skewers, scissors, steels.

"This one I like. It fits my hand so well."

"But that's not meant for fruit," the cutler protested. "The
ladies ought to have a silver knife for that."

"It is very sharp," said Carlóta in a caressing tone. She drew
it thoughtfully across the ball of her left thumb. The keen edge
cut deeply into the flesh and a line of blood sprang out and spilt
across her hand.

"I've cut myself!"

"I *told* the lady it was a knife for cutting meat—" The stall-keeper hurried out from behind his booth. Sally said nothing. She was ripping her clean white handkerchief into strips and deftly bandaging Carlóta's hand.

"Does it hurt, Madame?"

"No—no," said Carlóta, staring at the red stain on the white cambric. "It doesn't hurt at all. How strange! The cut was deep— I ought to feel some pain, but I feel nothing."

THE FRENCH TROOPS engaged in the battle of Noria de Custodio were the Chasseurs d'Afrique, commanded by Colonel du Preuil, and the Foreign Legion was still concentrated at San Luis Potosí. This much Sally learned from the *Figaro,* which she sent for as soon as Carlóta was returned to the care of her anxious maid. The few daily papers not directly or indirectly controlled by Napoleon III, however, dismissed Noria de Custodio as an unimportant victory. They stressed the new threat to the French in Mexico represented by a Juarista attack on the key town of Durango.

"We have every confidence in Colonel Cottret and his troops," one editorial ran, "but faced with the evacuations of Monterrey and Saltillo in the northeast, and the Imperialist collapse in the state of Sonora, the gallant colonel runs the risk of being completely isolated at Durango. The high command in Mexico can now rely on no base established further north than San Luis Potosí—and San Luis Potosí, we remind our readers, is only four hundred kilometers from the capital. Every step of the road south from Durango may be trodden in blood. We appeal to the princes who govern us to spare further slaughter of Frenchmen, and end this vain attempt to establish a new Algeria on the shores of the Gulf of Mexico."

Such comments, translated by Sally for those who spoke no French, could only increase the gloom of Carlóta's Mexican followers. The morning passed painfully in the grand salon. Three

French physicians waited on the Empress, pronounced her recovered from her "faint" and able to proceed to Rome, but the Empress herself remained in seclusion. For the first time, those who had accompanied her to Europe began to split into dissident groups and argue the right course to follow after the flat refusal of Napoleon III—given prominence in all his papers—to send more aid to Maximilian. Herr "Kuhacs," who took Sally and his wife to luncheon in the hotel dining room, was particularly strong against going on to Rome with a petition to the Holy Father.

"Doña Carlóta should return to Miramar," he said significantly. "If Don Maximiliano has any sense left he will send a cable message to tell her so, and then *we* could make our own arrangements."

"I wish he would send her any sort of message," Sally said. "I think she felt it very much, at St. Cloud yesterday, that his first cable was to the French Emperor, and not to her."

"Spoken like a true woman, dear young lady. Don Maximiliano has to toady to Napoleon before he starts singing *mañanitas* to his wife."

They left the dining room so late that the afternoon crowd was already dense in the Grand Hotel lobby. There was the usual hum of American voices, for the place was popular with the war-enriched tourists from the North, and also with such Southerners as had been wise enough to invest in European funds before the War. For a farcical instant Sally wondered what the effect would be if she went up to one of the stout, richly dressed matrons with daughters sheltering beneath her wings, and said,

"Please, ma'am, let me talk to you and ask for your advice. I'm afraid the Empress of Mexico is going mad and I don't know what to do."

Crazy! I shall go crazy myself soon, she thought as she followed Frau "Kuhacs'" plump form up the grand staircase. Perhaps the heat and the heartbreak are making us all a little mad.

"Such heat!" she said as they parted on the landing. "Paris is worse than Vera Cruz."

"It will be cooler after the siesta."

But for Sally there was no siesta. Alone in her bedroom, where the pink toile de Jouy and long lace curtains seemed to stifle her, she considered the wisdom of sending a telegram to Dr. Herzog. In the end she decided against it. How could she explain his arrival when three French doctors, leaders of their profession in Paris, were apparently satisfied with the Empress of Mexico's condition? Or had those doctors, summoned in the first place by Eugénie, given Carlóta permission to go on to Rome simply to get her out of Paris? Would they have given the same verdict if they had seen and heard Carlóta in the Marché St. Honoré?

Neither the affair of the "poisoned" orangeade nor the flight across the barranca "to take the child to Ixtaccíhuatl" had so impressed Sally with a sense of Carlóta's instability as that morning's incident with the knife. She remembered cutting her own fingers on a broken glass at Fayetteville and the sharp pain of it, recorded faithfully by healthy nerves, becoming the jangling pain when Andrew made her soak her hand in a weak permanganate solution. Healthy people, with healthy nervous systems, *must* feel pain; and in the market that morning, to see the deep cut and the welling blood—to hear Carlóta insist that she felt nothing, was to feel with the chill of absolute certainty that the Empress was deranged.

At half-past six, weary of herself and yet unwilling to return without a summons to the sad little group of Mexicans, Sally ordered her hipbath filled with tepid water and prepared to dress for dinner. It was very early; eight-thirty was the hour when Carlóta's pathetic court gathered in the grand salon, ready for the Empress to "make the circle," but some of the heat and worry of the day were dissipated in the cool water and the rub with eau de cologne which followed. Sally was dressed in her white crinoline, and had arranged her hair in the single curl which appeared to be in fashion at St. Cloud, when for the second

time that day the Empress of Mexico appeared unannounced at
her bedroom door.

"What? Dressed already?" she began abruptly. "I told the
chamberlain we wouldn't dine till ten. I need a rest from all the
gloomy hangdog faces staring at me everywhere. There's no escaping from them in the suite. One comes from the Minister, one
from the Papal Nuncio—it never ends. Then I thought of *your*
room—so small and neat, and everything in such plain view. . . .
Is there anybody behind that curtain?"

"Certainly not, Madame." Sally drew the curtains of the
dressing alcove open. "But I must apologize for some untidiness
—I was just going to ring for the maid."

"It's not untidy, and you look fresh and pretty, as you always do." Carlóta, in her crumpled gown, sank down on a sofa
beneath the open window. "I—I thought you might like to know
that I have had a cable from His Majesty, and he is well and
hopeful, and—missing me."

"I'm so glad to know you've had a message—"

"Sit down, my dear, and let me show it to you." The inevitable ragbag of papers was opened, and on Sally's table Carlóta laid out several documents, two clean pocket handkerchiefs,
an apple and—Sally saw with a sinking heart—the meat knife of
the morning, with the handle which so comfortably fitted Carlóta's grasp.

"We shall have to get you a leather sheath like the Indians
use, if you mean to carry your fruit knife with you," she said as
lightly as she could. "How does your cut hand feel now?"

"Better—I don't know," said the abstracted voice. "Ah—
here it is! You may read it, if you like."

Sally took the flimsy sheet. The message, which through
Matthew Maury's miracle had left Mexico less than a day before,
was a rigmarole of *Herz* and *Schmerz* and *Liebling* such as
Maximilian might have written by rote to a ballet dancer at the
Opera. Sally forced herself to smile.

"His Majesty expresses himself beautifully, Doña Carlóta—"

"And he means it all, you know."

Her trembling smile wrung Sally's heart. In it she saw a flash of the lost girl, trapped by ambition in the Imperial cage; and her own ambivalent feeling for Carlóta, always swaying between fear and sympathy, tipped down once more on the side of sympathy. Her heart, which had been beating furiously since Carlóta's entry, grew calmer. She took her courage in both hands and said:

"Then, Madame—since His Majesty is so lonely while you're gone—and you are not very well or happy here in Europe—would you not consider giving up the trip to Rome? You could return to Vera Cruz on an earlier steamer . . . and be home with Don Maximiliano within a month."

"Go home a failure? *Never*."

The lost girl slipped away, the hard embittered woman stared at Sally in the gathering dusk.

"All my life I've loathed the idea of failure! I wanted to succeed—to govern, as my father did; to win. I won't go back to Mexico defeated by Napoleon and Eugénie—I who always wished to be the best, the first, at whatever I undertook to do. *You* ought to understand me. You know that feeling very well."

Hesitatingly: "I always wanted to be first at school."

"It goes on all one's life, you know."

A little silence fell. The last colors of the day drained from the sky and the lights grew brighter along the Boulevard des Capucines.

"Shall I light the gas?" suggested Sally.

"I hate the smell of gas. There is light enough for us to talk by from these abominable new street lamps of Baron Haussmann's—to say nothing of those vulgar great shops and cafés. Or do you admire them, perhaps?"—pettishly. "Does the City of Light dazzle your young eyes? Does it seem much grander and more brilliant than the City of Mexico?"

"I think there's no comparison, Madame."

"Well—! That's frank, at all events—and bold, and—"

"Wait, Doña Carlóta. I expressed myself badly then. I should have said, there *can* be no comparison; the country, the setting, all is different. In Paris," said Sally, picking her words with care, "there's a form, a sense of style, a—a grandeur in all those squares and buildings, which—which we don't have yet, in Mexico. Oh, you have done wonders, I know that; and the new Promenade is far finer than the old Paseo. It will be quite as grand, when it is finished, as the Champs Elysées . . . but I'm not sure, really, that the European form suits Mexico. I miss the little old streets round the Plaza de Santo Domingo, with the people gliding along so quietly, not staring and chattering as they do here, and all this gray stone makes me long for the reds and rose of our tezontle, and oh! how I miss the bells!"

"The—bells?"

"The church bells, Madame; you may not hear them at Chapultepec, but they are so lovely, like water falling on the roofs."

"But you never go inside these churches to worship, do you—little heretic?"

"How can I, Madame?"

"How can you?" Carlóta echoed. "And—how can I?"

She laid her head back on the sofa and closed her eyes. Sally watched her warily. Have I said something wrong, she wondered, something that will . . . start her off again? That the European form may not suit Mexico—will that be taken as a criticism of *them?* But when the Empress spoke it was not in resentment.

"I have never gone to church, except when form or ceremony required it, since the Virgin of Guadalupe refused to grant my prayers for a child . . . Have you ever been to the Shrine of Guadalupe?"

"Never, Madame."

"To millions of our subjects, that shrine is the heart of Mexico. It stands on Tepayac Hill; there the Virgin laid a sheaf of roses in the poor Indian's cloak, and when he opened it before the doubting bishop, there were no flowers, but the imprint of Her face, brown-skinned like his own—they have the

336   THE CACTUS AND THE CROWN

cloak there still. It adorns the high altar. Underneath is written,
'I am the Mother—' " Her voice broke in a sob.

"Don't, Doña Carlóta—"

" 'I am the Mother of all you who dwell in this land.' "

Sally leaned forward to the couch and took Carlóta's hand.
The Empress, with a quick movement, shook her off.

"But *my* prayers She never heeded—never; all the weeks
and months of prayer. And so I turned away from her to Ixtaccíhuatl, the Sleeping Woman, who is older by many centuries by
far. Ask your overseer's wife! Ask any Indian woman! They go
on pilgrimages to La Guadalupana—but they keep Ixtaccíhuatl
hidden from the priest with their clothes and their maize querns,
part of their homes, near to their hearths."

It was the old tone, the wild manner; Sally sat paralyzed.
The warning bell which had struck when Carlóta fled with little
Agustín was ringing loudly now. The mystery of Ixtaccíhuatl
was about to be resolved.

"Have you never seen the Sleeping Woman?" whispered
Carlóta.

"You mean—the volcano?"—whispering too.

"I mean the Lady dressed in blue, with the white bark crown
that stands for her crown of snow, and the black streamers for
the forests on her flanks, and the young face, red-lipped with the
blood of children sacrificed to her in all the Aztec temples—"

"For God's sake, stop!"

Sally sprang to her feet, the Empress also; Sally could feel
the hot breath on her face.

"The Sleeping Woman came to me by night," Carlóta whispered, "and told me, 'A life for a life! To bear a child you must
sacrifice a child to me. To me, to me! Not to the meek one,
the Guadalupana, but to me!' "

I am taking the child to Ixtaccíhuatl.

High on the hillside, with Agustín crying, and Pierre pouring water into a tin cup—

"We thought you were going to the volcano," she said stupidly, and through the fear and horror heard somebody knocking at the door.

"Don't open it!" said Carlóta.

"I must, Madame." The table was between them. Sally whipped round it; and flung the door open on the apologetic figure of Señora del Barrio.

"I am so sorry to disturb Your Majesty"—with the ceremonious Spanish curtsy—"but a—a visitor has arrived who insists that her name be brought to you. I thought it wiser to come myself—dear Doña Carlóta—there is of course no reason why you should receive her at all."

"*Insists* that her name be brought? Is it—the Empress Eugénie?"

"*Madre de Dios,* no!" cried Doña Manuela. "It is Doña Alicia Iturbide."

". . . I see," said the Empress after a pause. "Of course. We could hardly be spared that, could we, Doña Manuela? Everything else is falling into ruin, everyone is exulting at our downfall; naturally little Agustín's mother wants to be in at the kill. I will receive Señora de Iturbide. Where is she now?"

"In the smaller anteroom, Your Majesty."

"Has she seen anybody besides yourself?"

"No one. Your Majesty postponed the dinner, so all were in their rooms—"

"But you remained on guard, my faithful dear."

It was said so affectionately that Doña Manuela cried:

"Don't see her, *querida Señora,* don't! You will distress yourself too much—you will be ill again—"

"Please do as I say, and bring the woman to this room—quietly. No doubt the story will be in all the papers tomorrow morning, but let us try to keep the meeting private, if we can."

When the Mexican lady had left the room, Carlóta said to Sally,

"Do you know how to light the gaselier?"

"I think so."

"Light it then."

There was a box of vesta matches on the candlestick by
Sally's bed. The lighting of the four fishtail burners inside the
pink glass globes was the first movement of any kind that the
girl had made since Doña Manuela's entrance, and she had
scarcely swung the gaselier back into place on its brass chain
when the Lady of the Palace was again in the room. This time
she ushered in a much younger woman, with the formal presentation:

"Princess Angel de Iturbide."

The woman who had borne Agustín Iturbide and given
him for adoption curtsied to her son's adoptive mother. She
was of average height, no more than average good looks, and
although with an unmistakably American chic, was very quietly
dressed. There was nothing in her which could possibly bear
comparison with the Empress Eugénie, and yet Sally was suddenly certain that she was wrong in thinking of Eugénie as the
stumbling block to Carlóta's peace of mind. This woman, who
had given birth to the child who called Carlóta "mamma" was
her true rival. Here was the one who could touch the dead center
of her pain.

She found herself involved in the curtsies and the rear-
rangement of the spindling gilt chairs around the sofa, on which
Carlóta had resumed her place. The triple reflections from
the three long mirrors made the room seem full of women. Three
Carlótas. Three Doña Manuelas in black, three Alicia Iturbides
in pearl gray and three Sallys in white—all twelve made up a
symphony of the muted colors of Paris, as Sally had just described them to the Empress. The tension in the air was entirely
Mexican—as charged as the Plaza de Santo Domingo on a fiesta
night, when the pulque took effect and the music played louder;
and the tortilla women, remembering mysterious grievances,
snatched and pulled at each other's hair.

"It is very good of Your Majesty to receive me," Alicia
Iturbide began. She spoke in Spanish, correct but with a perceptible American accent; her voice was low but firm. "You must

think it very strange of me to come here at this hour, unannounced, and without my husband."

"I think it even more strange," said Carlóta sharply, "that
you and he, who owe your wealth and titles to ourselves, should
not have paid your respects to me on the day after I arrived in
Paris."

"I would have come," said the American princess, "I would
have been on my knees to you at St. Nazaire, if I could have
persuaded my husband and his family to do what I have begged
them to do for nearly a year past. It was only today, when we
learned the position taken by the French Emperor, that I—I at
last succeeded; that I felt I had the right to come to you."

"Indeed!" said Carlóta, trembling. "And what decision have
the noble Iturbides arrived at now?"

"They ask you—the whole family asks you—to give me back
my little boy."

"Whom you sold to me," said Carlóta, "for one hundred
and fifty thousand dollars and five thousand dollars a year."

"We will repay the money, Señora. We will give up the
annual allowance—the titles, everything—if only you will give us
Agustín."

"Repay the money!"

"Señora," said the American princess, trembling—and Sally
guessed that she was embarking on a prepared speech, long and
carefully considered. "Just a year ago I committed the great folly
of my life when I gave away my little boy. It's no excuse to say
that Don Angel and his family overpersuaded me. I was his
mother, and I should never, never have let my Agustínito go. I
knew it, twenty-four hours after the Act of Adoption was signed
and we were on our way to Vera Cruz. You remember I turned
back from Puebla? You remember I went to Marshal Bazaine
and asked him to intercede for me? Of course you do. You were
furious. You were in a cold passion of rage which made me fear
even for my child's safety in your hands—"

I am taking the child to Ixtaccíhuatl, Sally thought. Safety
in her hands.

"And yet Agustín is very happy with his papa and me," said Carlóta. "He has quite forgotten you."

"Because you have taught him to forget us, then!"

"A child's memory is very short at three years old, Princess. And Agustín has so many other things to learn. He is very quick at his lessons, particularly French and German. He has a musical ear, and he has made a good start at the piano. His penmanship is not good as yet. He sits his pony well. I have been unable to ride much lately, so I have to take the head vaquero's word for that."

Sally saw the Empress on the black horse, thundering across the turf towards the child.

"Lessons?" said the child's mother. "Languages and penmanship—at three? You'll kill him."

"Nonsense," said Carlóta with an annoyed laugh. "He is the heir presumptive to the throne of Mexico, and princes must begin their studies early. *I* was only three when I joined my brothers in the schoolroom, and I assure you Agustín doesn't work as hard as I did. Ask Doña Manuela—she'll tell you he spends at least half his day in play."

"That is quite true, Doña Alicia," said the faithful voice. "Don Agustín is a very healthy, happy little boy, and he adores his papa and mamma."

"Miss Lorimer? Princess, I don't believe you know Miss Sally Lorimer. She came to Mexico with her brother some months after you left for Europe."

"Oh!" cried Doña Alicia, "is your brother the American doctor? My sister-in-law, Princess Josefa, wrote to me about you both. You gave my little boy his kitten—"

Suddenly she was in tears, with her gloved hands pressed to her contorted mouth.

"Tell the princess what you know of Agustín."

Carlóta's face was ghastly, the cheeks sunk under the shadowed eyes. There was something in the repeated taunts of "princess" from the one and "my little boy" from the other which made the scene more vicious than any exchange of insults or vulgarity. Sally moistened her lips and said:

"I've seen Don Agustín only once, Señora de Iturbide. He's very handsome . . . and very affectionate . . . and very brave. He came to my house, and seemed glad to have the little cat. He calls it El Tigre."

Doña Alicia smiled through her tears. "The darling," she said, "he has a tender heart for birds and beasts, I know. Thank you, Miss Lorimer. Thank you for understanding what my little boy would like."

"This is sheer sentimentality," Carlóta coldly said. "Princess, do I understand that you—and your husband—seriously expect me to accept a repayment of the money which you took so thankfully a year ago, in exchange for my adopted child?"

"With the money we will repay you, Your Majesty could raise four regiments of Cazadores—"

"The Holy Father will give me the means to raise a score," Carlóta said. "Princess, I have no wish to prolong this painful interview. Go with God; be satisfied with the great destiny to which we have called your first-born, and in due time other children will come to make you happy."

"Have *you* found it so easy to conceive a child?"

In the simple, deadly words was all of Doña Alicia's self-hatred and despair. Before the eyes of the watching women, Carlóta's face contracted as from a blow. They saw her summon all her dignity to say,

"You are impertinent, Princess de Iturbide. You may withdraw."

But Agustín's mother, whipping round, cried out:

"Miss Lorimer—you and I are Americans—you will tell me the truth! Do you think my boy will be happier in Mexico—or with me?"

Her abrupt movement set all the reflections moving in the mirrors. Three Sallys, three Carlótas, three ladies in gray, shaken with tears and anger, three Doña Manuelas all in black—a crowd of women, under the hissing gas. And with them the invisible rivals: La Guadalupana bearing miraculous roses, the Sleeping Woman with her crown of snow and her mouth of blood, following them to France from Mexico, never in this life to be shaken off—

"You may speak, Miss Lorimer," Carlóta said.

Sally paused. There was an equivocal answer, ready to her hand. There was a sentimental answer, which might appease them both. But Sally, with the sound of hoofs on turf in her ears, plunged headlong for the truth.

"I think . . . such a little child . . . would be happiest with his own mother."

"God bless you," said Alicia de Iturbide. "I'll tell Mr. Seward you said that." She touched Sally's hand. "Good-by . . . and thank you for your sweetness to my boy."

"So YOU ARE disloyal to me, like all the others," Carlóta said.

Señora de Iturbide had gone. Doña Manuela still stood by the door. Carlóta had risen from the couch.

"Not disloyal," Sally said, and began to tremble.

"You gave the answer that will please my enemies. Or was this melodrama arranged between you and the Iturbides? Did you rehearse your lines with Doña Alicia?"

"I never saw her in my life before," said Sally steadily.

"*You lie!*" screamed Carlóta, and at the sound all the glass prisms of the gaselier rang a discord. "You were a spy of the Iturbides! Planted in Mexico to win my son away from me! You can't deceive me now with your clever ways and your pretty face, Miss Lorimer! I see the plot—between the Iturbides and Napoleon—to hunt me down, me a failure, me the woman who could neither bear nor raise a child—"

She snatched the knife from the table and threw herself on Sally.

The attack was so sudden, like the final shift from reason

to lunacy, that Sally staggered under the weight of the mad-woman's body. All she was able to do, as Carlóta drove her back against the wall, and Doña Manuela shrieked, was to catch at the wrist of the hand which held the knife. The sharp blade grazed her cheek, but with all her strength she held it away from her throat, forcing Carlóta's arm back and up, and pushing desperately with her free hand at the tense body pressed against her own. Carlóta was as lean as a man, and madness gave her a man's strength. More horrible to Sally than even the fear of the knife was the epicene feel of the woman's limbs, now hard, now flaccid and melting, and the sound of the hoarse voice whispering lunatic accusations of vice and treachery. Then as suddenly as the thing began it was all over. The insane pressures gave way before the unimpaired strength of Sally's nineteen years, the mur-derous wrist grew limp in Sally's hand, and the Empress of Mexico crumpled like a rag doll at her feet.

Sally snatched up the knife and flung it through the open window. It rattled harmlessly on the stone roof of the balcony below.

"Look after her," she gasped to Señora del Barrio. She ran from the room—out of the Grand Hotel—into the street.

She had no idea what sort of apparition she was, flying through the hall with her white lace bertha torn and hanging from one shoulder, her hair loose, and a thin streak of blood upon her cheek. She was dimly aware that a lady in a silvery dress, escorted by a gentleman in a vast expanse of white shirt front, stood hastily aside to let her pass, and that a soft laugh followed her as she pushed out of the swinging door. She ran headlong across the street while drivers of fiacres shouted and reined in their horses, down the boulevard and into the narrow rue des Capucines.

Her whole instinct had been to put a distance between her-self and that nightmare room, to be surrounded by people who were sane. But as she struggled up the crowded street with her cheek stinging painfully and her breath caught short in fatigue, Sally began to doubt her own sanity, as well as the balance of all those around her. She was not running or walking any more; she was being carried along on an irresistible wave of humanity, pressing in on the quiet rue des Capucines from the new boulevards and roaring in unison:

"*A la gare St. Lazare! A la gare St. Lazare!*"

Sally had no means of knowing that Napoleon III, somewhat recovered from his attack of uremia, had that evening made in Paris one of the speeches of which he alone had the secret. He had spoken of France's mission of leadership in Europe—of France's civilizing presence in Algeria—of what Britain and the United States might learn from France—empty bombast which served to cover his real intention of asserting himself against the rising force of Prussia. For the Parisians, long poisoned by his oratory, this was a heady draught of glory. They had reacted by a concerted move toward the railway station from which two city regiments were to leave that night for land and sea maneuvers at the Channel ports.

So much Sally learned from the women who had now linked arms with her as they struggled across another of the wide new streets and came within sight of the station. She tried in vain to free herself from their affectionate clasp. To the sisterhood of the streets, tipsy and disheveled, Sally with her torn lace and bonnetless head was another of themselves. They saw that she was crying, and consoled her for the lover who had left her "in such a state." One woman, big and blowsy, even tried to press a few francs into her hand.

Money! She had left the hotel without her purse, and everything she possessed was in that room where madness and murder had touched her with their withering breath. And now, beneath the station lamps, was another madness, as the street rang to names she knew so well:

"*Vive du Preuil et la victoire de Noria!*" the crowd roared. "Hurrah! Hurrah!" Then from another part of the throng came the answering shout:

"*Vive Cottret et les défenseurs de Durango!*"

"Hurrah! Hurrah!"

A DOCUMENT IN MADNESS345

The crowd was torn apart by a procession of men wearing
masks—masks which discreetly hid the well-known faces of some
of Napoleon's cleverest propagandists—and carrying square
lighted lanterns on which words and slogans had been painted.
They bobbed crazily up and down before Sally's unfocussed
eyes: *Algérie française. Mexique française. Algérie française*
again. At last, a grinning turnip lantern with a spiked Prussian
helmet upon it to which some wit had tied a banner inscribed
"Allemagne française."

"A Berlin! A Berlin! A Berlin!"

The mob had found its slogan now. The steady rhythm of
the three syllables broke over the heads of the astonished troops.
They broke ranks. They swarmed among the crowd. Sally felt
herself caught off the ground, kissed by a grinning bearded face,
pressed close to a blue uniform which reeked of sweat and garlic.

"Pierre! Oh Pierre! Where are you?" she cried in fear.

There was a roar of laughter.

"The little lady wants her Pierrot! Will I do, *belle enfant?*"
"Or me?" "Or me?"

She broke away from them all and ran like a cornered hare
back to the boulevard. Some street boys ran after her.

"See her run! See her run!" An enterprising voice shouted
"Stop thief!"

Shouldering, twisting, doubling through the crowds, she
came out into a great space of golden light surrounding the new
Opéra. The Opéra! She knew, as far as she knew anything, that
it was no distance from the hotel. But which way? Which way?
She stopped an elderly man, well dressed, with a discreetly rolled
umbrella.

"Monsieur, will you please tell me the way to the Grand
Hotel?"

He sized her up quickly, looked this way and that, raised
his umbrella to summon a fiacre.

"Mademoiselle, I'll be delighted to drive you there."

"Oh, *no!*"

She shied away from danger. She saw the newsvendors

laughing at her. The laughter began to crackle round the brilliant Opéra square, where Sally Lorimer alone looked ragged and disreputable. Then from the passengers descending from an imperial, carrying bags and traveling rugs, one man detached himself. Took her hand, while the Opéra and the tall houses around rocked and settled back on an even foundation. Soothed her, as she had once soothed him, with a friendly voice—

"My dear," said Dr. Julius Herzog. "I see I very nearly came too late."

Chapter Eighteen

"AMONG THORNS, YOU"

THE MAN who loved Sally Lorimer was gifted with no psychic perception of her fear and danger, as he settled down to *la guerre aux adobes,* the mud war, in the mesa north of San Luis Potosí. After the shock of her abrupt decision, Pierre's cool, practical mind—the counterpart of her own—acknowledged the justice of her claim that he should be the one to wait. His only anxiety was that a Juarista bullet might cut the waiting short.

Yet Bazaine, for all his boasting at the grand review, did not lead the Imperialist forces to death or glory. After the shocking defeats of July and early August, he went back to Mexico, leaving the troops at San Luis Potosí to the routine work of protecting the Sappers who were digging trenches and throwing up earthworks around the mining town. It had become, after besieged Durango, the most northerly stronghold of Maximilian's power.

The Foreign Legion, fighting the mud war, began to resent its inactivity. Searching through Indian villages for caches of the American weapons and ammunition now pouring into Mexico, or nursemaiding convoys of wounded men and refugees coming down from the evacuated towns, was tedious work for soldiers who still burned to avenge the Legion's defeat at Santa Isabel. Their morale was good enough, although Pierre, like all the sergeants, had to watch carefully for outbreaks of *le cafard,* the madness of depression which could affect an entire barrack room as "the Beetle" bored and burrowed through the brains of men.

Several times Colonel Saussier ordered a surprise check of kit and
bedding for peyotl, the mezcal button which when chewed and
swallowed lifted the addict into a hallucinated world far above
thirst and fatigue. These checks were usually satisfactory, for
the Foreign Legion was in the process of building up a great
tradition, and the sacrifice at Camerone was too recent to be
dishonored by drugs and excess of drink. Even Légionnaires
who, like Pierre Franchet, had received a superior education,
were quite unaffected by the attempts of French liberals, from
Victor Hugo to Adolphe Thiers, to turn them from their duty by
pleading the cause of Mexican independence. Such appeals, uttered at the safe distance of Paris, were reprinted in the United
States and distributed clandestinely to the French Expeditionary
Corps, where—outside the Legion—they were responsible for a
growing number of desertions.

   The mud war, in which the Juarista guerrillas were increas-
ingly active, was not continuous for the Légionnaires, who regularly returned to rest billets in San Luis Potosí. In that attractive
mountain town French sentiment had been strong for over two
hundred years. After the capital, it seemed a carefree little place
to Pierre. Mining magnates and their families still made San Luis
Potosí the center of their social life, and the hotels were full of
those who had spent the summer, tranquilly enough, at the surrounding spas. The cafés did a thriving trade. Dances and con-
certs were frequent, and amateur theatricals got up by the
French officers were even more successful, in the eyes of the
fifteen-year-old Mexican belles, than the performances of Cal-
derón and Lope de Vega given nightly in the Teatro de la Paz.

   If Sally had married me, and come up to San Luis, thought
Pierre, she would have known no hardship. There are ladies
here; there are entertainments, good food, clean rooms; I could
have taken good care of my wife. If it hadn't been for that
damned *putain de Malinche*—

   He believed that without the revival of the Malinche story,
he could have persuaded Sally to marry him. But he had known,
as soon as he was summoned to the court-martial at Puebla,

that his old liaison, once it was made public, would come in some way or another between Sally and himself. He did not blame Sally. We all went wrong, he thought, as the Spaniards went wrong before us, when we seduced those Indian girls. It makes no difference that they were more than willing. Sooner or later our betrayal of them will betray us all.

It was only in San Luis Potosí, when he saw Mexican and European ladies sauntering with their husbands while the band played in the plaza, that Pierre ever thought of his cast mistress, and the trouble she had caused and might cause still. Out on the mesa, when he went the rounds of the bivouac after dark, his thoughts were all of Sally.

When the stars came out, and the shale glistened along the flanks of the silver mountains, it was easy to feel that she was close to him. He could hear her voice with the funny Rs, and see her in all her shapes and forms. Dripping the chloroform, pale-faced, at Río Frío; coming to meet him with her parasol over her shoulder under the trees of the Plaza Mayor—the only thing that worried him was that he could not clearly remember whether her eyes were brown or hazel. *Fauve*—they were *fauve* eyes, never more sparkling or more true than when she sat black Nelly on the hill above the hacienda and said, "This is my little world and motherland!" He wondered if there was the slightest hope that the fighting would not spread to Cuernavaca.

Darling Sally—so set on her independence, so determined in her idealism! So contentious too; Sergeant Franchet had never before met a contentious woman. The Mexican girls he had taken lightly, for a night or a week, were capable of making screaming scenes, threatening to murder or to die for love, but argument was beyond them, and Sally had loved to argue. Her decided opinions had more than once punctured his own naïve convictions of good and evil. "Why is it wrong to kill one man in hot blood, but praiseworthy to kill a hundred in Algeria?" He could hear the scornful young voice now. Into Franchet's disciplined mind the Beetle was never likely to crawl, but since his arguments with Sally he was not so certain as before of the necessity to pacify Algeria for the glory of the Emperor. He was no longer even certain that the Algerian rebels could be brought to an unconditional surrender. The French Army had been trying that for thirty years: it was Franchet's professional opinion that they might have to go on trying for thirty more. Almost until the end of the century.

"What will you be in the year nineteen hundred?" Sally had asked him once—why, he didn't know; he thought the words came from some parlor game she had been playing with Herzog and her brother—

In 1900 he would be sixty-one. An old soldier in some French village, reciting his stories of Tampico and the march to Monterrey for a litre of wine, like the Waterloo veterans he remembered from his childhood.

He was damned if he would be that.

For Sally had touched some spring of ambition, denied for eight years past, in the man whose keen bright mind had been turned into a single track, the soldier's way, expressing itself only by a fanatical devotion to a living legend, Napoleon III, and a legend in the making, the Foreign Legion.

Sally had whipped his mind and pricked his pride, and God knew she had roused him—Sally absent, Sally far across the sea —to an unslaked, fiercely recurrent torment of desire.

THERE CAME a day when, as he returned to rest billets, the regimental vivandière said to Pierre:

"Do you remember Parendel?"

"Parendel, who was with us at Cerro de Magordo?"

"Himself, and who was commissioned later by the *patron* at the grand maneuvers outside Mexico—"

"What about him?"

"You know he was severely wounded at Santa Isabel?"

"He recovered, no?"

"No." The little vivandière scowled, and shook her head.

"He was in hospital in Saltillo, some months. Then they started on the way down, his wounds broke out again, the fever rose, and—well, he lies in the San Francisco convent now, and they don't give him a day to live, that's all."

"*Dommage.*" There was never much more to be said than that: It's a pity. Too bad. "He was a good lad, the Parendel."

"He wants to see you, sergeant."

"Me? Why me?"

"Should I know? Weren't you together at Sidi-bel-Abbès?"

"We were, it's true—" remembering. "All right. I'll go this afternoon. San Francisco, did you say?"

There was another San Luis Potosí, side by side with the gay town of balls and masquerades. It came to life between two and five in the morning, when the ambulances creaked into the Plaza de Armas with their load of French wounded—sometimes of French dead. It breathed silently all day long in the convent and classrooms where a few Army doctors, and many more Mexican monks and nuns, nursed the sick back to health, or said the last prayers for the dying. In this other town, of Christian charity and mercy, the seventeenth-century church of San Francisco was an inspiring landmark. Frenchmen, Imperialist Mexicans, an occasional Juarista whom some act of unusual humanity had brought in with his enemies, were lying on beds and pallets, even on stretchers, in the halls and stone corridors of the adjacent convent, and in the garden convalescents were hobbling on crutches or propped up on the carved stone seats. Pierre asked for Lieutenant Parendel, 2nd Regiment the Foreign Legion, and after a long wait was confronted by a Sister of the Franciscan order.

"I'm afraid the lieutenant is much too ill to see you, sergeant—"

"He sent for me, madame."

In Sergeant Franchet the core of Calvinism was far harder than in Sally Lorimer. He came of old Huguenot stock, toughened and embittered in the Wars of Religion. He could never bring himself, for instance, to address a religious as "mon Père" or "ma Soeur," and that "madame" told the nun all she needed to know about Pierre Franchet. But when she looked up through her thick spectacles at his tanned face, hard and alert under the battered leather visor, the little elderly Sister, who had taken her vows many years before, was somehow aware of a masculinity, an authority not easily denied. She said:

"Wait, then. If he is awake, I will see what I can do."

Presently she led him, treading softly, through the room which had been the convent's library, with the great Spanish tomes still on the shelves, to a truckle bed in the bay window where, with three others, lay Franchet's former comrade of Algeria.

Guy Parendel was drifting out of life on a merciful tide of morphia, but his eyes were open and he made the faintest gesture with his bandaged right hand.

"*Comment ça va, mon lieutenant?*" There was a rush-bottomed stool beside the low bed. Pierre lowered himself to it gently, so that his face was within range of the drowsy eyes.

"*Ça . . . va mal, mon vieux.*"

"You're going to be all right, Parendel." Pierre saw that the less formal address pleased the dying man. After all, they had been recruits together in the Maison-Mère at Sidi-bel-Abbès. Indoctrinated, broken to the Legion together; but Parendel had been one of the ambitious ones, as Sally would have liked himself to be.

"I heard you were here, Franchet. From Lesdiguières—do you remember him? He died yesterday." The words came with an effort.

"Can I get you anything, Parendel? A cool drink, would you like that?"

"Yes."

There was a beaker beside the bed containing a mixture of molasses with vinegar and ice water. Franchet held a little of the drink to the lieutenant's lips.

"Are they taking care of you all right?"

"Soeur Marie-Antoine, yes, and Monsieur l'Aumônier have been very good. The curé . . . of Aranzazu . . . also."

Poor devil, Franchet thought. A deathbed repentance, a beautiful end, that's all the black crows want. He stirred uneasily. But Parendel (the Parendel of Sidi-bel-Abbès and the brothels of the Bazar d'Orléans, who used to cheer when a new batch of Kabyle heads went up on the gates at Blidah) had no religious message to impart. He raised himself a very little on his pillows and said:

"You—were right—about the barrancas. Remember—that night in Tía Juana's house in Tampico, when we were both sergeants—you said the danger in barranca fighting wasn't the cul-de-sac but the crossfire?"

"I remember all right." He remembered the naked brown girl on his knee, trying to make him drink tequila, and squabbling with Parendel's girl because the two drunk French NCOs insisted on discussing strategy.

"It was the crossfire did for us at Santa Isabel."

"You shouldn't talk too much, *mon vieux,* you'll tire yourself."

"No, let me tell you. You know de Briancourt divided us into three that day, one force of Mexican cavalry and two of the Legion. Escobedo," his voice grew stronger as the memory of that day came back, "Escobedo drew us on down the barranca towards the hacienda of Santa Isabel. Then he opened fire from the hill, the hacienda, and the convent on our right flank—oh, my God! De Briancourt stood up yelling in his stirrups, *'A moi, la Légion! A moi, la Légion!'* I can hear him yet. Then I fell, and when I came to, the Juaristas were mutilating the wounded . . . God knows how our boys were able to drag me off."

The dew came out on the white face, and Franchet laid his hard hand over the restless hands.

"Is there anything that I can do for you, Parendel? Any message, that I could deliver?"

"Would you write a letter to my father?"

"Monsieur l'Aumônier would do it better."

"But you *knew* me, Franchet. You know what to say."

"All right then, I can try."

"Guillaume Parendel, La Grave, in the Dauphiné, that'll find him . . . We have a farm there, did I ever tell you?"

"No. It doesn't matter. Never mind."

"I would have liked to see . . . the snow on La Meije again . . . and hear the Romanche down in . . . the valley—"

Soeur Marie-Antoine came from behind the screen with her finger to her lips. Pierre rose to go.

"Au revoir, mon brave! A demain!"

But Parendel was far away, in the cool shadows of the Meije glacier. He opened his eyes once more, and whispered: "No barrancas there!"

Soeur Marie-Antoine crossed herself and looked edified; she thought her patient spoke of heaven. But Franchet, sorry and embarrassed, knew much better. He had witnessed it so often before: the turning of a Légionnaire's heart, at the last, towards the France which had rejected him. The desire to communicate with the parents estranged, perhaps by his own fault, many years before. Well, he could give Guillaume Parendel, farmer, a true bill in respect of his son Guy, caught in the crossfire, *mort pour la France.*

"I think your friend will not be here tomorrow, sergeant," said the nun, outside the ward.

"I suppose not, madame. Please—don't let him suffer too much."

"He *has* suffered much for six months past. He was cruelly mutilated as he lay upon the battlefield. And yet, since he came to San Francisco, the grace of the Virgin of Aranzazu has led him to offer up his suffering to God."

She opened a small door set in the stone wall.

"This is the chapel of Aranzazu, sergeant. It is specially dear to all of us Sisters privileged to serve here, for we are from the Basque country, and Aranzazu is a word from our own tongue."

"Meaning?"

" 'Among thorns, You.' Will you not say a prayer in our beautiful chapel, for the passing of your poor friend's soul?"

The Capilla de la Virgén de Aranzazu glowed before Pierre's eyes. Baroque and Churrigueresque, perfectly united in a chapel of exquisite proportions, enchanted in the contrast between bare walls and bold raised traceries, offered a fitting home on earth to the winged company of angels and of saints. Pierre drew back from the threshold.

"I shall serve Parendel better by avenging his death, madame."

The nun sighed. She lifted a rush basket from a carved table just inside the chapel door, and held it out to the Frenchman.

"We will pray for you, my son. Take a Thorn from Aranzazu to remind you of that promise."

"Thank you, madame."

Pierre took a brown, wooden splinter from the basket and twirled it uncertainly in his hand.

"What is it meant to be?"

The eyes behind the thick spectacles grew stern.

"Are you a heathen as well as a heretic? It is a Cross. The monks gather thorns upon the mesa, and whittle them at recreation, for our visitors."

She looked at him expectantly. She wanted money, of course, the black crows always did. He thought of giving her a real, remembered the promise of prayer and put two into her hand. He thrust the sharp-pointed cross of thornwood deep into his pocket, and bade her farewell with a stiff salute.

Ten minutes later, at a café in the Plaza de Armas, with a glass of tequila in front of him, he was still thinking of Parendel's last words. Would his own thoughts, in extremity, turn towards the limestone crags above Aix-en-Provence and the silvery green olive grove round the low white *mas* where he was born? He hardly thought so. Eighteen years of hard manual work and hard study, ending in the shock of his arrest and sentence, had left him with no sentimental impressions of Provence. He was far more at home now in the Plaza de Armas at San Luis Potosí, with the sunset beginning to glow red in the sky and the white pigeons who nested in the Cathedral towers wheeling in the last flight of the day. Sally would love this place, he thought. And at once she was in his arms, wrapped in his cloak, with her lips parting beneath his kisses, under the white magnolia tree. Against the wrench of desire he forced himself to rise, flung a small coin on the table, and walked quickly back to his billet.

II

A FEW DAYS after the death of Parendel, the 1st Regiment was ordered south to Querétaro.

"We're pulling out, *sergent,*" said his corporal to Pierre as the barracks bags were packed. "*Le patron* is going to leave the north to Escobedo."

"Looks like it," Pierre agreed. "Maybe, though, it means we'll get a whack at Don Porfirio instead."

"At Diaz? *Parbleu,* you've had Diaz on the brain ever since you let him slip that time at Puebla—"

"He didn't slip through *my* fingers, Rossi," said Pierre, but he said it quietly, and the Corsican corporal marveled. It had been a favorite way to bait the sergeant—to remind him of Diaz' escape from prison at Puebla, when Franchet was one of the detail on guard. But Franchet was too good-humored, that day, to pick a quarrel. Moving nearer Mexico meant moving closer to the possibility of hearing news of Sally.

In spite of the opening of the transatlantic cable, dispatches on the Empress of Mexico's progress had practically disappeared from the newspapers. Her triumphal journey through France, her reception at the railroad station in Paris by Napoleon and Eugénie in person had been amply chronicled. A grand ball had been given in her honor at the Tuileries. She had been particularly fêted at St. Cloud. Then silence for nearly ten days.

About the end of August Pierre read in the *Diario* that "Her Imperial Majesty, fatigued by her arduous mission to Europe, had arrived at the Castle of Miramar for a short period of repose advised by her physicians."

It was then that he felt Sally, in Austria, was moving farther away from him. Still, the stay at Miramar could hardly be prolonged, if Carlóta and her suite were to return to Vera Cruz, as intended, by the middle of October. They were probably, Pierre thought, already on their way back to St. Nazaire. He checked provisions with a light heart. No wagons on the expedition meant no bread and French wine, which in turn meant trouble with the men over the tortillas and thin Baja California claret the supply sergeants would buy along the way. Cattle were to be driven and slaughtered to provide the regulation pound of meat a day. Sixty rounds of ammunition were issued to each man. Eventually they left San Luis Potosí at first light on the fifteenth of September—Rataplan, who had been stabled for weeks in the Calle de los Tumultos, kicking up his heels with joy as he carried Franchet out of the city gates and off across the mesa.

The Huasteca Potosina, across which their road lay from the Potosí mountains to the circle of hills around Querétaro, was a brown, burned stretch of land seamed with dry watercourses. Thorn thickets gave no protection from the sun. Cactus were twisted into tortured shape. The pulque maguey was here dwarfed by the tall columns of the organ cactus. The prickly pear, flower of purple and fruit of gold, abounded by the roadside. The road itself was in wretched shape and the marching regiment with its herd of cattle and the inevitable Imperialist refugees in their bullock carts covered less than fifteen miles a day. Each evening, as the sun began to set, the mounted sergeants were forced to ride up and down the weary ranks, crowding the stragglers back into step, and shouting the familiar,

"Allez, allez! Marchez ou crevez, marchez ou crevez!"
—Get on, or die.

They slept at night on the mesa, all camp fires extinguished,

with their cloaks wrapped round their bodies and the horses
blanketed against the mountain chill. They were nearly out of
the ravine country now, and the bare wide mesa offered little
opportunity for an ambush, but the officers were taking no
chances, and in the Indian villages there was always the risk of a
Juarista surprise. Not that there were any adult males to be seen
in the few villages they marched through by day. Only the silent
Indian women, surrounded by little children, stood in the doors
of their adobe huts to watch the Gringos on their march back
to the sea.

They were nearing the Querétaro province line when an
order came from Colonel Saussier to Pierre's company commander which caused him to frown and, after some thought, to
send for Sergeant Franchet. It was night. Captain Castaing was
in his tent, and the lanternlight showed faintly through the canvas
walls as Pierre walked quietly up. He heard, with an impassive
face, that a quarter company was to be detached from the
strength of the regiment next morning to make a detour by San
Miguel Allende, joining the main force later on the great highway to Querétaro.

In any other branch of the service, no more than this would
have been said, but the tradition of the Legion required the reasons for such an order to be explained, particularly to an NCO.
Captain Castaing thought twenty-five men too small a force for
the task in hand, and that he ought to have been sent to San
Miguel Allende himself; he was therefore careful to keep all expression from his voice when he explained,

"Lieutenant Malaval, from 'Two' Company, will command
the detachment. He has not been in the town before, so I'm
sending you, Franchet, because you know the terrain fairly well.
The bivouac will be on the Conde de la Canal's land as usual,
and the Conde will accompany Lieutenant Malaval on his visit
to the mayor."

"Very good, sir."

"Mayor García is heart and soul for Maximilian, and it

will hearten him and his friends if we show the flag in San Miguel
Allende. You understand?"

"Perfectly, *mon capitaine.*"

Par-fai-te-ment mon cap-it-aine. The hoofbeats spelled it
out next morning, when they cantered off across the mesa, riding
east into the sun. Pierre's spirits rose. The slow-plodding south-
bound trek had tired him, and for two days past his old wound
had given him some pain. The quick movement as part of a
mounted troop was cheering, even when the troop was commanded by Lieutenant Malaval.

This officer, known to the 1st Regiment as *"En Dentelles,"*
was unpopular in "Two" Company and seemed eager to extend
his unpopularity through his temporary command from Company "One." There was a row, before they had gone a mile, about
sombreros, why aren't the men wearing their sombreros, sergeant, they're courting sunstroke in those neckcloths; two miles
farther on the young lieutenant was inspired to call a halt and
check on the water bottles. Five water bottles were found to con-
tain tequila instead of water, and in the ensuing flurry Malaval
criticized the cleanliness of the tin *quarts* which each man carried by a strap around the top button of his coat. All the bearded
faces were scowling as they rode on, and Sergeant Franchet's
clean-shaven mouth was taut with temper. He was glad when
the lieutenant ordered him to ride rear guard. He went down the
ranks shouting *"Marchez ou crevez!"* with a zeal which deceived
nobody and even earned a few grins, and pulled Rataplan alongside Corporal Rossi, riding in the rear file.

"Lace Drawers is feeling his oats today, eh?" said Rossi
from the side of his mouth.

"He's showing the flag, that's all," said Pierre with a grin.

"Flag be damned, he's on the peyotl. Couldn't you see it
in his eyes?"

"Hein?" said Pierre, surprised. "I'll check on that, Rossi.
Thanks."

Till then he had taken Malaval as a necessary evil, one of
the many showered on poor troopers by the higher powers. He

already knew that the young officer, whatever his shortcomings, had a magnificent command of Spanish. Assuming this was why he had been selected to bolster up the Imperialism of the Mayor of San Miguel, Pierre thought it should be possible for seasoned troops to tolerate Lieutenant Malaval on a sortie which would last thirty-six hours at the most. But if there was the slightest possibility that he had taken to "eating the flesh of the gods," "plucking the singing root" or any other expression that meant peyotl, then Malaval might be a liability to the men at any hour they were in his charge.

Pierre Franchet checked his horse and looked across the mesa. Ahead, San Miguel was not yet in sight. Behind, there was nothing but the track along which they had come, the brown earth, and the tortured cactus arms. No sign of any danger there.

The trouble with himself was that he was growing obsessed by the need for Sally. He, not his corporal, should have seen the signs of the drug in the lieutenant's eyes. But he was letting his thoughts wander to her, thinking of what she would think of all the new sights, as Mexico opened out before her.

She would have done something about that Indian baby's eyes, at the door of the mud hut half a mile back—

And had that dirt-encrusted pig, with its snout poking round the baby, out of the hut in double-quick time—

There was a flower which grew in this part of the mesa, which had often caught Sergeant Franchet's eye as he rode along. It charmed him by its contrast with the tall plants of Spanish bayonet under which it grew. It was a type of thistle, with closed creamy buds rising from a circle of spiky, silvery green leaves, and in a strange way it reminded him of Sally. Cool and intact, with the prickles of her independence all around her—

"My little Scottish wild rose," he had called her once.

"Your little Scottish thistle," she had said.

Oh, Sally, *flor de mi corazón, flor de la mesa,* there is no one like you in all the world.

THE GREAT GATES of the Conde de la Canal's hacienda, which for years had opened hospitably to every French troop, were locked and barred.

"What now, sergeant?" said Lieutenant Malaval. "On into the town and requisition the posada?"

"It might be wiser to pay our way, since the alcalde is so well-disposed," hinted Franchet. "Would the lieutenant wish to make a detour by the back of the casa grande first? We might get news of the Conde de la Canal at the lodges or the stables."

They jogged at a foot pace round a winding rutted track to the back premises, to be confronted by more padlocks, more bars, and a bristling *chevaux de frise* of spikes above the gates. Clearly, the residence of the de la Canal family had been emptied of all its occupants.

Round the corner from the last lodge, and in the last light of the day, they came upon a stone fountain where three worn steps led up to a water trough which bore the inscription

EN MEMORIA DE 16 DE SEPTIEMBRE DE 1810

"Too bad the horses—" Pierre began, and then broke off. *"Olé, niño!"*

In the shadow cast by the pillared fountain, a boy was lurking. He was barelegged and barefoot. He wore, with a swagger, a French drummer boy's blue cutaway coat.

"My God," said Lieutenant Malaval, "is he one of ours?"

"An Indio, sir; he stole the jacket—listen to him."

"Olé, señores gringos!" The childish voice came insolently above the noise of the water jet. "What will you pay to know where the Conde de la Canal has gone?"

"A quartilla," said Malaval, naming the lowest coin in the currency. But the boy caught the medio which Pierre flung down, and shouted *"Gracias!"*

"He's gone to Havana, *Señores Franceses*. To be with all the other *Mochos,* waiting for their sovereign lord and king, Don Maximiliano."

"Ride on, men," said Malaval with an oath, and urged his horse forward. The Mexican boy in the blue coat leaped on the stone coping of the fountain to watch them go.

The Posada de San Francisco, in the plaza of San Miguel, was the only building showing lights that night. The last rains of the season came sweeping down over the little town, turning every narrow lane into an arroyo, and Lieutenant Malaval decided that the prestige of the French Army required that the well-disposed alcalde should wait on him at the posada. An inn servant was sent for Mayor García, who came at once and cheerfully; he and the lieutenant dined apart, and sat over their wine until after ten o'clock. The innkeeper, while making no pretense to be glad to see the troopers, piled their plates with stewed fowl and rice and kept their glasses filled. It was a better billet, after all, than the Conde de la Canal's barns. Franchet, however, was uneasy. He was acting stable sergeant, to make sure that after they were properly cooled off and blanketed the horses had water drawn only from the well used by the innkeeper's family. He saw a warm mash prepared under his own supervision. He tested the bars of the stable door before ordering Corporal Rossi and two soldiers to sleep in the clean straw beside the animals. He had decided to take no chances in San Miguel Allende.

The small posada was easily guarded. He set two sentries at the doors and a third at the staircase from the patio to the upper rooms where the family and their servants slept. There were no other guests that night. Lieutenant Malaval had retired to a small bedroom on the ground floor, and the men not posted lay sleeping with their weapons close to their hands, on the sala floor.

When the cathedral clock boomed out its twelve strokes across the plaza, the posada had long been dark and silent, except for the tread of sentries on the wet cobblestones. Pierre passed with the light step the desert had taught him from sala to

stable, stable to patio, and then to the door of the lieutenant's
room. He knocked. He turned the handle softly.

"Mon lieutenant!"

Malaval was lying on a low bed covered with a red and
black Indian blanket. A bottle and a glass, half full of French
brandy, stood on the floor beside a leather satchel and his heavy
riding boots. He had taken off his frock coat, but still wore his
shirt and trousers. His face, in the faint light of the shuttered
stable lantern Franchet carried, looked almost too young for the
dark mustache and small imperial. St. Cyr, class of 1864; a brief
home posting to Romorantin, and then straight to the complexi-
ties of Mexico—that had been the making of this soldier, sleeping
too soundly to hear his sergeant's voice.

"Mon lieutenant!"

Franchet knelt down beside the sleeping man. He bent over
Malaval's face, with a gentle inhalation of the breath. Yes—he
had chewed peyotl before sleeping. Lace Drawers was now far
away from San Miguel, in a hallucinated heaven.

There were two mezcal buttons, still tufted with silky hairs,
lying in the mouth of the open leather satchel. Pierre sniffed at
the liquor in the glass, and tasted it. No—no peyotl there, thank
God. If he'd put the stuff in his drink, he thought, he'd have been
empeyotado, and shouting for every whore in San Miguel. But
—what sort of shape will he be in tomorrow?

He went noiselessly back to the sala and laid another pine
log on the fire. Six thousand feet up in the mountains, and as
cold as a Christmas night in Provence. No sound but the sentries'
tread. Was he overcautious, worrying unduly? What harm could
come to twenty-five armed men in a township where the mayor
was friendly? His head nodded sleepily in the warm firelight.

It was then he heard the shuffling feet, like autumn leaves
blowing, and the sentry's sharp *"Qui vive?"*

Franchet jerked the window shutter open. Two paces away
stood the sentry, a Corsican named Gavini, with his finger on
the trigger of his carbine.

Franchet took in the scene at a glance.

"For God's sake, don't fire," he said, low. "They're only children!"

The little plaza was filling silently. Not many girls, but not a few young women, with rebozos tightly pulled round their heads, mingled with at least a score of boys of ten and twelve years old. Lean, hungry, and in rags, they gathered between the posada and the ugly squat cathedral. Lit by the fitful light of a clouded moon, looking with glinting eyes at the house where the Frenchmen lay, they were singing in a broken chorus:

> "Mexicanos, al grito de guerra,
> El acero aprestad y el brindon."

"You are on sentry duty, Soldat Gavini," said Pierre from the sala window. He had his pistol in his hand to cover the sentry if they rushed him. The Corsican resumed his tread, twelve paces to the right and back, twelve to the left and back, covering the whole front of the little posada, and the singing children came no farther than the near edge of the square.

> "Y retiemble en sus centros la tierra
> Al sonoro rugir del canon."

Pierre watched the lad wearing a French drummer boy's coat who appeared to lead the song. He remembered that this town, where the mayor was friendly, was one of the cradles of Mexican independence—commemorated by the fountain, and by the name, Allende, of one of the patriots of 1810. Dolores Hidalgo, the sacred place of independence, was only a few miles to the north. In this very street the priest Hidalgo had met with Allende, and with a woman—he had forgotten her name—when they were plotting to overthrow the rule of Spain. Here they had schemed for, here they were asking still, that which he admired so much in Sally—independence.

"DID MALAVAL LEARN from the alcalde where the men of this village may have gone?" Rossi asked Pierre next morning while the horses were being saddled.

"They're all at work on the outlying farms, he says. In fact, García swears not a single man in San Miguel has gone to join the Juaristas."

Lace Drawers was in better shape than Franchet had expected. Peyotl was not as yet a habit with him, and the cold water which he had made one of the troopers throw over his head and torso had thoroughly aroused him. Pierre, with his passion for pipe-clay and gleaming harness, could only approve of the young lieutenant's insistence on spit-and-polish, and the little troop showed the flag in fine style when they assembled in the deserted plaza. The sun was shining, and the high plateau of Guanajuato stretched golden on all sides to the distant mountain peaks, serrated, umbered with cloud shadows—the landscape which so many of the Spanish Viceroys had loved for its evocation of Castile. The road to Querétaro took them across level ground, between more prosperous casitas with well-stocked corrals. It then sloped down to the ford at Atascadero, where a narrow river ran in a deep ravine.

They were out of the barranca country proper—and yet any gulch or gully could conceal a trap. Pierre, spurring up to the head of the column, saw across the river the hacienda of Atascadero, with a puff of smoke coming out of its one chimney. He saw on the left of the rising ground beyond the ford a small adobe church with a belfry and a cross. He saw on the right a stone hut like a sheepfold, built at one side of a large corral.

Something in the relation of the buildings reminded him of Parendel. "A convent—and the cerro—and the hacienda up ahead"—such had been the deathtrap of Santa Isabel. He pulled Rataplan alongside Lieutenant Malaval as Lace Drawers was about to lead the way across the river.

"Mon lieutenant—excuse me—I wonder if we should go back towards Celaya and cut northeast across the mesa, instead of fording the arroyo?"

Lace Drawers checked his fine bay mare.

"Go back on the Celaya road—are you crazy, Franchet? Ride back through the town, and put ten miles on to our day's journey? Follow me, and give the order to ride in close formation; I'm as eager to get out of this ravine as you are."

Franchet shouted *"Serrez!"* The horses began to crowd together, the muddy water rose round their hocks. *"Allez, ser—* My God, sir, look!"

They were near enough to the far bank to see the horror roped to a great thorn tree. To see the body of the mayor of San Miguel Allende, stripped to the waist and bleeding from many knife wounds, with deep cuts on the forehead, and the right hand, with which he had shaken hands with the French officer, missing from his bleeding arm.

"Dismount! Dismount!"

"Cut him down, for God's sake!"

"He's cold, sir; it was done hours ago—"

The Frenchmen crowded round the body of the Mexican who had paid with his life for his faith in Maximilian.

"Are those *letters* on his forehead, sergeant?"

"Yes, *mon lieutenant*. T.A.M., for traitor to Mexico. I've seen this done before."

"You may have, but this is the worst I ever saw—"

"Would the lieutenant consider sending a picket back to San Miguel to tell his wife, and bring his servants here?"

"No," said Lace Drawers with decision. He had been badly shaken, and he showed it, but he was prepared to take command of the situation now. "We'll ride to the hacienda yonder, and get the people to carry up the body. We must not be late at our rendezvous with the regiment. Prepare to mount!"

The troopers, with a few looks in Pierre's direction, obeyed the officer. They mounted, the horses pawing for a foothold in the mud of the river bank. Malaval's splendid bay ran out ahead

of them. Pierre, flinging his leg over Rataplan's back, saw the
flash from the stone hut and heard the sharp crack of the Springfield rifle.

He saw the lieutenant fall, shot through the head.

"Back! back!"

The troop galloped down to the ford in a jostling mass,
splashing into the river, out of rifle shot, and cursing. The echo
of a concerted yell of triumph followed them.

"All right," said Pierre quietly. "Dismount. Tether the
horses. Rossi, take ten men; the rest follow me."

He gave orders that they all knew well. It was the old Algerian technique for smoking out the Kabyle strongholds; he wasn't
sure if it would work this time. If the enemy was in strength up
there, the troop had a good chance of being wiped out entirely.
The Massacre of Atascadero, he thought grimly. It'll look well
in the regimental records.

As it turned out, the climb up through the thorns on the
steep bank of the little ravine was the most difficult part of the
operation. There was no General Escobedo to direct the strategy
of an enemy who had made the error of placing only two men in
the hut, which was easily rushed and occupied, and concentrating
ten in the hacienda. The two Corsicans, who excelled in such
tactics, led the attack on the back of the farm, while Franchet
drew the fire at the front. There were fifteen minutes of heavy
firing at close quarters, and then the farmhouse fell to the French,
who entered with their sabers drawn.

They carried their own dead out and laid them on the grass.

"Get Malaval's body," said Pierre, wiping the sweat from
his face. "Get the prisoners started digging the graves. Have the
mayor's body carried into the church. You, Padre, get out of the
way."

An old priest, in a brown cassock, with his arms upraised
in protest, had appeared in the open door of the little church.
Behind him, Pierre saw the skulking figure of the boy in the
drummer's coat.

"You boy, come here!"

The lad hesitated, swerved, and broke for the road down to the ford. Pierre caught up with him, and with one blow with the flat of his bloodstained saber knocked the boy senseless on the turf.

"Do the French make war on children, señor?" cried the old priest, hobbling up to them.

"Child?" said Pierre. "That little devil? I'll not leave him free to run to San Miguel for help."

"There are millions of such children now in Mexico," the priest said slowly. "All they want for their country is what *your* country taught the world to need—"

"An Emperor, do you mean?" jeered Franchet.

"I mean Liberty, Equality and Fraternity."

Pierre turned on his heel. The troopers were standing guard over the prisoners and the dead—all but Corporal Rossi, who was kneeling beside the body of the soldier Gavini, and weeping bitterly. Pierre remembered that they had been blood brothers in some obscure Corsican vendetta, which had filled several graves in Ajaccio and given two worthy recruits to the Foreign Legion.

"He was a good soldier, Rossi," he said.

The corporal drew his hand across his eyes and started up.

"He was," he said. "Avenge him! Execute the prisoners!"

"Execute them? I'll take them into Querétaro. We might get information out of them—"

"There's no more information needed about San Miguel Allende," said the corporal, with a curse. "Remember, you are the *chef de la troupe* now, Franchet! And under the Decrees, you *must* court-martial them!"

Franchet was silent. He had always thought the Black Flag Decrees Maximilian's greatest error, and the summary execution of prisoners of war a hateful task. But he knew by the growl of assent that the Légionnaires were all behind the Corsican. He remembered the mutilated mayor, and the dying Parendel, and he said:

"Is there a manual in Malaval's *musette?*"

There was. He turned the pages in silence while the four

prisoners dug four shallow graves. The women came shrieking
out of the hacienda, and he bade the old priest leave the dazed
and trembling boy and go to them, while the papers and small
possessions of the dead Frenchmen were collected for the records
and the relatives. Then the bodies of Malaval, Gavini, Lachaume
and Bertholet were committed to their graves in the soil of Mexico, while the old priest read the burial service in a trembling
voice.

It was Pierre's turn to read aloud after that.

"By virtue of the Articles of War and the authority dele-
gated to me by François Achille Bazaine, Marshal of France
and Supreme Commander of the Imperial Forces in Mexico, I
hereby declare that all individuals forming part of armed bands
shall be condemned by a court-martial and executed within
twenty-four hours. The same shall apply to all prisoners of
war . . ."

The Black Flag Decrees were read to the last word. The
drumhead court-martial followed. The verdict of all the Légionnaires was guilty.

"I hate to waste good ammunition on the dogs," said Rossi.
"There are lariats in the stables; shall we string them up?"

"Fall out a firing party," was Pierre's rejoinder. "And you,
señor cura, confess your parishioners; we're in a hurry to be on
our way."

"But surely," said the old man, bewildered, "you cannot
mean to destroy men who surrendered to you, and are your
prisoners?"

"They knew the risk they took when they opened fire,"
said Pierre Franchet. "Four of our men are dead. A life for a
life, *señor cura:* I've heard that called a fair exchange."

"My son," said the old man gravely, "only God requires a
life for a life—not man."

He took one of the Mexicans apart. The others waited in
the sun. They did not seem much moved; the obsidian eyes
stared with a queer fatalism at the ring of weeping women and

the familiar buildings of Atascadero. The firing party leaned on their carbines, and waited.

They fired, when Pierre jerked out the word of command, point-blank, and there was no need of a *coup de grâce*. Then the incident at Atascadero was concluded, and Pierre was free to think of the interviews which lay ahead, when the sergeant who knew the terrain returned to his regiment without his young lieutenant and three of their best men.

The women were howling over the bodies, of course, before the horses were brought up from the riverside. But the old padre paused in his prayers to stand in Rataplan's path for a moment, and make the sign of the Cross in the air with his forefinger.

"May God have mercy on your troubled soul, my son," he said.

They rode away from the place of death in silence. Nearly all of the men bore some mark of the fighting: two, indeed, were bandaged and swaying in their saddles. They were going to be half a day late at the rendezvous.

In spite of that Franchet meant to halt them when they had got a few miles away from San Miguel Allende. They all needed food and drink; some, he saw, had already lighted cigarillos as they rode. He put his hand in his pocket for his own pipe and tobacco. His fingers encountered something with sharp points which drew blood even from his calloused hand as he pulled it out.

It was the Cross from Aranzazu. He had seen the old priest holding up a larger Cross, carved from the same brown thorn-wood, before the eyes of the Mexicans condemned to die.

"May God have mercy on your troubled soul, my son."

Among thorns, You.

Chapter Nineteen

THE LOST CAUSE

THE PIERRE FRANCHET who strode down the main street of Orizaba on a warm afternoon late in October was a different Pierre from the weary, anxious sergeant who led his little troop out of the ambush at Atascadero. He was alert and confident in a spruce white uniform, freshly barbered, with a cheerful word for acquaintances in the steadily moving crowd around him. The pretty town at the foot of the Peak was not only a vast transit camp for the Imperial Army. It was, and had been for three days past, the seat of the Imperial Government. Maximilian, by the grace of God Emperor, was in residence at his little hacienda of Jalapilla, and the town was full to overflowing with his body-guard and friends.

There was, as always, a little crowd of loungers and beggars round the white picket fence of the Hotel de France. Pierre signaled to a couple of vaqueros in a nondescript livery of what might once have been brown and yellow, and cried above the heads of the bystanders:

"No sign of the conducta?"

"Not yet, señor." A slow smile creased the copper-colored face. "Don Juan will not delay much longer on the road."

Pierre consulted the silver turnip watch held in his breast pocket by a leather strap. Inside the garden of the Hotel de France he saw a woman holding court, and recognized her as the most sensational arrival in Mexico for many a day. Princess Felix zu Salm-Salm, once an American circus rider and now the

wife of a German princeling who had thrown in his lot with
Maximilian, wore a gray and silver habit cut on the style of the
Belgian uniform. She was smiling with a great display of teeth
and fondling a black and tan terrier, whom she called Jimmy
after the owner of the *New York Tribune,* who had presented
him to her. The men around the princess were nearly all Americans, wearing the short gray patrol jackets of the French Counterguerilleros.

Pierre turned away. He was waiting for just one girl, who
had no need of a uniform to prove her spirit. And the time of his
waiting, which he had feared might be prolonged for weeks yet,
had been miraculously shortened since that day at noon, when
two of John Halkett's vaqueros, riding well ahead of their conducta, had come in to Orizaba to tell him the Scots mine manager was bringing Miss Sally Lorimer up the great highway from
the coast.

The silver trains still went down with their loads of bullion
to Vera Cruz, now the only port remaining in Maximilian's
hands. Their passage was almost the one constant feature in the
changing face of Mexico. That it was maintained in a land at war
—that the coarse sacks of maguey fiber, each holding three thousand dollars worth of silver—were carried and shipped in safety
was a tribute to the perseverance of the mine managers, nearly
all Scots or English, who were as little affected by the decline of
Maximilian as by the collapse of a dozen Mexican Presidents
before him. Pierre had taken the movement of the silver trains
for granted. He had never before, in three years of the great highway, strained his eyes through the moving mass of men and
vehicles for one convoy—one train of wagons, piled on the return journey with goods and stores, with one especial mule cart
traveling in the middle. When it came, and the cart stopped at the
gate of the Hotel de France, and Sally got out, he was speechless.
He could only stammer like a schoolboy and bow over her
hand, all his self-assurance gone, and himself aware that the
American volunteers had turned from Princess Salm to admire

the slim girl in a grayish-green dress, who wore a hat veiled with cream lace upon her shining hair.

Somehow, he made himself shake hands with bluff John Halkett and his sister Ann, a tall grenadier of a woman, laden with small awkward parcels; somehow he handed Sally up the path to the private sitting room reserved since the Halketts' outward journey, and shut the door upon the world. Then she was in his arms again, pressing his head down to her with fierce small hands, taking his kisses like a parched plant opening to rain. And the words were kisses, the kisses words, when she murmured her confession.

"Oh Pierre, oh Pierre, I've missed you so!"

"Sally! my God! I adore you!"

There was something Pierre had wanted to make sure of, for weeks past. He tilted up her chin with one hand, to look into her eyes. And they were brown, not hazel, but the brown was flecked with gold and green, *fauve* eyes, just as he had remembered them when the moonlight shone down on the mesa. So he kissed her eyelids and her little ears, till Sally pulled away from him breathless, setting her smart hat straight.

"Have I rumpled your fine feathers?" he said with his crooked smile. "Let me look at you, *ma belle Parisienne!*"

His keen, appraising eyes, so quick to sum up what a woman wore and how she wore it, were quite simply dazzled by her. Sally was paler than when she went away, but the shining curl on her shoulder, the touch of coralline salve on her lips— even the pink polished nails of the hands he held in his, gave her a sophistication which the Sally of Las Flores never had. She was a Parisienne on the surface, but then—she had come back to him!

"You're so lovely, Sally," he said huskily, "I wonder the Empress of the French didn't kidnap you, to be one of the beauties of her court."

"Oh, Pierre! This is my *only* Paris dress! Lady Laura—Mr. Fraser's wife—gave it to me as a farewell present. She was kindness itself to me. I oughtn't to be wearing it for traveling," Sally was talking in an effort to regain her composure, "but I wanted Andrew—"

"You wanted Andrew to see that you'd come back with the honors of war; quite right," said Pierre. "But he knows it, darling. He was quite aware of it, when I talked to him here ten days ago."

"You talked, and didn't quarrel?"

"Of course not." Pierre tried to smile. "He saw that I was—desperate for news of you. He told me, quite pleasantly, that you were crossing with an English family, and meant to spend a few days in Havana. You'll find him a good deal changed, Sally. He's been worried about you, since the truth began to come out about Carlóta."

"Was Andrew in Orizaba ten days ago?" she said. "I thought the Emperor had only just arrived."

"Perhaps he came to make arrangements—I don't know. I'd only just arrived from Mexico myself," said Pierre easily. "But Sally—*your* letter—the one I got at Querétaro; how can I ever thank you for it? It came when I was in bad trouble; we ran into an ambush on the way down, and I was held to blame, but your letter made up for all of it. To know that you had left the Empress, and gone to stay with your own relations—that meant everything to me. I knew then that you were safe and well."

"Yes, I was safe," said Sally slowly. "But I didn't tell the whole truth in that letter."

"You didn't?" suddenly alert.

"You say the truth came out about Carlóta? How much *do* you know?"

"Pretty nearly everything, *chérie*. It's known, of course, that the first stories of her trip were lies, that Napoleon rebuffed her and her mission to Paris failed. Everything changed, you see, after the cable service started and newspaper correspondents began coming into Mexico. It can never happen again that a war is begun and ended in Europe before we even know about it here, or—well, never mind. Right up to the time Carlóta left Paris for Miramar, it was given out that she was well and prospering. But they couldn't make a secret of her trip to Italy. Everybody knows she went off to appeal to the Pope of Rome, and went stark mad in the Vatican. That her brother turned up at last and took her back to Miramar—"

"She didn't go mad in the Vatican, Pierre."

"Oh, come now, Sally—"

"She went mad in the palace of St. Cloud."

"What!"

"You were right, Pierre, and I was wrong." The words so hard for Sally Lorimer to say, were out at last. ". . . I want to tell you everything that really happened. But only you and Andrew are to know. Not anybody else. Not even the Halketts. Where are they, by the way?"

"He's seeing after his men and the wagons, and she's a wonderful dueña—knows when to keep out of sight. Sally, go on!"

Very quietly, and at first unemotionally, Sally described her last two days with the Empress of Mexico. The delusion of the poisoned orangeade, the episode of the knife in the Paris market, were narrated quickly and calmly. But before the end of the story, when Carlóta at last numbered Sally among her persecutors, Pierre had taken her back into his arms, and as she described her nightmare flight through the streets of Paris his hard cheek was against her wet one and his clasp had tightened as though he would never let her go.

"Thank God for Herzog," he said when all was told. "You mean he grew so uneasy about the situation that he left Vienna and went to Paris of his own accord?"

"After he read that Carlóta had failed in her appeal to Napoleon."

"And so he took you back to the hotel—what happened then?"

"I spent the night in Señora del Barrio's dressing room, in an easy chair. I couldn't have gone back to my own room until daylight, not to save my life. Señora del Barrio was extremely kind to me, bless her; I'd worried so, in case she would blame me for what happened—"

"Nonsense!"

"I blame myself, Pierre."

"None of that," said Franchet roughly. He made her lift her head and look at him. Lights from the garden, where paper lanterns had been hung from the trees, showed his face strained and weary, with new lines round his eyes and mouth, but he smiled at her with confidence.

"You mustn't shoulder other people's guilt for poor Doña Carlóta," he said. "We are only required to be responsible for our own."

"But this may *be* my guilt! Supposing what I said about poor little Agustín was the thing that pushed her over the edge into madness?"

He saw the pent-up wretchedness in her face and spoke hastily,

"She was mad already, Sally. I told you so, the day we found her in the barranca."

"Yes." She gave a long sigh, like a child, and relaxed in his arms. "After it was—all over, I couldn't be sorry that I ran out into the streets, and was so lost and frightened for a time. Because then I understood what *she* felt like that day, when she ran away from La Borda. I understood what it could be like—to go mad."

"God!" breathed Pierre. "If Herzog hadn't found you! And he took you straight to your relations?"

"As soon as he found that the Mexicans had quarreled among themselves after the mission failed. You know, don't you, that only a few of them went on with her as far as Rome? Señora del Barrio did . . . but even Señora del Barrio wouldn't risk letting her see *me*. So Dr. Herzog telegraphed to the Frasers, who were on holiday at Houlgate, and later he took me down to them by train. I think Lady Laura was rather shocked when I arrived with an unmarried gentleman for escort, but she unfroze after a bit and was very kind. So was Mr. Fraser. We stayed for a week at Houlgate and then we all went back to Paris."

"Dr. Herzog too?"

Opening wide eyes: "He'd gone back to Vienna, of course."

"Didn't he try to make an honest woman of you, after this compromising excursion by slow train to the English Channel?"

"Pierre!"

"Didn't he ask you to marry him, darling?"

"How could you possibly think of such a thing?"

"You forget that in my dishonorable way I overheard a conversation between the two of you in the garden at Chapultepec. There is a certain tone in a man's voice when he is interested in a lady—I heard it in Dr. Herzog's voice that night."

"Most of that conversation was about yourself," retorted Sally.

"*Touché!* But seriously, am I right about the worthy doctor's hopes?"

"He did ask me," Sally admitted. "Don't make fun of him, Pierre!"

"The student of the brain. Why wouldn't you have him, Sally? Didn't you fancy the idea of Vienna? You'd have been the Frau Medicine Rat, or whatever they call it, with a place among the intellectuals, and your own carriage and pair—"

She hid her face against his shoulder and murmured something he pretended not to hear. Pretended, for the aching joy and triumph of making her repeat it.

"My place is here in Mexico with you."

There was healing for Sally in Pierre's arms and his lips. She could hear John Halkett's robust voice uplifted in the garden, shouting to a servant to bring a bottle of whisky, and the knowledge that he and his sister were there within call added to the delicious sense of being protected and sustained against the world. But Pierre's broad shoulders were her first defense. She let her hands move over them, caressingly, from epaulets to high-hooked collar up to the place where his ash-blond hair was most closely cropped, and back again across the smooth white linen . . . Her hands stopped.

"What's become of all those leather straps you used to wear?"

"What indeed?" said Franchet, bending over her. The white scar on his jaw stood out clearly in the lamplight from the garden.

"Have they issued a new tropical uniform at last?"

"Yes."

There was something in his tone that brought her to her feet.

"Light the lamp," she said quickly. "Or are there candles? The Halketts mustn't find us sitting in the dark."

Pierre obeyed. He drew a shade across the open window and struck a light. On the white-spread table, between the pottery bowls of fruit, an oil lamp flowered into gold.

Sally saw Pierre in his new, close-fitting white tunic, with long white trousers strapped under short riding boots, and without the blue sash, the pistol, the red trousers of the Legion. She took in the captain's gilt bars on his shoulder, and she became aware of a high shako lying in the chair where he had tossed it when he first brought her into the posada. She found her voice,

"A *Whitecoat?* Is that an Austrian uniform, Pierre?"

The haunted look on his face gave way to ironical amusement.

"Oh now, Sally, things aren't as bad as all that! The Whitecoats indeed! This is the dress uniform of the *Cazadores de México,* in which I hold a captain's commission, signed by Maximilian Emperor and countersigned by Bazaine, Marshal of France. From sergeant to captain in twenty-four hours! At the Mexican rate of promotion, I'll be a general before Christmas."

"You transferred to *them?* From the Foreign Legion?"

"If I hadn't, *ma chérie,* you might have passed Rataplan and me slogging downhill through Tierra Caliente, as you came up from Córdoba today . . . Or else the transport taking us to Europe might have hailed the *Clotilde* as she passed us in midocean. Or else—oh, Sally, don't you know what I'm driving at?

I exchanged to the Cazadores because it was the only way to stay in Mexico and keep the promise I made to wait for you."

"But will this make any difference to the terms of your enlistment? To the two years more you have to serve?"

He nodded approvingly. Trust Sally to put her finger at once on the weak point in the whole transaction—the point debated round many campfires, up and down Mexico, by the fifteen hundred officers and men of the French Expeditionary Corps who had transferred to the Mexican Chasseurs.

"Well, it seems that's still in doubt," he said. "Officially, I was discharged from the Foreign Legion before I could be commissioned in the Cazadores. But I believe the War Ministry has to give its approval of the deal. Meantime, Bazaine is paying us, when he remembers. I get three thousand francs a year now, instead of one—and I daresay the war will be over before we ever hear a word from Paris."

"But *isn't* the war over?"

"Over—how?"

She looked at him aghast.

"Yesterday in Vera Cruz," she said, "I met the British Minister at luncheon. He was at the posada, and he came over to talk to me about—Doña Carlóta. He told us, he said he wanted as many Mexicans as possible to know it, that he had advised Don Maximiliano to abdicate *at once* and return to Europe. He even pointed out an Austrian boat, a corvette I think he called it—I know its name was *Dandolo,* which was coaled and ready to take Maximilian right back to Trieste. I thought the thing was finished, Pierre: what is the sense in going on?"

"You may well ask," said Captain Franchet. "You might think that a man with an insane wife, no allies and an empty treasury would have the tact to make his bow and head for home. But Max is just stupid enough and just stubborn enough, to want to persevere. You know Diaz gave the Austrians a tremendous hammering in Oaxaca a few days ago?"

"At La Carbonera—Mr. Halkett told me."

"Well, our orders are to follow Diaz across the province

and try to stop him from reaching Oaxaca city. Oh, my darling girl, don't cry!" For Sally had sat down abruptly and buried her face in her hands.

"Sally! Darling! You're overtired. You shouldn't be worrying about all this now. Shall I call Miss Halkett? Shall I get you a glass of wine?"

"I'm all right," she said dangerously. "I only—the whole thing is such a murderous *farce!* Silly men, moving about like rooks on a chessboard! Juarez is in Chihuahua. Bazaine is in Mexico. Maximilian in Orizaba. Diaz in Oaxaca. You've joined the Cazadores and the Foreign Legion is on the way back to Algeria. And I—where am I? I went to Europe with a lunatic. *Not* to enjoy myself. Just to earn some money to buy machinery. Do you know where that machinery is now, Pierre? The boilers and instruments for my refinery, shipped f.o.b. New Orleans on the first of August, according to the bill of lading? I found them rusting in a bonded warehouse, if you can call it that, on the wharf at Vera Cruz. It was considered too big a risk to ship them up to Cuernavaca 'in the unsettled state of the country.' And next month, early next month, is the time the refinery should be operating. When I was in Havana I arranged with Mr. Wilkinson to send over a competent sugarmaster for the season. A nice fool I should have looked if his equipment had still been under lock and key at Vera Cruz!"

"You mean you got it out of bond?"

"Of course I did. And had it loaded on the empty silver wagons, with Mr. Halkett's help. I've been through hell for that machinery," said Sally defiantly. "Naturally I brought it with me!"

SALLY WAS awakened early next morning by the familiar sounds of departure in the street below. Her bed was near the window, and by raising herself on one elbow she could see not one but three coaches of the Diligencias Generales, loading baggage and travelers whom she had not seen the night before. Among them were young women with saucy painted faces and feathered hats, who were waving and screeching agreeably to a group of the Counterguerilleros in the gray uniform which Pierre had pointed out to her as they sat at dinner. She could read part of the address marked in large white letters on their trunks and boxes,

MAZEPPA COMP
TEATRO IMPER
MEXICO.

That'll make a nice change from the *Domino Azul* and *Don Juan Tenorio,* she thought without sarcasm. Somehow, in this changing Mexico, it was cheering to think that a company of American players was heading for the capital. She sat up in her white bed to watch them. The coaches got under way with the usual cracking of whips and shouting of the guards. The American boys in the gray uniforms began to cheer and sing:

"Oh say shall the star-spangled banner yet wave
O'er the land of the free—and Jeff Davis's grave!"

"Oh, *pooh!*" said Sally, jerking down the window shade. She looked apprehensively at the other bed. Neither the shouting outside nor her own impulsive exclamation had roused her latest traveling companion, Miss Ann Halkett. The Scotswoman's large form, in shape resembling a sea lion, lay motionless except for the quivering of her short brindled pigtail. In her capacity for slumber, Miss Ann was a great improvement on the peevish, wakeful English spinster with whom Sally had shared a cabin on the voyage home.

Not the least of the lessons Sally had learned in the months since she left Mexico had been to adapt herself, as best she could, to other people. She had set out prepared to be at the beck and call of the Empress of Mexico; she had not reckoned on the vagaries of Lady Laura Fraser, nor of her English chaperones, nor even on a presence as silent and sympathetic as that of Ann Halkett. Her independent spirit had often rebelled at being under an obligation to all the strangers, kindly and well meaning though they were, who had come to the rescue of a girl stranded in a foreign country.

The night before, in the joy of her reunion with Pierre, she had not experienced the feeling of anticlimax which the morning brought. Then, her only disappointment had been Andrew's absence; for in spite of two messages sent to the Emperor's hacienda, her brother had failed to put in an appearance at the Hotel de France. Now, she realized how childishly she had pictured her return to Mexico as the start of a new play, with all the inconvenient characters removed to the wings, and the limelight full on Pierre and herself in the peace and prosperity of Las Flores.

It was not so: Pierre with a different rank and uniform was still a soldier, still waiting for his marching orders. The Emperor was still vacillating, still putting off decisive action, and Las Flores, as the war crept farther south, seemed farther out of reach than ever. But Sally, as the noise and bustle of the day began to spread through the posada, was not despondent. For all the difficulties which lay ahead, she was back in Mexico . . . and Pierre was coming to her as soon as parade was over.

She fell asleep again, with innocent sensuality dreaming of his kisses, and woke two hours later to find Ann Halkett standing by her bed with a small tray in her hands.

"Ye'll need to jump, ma dearie," the Scotswoman said. "Your brother's come. Here's a cup o' coffee; drink it while ye put your clothes on, for the doctor seems gey hurried like, and willna sit down to tak' his breakfast. He's waiting for you in the yard outbye."

Their parlor of the night before was no longer private, for Mr. Perry, the correspondent of the *New York Tribune,* had reserved it for a breakfast party of the foreign newspapermen now gathering in Orizaba to write the story of Maximilian's expected abdication. Princess Salm was there, this time escorted by her husband; Sally heard her high laugh and the barking of her dog as she went past the door.

Andrew was walking up and down in the garden near a pergola of the roses for which the province and town were famous. He was dressed in a tropical suit of white linen, much rumpled, with a scarf at his neck, Mexican fashion, instead of the usual cravat. There was dust on his short riding boots and some brown horse hairs on his clothing, as if he had ridden further that morning than the short way from the hacienda of Jalapilla.

"Sally, how are you?" There was a constraint in his manner, as he shook hands, which made her glad no critical eyes were watching their reunion. "I'm sorry I wasn't able to be here when you arrived."

"We thought the Emperor might spare you for a little while, but they said you weren't at his house at all—"

"Did they? No, that's so; I was out on a case," he said readily. "Dr. Basch attends the Emperor now, and I'm more free to come and go. How was your journey up from Vera Cruz?"

"Very good; but oh, Andrew! We met half those poor people from the Carlóta Colony on the highway, just before you come to Mule Pass. They're afraid to stay on in Córdoba since Diaz won his big victory."

"Have you any idea where they're going?"

"Some of them are going to try coffee-planting in Brazil."

"Poor devils." He spoke quite without feeling. Sally studied him covertly as they sat down at a white-painted table in the rose arbor. She saw what Ann Halkett had meant by the word "hurried," for although her brother sprawled in his seat like a man of leisure, there was a driven look in his face which she had never seen before. He was very pale, with all his ruddy color gone, and there were shadows of sleeplessness beneath his eyes.

"I want you to tell me about the Empress." His first inquiries had meant nothing, of course; this was the question she had known he would ask first, and she was ready for it. As rapidly, but also as completely as possible, she repeated the story she had told Pierre Franchet. Andrew sat slumped over the table, shading his eyes with his hand.

"I owe you an apology, Sally," he said when she had finished; and that cost Andrew as much of an effort as for Sally to confess herself in the wrong to Pierre. "I—Herzog was right about her all along, and I refused to see it. I was positive that if I could heal her body, her mind would heal itself. Herzog knew that in her case the mind came first."

"You weren't the only one," she comforted him. "At least three French doctors thought her well enough to go on to Rome."

"Did you know she had been *certified* insane?"

"No!" startled. "When did you hear that?"

"The telegram came from Riedel, the Viennese alienist, just before we left Chapultepec."

"It must have been a terrible shock to Maximilian."

"Basch was with him at the time, and said he took it very well. He should have been expecting it, after her brother's letters—after Rome. By the way, he wants to see you, Sally; I'm to take you to him, later in the day."

"I'd rather not," she said, shrinking. "I want to forget the whole thing, if I can. But Andrew—after all that—doesn't Maximilian mean to abdicate?"

"God knows! Mexico is a lost cause, they all think, but he holds on somehow through it all. At the time of the Austrian defeat, he seemed to have an idea of going back to Europe, but only as Emperor of Mexico, and his brother made it clear there wasn't room for two Emperors in Vienna. Right now he's recovering from an acute attack of dysentery, and Basch and I are trying to get him in shape to meet the Cabinet next week. The Diaz sensation—"

"I beg your graces' pardon, by your leave—"

Neither of them had heard the soft-footed approach of an

Indian in livery. He stood deferentially before them, with his sombrero and a letter in one hand.

"I missed you at La Fortaleza, señor doctor," the man said. "At the posada they said you left an hour ahead of me. I have an urgent message from the Quinta Vega—"

"Give it here!"

Andrew had started to his feet, and his face, which had been so pale, was suffused with color. He did not look at Sally. He read the brief note hastily.

"Ride back at once," he said to the vaquero. "Tell the lady I am on my way."

When the man had gone: "Is it Silvia?" said Sally anxiously. "Has she been taken ill?"

"I don't know," said Andrew slowly, and then he passed the written page across the table. "I—you'd better read it, Sally."

"It was impossible to send to you last night," the message ran. "They had a quarrel. Please do not leave La Fortaleza until I come."

It was signed "M.C.R."

"Andrew, who—?"

"Maria del Carmen Ramirez," said Andrew. "The Tía Maria Beata."

"Is that her real name? I never knew." She thought inconsequently how ill the name suited Silvia's dueña. Carmen—it was a vivid name, much in favor among the lower classes in Mexico. *"Olé, Carmen—cita!"*—it had been a frequent shout at the fountain of the Plaza de Santo Domingo.

"I must go," said Andrew. "If—everything is all right—I'll see you later, Sally."

She detained him.

"Did you spend last night at La Fortaleza, Andrew?"

"Yes."

"And you were there ten days ago, when Pierre saw you?"

"I was."

"Hoping for a meeting with Silvia?"

"I haven't seen Silvia for three weeks."

"But you're her lover, aren't you?"

"I can't answer that question, Sally."

He had answered Sally by his refusal. She remembered Vera's cynical words after the picnic at Las Tres Marias. She remembered that the Tía Beata—the experienced go-between—had been sent to Silvia by Vera. In Andrew's miserable face she saw the whole intrigue.

"Let me go, Sally. God only knows what may have happened there by now."

"If you go to the Quinta Vega," said Sally, "I'm going with you."

. . . He found it impossible to shake her determination. Silvia might be in trouble and would need a friend. This she repeated, while Pierre Franchet came off duty and hurried to her side; while John Halkett ordered horses saddled and said with equal decision that they should all four ride to the Quinta Vega without delay.

"For if there's illness in the house, and you're detained there, doctor," he said with rough tact, "somebody will be needed to bring poor Sally back to Orizaba, and let Annie and me see her safely on her way. We'll wait at the gatehouse if you like, but we're going with you, and that's flat."

They took the road which Andrew knew by heart. In the four months since his journey with Carlóta's suite, he had gone at least every ten days by coach to Orizaba, had hired a horse and ridden on to the little township at the Vega gates. Had waited in the inn parlor for the message from the Tía Beata, or for the woman herself, to tell him where on Don Felipe's vast estates he could find and possess Don Felipe Vega's wife. In tropical rains, in humid nights when the whole province seeemed bursting into flower, oblivious to his profession, to the fate of Mexico, to the needs of his countrymen at the Carlóta Colony whom he had once desired to serve, Andrew Lorimer had gone to the repeated, the frantic consummation of his love. Had passed, inevitably, from the first rapture to the first chill: the knowledge that even now she would not trust him, would not fly with him to Cuba, feared her father even while she loved himself. At their last rendezvous, early in October, she had wept that her father was to visit the Quinta Vega, and so *he* must keep away; must not compromise her—all this while her arms were round his neck, and choking him.

He rode now beside John Halkett, saying nothing: bucketing along the road he had come earlier that morning, when he had given up all hope of having word from Silvia. Ahead of them Sally and Pierre were setting a sharp pace. Sally, he saw, rode easily and well. He heard Pierre laugh and say something inaudible, and Sally's gay rejoinder,

". . . rode quite often in the Bois de Boulogne!"

"Weren't you glad I taught you on a European saddle?"

Andrew saw their hands go out, and link between the horses, as the roofs of La Fortaleza came in sight.

They went through the little town without drawing rein, although Sally saw the innkeeper and his wife at the door of the posada, who eyed them curiously as they rode by. In a few strides more—Rataplan leading, and champing at his bit—they were on the Vega estate proper, where peons were gathering the coffee crop, and all appeared so normal that Sally unconsciously relaxed. From horseback she could see much more than from the coach of her previous visit, of the domains over which Silvia was mistress. The buildings of a great, self-supporting hacienda, compared to which her own Las Flores was a gardener's cottage, were strung out along the road. The sawmill, the flour mill, the rice mill, the meat market, the curing sheds, the blanket manufactory, led them on to the belt of giant trees which sheltered the hacienda, and the gatekeeper came out, bowing, to admit them to the orchid avenue.

The Tía Beata was running down between the palms to meet them. Her black veil was undone and her short grizzled hair revealed. Her mouth was open and gasping, her hands outstretched.

The men were off their horses instantly. Andrew was the first to reach her.

"Señorita!" he cried. "Silvia! where is she?"

"Oh *Madre de Dios,* Don Andrés," she said. "He has killed her."

THE HOUSE SERVANTS were weeping and wringing their hands outside the room where Silvia Mora's fate had been decided once and for all. The major-domo, who had been told that a doctor was on his way, had refused to let anybody enter, although both he and the Tía Beata knew that no doctor could help the man and woman who lay on the Moorish rugs of the splendid room. He told John Halkett and Pierre, far more coherently than the dueña, of Don Felipe's unexpected appearance in his wife's apartments while her maid was pouring out her morning chocolate—of the maid's having been sent out of the room as the voices behind the heavy door were raised—and finally of the two shots which, about an hour before Andrew's arrival, had terrified the house. The soldier and the Scotsman listened to the man in silence. The thoughts of both men were with Sally.

Sally had not been allowed to see the body of Don Felipe Vega. After he had shot down his wife, he had blown his brains out, and Andrew's first intelligible order had been to have one of the thick rugs thrown over the ghastly sight. But he let his sister kneel in tears by Silvia, lovely in death as in life, with one bullet hole beneath the spot where the Querétaro opals held together the laces on her breast.

She must have snatched up the brooch to pin her *negligé* when her husband came into the room, for her jewel case was overturned on her bedside table, and a stool, lying on its side, showed where she had tried to escape from him at the climax of their quarrel. The bullet had gone through her body, for there was much blood on the carpet when Andrew lifted her up and carried her to another room where white sheets had been spread upon a low divan. The flow had stopped when he laid her down; there was blood on his coat sleeve, but not much, and Silvia lay on her bier as calmly as he had seen her lie, after love, in his own arms.

"I want you to leave me with her, Sally—will you?" he got out. He heard her sobbing as she obeyed him, and then the soft click of the door. He was alone at last with his true love.

"Silvia!"

He fell on his knees beside the couch and buried his face in her side. She was still warm and yielding when he flung out his arm and gathered her closer to him, kissing her dead face desperately, bruising his lips on the opal brooch.

The laces of her robe fell open and her white throat was waiting for his mouth. He saw the blue veins, clearly marked as never before, and the enlarged breasts beneath the thin night-gown. He knew then what her murderer had suspected, and had seen, when he came on his wife propped up on her pillows in the morning light.

His child—his love had given her the promise of a child, and now child and mother lay dead together, and his own life lay in ruins at her feet.

Much later, as it seemed, the Tía Beata came to him, and knelt by his side with her rosary in her hand. Only then had Silvia's lover the power to rise to his feet and raise the kneeling woman to confront him.

"You have the rest of your life for prayer," he said sternly. "Tell me, before we leave this room, why you failed to come for me last night."

"Don Andrés," she said, "I *will* tell you; it is only right that you should know. Silvia meant to come to you herself. She had been ailing and capricious for some weeks and afraid to see you, but last night I think her mind was quite made up. Then he made a scene about her father's visit; said he had written to Don Antonio about her—and that Don Antonio would arrive today. Then she grew nervous, and wept much, and was afraid to leave the house."

"But she meant to come away with me?"

The Beata bowed her head. "This morning he came to her room. It was the first time, señor; the first time for many weeks, because she had resisted him when she was—happy; and after the beginning he seemed more interested in his gardenias than in her. But today he came upon her unawares—he realized . . ."

There was no need to say more. Andrew looked at the Beata, and saw that her knowledge was complete.

"I want you to promise," he said painfully, "that only your hands shall dress her for her grave."

"I swear it, Don Andrés. And though they put me to the torture, I shall never, never tell."

"They will not torture *you*," he said. "The torture will be reserved for me."

Chapter Twenty

THE PEDREGAL

"TAKE CARE of my sister, Halkett. Get her away from here as fast as possible."

It was Andrew's express order, and it was carried out to the letter by John Halkett, with the full approval of Pierre. John never told Sally of his personal relief at seeing Don Antonio Mora's carriage go through Orizaba without stopping while she was taking an agonized leave of Captain Franchet. He felt that it was well for all of them to avoid a painful scene with Silvia's father—who was, incidentally, his own son's father-in-law. "The doctor will need to take his medicine like a man," he said grimly to his sister. "That lassie has plenty on her plate already."

Sally indeed was broken with grief and anxiety when Mr. Halkett's silver train resumed its slow progress to the north. Miss Ann wisely let her cry, and then held Sally in her arms until she fell asleep, as the mule cart picked its way through the convoys of army vehicles which in those days seemed always on the move. At the first halt John Halkett asked Sally to go with them to the Mine House. He did not insist when she refused. "I must go back to the Plazuelita," she kept repeating. "Andrew's house must be ready for him when he comes home."

But Dr. Lorimer did not return to Mexico for several weeks. He remained with the Emperor at Orizaba, sheltered to some extent from the storm which broke over his head when the Vega murder and suicide were made public. The time was past when such a scandal in high life could be hushed up by the families concerned. As Pierre had told Sally, it was a changed Mexico, where news traveled fast, and the presence of so many foreign correspondents at Orizaba made it inevitable that the Vega scandal would be given promptly to the world. It was the biggest sensation since the Praslin case of 1847, which had rocked Paris and helped to bring about the downfall of King Louis Philippe, and it was used in the same way by the Northern press in the United States. It was an example, said Northern editors severely, of the decadence and degeneracy of society which might be expected when a foreign archduke was permitted to usurp a throne south of the border. The part played by a Southern filibuster, Dr. Andrew Lorimer, in breaking up the happy marriage of the Marqués and Marquesa de Vega was also heartily condemned.

Don Antonio Mora, in his grief and anger, had forgotten to be discreet, and a few questions put—notably by the *New York Tribune*—to the innkeeper at La Fortaleza had done the rest. Sally, almost alone in the home for which they had set out with such high hopes, had the added pain of knowing that her brother's name was not only notorious in Mexico but had been dragged through the gutter press of the whole world.

She was not quite alone, for kind Ann Halkett stayed on to keep her company until Andrew came, and the English governess, Miss Keane, was glad to leave her apartment in the Calle de Santo Espíritu and occupy one of the bedrooms at Four, Plaza de Santo Domingo. Together, the older women helped Sally to endure the Day of the Dead, kept that year with particular solemnity as the tide of war lapped inexorably over Mexico. On that day Sally, with her black mantilla folded over her black dress, ventured into Santo Domingo's church to look once more on the Virgén del Rosario who so strangely resembled Silvia Mora. For the tragedy of Silvia weighed heavily on Sally. Being a woman, she blamed Silvia more than she blamed her brother. If only, she thought again and again, she had listened to me! If only she had eloped with Andrew months ago, as Pilár did with the man she loved! But in the church, looking up at the subtle Virgin, now bejeweled in a dark-blue velvet crinoline,

Sally could only remember the lovely girl standing before the altar of the Child of the Cactus, and weep for her.

The only gaiety in Sally's life at that time was provided by a child. Chapultepec castle had been closed when the Emperor left for Orizaba, and no one walked now in the patio of the Boy Heroes, or on the sunrise-facing terrace where Carlóta had watched the progress of her great new avenue to Mexico. Little Agustín Iturbide had been one of the first persons to drive along the promenade when his aunt, Princess Josefa, brought him into the rooms prepared for them at the National Palace.

There Sally went to play with him and with El Tigre, now grown a fine large cat with a sense of humor delightful to his little master. Agustín at nearly four was affectionate and outgiving; he asked Sally every time he saw her "when papa was coming back." He never mentioned his mamma: on his lips, as on those of everyone who had known her, the name of the Empress Carlóta was stilled forever.

There came an afternoon when bluff John Halkett, with his Scotch bonnet on the back of his head, reappeared in the Plazuelita, with a small company of his mule drivers and the wagons containing the refinery equipment which Sally had taken out of bond at Vera Cruz.

"Are ye ready for the road again, my lass?" was his cheerful salutation. "I'm willing to tak' you down to Las Flores tomorrow morning. Your sugarmaster's on his way; he was to sleep tonight at Río Frío, and he may verra well catch up with us at the Tres Marias, if you're still keen to make a start."

"Keen!" said Sally the next morning, as they drove out of Mexico, "if you only knew how eager I am to see this sugar crop refined! You see, I never had time at Orizaba to tell Pierre my plans for the hacienda. He laughed his head off when I told him I'd brought the machinery along with me—"

"But you took it in good part. I mind you were laughin' like two bairns when Ann and me came in to our suppers. Aye, yon was a happy evenin', right enough."

"And next day brought such trouble," said Sally pitifully.

"How could I talk about refining sugar in the middle of all that? But the fact is that I've already sold the entire crop—refined—to Mr. Jonas Wilkinson at Havana. I told you about him—the man I met on the boat, who sent over the sugarmaster—and he gave me his check for it in advance. I deposited it at the New York City bank as soon as I got home."

"Paid in advance?" with raised eyebrows. "He took a risk."

"No more of a risk than I took, going to Europe," Sally retorted. John Halkett eyed her quizzically. She was rising above her troubles, he could see, as if some wellspring of courage and optimism had begun to bubble again inside Miss Sally Lorimer. She even looked better, as the mountain freshness touched her pale face with color, and she looked about her joyfully at the sentinel peaks above Cuernavaca.

"Mr. Wilkinson wanted to help me," she said simply. "I told him about the peons and their debts to the hacienda, and he agreed that I should remit them if I could. With his advance on this year's crop, and what I have in hand, I can just do it—and I will."

"Ye won't have much left to start your next year with," was Halkett's comment.

"I'll have a clear conscience, anyway. And besides, I'm going to make Martínez plant the next crop in January. No more waiting for Holy Cross Day to start planting."

"Speeding up your operation, eh? You put me in mind o' your grandfather, Sally; he was considered the fleetest worker in the parish o' Tyrie."

"My grandfather Sandhaven?"

"Na, na, not the auld lord. He was fit for nothing but blastin' at the hares and rabbits wi' his gun. Na, I meant your father's father, Sandy Lorimer, that had a meal mill at Tyrie when I was a little lad."

"I don't know much about my grandfather Lorimer. Andrew thought he owned farms in the north."

"Poor Andra wouldna think the meal mill very genteel, I doubt. But a miller he was; a little red-headed energetic mannie, and they said the proverb about the miller's thumb was fair appropriate to auld Sandy. Keep you a good watch on *your* weights and measures, Sally; this sugarmaster lad will likely be worth the watching."

The young man from Havana, however, passed Halkett's tests of honesty with flying colors. Under his directions, with the overseer's willing assistance, the canes which had grown twelve or fifteen feet tall through the summer were cut into three lengths and put on the feed board to the cleaned and overhauled carrier, which crushed the cane by water power from the arroyo. Sally looked on fascinated as the "train" was started over the furnace, and for the first time in years smoke belched from the tall brick chimney. The "temper" of cream of lime was added by the sugarmaster, who while the peons skimmed the boiling juice in the new copper kettles shipped from the United States, carried out his acid tests with litmus paper. The new earthenware cones were set on their pointed ends, filled with liquid, stoppered with wood and the crystallization process began.

In the end the clayed sugar was to be packed into boxes each of four hundredweight to be exported, not to Cuba, but to a market the sugarbroker was about to open in the United States.

"If Mr. Wilkinson handles the deal right, you'll be the first planter in Mexico to export sugar," said John Halkett, when the time came to return to town.

"If I can only get the sugar safely down to Vera Cruz, I'll be quite happy."

"It'll get there all right, for I'll see it goes down with my next conducta. You're a game one, Sally. Miller Sandy would ha' been proud of you, though I don't know what he would have said to givin' away your siller."

"I'll have something over, after all. It was a very good crop, you know."

She had kept her quixotic ideal before her eyes, night and day. In the hard days in Paris, on the ocean, in the desolate city, Sally Lorimer had dreamed of the moment when she would set her peons free. When it came, it was quite undramatic. She had the bell rung, and the men brought into the courtyard, because she wished all to be present, and to understand. But there was no speechmaking, no formal expression of thanks. Sally could not trust her voice to say what she had once planned to say, that this was being done "in agreement with the intention of the Empress Carlóta, who had loved the Indians and desired to set them free." She told them only, in the simplest words, that their own debts to the hacienda, as well as the debts contracted by their fathers, were canceled as of that day. All the purveyors who supplied goods to the tienda had been paid in full for accounts reaching years back, and in future articles sold in the tienda would be sold for cash or not at all. There was to be a clean slate at the Hacienda de las Flores, and any man who wished to go away and find employment elsewhere was free to do so.

The broad Otomí faces were impassive. There were some doubtful smiles, some shuffling of feet, and one man ventured, "Gracias, señorita." Then the foreman of the peons, Mariquita's husband, took off his sombrero and said,

"We thank La Niña. But this is our little world and motherland: here we were born, and here we shall remain."

That was all. They went back to the village quietly. And Sally went by herself to the magnolia at the foot of the garden, imagining Pierre's arms and Pierre's kisses, and remembering how they had called the place their *"tierra y patria chica"* on the day they planted the olive trees.

It was hard to leave Las Flores the next morning, with the Martínez family and the house servants begging her to stay, and the garden glowing in the perfect weather of November. All around the village Xochitl's own flowers were breaking into crimson blossom—the cuetla-xochitl, which the Spaniards had called *la nochebuena* and an American ambassador to Mexico had named for himself, Poinsettia. By any name it was most beautiful, and Sally gathered an armful in memory of Las Flores be-

fore she said good-by to the sugarmaster and took her place in
the mule cart.

"I'm sorry to tak' you back so soon," said Mr. Halkett,
"but faith I dare not bide away from the Mine House for another week. The foreman's a reliable man, but he counts on us
if anything goes wrong, and my boy Tony's but fifteen, and too
young to take the whole responsibility. If George had but stayed
beside me, it would have been another story."

"Maybe he'll bring Pilár back to Mexico when the war is
over."

"I'm not so sure. There's a bairnie on the way up there in
Arizona, and Mrs. Pilár will be making her own nest north of
the border. No, I dinna count on George—even if Don Antonio
would consider hiring the lad that ran off wi' his lady daughter."

"But Don Antonio never showed any resentment in his relationship with you?"

"That's entirely different. He kens fine he could get nobody
to run the mine as well as me."

It was said with all the Scotsman's majestic self-assurance,
and Sally smiled.

"If only Silvia had been as brave as Pilár when she fell in
love!"

John Halkett made no rejoinder, somewhat to Sally's relief. I shouldn't have said that, she thought. If only—if only—I'm
saying that too often. I'm as bad as Andrew and those poor
people on the *Jupiter,* who never stopped talking about if only
Longstreet, and if only Lee . . .

If only Maximilian would make up his mind to abdicate . . .

They halted briefly in Cuernavaca. There was still an Imperialist garrison in the Cortés barracks, but all the troops were
Mexican—there had been no French there since June, a bystander told John Halkett. He eyed the soldiers shrewdly. Undisciplined, lounging, possibly disaffected—he didn't think they
would stand fast if the Juaristas made a really determined drive
on the province of Michoacán. And they could invade now, quite

easily, by way of Acapulco, for since their capture of Mazatlan
and the French evacuation of the northwest the southern Pacific
coast would be their easy prey. He wondered if Sally had ever
considered that, when she planned the future of Las Flores.

The center of Sally's thinking was somewhere further south
than Acapulco. Diaz, after his victory over the Austrian brigade,
had shown a clean pair of heels to the Cazadores, whom the
Emperor's indecision had kept too long at Orizaba. Before
Pierre's regiment could come up with him, General Diaz had
recaptured the city of Oaxaca, and with the south solidly behind him would soon be in a position to march on the north.
The Cazadores had been ordered to fall back upon Puebla,
where the defense works breached by the French in 1863 were
being hastily strengthened.

This much Sally learned from one of Pierre's terse letters,
which to her joy was waiting when she returned from Cuernavaca. It was followed, just before the end of November, by the
tidings she had so long dreaded. Maximilian had announced his
intention to return to Mexico, to reorganize his shrunken army,
and to lead it himself against the troops of Juarez.

He returned to his capital two weeks later, and in his entourage came Andrew Lorimer.

The young doctor came back to his own house in the brief
Mexican twilight, just as the pulque shops were beginning their
brisk trade and the Customs House opposite was shutting its
doors for the night. He came on foot, and quietly, but the letter
writers at the corner of the arcade recognized him. The *es-
cribiendos,* who next to the Lorimers themselves were the most
literate persons in the Plazuelita, had read many highly flavored
versions of the loves of Andrew and Silvia Mora in papers with
such suggestive titles as *Kick, Spur* and *Flea,* and there was a
buzz of talk and some loud laughter as Jorge admitted the señor
doctor through his own front door.

Miss Keane was reading in her room, and Ann Halkett
slipped away discreetly as soon as she heard Andrew's greeting
to his sister in the hall.

"Why, Sally! Do you want to shake hands with the family disgrace?"

Her answer was to put her arms around him, and standing on tiptoe to kiss him far more warmly than she had kissed him since Helen's death. Then she took him into the sala, where all the things that looked like home were in their place; and as soon as he had slumped into his own chair Sally drew his head against her shoulder and whispered, "I'm so glad you've come back, Andy dear!" She saw that there were gray threads in the heavy locks of red hair behind his ears.

"Has it been bad for *you*, Sally? Have people here been mean to you because of all this scandal?"

"Mean to me? I'd like to see them try!" cried Sally so belligerently that Andrew achieved a laugh.

"And anyway, all the talk is over now," she added, practically. "People have other things to think about."

"I'm afraid the whole thing will start up again. Silvia's brother has challenged me to fight a duel."

"Oh, Andrew, *no!*"

"He's right of course. Don Antonio himself could hardly call me out, and the eldest brother took it on himself to avenge the family honor—"

"Hilarión? He's still stationed at Acapulco, and I hope he stays there! You never fought a duel in your life—did you?"

"I can hold a pistol if I have to," said Andrew indifferently. "Don't worry, Sally; it won't come off this week or the next. Now call Lupita and tell her to send up a good supper; we've been living on the same slops as Maximilian and I'm sick to death of cereals. He wants to see you, Sally, and this time you must go."

"To talk to him about Carlóta?"

"No, to talk about the little boy. That was a very good letter you wrote about him. I showed it to Maximilian and he liked it. He wasn't very willing, at first, to give the boy back to the Iturbides, and he's quite determined to refuse their money offer; but I think now it's going to be a fight to the death here, he feels the child is better out of danger. That's about it."

"Is he going to send Agustín all that way to Paris by himself?"

"No, the parents have come out to Cuba, didn't you know? Princess Josefa is going to take him over. It was all settled this morning, as soon as we reached the National Palace. It really was pathetic, Sally—to see him with that child."

"Sometimes I can't help feeling sorry for him," said Sally thoughtfully.

She was sorry the next day, when she curtsied to the Emperor of Mexico in the palace of the Plaza Mayor. He was in a small anteroom to the great Iturbide Salon, which Maximilian in his tactless recall of the First Empire had renovated and named for his unlucky predecessor. He was accompanied by Agustín's Aunt Josefa and a few courtiers.

"How do you do, Miss Lorimer?" The Emperor held out his hand. Sally thought him changed, for the repeated attacks of dysentery had shaken even his splendid frame; but his blue eyes were mild and gentle. "I hope we can have a talk, some day, about your journey to Paris, and your kindness to my poor wife. She was fond of you, I know; and it was not your fault that she was driven too far, and went where no kindness of ours could reach her."

"But they take good care of her, Sir, at Miramar?" said literal Sally.

"Indeed they do; I can trust her to her brother," declared Carlóta's husband. "But I asked you here today to say good-by to your little friend Agustín. You are a great favorite of his, I know."

There was silence in the room as the little boy came in. He was dressed in a gray suit, and carried his cat in a wicker basket. His chestnut curls were bobbing as he ran to Sally.

"Oh, Doña Sarita, my papa came back. Now you can play with both of us."

"Hallo, Agustín." Sally knelt down and put her arms around him. "I don't think we can play today, you know."

"Why?"

"Because you're going away on a lovely trip with Aunt Josefa. And you'll have to take great care of El Tigre."

"Why?"

"Because you're going to spend a few days on a boat, and cats don't like boats much; if they get out of their baskets they rush around, and might fall in the ocean, or get stuck at the top of a mast, and then what would you do?"

"El Tigre loves his basket." The boy lifted the wicker lid a little way and let Sally look in. The striped cat, now an experienced traveler, was lying curled up, and purring.

"Agustín, come here," the Emperor said gravely.

"Yes, papa."

He stood the boy between his knees, and kissed him.

"You are going to make a journey, as the pretty lady says. You are going back to your mother—"

"To mamma?"

"No, not to poor mamma. To your own father and mother, who love you dearly, and miss you very much—"

At the grave words *padre y madre* the child's eyes opened wide.

"But I love *you*, papa—"

Maximilian gathered the child closer to him and the chestnut curls mingled with the golden beard as the Emperor hid his face in the boy's hair.

He really loves him, Sally thought. She noticed with distaste that Princess Josefa was ostentatiously wiping her eyes with a lace handkerchief.

"You will soon forget your old papa," said Maximilian. "And it is better that you should." Then, as the child looked up at him wonderingly, he said in a still lower tone:

"Tell papa your name, my dear."

"Agustín Iturbide!"

The name—the ill-omened name—rang out so proudly that it seemed as if an older voice had spoken in the silent room.

"Do you know who was your father's father?"

"Agustín the First, Emperor of Mexico!" He lovingly

stroked Maximilian's cheek. "Mamma taught me to say that, you know."

Sighing: "You have your lesson pat. And now listen to what *I* have to teach you, and repeat it often; never let anyone persuade you to try to regain his throne!"

The tone, the uncomprehended words were too much for little Agustín. His lower lip quivered. He tried to wriggle out from between his adoptive father's knees.

"Sir," said Sally swiftly, "let him go! He is much too young to understand."

"You think so?"—wearily. "It is a lesson he can never learn too soon. But say good-by to the ladies and gentlemen, my Güsti, and then go back to the nurseries and wait for Aunt Josefa."

Agustín obeyed. He kissed Sally fondly, and bowed to all the rest of the little company. He lifted El Tigre's basket from the floor. Thus, with a few memories soon to be forgotten, and a striped cat for his sole inheritance, the grandson of the Emperor Agustín started on his way back to his mother's arms.

. . . They heard later that Maximilian had ordered a Sovereign's Escort as far as Ayotla for the child whom he had declared his son and heir. In this, the little boy was only by some degrees more distinguished than the hordes of refugees now streaming down the highway to the last exit at Vera Cruz. Durango had fallen at last, and San Luis Potosí had been evacuated; even in Yucatán, the loyal province in the south, there were rumors of a Juarista rising. Benito Juarez himself, traveling in his little black carriage, moved into Durango as soon as the French had left, and Zacatecas, it was said, would be the next halt on his slow but steady movement to the south. The British Legation (and in its train Sally's old friend Miss Keane) removed to Vera Cruz. Baron Lago, the Austrian Chargé d'Affaires, undertook the repatriation of his nationals. Marshal Bazaine announced that transportation would be arranged for all French civilians, as well as military personnel, desiring to return to Europe.

As fast as the Europeans and wealthy Mexicans moved

out, the Americans moved in. It was true that the newly appointed American Minister, Lewis D. Campbell, had not yet ventured nearer Mexico than Cuba, but each day saw more money and munitions poured across the border in support of Juarez, and more Union veterans enlisting under the Republican banner.

There were Union men on the Imperialist side too, and often in the streets of Mexico Sally heard bearded boys singing or whistling "John Brown's Body" or the version of "The Star-Spangled Banner" which had annoyed her at Orizaba. The war seemed to be entering a new phase of confusion, but Sally herself, as the momentous year moved onward to its end, began to pluck up hope for the future.

One ordeal she had been spared—the long-threatened interview with Maximilian. After sending Agustín away, he had been seized with another attack of acute dysentery which taxed the combined skills of Andrew and Dr. Basch to cure. When Sally heard of some of their prescriptions, which ranged from Dover's powder through opium pills to enemas of laudanum and copper sulphate, she privately wondered how the Emperor continued capable of seeing his remaining Ministers, or organizing his remaining troops into three army corps; but the medicines of the time were drastic, as she observed daily at the Hospital of Jesus the Nazarene. Andrew was now a regular member of a busy hospital staff which had no interest in his private affairs, and Sally, at her earnest request, spent many hours there daily, helping the overworked Sisters of St. Vincent. The French army hospitals were closing as part of Bazaine's great evacuation scheme, and the ancient city lazarettos, dark and insanitary, were filling with the overflow of patients.

It was not an unhappy time for Sally. Her mind was at ease about Pierre, whose regiment now formed part of the garrison at Puebla. She also had the great satisfaction of knowing that the consignment of Las Flores sugar had left the country safely and that planting of the new crop had been begun. She had a sense, as she walked to and from the hospital or market, of a continuity of life in Mexico which would outlast the greedy struggles of the generals and the indecisions of the Emperor.

At last there came the news of an attack on Acapulco. It was the first Juarista attempt to seize a port on the lower Pacific coast; and it was beaten off. But in the skirmish Colonel Hilarión Mora, second-in-command of the garrison, lost his life, and the duel he had wished to fight with Andrew Lorimer was destined never to take place.

The supper table at Four, Plaza de Santo Domingo that night would have been utterly silent without the few amiable remarks offered by Miss Halkett. Andrew had been able to forget Silvia for as long as an hour at a time in the absorption of his work; but the wound of her tragic death broke out and bled afresh when he heard the news from Acapulco. As for Sally, the idea of any attempt to invade the province of Michoacán, even down on the coast, made her tremble for the safety of Las Flores.

There was no word of fighting on any of the fronts for a few days. Then, exactly a week after the first attack on Acapulco, Captain Franchet arrived in the Plaza de Santo Domingo.

There were no shouts of "Death to the French" as Rataplan picked his way across the dusty square. The rider in the soiled uniform was scarcely identifiable as a Frenchman; moreover, the loungers knew that the day of the French in Mexico was nearly over. Pierre dismounted stiffly and gave Rataplan to old Jorge's care, as Sally came running to the top of the stairs to greet him.

"Keep off, my darling; I'm not fit to touch you," he said wearily, as she lifted her face to be kissed. "I haven't been out of my clothes for five days. But I had to come straight to you —I had to see you, Sally—"

"Of course," she said, hiding her dismay. He was grimed with powder and the dust of the highway, unshaven, the white Cazador uniform saddle-stained and torn. "Lupita! El Señor Güero has come back! Get hot water and a clean shirt—and a razor—"

"I never thought *you'd* call me El Güero," said Pierre with a flash of his old spirit, as he followed her into the sala and fumbled at the strap of his heavy saber belt. "May I take this off here, Sally? I'm tired."

"Have you been in action, Pierre?" she asked fearfully.

"We took a drubbing up at Cuatla, yesterday morning," he said briefly.

"At *Cuatla?* You mean there's fighting in Michoacán?"

"You haven't heard, then? They've got Acapulco—got it on the second try—and they came right up from the coast to Taxco without a fight. The province is going to declare for Juarez, I'm very much afraid."

"Then—Cuernavaca, Pierre?"

"We were trying to cut them off from Cuernavaca, but—damnation, we always arrive too late! Too late at Oaxaca, too late at Cuatla; General This says march and General That says halt, and it's *mañana, mañana,* tomorrow, while the Juaristas win today!" Pierre's cracked lips tightened in a grimace of contempt.

"Never mind, my darling. I don't care what else happens, as long as you are safe." She watched him stumble off to the back bedroom where Lupita had set a basin and hot water and ran down the kitchen stairs herself. Trouble, she was learning fast, might take the edge off a woman's appetite, but men were comforted by food and wine; and though good food was in short supply now there was always a cazuela simmering with some tasty stew on the back of the charcoal stove, and a bottle of the Old Doctor's Burgundy to be brought out of the locked cellar.

"This puts heart into a man," said Captain Franchet, half an hour later. He looked gratefully across the clean white cloth at Sally. But there was still trouble in his tired face.

"Now you must smoke," she told him with a smile.

"In a lady's parlor, mademoiselle?"

"Andrew does! And how many pipes did you smoke here when it was your billet, pray?" She brought him a box of cigarillos and the vesta matches. "Do smoke—Miss Halkett won't object; and anyway she's gone to market."

"She'll find it closed, then, if it's Lagunilla; they've requisitioned the market sheds for us." He lighted the cigarillo and inhaled deeply.

"You aren't quartered at Buena Vista?"

"No. I'm not a Frenchman now, Sally—did you know that?"

"You mean you're no longer a Légionnaire?"

"I said I'm not a *Frenchman.*" He raised his voice slightly on that *je ne suis plus Français,* and Sally caught her breath. "I see you haven't heard—well, the order only came the day we left Puebla. Napoleon has thrown over men like me. He's so determined to get us all out of Mexico—to have us give up the job he sent us here to do—that he gives us notice to turn in our arms and leave Vera Cruz on the French transports . . . or else be deprived of our citizen rights for all time to come."

She could not quite see it as a tragedy. But that it was a grief and disillusionment to the man she loved, she clearly saw.

"There's no way round it, Pierre?"

"Only to submit. And I won't do that, Sally. I won't leave *you.*"

"Darling!"

He stubbed out the cigarillo, came round the table, and knelt beside her chair. The brown face, the smoky eyes, looked up at her with pleading.

"Why did he do it, Sally? The Emperor? Why would he abandon men who fought at his command?"

She saw that the dream was shattered; the identification of the Emperor with France which had begun in a prison courtyard at Montpellier nine years before. She said gently,

"What exactly does being deprived of citizen rights mean? That you can't vote in the Emperor Napoleon's plebiscites?"

It was the shrewd, logical Sally who had punctured his romantic version of a life dedicated to the Emperor who had saved him from the guillotine. In spite of himself Pierre laughed a strangled laugh, and said:

"I never thought of that. And I never expected to go back to France to live—with you or without you, Sally dear. It's the feeling of being thrown over that I can't endure. Having my country taken from me—at one man's whim—"

"But our *tierra y patria chica* is still waiting for us both!"

The next day but one, that dream too was ended, when it was officially admitted that Cuernavaca had fallen to the Juaristas.

"I don't care, I don't care," sobbed Sally in Pierre's arms, "if only the Martínez are safe, and all the poor people in the village!"

"They'll be all right. They wouldn't have put up a fight, you know. They'd have melted away, down the canyon and into the woods. That's what the Juaristas used to do, when *we* were the stronger—just melted away into the barrancas; it was like fighting with the clouds. But the house, Sally, and the refinery—" He shook his head.

"The reports say they set fire to La Borda. Maybe they didn't go Las Flores way."

"I hope so, darling, for your sake. Because it cost a lot one way or another, your refinery."

"I'm so thankful, so grateful to Providence, that it wasn't quite in vain. That I was able to remit their debts, before—this happened. Because it'll be such a help to have a clean slate when we start again."

"Sally, listen to me. If it's not possible to start again? If the place is wrecked beyond recall, like the Southern plantations your brother talks about?"

"We'll start again somewhere else, that's all."

"Would you come to Tampico with me?"

"To anywhere!"

"Will you marry me now? Now, when we've both lost so much? When we have nothing but each other in the world?"

"Yes, I will, Pierre."

There had been passion between them in the past, and both knew that it was only held in check. But it was the spirit, not the body, that triumphed in that quiet answer, and inspired Sally to go on,

"I was a coward when you asked me first, six months ago. I was afraid of being left alone, perhaps alone to bear your child, and Pierre . . . then I still liked to have my own way best. But since Silvia died I've thought of her so much, and how all that tragedy could have been spared if she had been brave enough to choose Andrew at the beginning, and stick to him whatever they said . . . I'm still afraid of being all alone. But I'm brave enough, now, to want to be your wife."

. . . When they heard Andrew Lorimer come home, and shut himself into the surgery, Pierre went to him with a formal request for Sally's hand.

Andrew heard him out in silence. Pierre thought that among all the careworn men around the Emperor, Dr. Lorimer showed the most marks of strain.

"Are you asking me, or telling me?" was all that Andrew said. "Who am I, to withhold my permission for Sally's marriage?"

"Nevertheless, we should both be glad to have your approval, monsieur."

"Approval? I don't disapprove, that's all. I only hope the Halketts will look after her, when Maximilian has led us both to our death up at Querétaro."

"I agree with you it's madness to go north. If he means to fight he should go south, to Puebla; but when has Max ever done the sensible thing, since he left his homeland? *You* don't have to go to Querétaro with him though!"

"He has asked for me, and I can't refuse him. Not after he gave me his protection last October. I feel bound to him now, somehow. But *you* could ask to stay with the garrison in Mexico—"

"I could," said Pierre, "but that's not possible. I've been called a few things in my time, but never a coward; and Sally knows I must see the fight out to the end."

She knew it very well. But it was hard to accept it, in those few days before their marriage, which seemed to Sally like the worst days of the Civil War. The city was full of movement as

Bazaine completed the huge French evacuation of eleven hundred officers and twenty-two thousand men. The Marshal ordered the destruction of all ammunition unsuited to the Mexican smooth-bored arms, and while all the French powder was dumped into the Sequia, the capital reverberated to the sound of exploding projectiles. Wagons, vehicles, harness, uniforms and all surplus stock were offered first to the Imperial Government and then put up to public auction. The army horses were put up for sale, and Pierre, after a long haggle with the Remount Board, was able to purchase Rataplan for fifty dollars.

"They'll go for twenty, down at the Mule Pass railhead," he told Sally, "but I can't let Rata fall into the hands of some Hot Country ranchero, can I, dear?"

"Of course you can't." Sally had lost her fear of the big chestnut since he had condescended to take sugar from her hand. "It's too bad Rataplan can't be at our wedding! We *could* hold it downstairs in the stable, if you like—"

"Oh, *you—!*" He caught his laughing sweetheart as she dodged away, and kissed her.

"I bought something else today, Sally. It's an odd kind of wedding present, but I want you to have it. Take it with you to the Mine House when we go, and one of the Halketts will show you how to fire it."

She looked from his face to the small revolver which lay so easily in the palm of Captain Franchet's hand.

"Remember the night we came on you outside the barrier, lugging that small cannon of Don Antonio's?" said Pierre with his crooked smile. "This is more your weight, darling. Liége workmanship—the finest; I bought it from one of the Belgian heroes on his way back to the coast. Don't be afraid of it. It isn't loaded."

This was the bridegroom's gift, and Andrew gave the wedding dress of pearl-colored silk, bought just before the last French boutique in the Plaza Mayor closed its shutters. But it was Miss Halkett who found the minister, a missionary from the American and Foreign Christian Union, which continued to preach the Gospel to Protestants remaining in the capital, and Miss Halkett who, with some help from Lupita, dressed the bride for her wedding.

To Lupita and Jorge, who were invited to be present in the sala, it was the strangest wedding they had ever seen, with no firecrackers and no music—and no tears. Sally's lips trembled once, when the flat Ohio voice of the missionary recalled *"Our Lord's gracious presence and first miracle at the wedding in Cana of Galilee,"* and she looked at Andrew, again giving a sister in marriage, to see if he too were thinking of their father. But she made her responses clearly and so did Pierre, to love and to cherish until death them did part; and *"before God and in the presence of this congregation"* Sarah Elizabeth Lorimer and Pierre Jean Louis Franchet took one another to be man and wife.

Their wedding journey was not long. A deep calm lay upon the city as a hired carriage took them along Tacuba Street, past the cottonwoods of the Alameda, to the ancient Hospederia de Santo Tomás Villanuova, where Pierre had engaged rooms opening off a balcony hung with flowers. There were few other guests in the ancient posada, and no inquisitive looks were given to the table, spread in a corner of the patio, which Pierre had ordered to be decked with white flowers for his bride. The lighting of a small log fire on two andirons, and the persistence of the guitarist who wandered round the patio with his instrument slung from his shoulders were the only extra attentions offered to Madame Pierre Franchet.

"You're sure you wouldn't have preferred to dine upstairs?" asked Pierre.

Sally shook her head. "I like it here. It's so much *Mexico.*"

He knew what she meant. The patio was open to the stars, twinkling in the milky dark blue which so often hung over the valley of Mexico, and the scent of the burning logs recalled all the wood fires of the Indians which they knew so well. He heard the plash of a little fountain; he smelled the flowers, and he wondered if behind that vivid face, so enchanting when framed in

the white mantilla Sally wore so well, there lurked a sad thought
of the garden at Las Flores. But his wife's high heart held no sad
thoughts that night. Even when the guitarist, his eyes liquid with
romance, sang "La Paloma," she yielded to no memories of Silvia Mora. This was her night, and Pierre's, and she let her fingers
lie in his while the Mexican sang for them alone:

> *"If a dove should hover*
> *At thy window wide*
> *Give it love, my lover,*
> *It is I, thy bride!"*

The haunting tune followed them up the old stone stair.
But there was silence, deep and absolute, over the patio where
only a few golden sparks still flickered from the burning logs
when the silks and laces of the bride were laid aside, and the
girl became a woman in her husband's arms.

Gave herself to him, received his long-suppressed intensity
of passion without shock or pain, and fell asleep with smiling
mouth pressed to smiling mouth as midnight struck, and in
blessing over their marriage bed rang the familiar, golden
cadence of the bells of Mexico.

THREE DAYS later she bade him farewell, and he followed Maximilian north to Querétaro.

Andrew Lorimer saw her as the army of eight thousand
horse and foot marched out of Mexico. She was with Ann
Halkett, in a hired carriage, halted where not a few other women,
and mothers with young children, had driven out to see the last
of husbands and lovers. It was at the farthest safe limit of the
city, on the edge of the waste called the Pedregal, where thieves
and outlaws still had their abiding place; and he had thought, as
he rode up to it, how well that desolate place under Xitle, the
extinct volcano, suited the beginning of what might well be for

all of them a march to death. But in the jagged, tortured mass of lava, broken by cliffs and miniature barrancas eight to ten feet deep, there grew over all a bright red flower, and Sally, he saw as he came abreast of her, held a few of those wild flowers in her hand. He knew that Pierre and Rataplan, riding ahead, had already passed her, and wondered at her steadfast smile. Then he realized that she was watching for him too; was keeping one brave look for him; and he pulled out of the ranks by half a length, and raised his hat.

Andrew saw in Sally the face of true love, truly fulfilled, and he bowed low above his saddle, without speaking, as the tide of soldiers carried him along. He knew now what he must salute in Sally: a heart far stronger than Silvia's; stronger, always, than his own.

Chapter Twenty-one

"A MOI, LA LÉGION!"

FOR HIS ENTRY into Querétaro, Maximilian chose to ride. The lively bay, Orispelo, was too much for him to manage in his enfeebled state, but his gentle horse Anteburro was brought up to his traveling carriage, and he mounted just before the Imperialists entered the pretty town nestling in its encircling hills. It was the nearest approach to a triumphal entry he had enjoyed for months. The population was enthusiastically loyal to the Emperor, and he and his officers rode into the central plaza under a rain of flowers.

Among the troops who followed them there were many who looked up at those hills with anxious eyes. The Hill of the Bells, San Gregorio's Hill, the ominously named Hill of the Cemetery all dominated the town, and—in the possession of the enemy—would turn it all too rapidly into the deathtrap it had been already called. But the enemy was still far distant on that first night, the nineteenth of February, when Maximilian, in something like a holiday mood, bivouacked among his men on the Hill of the Bells.

"You and Basch have cured me, friend Andrew," he said in his charming way, when he met the American doctor in the course of an inspection tour next day. "I feel better here than I have done any time these past four months."

"I shouldn't recommend many more outdoor nights, Your Majesty," warned Andrew. "It's warmer here than in the capital, but still a long way from Orizaba temperatures."

"Colonel Lopez said the very same thing this morning," Maximilian said good-naturedly. "We must find more suitable headquarters in the course of the day."

But of course there was no hurry, there never was. In the spirit of *mañana,* the decision on a headquarters was put off until next day. Don Cuyatano Rubio, who owned the "Hercules" cotton manufactory—the largest industrial concern in Mexico—had arranged one of the alfresco picnics in which the Emperor delighted, and by noon the whole Staff was pleasantly occupied at the baths of La Cañada, five miles outside the town. It was not until the next day that Dr. Lorimer learned that Maximilian had taken up his quarters in the Casino.

Some of this holiday mood continued at Querétaro for the next two weeks. Maximilian visited the Hercules mills, lunched at another and smaller manufactory called La Purísima Concepción, and even drank wine at the Esperanza mine from which had come Carlóta's unlucky gift of opals. He went again and again to the thermal springs at La Cañada, with the full approval of his physicians. He used the Casino billiard tables for an occasional game, and sometimes of an evening walked through the rough cobbled streets to the Square of Independence, where he sat smoking his meerschaum pipe on the curb of a memorial fountain. He looked very much the Austrian there, in spite of his big Mexican sombrero; very much the village elder, with his gentle smile and flowing golden beard. The brown Indian children made little flower wreaths for him, and he threw a handful of coins among them whenever he rose to go away.

"What does he do when he's not amusing himself?" enquired Captain Franchet of Dr. Lorimer, when he met his newly acquired brother-in-law in one of the wooded avenues of Querétaro.

Andrew shrugged. "He doesn't have much leisure for enjoyment."

"Eh? He talks to his generals all the time? Miramón, Mejía, and What's-his-name—that jackal Marquez? Doesn't he know they're the dedicated rivals of each other? Escobedo and

Corona will join forces on the hills before Max decides to move to the attack."

"I don't know anything about General Escobedo. I'm here to set up a field hospital; it's much the same routine in any country, and they don't ask my opinion on the enemy's dispositions."

"You've no idea when we're likely to attack?" persisted Franchet. Like a true Frenchman he could not believe that anyone who occasionally shared the Emperor's frugal meals, or was in daily contact with his aides, should not be aware of their intentions.

"None at all, I'm afraid."

"Our vedettes say Max sent secret messages to Escobedo across the lines last night."

"What the devil would he do that for?"

"For the same reason as he tried to get in touch with Diaz, and even with Juarez, before we left Mexico. That was common knowledge at the time. He doesn't seem to realize that it's no use trying any attempt at conciliation with those men. They're out for blood, and my God! they're bringing some real killers down from San Luis Potosí. Did you ever hear of a Juarista battalion called the Supremos Poderes?"

"Colonel Lopez was talking about them in the mess last night. Ruffians—thoroughpaced brutes and mutilators, was what he called them."

"They were in that shambles at San Jacinto last month, when Escobedo shot a hundred French prisoners."

Andrew said: "It doesn't look as though we need expect much mercy from General Escobedo if we lose."

"We won't win by sitting on our backsides doing nothing."

Andrew left him with a nod. Pierre's phrase "the real killers" rang uncomfortably in his ears. That was what *he* had called the Légionnaire, in the cocksure days when he had forbidden Sally's marriage. Pierre, with his more equable temper, had never shown that he remembered the scene.

A few days later the encirclement of Querétaro was complete, and Escobedo and Corona were joined by Riva Palacio,

who had conquered the west for Juarez. Their forces were as
yet very thinly scattered along the ridges above the town, but
reinforcements were coming in every day. Benito Juarez himself
had made a long move on his way south, and was about to be
established where Bazaine had once had his own forward headquarters, at San Luis Potosí.

Now was the time when Maximilian was bedeviled by divided counsels among his own three generals. Mejía, the Sierra
Gordo Indian who was one of the best men on the Imperial
side, took little part in the bitter arguments. But the dashing
Miramón, himself a former president of the republic, was all for
breaking out and attacking while the enemy lines were still thin.
Marquez, who was afraid for his own skin, argued that this
would be too dangerous until reinforcements of their own were
sent from Mexico.

On one thing all were agreed: Maximilian must leave his
totally undefended quarters in the center of the town. He moved,
on the thirteenth of March, to the solid old Convento de la Cruz,
on the eastern side of Querétaro, which had walls thick enough
to resist cannon-shot, and a fountain fed from the great aqueduct which carried drinking water to the town. There, Maximilian's quarters were cramped indeed. When Andrew Lorimer was
sent for to attend him on the night after his establishment at La
Cruz, he found the Emperor in a little upstairs room in an inner
court, with a stone floor, whitewashed walls, and a small window
crossed by three iron bars. It had once been a monk's cell. It
now looked ominously like a prison.

The Emperor was sitting at a plain wooden table, writing
letters. Mail had arrived that day by the hand of an Indian
courier who had taken devious ways through the Juarista lines,
and Andrew saw letters with the Austrian royal arms and stamps
lying at Maximilian's elbow. Dr. Basch was with him, and a new
intimate, Colonel Miguel Lopez, was lounging against the wall.

Andrew entered, stooping—the door was too low for a man
of his or Maximilian's height—and made his bow.

"Come in, Andrew," said Maximilian cheerfully. "Support

me against Basch, who has been trying to persuade me to go to bed."

"There has been a slight return of the dysentery, doctor," said Basch professionally. "I think His Majesty would be more comfortable in bed."

"I have letters to answer," said the Emperor. "Letters from my mother—and from Miramar. Give me some of your nostrums, gentlemen, and let me work."

The doctors conferred quietly, and a soothing draught was administered to the Emperor. Presently he signed to Basch and Lopez to leave them, and offered Andrew Lorimer a glass of wine.

"It's pleasant to have a word with you," he said. "This is a pleasant moment of the day."

Golden sunset light was drenching the adobe rooftops of Querétaro, and on the stonework of the convent walls the pigeons were cooing quietly. Maximilian sighed.

"I had news of my poor wife today," he said.

"How is she, Sire?"

"There has been no change—no change at all. The assurance that she was quite recovered was as false as that other story of her death."

"These ups and downs of hope and fear have been very hard for Your Majesty."

Maximilian sighed. "If only I could be certain that she is cared for—tended with love, and not as a duty. I *did* love her, you know—in my own way."

"I know you did, Sire."

"If she were here now, she would agree with Miramón. She'd have us make a sortie, and march out to face the enemy, wouldn't she?"

"I think she would, Your Majesty."

Later, as Andrew was leaving, he saw something vaguely disquieting. It was a plaque set in the ancient wall, which chronicled the departure, from that very monastery, of Fray Junípero Serra on his Christian mission to California in 1773.

But underneath, newer, larger letters commemorated a victory
of Agustín Iturbide on that spot "which ended the Viceregal
government of Spain in Mexico."

Andrew was not superstitious. But "the ill-omened name
of Agustín Iturbide" rang in his ears all the way back to the
small field hospital which he had fitted up, with two Mexican
assistants, in a requisitioned house near the Casino.

It was empty then, but within a few days it was full of
groaning men, when Escobedo took the initiative and captured
the Hill of San Gregorio. And Dr. Lorimer tied on his tarpaulin apron again and set to work with knife and saw, while
priests moved among the dying, and nuns bandaged the walking
wounded at his aides' direction. Military surgery is all I am fit for,
or can be employed at now, he said to himself more than once
during that long day.

When the work had started, it never slackened. Sortie after
sortie was attempted by the beleaguered garrison and easily re-
pulsed by the Juaristas. It was not until the night of the twenty-
second that a successful feint was made under the leadership of
Prince Salm in one direction, which allowed General Marquez
to slip out of Querétaro in the other.

Some hours before the joint operation was due to start,
Captain Franchet came to the emergency hospital to say good-
by to Andrew.

"I'm off to Mexico tonight," he said jubilantly. "Had you
heard?"

"I heard they were going to select a thousand of the best
horsemen to ride with Marquez. I thought you ought to qualify
for that."

Grinning: "About number nine hundred, maybe? No,
Rataplan qualified, not me. 'Smart-looking horse, that,' says
Marquez, the last time he rode down our lines. 'Yes, *mon gén-
éral,*' says I; 'and all my own!' So, thanks to Rataplan, I'm
getting out of here. Honorably discharged from Querétaro, that's
something to be thankful for."

"We may see you back again, when Marquez brings up the reinforcements."

"*If* he brings them up," said Pierre knowingly. "It's my belief the old Tiger hopes to get the Mexico garrison to 'pronounce' for him as President. Querétaro is a forcing house for such ambitions."

"You and Sally really are a well-matched pair. You always have the answer to everything in politics."

"Sally . . ." Franchet's hard-bitten face grew tender at the mention of her name.

"Are you sorry now you insisted on her leaving town, and going to the Mine House?"

"No, ten thousand times. I wanted her out of Mexico. But I can write to her when I get into town—"

"Give her my love."

"I will . . . You wouldn't think of coming out with us to-night?"

"I'm going to stay as long as *he* needs me."

"Then good-by, André. Good luck."

"Good-by, Pierre. Take care of Sally."

"As long as I live."

For the first time they shook hands in friendship.

PIERRE FRANCHET was glad of that when he rode out of Mexico behind General Marquez a week later. He was glad to think that he had parted from Sally's brother cordially, and that in the city he had made a will in Sally's favor, leaving her his land at Tampico and his horse Rataplan. For the adventure they were now embarked on looked as if it might be the last engagement for Pierre Franchet.

He had not told Sally so in the letter sent to the Mine House by way of Río Frío. That part of the highway was still open, and he had no doubt she would receive it long before he was within sight of Puebla. For General Marquez, whatever his ambitions, had not found the politicians willing to "pronounce" for him. On the contrary, they had ordered him south to Puebla, the third of the four towns which were all that remained of Maximilian's Empire, where General Noriega was being besieged by a relentless enemy.

The enemy at the gates—once the staunchest defender of that very city—was Porfirio Diaz.

As Pierre had written cheerfully to Sally, he had "always known" that the last round would be played with General Diaz. Now, riding with his hang-dog troop of Cazadores, he had very little doubt of what the outcome of the round would be.

If he were advancing with the Foreign Legion now. . . . But the Legion had embarked for France many days ago, standing out to sea between San Juan de Ulúa and the Island of Sacrifices—clear of the Frenchman's Graveyard for good and all.

Marquez was taking them along as slowly as he could. He was marching by the old road across the Plains of Apam, easier than the mountain passes for artillery, but still bitterly cold for troops clad in the rags of summer uniforms. Pierre had pulled on his blue French Army cutaway, with the epaulets and insignia removed, and even his old képi. There were many others in the motley brigade who wore old uniforms, including the Red Hussars whom Colonel von Kodolitsch was paying out of his own pocket. The other "K," Sally's friend Khevenhüller, was riding in the van with his old comrade-in-arms.

Who would have thought the Whitecoats had it in them, Pierre thought. At least that couple didn't rat on Maximilian, like de Thun and all the rest.

He looked about him wistfully as they came round the flank of the mountains which towered over Río Frío. Somewhere among those peaks the Mine House sheltered Sally; and if she was dear to him when she was the white flower, inviolate in its prickly leaves, how much more dear was she now that the flower was gathered, and their love fulfilled! With all his heart Pierre clung to life and Sally; with all the good impulses which had been born in him since the ordeal on the mesa, when he first understood the meaning of the thornwood Cross, he longed to lead with her the life of faith and works and be done forever with the soldier's trade. But Marquez led them on, however slowly and unwillingly, until they came within sight of the towers of Puebla.

It was late afternoon and clear with the sharp brilliance of the Cold Country. The twin volcanoes, Popocatépetl and Ixtaccíhuatl, raised their snowy crests above the road that led into Puebla. Pierre with a superstitious thrill remembered the name of the third mountain on their way, covered with the deep green of its pine forests—

La Malinche.

To Pierre the green mountain seemed to dominate the whole landscape. He knew, now, that at Cholula, not many miles away, the Malinche who was Cortés' mistress had betrayed two thousand of her own Indian people as they plotted an ambush for the Spanish conquerors; but his thoughts on that night outside Puebla were with the living Malinche, who had betrayed the French.

He had heard of her during the winter; now here, now there. Sometimes with the troops of Diaz, sometimes with Perez the Plateado bandit, whom rumor called her brother: spying, cajoling, restless and resentful still. It was said, while he was quartered at Puebla, that La Malinche knew her own way in and out of the city, and flouted the standing French order for her arrest. He would have handed her over—the hell cat—if she had ever crossed his path. Now he took it for an evil omen that they had to turn the flank of the mountain which bore her name on the march to their last battle, and must bivouac that night in the shadow of La Malinche.

At first light, the Imperial troops knew their march had been in vain. The Tricolore had been hauled down from the tower of Fort Loreto, and Noriega was defeated before the reinforcements could arrive.

It might still have been possible to attack Puebla from

the north, and challenge the weary troops whom Diaz had used to win his hard-fought victory. But Marquez, still intent upon his own safety, procrastinated; dallied at San Lorenzo, while Diaz, his men refreshed by sleep and a day's looting in the captured town, came out of Puebla like a whirlwind and caught up with him.

The issue of the battle of San Lorenzo was never in any doubt. General Marquez himself led the retreat from the field. Only the Red Hussars, as a single disciplined body, charged the Juaristas again and again.

Pierre had posted his sharpshooters round the adobe huts of San Lorenzo, and among the Cazadores under his command these did their duty well enough. The rough-riders mutinied; flung down their sabers and fraternized with the Juaristas; of his whole company only ten men charged with him at the vanguard of the foe.

"Ride with us! Franchet, ride with us!" Colonel von Kodolitsch was alongside him on a raking bay. "Keep your men together—are you hurt?"

"Only a saber nick, *mon colonel*." He hardly felt it, a little cut above his left ear, with an awkward drip of blood down his old blue collar. "Ride, my lads! *Marchez ou crevez!*"

The Mexicans came pounding after him. And after the Imperialists came their own countrymen, their dark faces swollen with triumph, overtaking them quickly on the great highway to the capital.

Cholula fell behind them on the left. San Martin came up ahead, pursuers and pursued were forced to check their speed. The blown horses had done all they could. But far ahead, where the foothills began and the highway ran between a double row of plane trees, the Imperialists could see their own artillerymen abandoning their guns, cutting the traces, mounting the gun horses to continue the flight to the city.

"If we can get our own battery through, we can make a road block with the cannon. Come on, lads!"

The dandy Austrian colonel was a man transformed. Following von Kodolitsch, the remnant of General Marquez' army rode forward with new inspiration.

"Where will you make a stand, *mon colonel?*" yelled Pierre above the thunder of the hoofs. They had had a brief respite while the cannon and the limbers were hauled into place. But the vanguard of their pursuers was already off its horses, as a quick look backward showed, and the obstruction was being pulled away to the sound of singing—

> *"Mexicanos, al grito de guerra*
> *El acero aprestad y el brindon,"*

Prince Khevenhüller was riding neck and neck with Pierre. "Colonel Kodolitsch will take the mountain battery up the Pass," he panted. "He can hold them for an hour at the Puerto del Aire—"

"A vos ordres, mon colonel—"

"And we'll make a stand—at the bridge—at Río Frío—"

Pierre thought it was the pain, now sharp, above his ear, and the slow drip of blood which made him faint and giddy.

"Mon colonel," he got out, *"ma femme est là*—my wife is with her friends at Río Frío."

"Dommage." There was a quick look of sympathy on Khevenhüller's blackened face. But what else could he say beyond *dommage,* a pity; it was all a soldier ever said . . .

"Mon colonel!" Pierre shouted after the Austrian. "The church! At Río Frío! Better than the bridge!"

But there was to be no time to man the church, although the church so like a fortress was already within view. They were near enough to see the little yard where he had sat with Sally—

Sally, my darling, to be so near you, and to have at my heels such men as those, who would destroy the Mine House without pity—

They were at the bridge, and, amazingly, they had reinforcements. Twenty terror-struck Mexican foot soldiers, with their carbines in their hands—

Pierre stood up in his stirrups, and as de Briancourt had shouted in the ambush at Santa Isabel, he called:

"*A moi! A moi, la Légion!*"

The cry echoed from the deep pinewoods, down the valley of the river, reverberated against the yellowish slide of shale.

"*A moi, la Légion!*"

But the Foreign Legion was far out at sea.

He shouted to the men beside him, to the scared auxiliaries, hustling them into a ragged formation.

"Kneel and fire, men! Kneel and fire!"

The Río Frío men dropped on one knee to fire. The horsemen drew up behind them. Pierre fastened his reins round the pommel of the saddle, unslung his carbine and took aim.

"Now steady, Rataplan!"

The chestnut stood firm at the first volley. But at the next a Juarista bullet grazed his shoulder, and he shuddered aside while Pierre fired again.

"Stand, boy!" Bullets out of the *cartouchière,* quick, reload and fire.

Then the thundering pain, as something pounded and burned its way between his own neck and shoulder. The sense of reeling backward even while knees still kept their accustomed pressure on the saddle leather—

The helpless loss of direction as Rataplan whinnied and galloped free, away from the smell of powder, terrified of the rain of his own master's blood.

Oh, Cold River, Cold River, that could lead me to Sally, is this to be the end?

—The headlong, senseless fall to the river bank.

Chapter Twenty-two

LA SOLDADERA

THE NOISE of firing from the bridge at Río Frío was almost inaudible at the Mora mine. What drifted up above the evergreens was an irregular rat-tat, soon dying away, and followed only by the echo of hoofbeats on the road.

In less than an hour came the sound of heavier firing, as Colonel von Kodolitsch's mountain battery offered the first serious resistance to Diaz' advance on the capital. Then, nearly all the inhabitants of the Mine House came out to the cleared space between the square stone mansion and the hovels of the peons, and stood listening anxiously to the sounds which came drifting down the wind.

Sally walked to and fro, with her chilly hands wrapped in the deep hem of her thick wool rebozo. It was always cold at the Mine House, which was the highest inhabited dwelling between Vera Cruz and Mexico. It had snowed several times since she arrived from the capital, and great pine log fires burned all day long in the comfortable homely sala. On this April evening there was something chilling to Sally's spirit in the fall of darkness and the crystallization of frost particles upon the firs, which accompanied the sound of distant cannonading.

Since the arrival of her husband's letter from Mexico, Sally had been restless and ill at ease. It was agonizing to know that Pierre had gone south by San Bonaventura and the plains of Apam with no possibility of halting at the Mine House, while passing only a few miles from her temporary home. The sense that the Intervention in Mexico was approaching its tragic climax had halted her enjoyment of the strangeness of the silver mine and the kindness of the Halkett family.

"What do you think can be going on down there? Oh, what?" she besought John Halkett several times that afternoon, as the rumble from the little Imperialist battery and the heavier guns of Diaz rolled among the trees. The Scotsman seemed unwilling to commit himself. It was his boy Tony who was bold enough to say at last:

"Bide you until the dark comes down, señora, and I'll go by the village and find out."

She looked at Tony gratefully. This second son of John and Bessy Halkett resembled neither his assertive father nor his bustling, capable Northumbrian mother, still less his brother George. At fifteen he was already adult, with a dark line of mustache on his upper lip; dark and slender, like a Mexican boy, and a woodsman to the finger tips. If his father paid the peons their wages, and ruled everything below and above ground at the mine with a rod of iron, it was young Tony who was made welcome in the hovels round the ore crushers and the mule yard, and brought home all the news of the highway from the posada and cantinas of Río Frío.

"I'll come with you, Tony"—said Sally eagerly.

"You'll do better to come in and have a nice warm at the fire, love," said Tony's mother. She had been locking the poultry houses, and came to warn them that supper was nearly ready.

But when darkness fell, Sally was no longer to be restrained. John Halkett took out a light cart, and harnessed a pair of mules, by which Sally knew that he too was anxious, and would not allow them to go alone to Río Frío. Tony most often came and went by the river bank, for the mountain stream ran far more directly from the Mine House to the village than the excellent road which Don Antonio Mora had caused to be made for the passage of his silver trains; but his father preferred the more conventional track, and Sally was afraid of wrenching an ankle among the tree stumps by the stream.

Both the Halkett women came out to the yard to see them start. They made Sally wrap up warmly, with a pointed wool quexquemetl over her dark stuff dress, and a rebozo folded tightly over all.

"Ye'll not sleep this night unless ye get some news of your man, ma dear," said Ann. "But try and not run into any danger!"

That danger for them all might lie ahead was evident as soon as they came down the mountain. They could hear laughter and shouting, the rolling of wheels and the sound of music, and even see between the trees the sparkle of the firecrackers which accompanied any Mexican fiesta. Halkett pulled the cart into a clearing, made for turning vehicles, at a bend of the road.

"It looks to me as if some folk are celebratin' a victory," he said. "We'd better go forward canny until we know which side."

They walked downhill in the darkness. Ahead, the church was lighted at every window, the posada too. Men with linked arms, drunk with victory and pulque, were parading between the inn and the Cantina El Especial and shouting,

"*Viva Diaz! Viva Diaz!*"

"That settles it, then," said Halkett in a low voice. "Sally, we'll be wise to gang back to the Mine House and let this night go bye as best it may."

"I'm going *on.*"

He could only see a triangle of her pale face between the folds of the rebozo, but he knew that it wore the mulish expression of the Sally who had never shirked a journey yet. He said:

"It's not safe even for us, and I'm verra well sure it's not safe for you."

"I'll go to the barracks—they'll take me for one of the *soldaderas.* Wait for me!"

She was gone before the father or the son could stop her, stepping lightly over the stones which made a passage across Cold River to the cuartel. She had seen, in the uncertain light, that a rabble of the wretched women called by courtesy camp followers were coming and going freely at the barracks, some weeping, some clutching their infants, some carrying food and drink to whoever might be inside. Sally hesitated. There were no sounds of revelry from the cuartel, that was all reserved for the cantinas, and a number of mule carts lined up in front of the low adobe building suggested that the wounded might have been conveyed there. Sally conquered her fear and slipped inside.

The barracks room was full of wounded men. Most of them were the Imperialists who had attempted to hold the bridge with Pierre, and it was to them the weeping *soldaderas* carried food and water. But there were also many Juaristas, who were receiving the first attentions of a medical orderly in a filthy white uniform with the insignia of Diaz' Oaxaca brigade. He paid no more attention to Sally than to any of the other women in the room. She moved quietly from pallet to pallet, man to man, holding her breath in fear. At any moment she expected to come upon her husband. She was possessed by the belief that here at Cold River, where they had met first, they would meet again.

The eyes in which she saw recognition were the eyes of Colonel Khevenhüller.

He was half-lying, half-propped against the wall, with a bloodstained bandage round his head. He was deathly pale, but they had given him a mug of wine, and he had strength to say, too loudly,

"Miss Sally!"

"Hush!" She dropped to the mud floor beside him. "Speak Spanish, señor, please! Are you much hurt?"

"No, I'll do very well, if they don't start shooting prisoners. But you, señorita, what are you doing here?"

"I'm married, señor. I was married to Captain Franchet only a few weeks ago. Oh please, can you tell me anything about him?"

Into the weary blue eyes of the Hussar came a look of compassion.

"I can—I wish it could be good news—but you must be brave . . ."

"Go on!"

"He was hit at the bridge, señora, when we were covering the retreat. His horse bolted with him into the woods above . . . I saw it, just before I was hit myself . . . You can never find him in the dark, Miss Sally!"

He had said her name again, incautiously, and it was well for Sally that the Juarista orderly was busy with his patients. For her rebozo fell back as she rose to her feet, and it seemed to the wounded man that her hair blazed like an aureole round her pale face as Sally said,

"With God's help, I will!"

. . . In the end it was Tony Halkett who found Pierre, halfway up the mountain, not far from the pathway along the river bank. It was Tony's quick ear which first heard the tiny jingle of harness as Rataplan moved his weary head above his master's body, and slid into the undergrowth to the spot where horse and man had ended their campaign. Pierre was lying on his back, as he had fallen, his head contused, his tunic soaked with the blood from his ear and neck. His face, when Sally touched it, was covered with cold sweat. His pulse, when she slid her fingers round his wrist, was just perceptible.

After the first sob, quickly stifled in her rebozo, Sally wasted no time in weeping.

"He is alive," she said, "we must get him to the cart, and up to the Mine House; how?"

"I canna so much as lift him," confessed John Halkett, with Franchet's heavy shoulders against his arm. "Tony'll need to gang up to the house and bring back some sort o' a litter—"

"There's no time for that." Sally spoke with authority. "My brother used to tell me how they made litters when he was a field surgeon. With a man's coat, and a bayonet—where's his bayonet?"

It was nowhere to be found. But Sally went up without fear to Rataplan and unbuckled Pierre's saber from the stirrup rest.

"There's blood on it too!"

The fitful starlight, shining through cloud, allowed the men to see her with the heavy saber, sticky with the blood of the fight at San Lorenzo, half in and half out of the scabbard.

"Let me do that, for God's sake!"

John Halkett had already taken off his heavy frieze coat. He ran the saber, with the cutting edge protected by a scarf, through one long sleeve, the scabbard through the other. He took Franchet's shoulders while Tony and Sally together lifted his legs, and between them they moved the inert body onto the improvised litter, and started across the hillside to the cart.

Sally stumbled behind the stretcher bearers, leading Rataplan. She had felt dried blood on the chestnut's shoulder as she groped for the saber, and knew that he had been wounded slightly, but he moved well enough, and once nuzzled her rebozo as if he meant to offer her his own form of comfort. When they reached the road and the cart, Tony undertook to walk him home and see to him; Sally sat down on the floor boards and took Pierre's head in her lap.

He was still breathing when the house servants carried him into the Mine House.

"Bring him into the little back parlor," said Mrs. Halkett in her capable way. "That's where we nursed the Belgian gentleman. It's handy, and there's a good light. Annie, put a match to the fire."

The glance she gave her sister-in-law seemed to say that not much nursing would be required for Pierre Franchet.

They cut away his tunic, removed his boots and wrapped him in warmed blankets. Miss Halkett, murmuring comfort, bathed and dressed the saber cut above his ear. But the concussion he had suffered when he fell to the ground had left him in a deathlike coma. His eyeballs were glassy when they tried to lift the blackened lids. His breathing grew steadily slower and more feeble.

"Can you not bring him round wi' brandy?" whispered John Halkett, hovering with the bottle in his hand.

"We've tried brandy, love. Ammonia too," his wife whispered back.

There was no danger of arousing Franchet. They had lowered their voices in pity for the pale girl kneeling by his side.

"Is it possible to get a doctor here?" said Sally, looking up at them.

"There's a Mexican *curandero* down at St. Martín, that lanced a boil of Tony's, real well. I doubt we canna get him here tonight."

"No." She considered. "But we have to get the bullet out, you know."

Mrs. Halkett made a gesture of despair. They had applied clean wet cloths to the wound, from which the blood still welled, but the large ugly hole between Pierre's neck and shoulder was surrounded by blackened tissues, and the swollen area seemed to increase as they looked on.

"Can you do it, Ann?"—appealingly.

"My poor lassie, I can nurse him day and night if he's spared to you, but to tak' out a bullet—no, I never—"

"Then I must try," said Sally. "I have a little surgery kit of my uncle's—and I've seen it done in the hospital—"

But when Sally took the silver bullet probe from the Old Doctor's kit, her courage failed her, and she began to cry.

"I can't use this sharp thing. I'm afraid of hurting him!"

"We'll try to get a doctor in the mornin'—"

But the flickering pulse was very low.

"I've read Chisholm's *Manual*. It says you can do it with your fingers—"

"Sally, are you sure?"

"Yes, I'm sure."

Sure of herself. Certain, as she turned from them to rub her hands with cactus soap and plunge them in one of the basins of warm water which had been brought to the bedside. Gently, surely, she inserted the fingers of her right hand into the dreadful wound. Pierre groaned.

"Oh, my darling, God help me not to hurt you!"

She could feel the bullet. It was not impacted in the shattered bone.

They saw her lips move and believed that she was praying. But Sally was repeating to herself the next step laid down in the old Confederate manual of military surgery which Andrew had brought with him to Mexico. There were shreds of blue cloth to be picked out of the cavity; there was gentle pressure by the left hand to squeeze the bullet free. It came out at last in Sally's fingers, dripping red.

"A Yankee bullet!" said John Halkett in disgust.

"The wet dressings, please." A young field surgeon, behind the lines at Gettysburg while the amputated limbs piled up, could have spoken no more calmly. Sally packed the wound with lint soaked in a weak solution of creosote, and wound the heavy bandages, always at hand, round Pierre's neck, upper arm and shoulder. Then she stood back, trembling, while the older women packed the bed with the stone hot-water bottles which frightened maids had been preparing in the kitchen, and Ann Halkett began chafing Pierre's naked feet. About an hour later they were able to get a little stimulant between his lips.

It was not very long before they saw his eyelids flutter and his lips move, and Sally in an agony leaned over him to catch his first weak whisper.

"He's speakin' French," murmured the watching Halkett. "What does he say?"

"He said *'marchez ou crevez!'*"

THEY WERE to hear many of the Legion commands, and a torrent of the Legion oaths from Pierre's blackened lips in the hours and days which followed, as the fever of his wound mounted and ran riot. There was no question of fetching the doctor from St. Martín Texmelucan: it was not possible to reach his village through the rabble of camp followers, foot and horse soldiers, mules and vehicles, trailing in the rear of the army of Diaz. Tony Halkett, who slipped down to Río Frío at first light, could learn nothing about the fate of the Imperialist wounded in the cuartel. They had been removed, no one could tell him where: what was several times reported, if not confirmed, was that in Puebla many Imperialist officers had been shot out of hand as soon as the Juaristas took the city.

Tony's father looked grave at this news, but Sally paid little attention. She was hanging over Pierre, watching for the symptoms of pyemia, which so often followed a suppurating wound. His wound was doomed to suppurate, having been caused by a rifled bullet, which invariably did more damage than a musket ball. His right collarbone was fractured, Sally could not tell how severely, but once a pad of toweling had been placed in the arm pit, bandages securely fixed and the patient's right arm strapped to his chest, his nurses concentrated on keeping down the suppuration from the wound. "Laudable pus" was always welcomed by military surgeons, but the spread of pus into the blood, which caused pyemia, could seldom be checked in the crowded and insanitary field hospitals. Pierre, like Dr. Herzog and Baron Bompard before him, had the advantage of clean surroundings and good nursing; but although Sally tried to tell herself that his rigors and shiverings, followed by drenching sweats, were due to his long exposure on the damp ground, she knew that they were also symptoms of the dreaded poisoning. She did her best to keep the suppuration in check with lint dressings soaked in cold water to which perchloride of iron was added from Mrs. Halkett's medicine chest. The patient seemed to grow a little calmer, each time these were applied.

He marched, in the delirium which followed shock and exposure, for hundreds of thousands of miles. He dragged his heavy boots through the sands of the Algerian desert, and begged them to find an oasis where he could fill his water bottle, and quench his thirst. He marched again with Jeanningros, on that historic three-hundred-mile trek from Tampico to Monterrey, and bragged in a hoarse whisper that Douay's division had marched nineteen thousand miles in seven months when the French first came to Mexico. Then for a time his mind ran much on Diaz at Puebla, and they thought he was babbling of the

recent defeat until he warned them to keep a sharp lookout on
the roofs of the Convento de la Compañia, because the attempt
to rescue Diaz was bound to come from there.

"I never took his bribe, never!" he asserted over and over
again. And each time Sally would answer steadily,

"No, darling, I know you didn't." She was always calm
at his bedside, always answered him rationally, although she
knew she was nothing but a voice and hands to him—not recog-
nizable as Sally. Once only, she thought she had found a way
to bring him nearer to full consciousness. His old blue cutaway
was to be destroyed, and in turning out of the pockets such items
as his pipe and his flint and steel, Sally came upon the thornwood
Cross from Aranzazu. Awed and touched, she laid it in his left
hand and closed his fingers round it. To her dismay, this pro-
voked at once his worst delirium, in which the names of Atascadero and "En Dentelles" were inextricably confused, and it
took John Halkett's strength to hold him still in bed. But that
was the last crisis. From then on, he began to mend. The day
came when Pierre was able to lift his wife's hand to his trembling
lips and say, "I love you!"

"Put a shawl over your head, Sally, and come out for a
breath of fresh air," commanded John Halkett, on the day when
Pierre was well enough to be shaved for the first time. "Ye're
losing your good looks, hangin' over your goodman's bed all
day and all night. He's on the mend now; faith I think he's like
a cat wi' nine lives, ye canna kill him."

"He owes his life to you and yours," said Sally. "Dear John,
how can we ever thank you?"

The Scotsman took her arm as they went out into the courtyard. He thought Sally looked exhausted. Her hair was flat and
dull beneath the dark-blue rebozo, and her cheekbones stood out
in her pale face, but the golden lights were dancing in her eyes.

"Never let the word 'thanks' be spoken between you and
me," he said. "Ye ken fine that if it hadna been for your uncle
we might ha' starved in Scotland. He gave me my chance in life,
and nothing I could do for you or Andra' would ever balance

the account. Not, mind you, that Andra's an easy one to help."

"I wish we had some news of him," said Sally. She lifted her face to the May sunshine, as if becoming aware that there was a world outside Pierre's sickroom—a world where there was new green at the tips of the pine branches, and a film of green over the cultivated land which lay round Río Frío.

"I wish we had some news o' anybody," said Halkett. "We're kind o' cut off from the world up here. But whatever may be going on at Querétaro, there's nae doubt but that Mexico is still holding out for the Empire."

It was confirmed beyond a doubt that the attempt to hold the bridge at Río Frío had not been in vain. That check to the Juaristas, slight though it was, had allowed von Kodolitsch to prepare the much more formidable barrier of the mountain battery at the head of the pass, which in turn covered General Marquez' headlong retreat to the capital. The General had fought his way through American opposition at Texcoco and led three thousand of his army back to Mexico. Against the strong fortifications which the French had erected round the capital, Porfirio Diaz had so far thrown his troops in vain.

"It's a God's mercy that Diaz took the most o' his rabble up the road wi' him," said Halkett, "but there's still too many of the rascals stravaigin' the countryside for my peace o' mind."

Sally saw that the great gates of the hacienda proper, which, as on a much smaller scale at Las Flores, surrounded and enclosed the Mine House, had been closed and bolted. Two of Halkett's most trusted peons, armed with old snuffbox muskets, stood on guard by the smaller gate, which remained open. The sound of the ore-crusher, which had moved at a steady beat when first Sally came up the mountain, was faint and intermittent.

"You have a fearful responsibility, John," she said, struck.

"I have that. I've a fortune in bar silver in my keeping, and it can only accumulate until I get the next conducta out —dear knows when!—because although I'm only workin' at half-time, I darena stop the work entirely. If a silver mine is out of operation for forty-eight hours, it becomes the property of the government—did ye know that?"

"No, I didn't. Do you mean any government? Imperialist, Republican, or what?"

"The Government of Mexico, whatever it may be. Now ye see why I couldna take Bessy and Ann to Cuba at the New Year, and put them out of danger. I dare not leave the mine that long; Don Antonio appointed me his manager, and here I bide until I've news of him."

"Perhaps *he's* gone to Cuba?"

"The señora and the young ones went; not him. He's still in the capital, as far as I know. Lord, Lord! I wish I had George beside me at a time like this."

John Halkett still regretted his elder son's departure. But Tony was a tower of strength, especially in his dealings with the sullen miners on whose loyalty the lives of all at the Mine House depended. Sally sometimes thought, with a happy fluttered glance into the future, that some day she and Pierre might have a son like that—a boy born in Mexico, who while thinking and reacting in some ways like his foreign parents, would be Mexican in ways that they could never be. It was Tony who came back from one of his silent expeditions to Río Frío at the beginning of June with the news that the Emperor Maximilian had been killed at the head of his troops while leading a sortie from Querétaro.

"That I don't believe for one single moment," said Halkett emphatically. "Cheering them on from the rear, that's more Max's style; but there's been broken crowns up there, I doubt. Tony, go down to the kirk the morn's morning, and see if Father Francisco is there to say the Mass. We'll get the rights o' it from him."

Then, as Sally looked surprised, he added,

"I've no special fancy for the Popish gentry, but the padre and me are old friends. Because Pope or no Pope I do *not* like to see folk persecuted, and when Juarez was in power, and hunt-

ing down the clergy, I gave Father Francisco shelter in the mine
for a while. But that's another story."

It was the true story of Querétaro which the stout old padre
had to tell next day. When, greatly daring, he had said Mass
in the church which the troops of Diaz had used for every purpose but that of worship, he walked quietly up the mine road to
the turning where Tony Halkett was waiting with the mules, and
so to the sala of the Mine House where food and wine were
ready.

"There's no doubt at all, I fear," he sadly said. "Some of
the more intelligent staff officers of General Diaz are at Xoquiapan, and they have the details complete from Querétaro. The
city was absolutely starved out; the water supply was finished
when the Juaristas cut the aqueduct . . . and of course, they
had at least four times as many troops as Maximilian. It seems
he planned a sortie for the fifteenth of May. In all probability it
would have been no more successful than the others—"

"They made a lot of sorties, eh, padre?" young Tony interrupted. His eyes were gleaming at the thought of battle.

"Five, I think, or six. There was a Prussian officer with
Don Maximiliano—Prince Salm, or Schalm, or some such a
name, who fought in the *Norteamericano* war, and was skilled
in such fighting; he did well, they say. However, in the night
before the sortie, the Emperor was betrayed. One of his intimates,
Don Miguel Lopez, admitted the enemy to the Convento de la
Cruz in the middle of the night, and after a brief resistance the
Emperor was taken prisoner and the city surrendered!"

"Colonel Lopez!" said Sally. She remembered the review,
and the blond, handsome officer riding so close to "Madame
Dictator's" carriage. "The man who is Madame Bazaine's
cousin, and a relative of Juarez?"

"I don't know, señora." The old man turned courteously to
Sally. "Lopez is a very common name in Mexico."

Maximilian betrayed, and Querétaro in Escobedo's hands!
There was enough matter for speculation and anxiety there; but

Sally slipped out of the room after Ann Halkett, who was going to give the maids an order, and whispered,

"Don't let Pierre know any of this. He's not strong enough yet."

"I havena lived so many years in Mexico," retorted Miss Ann, "to begin now with worrying a sick man about their politics. Don This and Don That, and betray here and bribe there—it aye comes to the same thing in the end: somebody's shot or knifed. It's a pity for that poor misguided Maximilian that he didna bide at home."

Pierre was awaking from a doze when Sally went back to his room. He was already at the fractious stage of his convalescence, and his first words were a request to know when he was to get out of bed and put his clothes on.

"Not for a long time yet," his wife said decidedly.

"You want to keep me here at your mercy, don't you—little tyrant!"

With his sound hand he drew her down until her head lay by his on the pillow. He ran his fingers through the thick tawny curl which fell across his breast.

"How is the *señora soldadera?*" he said teasingly.

"Pierre!"

"I can't get over it—you walking into the cuartel as bold as brass with all those poor trollops, and finding Khevenhüller. Did you have a turkey on a string for local color?"

"No, and I didn't have a *baby,* either," she said emphatically.

"Next year, maybe?"

"We'll see."

Pierre turned his head cautiously and kissed her.

"You're getting to be pretty again, my darling—"

"So are you," she said impishly. Pierre had been shaved that day, but his hair had not been cut since he left Mexico, and instead of the army crop he affected it was in long fair locks, falling like Andrew Lorimer's behind his ears and even across his brow. The fever which had paled some of his tan had for the time being subtly altered the structure of Captain Franchet's face. Sally could now see in it something of the boy who had left Aix-en-Provence for Montpellier, nine hardlived years ago.

"You mean I need a haircut; what's to be done?"

"Mrs. Halkett clips Tony's hair round a pudding basin."

"That's just what it looks like. With a headband and a feather cape that kid would make a pretty good Indio."

"Oh hush, they'll hear you!"

"I'm sick of being hushed," said Pierre vigorously. "Sick of lying here like a log. *Mon Dieu,* I'm not much of a husband to you, am I, Sally?"

She murmured something inaudible.

"Sally, do you remember. . . ."

THE NEWS of Maximilian's capture was confirmed; the soldiers of Diaz, raging up and down the land, were unrestrained in their jubilation.

"How's Pierre after his turn round the stables this afternoon?" asked John Halkett abruptly, coming in from the mine tienda, where he had been supervising the evening sale of goods.

"Very tired, but none the worse, I think," said Sally, laying aside her needlework. "He was so glad to be out of doors again, and see his beloved Rataplan."

"That beast needs exercise . . . But look here, Sally, I confess I'm worried. Some of the stable mozos were putting it about that there was a French officer in the barns today, and I overheard some talk in the tienda that I didna like the sound of. I canna trust the peons as I trust the indoor servants."

"I know you can't." She thought of the three hundred mine workers: tentateros, barenadores, and all the tools and gunpowder they had at hand in the silver mine if they chose to mutiny against the foreign manager and the owner who had been one of Maximilian's Councillors. "Oh, John, we ought to go away!"

"Where would ye go, my lassie, even if your man were fit
to travel? Na, ye canna go down the mountain yet. But I've been
thinking that just for a wee while ye ought to go *inside* the mountain, like Father Francisco did when he was on the run from
the priest-hunters, years ago. It's dark and eerie, I'll admit, but
the air is pure, and it's not unhealthy—"

"For the miners perhaps." Sally's voice was very doubtful.
"But Pierre has been so ill, John—do you think it's really a
good place for him?"

"It's that or the blank wall and the firing squad, if he falls
into Juarista hands."

After the household had gone to bed on the next night, a
platoon of Diaz' Puebla regiment demanded admittance, and
searched the Mine House from floor to attic. Failing to find any
trace of a French officer, they withdrew without apology, having
demanded for their pains the contents of the till at the tienda,
and as many bottles of mezcal as they could carry away. But
they made no attempt on the silver strong rooms, and John
Halkett, who had kept one hand on his pocket pistol throughout
their visit, sighed with relief as he saw them go. It was only a
few hours since he and Tony had helped Pierre and Sally down
three hundred of the eighteen hundred steps which led to the
lowest level of the mine workings, and established them with
blankets and pallets in a spur of one of the galleries which hon-
eycombed the mine.

Sally, too, had her gun in her dark-blue camisa when she
climbed to the mouth of the shaft for a basket of hot food next
day. She had spent the daytime hours in a state approaching
terror. In the night the novelty of their situation, and the joy
of being alone with Pierre after those weeks of living in close contact with the Halketts, had kept fear from her; and by night,
too, they could light the curious old lamp of beaten silver which
Bessy Halkett had given them. It was a treasure from Taxco, set
with such cuttings from semiprecious stones as Sally remembered
in Don Antonio Mora's Cactus shrine, and the light passing
through the tiny panes of topaz and amethyst fell strangely on

the rocks about them, worked out long ago, which still glittered here and there with the precious ore. If this was the heart of Mexico, as John Halkett had once said, it was a luminous heart, shining with treasure; but there was fear and danger in it too.

By day, Sally heard the voices of the tentateros, grumbling as they climbed the endless stairs with the ore-sacks, more than two hundred pounds in weight, on their naked backs, and balanced by a leather strap bound round their brows. She heard the distant explosions which meant blasting, and felt how completely they were now at the mercy of a people who had no cause to love their masters. But she became less nervous after a day or two. No peons came into the old working where Father Francisco had been sheltered in the religious troubles. Nobody came near them except John Halkett, who every day had to tell them that the future looked darker than ever for all those who had fought for or supported Maximilian, now on trial for his life for crimes against the state.

"If only we could get out of here," said Pierre, a week after they had gone underground. "I'd rather face whatever's coming to me than be taken here like a rat in a trap."

"Where would we go, Pierre?"

"We'd go to Diaz," he said confidently. "He's always generous in victory—if one can get to himself, and isn't kicked around by his lieutenants. He'd give us a safe conduct, I believe, and once the siege of Mexico is raised we could go back there, if you like, and wait for André."

"But how could you get to wherever Diaz is now?"

"I could ride Rataplan, if Halkett would lend you a horse."

She doubted it; he walked a good deal up and down the gallery, but his limbs were still weak, and he tired easily.

"You talked a lot about Diaz, when you were sick."

Alertly: "Did I? What did I say?"

"You talked about a cell at Puebla, and the Convento de la Compañia—"

"Oh that." She could see the wry smile in the light from the silver lamp. It was night, and he was lying partly undressed, on his pallet, with a serape round his bandaged shoulder. Sally was huddled in her rebozo by his side.

"Won't you tell me the whole story?" she coaxed. "I thought I knew all your stories about Diaz, but not this one!"

"I never told it to you. Not for my own sake, but because it doesn't reflect much credit on some of my countrymen. Look . . . did you ever wonder how I got this?" He took her hand and ran the fingers along the scar on his jaw.

"At Tampico, wasn't it?"

"No, no, it was at Puebla. And Porfirio Diaz gave it to me, *chérie;* your husband has had the honor of being knifed by a Mexican general."

"The horrible wretch!" Her anger was so fierce and sudden that Pierre laughed.

"It was fair enough. It was in September '65, the second time he was our prisoner, and this time I was on guard duty at the prison. Well, his friends offered us all bribes to let him escape—"

"Which you refused."

"Of course. But my captain accepted, damn him, and they threw in ropes to Diaz' cell over the convent roofs and had the way all clear. He was going out as I went in, so we had a scuffle, and he pulled a knife on me. Well, that's their natural weapon; they all carry it, and he ought to have been searched more thoroughly. I kicked him in the groin, so he missed my throat, but someone hit me on the back of the head at the same time, and when I came round our boy was gone. So that's the story, Sally, and I don't bear any malice . . . let's hope, neither will Diaz!"

He told his story lightly, but Sally could see that he was agitated. When he fell into a doze she felt his forehead. It was quite cool. Cooler than she felt, as she contemplated once again the extraordinary set of values by which men ruled their conduct. Pierre apparently expected Diaz to greet him like an old friend, not because he had accepted a bribe, but because he had not. It was inexplicable! Sally went to a bay in the gallery where they had made some rough and ready toilet arrangements, and washed her hands as if she were wringing the neck of Porfirio Diaz, who had given her husband one more of the scars which he would bear away from the war in Mexico.

It was while she stood there in complete darkness that she heard the soft footfall.

"Ann?" she said with her heart in her mouth. "Is that you, Ann?"

There was a pause, and then the woman's step came softly on.

"Bessy?"

"It is I!"

In the light of the silver lamp, where the patches of gold and mauve flecked the glittering walls, stood La Malinche.

Sally came out of the darkness, and halted by her husband's bed. Malinche had not raised her voice, neither did Sally. The man between them stirred in his sleep and muttered. He did not waken.

"What are you doing here?"

"I came to see you, Gringa, and your wounded hero."

"Following your old trade as a spy? They were looking for you in Puebla to arrest you."

"The *French* were looking for me," said La Malinche superbly. "I can be the queen of Puebla now, if I choose."

"You were glad enough to hide out in Orizaba province, not long ago, and dance with the gipsies at the Quinta Vega."

"Were you there that night? I went to see how the land lay, and if I could do harm to my wretched sister. But I could safely leave her to your brother's hands. He ruined her without any help from me."

"Your *sister?*"

"Don Antonio Mora was my father, Gringa."

"One of your twenty fathers, *hija de putana*. How do you like to be called what you once called me?"

La Malinche smiled. She was not in her Poblana dress; a dark green cloak covered her from head to foot, but her own quality of incandescence made her beauty blaze in the dark gallery. Sally felt that at any moment the sleeping man must be aware of it.

"The time for insults is over between us two," Malinche said. "Tomorrow you will both be taken down to Río Frío. The tentateros know you are sheltered here; if Señor Halkett is not to die, El Güero must. And you shall suffer too, Gringa, because you took my lover from me."

"*Your* lover!" said Sally contemptuously. "You little tramp, he may have gone to bed with you once or twice because you importuned him; but he is *my* lover, and *my* husband, and nothing you can do will ever come between us more."

"I shall see you die tomorrow, with great pleasure," said Malinche. "Wake him now, and enjoy your last night of love together."

"I will not let you go from here alive," said Sally. Each word tasted like acid in her mouth. She saw the flash of a knife, the natural weapon, in Malinche's hand. She saw Pierre raise himself on his pillows with a cry. She saw the woman turn on him with the knife upraised.

She drew the Belgian pistol from her breast, and fired twice.

Chapter Twenty-three

THE HILL OF THE BELLS

ON THE NIGHT when the dreaded soldiers of the Supremos Poderes, Benito Juarez' brigade of killers, burst into the Convento de la Cruz at Querétaro, Andrew Lorimer was asleep in his little hospital. He was awakened by the drums and bugles of the Imperialists sounding a flurried assembly, and by the tramp of troops making a last vain sortie outside the town. Dressing hastily, he was in time to see Maximilian riding quickly by with his two loyal generals, and almost as soon as the gunfire was heard on the Hill of the Bells he was called on to give first aid to General Miramón, who had been wounded in the face. Hardly more than twenty casualties had been brought in before the firing ceased. The word went through the hushed city that the Emperor had given up his sword to General Escobedo, and in half-an-hour more the Juaristas, laying down their arms, manned the belfries to send a jangling peal of victory over Querétaro and its encircling hills.

"I'm glad the affair ended with so little bloodshed," said the Emperor tranquilly, when Andrew was allowed to see him. He was back in the rooms which had always looked like a prison, and it was only different from yesterday in that two scowling guards of the Supremos Poderes were standing with fixed bayonets at the door.

"I told General Escobedo that I was quite willing to abdicate," he went on. "The distress of the good people of Querétaro in the past few weeks has been very painful to me. If my leaving the country now means that they would be given food and water,

I said to Escobedo, I will leave at once from any port you choose to name."

"What did the general reply, Sire?" said Dr. Lorimer uncomfortably. He had seen the look which Prince Salm exchanged with Dr. Basch.

"He said he would transmit my request to Señor Juarez." The Emperor parted his beard and twirled it meditatively. "I understood, of course. A serving soldier could hardly make such arrangements without referring to his Commander-in-Chief . . . I suppose Juarez *will* be elected President, and become Commander-in-Chief, eh, Salm?"

"I really couldn't say, Sire. If Your Majesty had but listened to me a month ago . . . then that traitor Lopez . . ."

Maximilian held up his hand.

"Let us have no recriminations," he said. "I take all the blame for our defeat upon myself. After all, I have been treated with courtesy, and am at home here in my own snug quarters—"

But after forty-eight hours Escobedo decided that the quarters were too snug, and far too close to the people of the town, who loved the Emperor, and might suddenly decide to stage a dramatic prison break. He was moved once, and twice, within the next few days, and both Andrew and Dr. Basch were with him when he arrived at a Capuchin monastery requisitioned by the Juaristas as a jail.

There had been an alarming return of the dysentery, and Maximilian was weak and ill when he was taken before the prison commandant.

"I trust you will allow my physicians to share my rooms with me for a day or two, *señor comandante,*" he said in his amiable way. "I have not been very well, I regret to say, and need their services."

"*Rooms?* What rooms?" barked the Mexican. "I have the strictest orders from San Luis Potosí to treat Maximilian von Hapsburg, Archduke of Austria, as a common criminal awaiting trial. You must make the best of such accommodations as criminals are usually offered, and without the services of your flunkies—"

"Señor," said Andrew Lorimer. "I am an American and a qualified physician, and I shall see to it that General Escobedo is made aware of your harsh treatment of an ailing man."

He knew that these potent words, *I am an American,* would have their effect upon the fellow, for Juarez prized above all things the support of the United States. But the commandant backed down only so far as to say,

"You can stay with him tonight then, if you are so anxious to see the inside of a prison. Warders, take them both down to the crypt."

The staircase to the crypt of the Capuchin church was broken, wet and narrow. The place itself was in darkness, lit only by the candle which the warder left on a stone tomb. Maximilian stared around, and as his eyes became accustomed to the darkness, he started, and crossed himself.

"Are those—coffins?"

They were: black and moldering, some fallen open, revealing here and there the dreadful traces of mortality.

"This is a vile place!" said Andrew. "You shall *not* stay here! I'll shout—I'll call the warder back—"

"No." Maximilian restrained him. "It will do me no harm to spend a night among the tombs. This is the crypt of the Capuchin church, you say: how very apt that they should confine a Hapsburg here! In the Kapuzinerkirche in Vienna the crypt is the great mausoleum of our House. Our ancestors are buried there: Franz Josef, Emperor, will be buried there some day—"

"Sire, pray be calm—"

"And so shall I!" cried Maximilian in an agony. "*That* will be how I shall go home again! When they carry my dead body to the vault of the Kapuzinerkirche, with the organ pealing, and the cortège dressed in black with handkerchiefs to their eyes for Maximilian. Only a few weeks from now, when it's still summer in Vienna, the *Novara* will carry me home again, and the Viennese girls will cry for Maxl, the victim of Benito Juarez! The victim of his own weakness and his indecision! The victim—"

He mastered his hysteria. Neither then nor ever did Andrew or any of those close to him hear Maximilian add: the victim of Carlóta.

Much later, when he had taken some of the remedies Andrew always carried, Maximilian slept. Andrew saw him, by the last light of the candle, lying with his long beautiful hands folded on his breast; and it seemed to him that they were already what Carlóta saw in her dreams at Puebla—the hands of a dead man.

"YOUR NAME, SEÑOR?"

"Andrew Fraser Lorimer."

"Your residence?"

"Four, Plaza de Santo Domingo, in the City of Mexico."

"Your occupation?"

"I am a physician."

"Serving as a field surgeon with the Imperial Army?"

"You can say so."

"Your nationality?"

"I am an American citizen."

"Have you proofs of that statement?"

"Proofs?"

"A passport, a *laissez-passer,* a document?"

"I have no passport."

"Why?"

The War Criminals Board of Querétaro was enjoying itself hugely. All four members scratched their paunches, or spat, or rubbed their bare toes thoughtfully as they studied the tall young man with the well-brushed red hair, the black stock and the immaculate white linen, who for the moment was completely at their mercy.

"Why, señor?"

"I was deprived of it last year at New Orleans, señores."

"On a criminal count?"

"As a Confederate veteran, desiring to emigrate to Mexico."

There was a consultation, and some sniggering laughter.

"Are you satisfied with your performance as an immigrant, señor doctor?"

"No, señor presidente."

"We can arrange that immediately. The sentence of the court is Deportation, with all property in Mexico forfeited to the Republic. Next case!"

. . . Andrew came out into the sunny street, settling his sombrero on his head. His temples ached. Thanks to his work at the hospital he was free to come and go alone, but he saw a guard watching him as he approached the courtroom gate.

He said, "What are they busy at across the way, hombre?"

"They are erecting stands for the populace, señor. So that all can watch the arrival and departure of the traitor Hapsburg."

"His trial is to be held in that building?"

"Sí, señor."

Andrew looked across the street. He had never been in this part of town before. He did not recognize the little building, with its three arched iron grilles beneath a graceful wrought-iron balcony ornamented with a lyre, a trumpet and a violin.

"Is it a concert hall? An opera house?"

"It is the Iturbide Theatre, señor."

From his palace to his prison to the scene of his court-martial, *the ill-omened name of Agustín Iturbide* haunted Maximilian to the last.

WHEN HE WAS sentenced to death in that courtroom, on the thirteenth of June—in his absence, and by a court of young lieutenants—the Emperor of Mexico refused to believe that Juarez would insist on the full punishment.

"He will commute the sentence—you will see," he said comfortably. "Juarez will never dare to have me executed. Perhaps a short term of imprisonment, such as President Jefferson Davis received after the fall of the Confederacy . . . Well, I could endure that. But Juarez will never dare to alienate the world by killing me."

Juarez could, and did. While all the Great Powers sent their diplomatic representatives to beg for Maximilian's life, or telegraphed urgently to San Luis Potosí—while the irrepressible Princess Salm traveled north to intercede in person for Maximilian and General Miramón's distracted wife flung herself at his feet to beg for her husband's life—the Aztec Indian remained immovable. Maximilian had been the chief instrument of the French Intervention, and had usurped the sovereignty of Mexico. Maximilian von Hapsburg must die.

When he understood that this was so, Maximilian called to his aid the dignity of his illustrious ancestors, and some inherent nobility, latent beneath all his faults, which enabled him to meet death bravely. Having done what he could to save or protect his faithful followers, he made his peace with God and man, and prepared to die.

Andrew saw him, and received his thanks "for all you tried to do for me," on the night of the eighteenth of June. It was a short meeting, for the Emperor had many letters to write to his mother and family. Still Andrew could not leave the garden of the Capuchin church. He sat down on a gravestone, thinking of the coffins in the crypt below, where he and the Emperor had spent one night, and of the vault that would open in the Kapuzinerkirche when Maximilian went home again to Vienna. He thought of the immense failure of his own life in Mexico: his uncle's warning disregarded, his uncle's property scattered, his false diagnosis of Carlóta's malady, the loss of Silvia all rose to torment him in that evening hour.

Presently he took a letter from his pocket, which Julius Herzog had addressed to him from Vienna nearly a month before, and began to read.

My dear Andrew,

I am sending this letter to you in care of Baron Lago, the Austrian Chargé d'Affaires in Mexico. Now that Querétaro has surrendered, the city will be open to diplomatic communications of all sorts, and Herr Lago should be able to transmit this to you without difficulty.

It is thanks to Madame Franchet that I know your whereabouts. She was good enough to write to tell me of her marriage soon after it took place, and she added that you and Captain Franchet had gone to Querétaro with the Imperial Army. I write this in the hope that you, as a surgeon, will have been serving on this occasion behind the lines.

If Captain Franchet has survived the fighting, then I have no fears for him and his wife. As I once remarked to Miss Sally Lorimer, they are two of a kind, and if the Republic brings peace to Mexico, they are certain to make their way successfully in that country. They will be valuable members of the community under the new régime, and I predict that in a few years they will be both influential and extremely rich.

But yours is the life of value to the world.

From the extreme bitterness of the letters you wrote to me after the Marquesa de Vega's tragic death, I realize you feel that, professionally, your year in Mexico has been entirely wasted. It contained, however, one outstanding success which I think, in the pressure of recent events, you have to some extent forgotten.

I refer to the ovariotomy you performed on your English patient, Mrs. Dixon.

When I was in Paris last July I showed your account of it to Professor Stephane Tarnier—a pioneer as you know of that operation, and he declared that, given the conditions at the Maternity House of Mexico, the result you achieved was remarkable. He was confirmed in this opinion by the postoperative notes you made on Mrs. Dixon's case from June to last October, which I passed on to him.

Professor Tarnier now offers you an internship at the

*Paris Maternité, working in the group which he directs. It may
seem to you that this is a step backward to the beginning of your
career. But Professor Tarnier is a young man, not yet forty, and
promotion is certain to come quickly. Look on it rather as the
true beginning of your medical career.*

*I have seen something of your sympathetic influence over a
woman patient, and I am convinced that in Europe, as an as-
sociate of Tarnier, you will be a life-giver to thousands of future
mothers and their unborn children.*

*The suffering of your mother and sister, and the experiences
you have survived in Mexico, will in the long run inspire you
to leadership in this noble branch of Medicine.*

*I am sending copies of this letter to Baron Lago, to inter-
cept you at Mexico or any possible port of embarkation, and I
will meet you, on receipt of a telegraphic message, at Antwerp,
Hamburg, or St. Nazaire as you shall choose. In the meantime
believe me,*

Always your friend,
Julius Herzog

He hadn't quite taken the whole thing in, of course. One
phrase had stunned him at the first reading—that anyone should
think *his* life of value to the world.

But he was going to Tarnier—in all humility; and to his
steadfast friend, with gratitude.

He was going to be a life-giver. Moving away from death.

The suffering of his mother and sister—it was very touching
that Julius should have remembered that. The mother, the sister
dead in childbirth *ought* to be his inspiration—

And Silvia, who died before their child was born—

Herzog would never know that secret grief. But Silvia would
be there as part of his inspiration; guiding his hands and mind,
forever.

. . . Andrew saw Maximilian for the last time at six o'clock
on the following morning.

The Emperor had made his confession, and heard a Solemn

Mass in the monastery. He had eaten some breakfast and said good-by to the weeping servants who had been allowed to wait upon him to the end. He was very pale, but his face was calm and cheerful as he shook hands with Dr. Basch and Andrew.

"I wish you both Godspeed," he said, "my faithful friends." He was put into a carriage with the two generals who were to die with him. The others followed in hired vehicles, through the cobbled streets where every house was draped in black, and the people, who had loved him, wept as he went by.

The Hill of the Bells, the scene of his first bivouac and last defeat, had been chosen as the place of execution. The carriages stopped at the foot of the hill. Looking up, they could all see a rough adobe wall, newly built, against which stood three wooden crosses. Beside the crosses three black wooden coffins lay open and waiting. And Andrew thought of Carlóta's nightmare of the three headless men on a bare hillside in the sun.

The Emperor looked about him. "A beautiful morning," he said with a smile. "I've always wanted to die on such a day as this. Gentlemen, shall we go?"

The guards turned to bring the condemned men up the hill. General Miramón walked erect. General Mejía, weak and wounded, was half carried to the place of execution.

"They'll shoot the Emperor first," Andrew heard one of the officers say. Dr. Basch was tugging at his sleeve.

"Look at his coffin," he said urgently. "It's far too short. They'll have to break his—"

"Don't, for God's sake!"

Andrew saw the Emperor take off his sombrero, his fair hair and beard touched by the light morning breeze. He turned away; he could not watch. He looked down at golden Querétaro in her deadly ring of hills, and the background of the beautiful merciless land.

He grasped a bough of the tree by which he stood and put his head down on his arm with a whispered prayer.

"Our Father—which art in Heaven—"

Presently he heard the volley.

Chapter Twenty-four

THE MASTER OF MEXICO

"Is SHE DEAD, Pierre? Have I—killed her?"

Her own whispered words seemed to Sally to reverberate from the walls of the cavern where Pierre knelt beside Malinche's body.

"Yes, she's dead," he said. "Sally—for God's sake, you mustn't faint now! I'll go for John—"

"Don't leave me alone with—her—"

"I must." He helped Sally to the pallet bed and wrapped the serape round her shoulders. "Sit down, my darling. I'll be as quick as I can. And Sally—I'll tell John it was *I* who shot her—let me go."

She crouched by the pallet, when he had left her, with chattering teeth, keeping as great a distance as possible between herself and the motionless body in the dark green cloak. But when John Halkett came she flung herself upon him,

"It wasn't Pierre who killed her, John! It was me!"

Then she was lifted in the Scotsman's strong arms and carried up the dark stairway and through the yard to the familiar sala where Tony was coaxing the fire into a blaze. And she was aware of only one thing that he said before the blankness of fatigue overwhelmed her,

"I kent fine it was you, my lassie. Pierre's not left-handed."

. . . I have taken the life of a human being. That was the thought to which Sally had to awaken two hours later. It was still night, the fire was burning brightly, and steadfast John

Halkett was sitting near the couch where he had laid her. He saw the shock and terror in her eyes and said at once,

"It's all right, Sally. It's all right, and Pierre is resting; you're not to fret about him. And Tony and me has seen to everything."

"But what have you done with—with—"

"The silver mine has always kept its secrets well," he said. Sally covered her face with her hands.

"*She* said the miners knew where we were, and had betrayed us . . . And some of them must have let her into the courtyard, for the gate was locked—"

"I think she was telling lies, as usual. There's more than one way into the mine, for the galleries run far back, and there were shafts and drillings made a hundred years ago that are never used now. I found out some queer things at the time of the religious troubles, and I've aye had a notion that the Plateado boys knew their own ways from the Black Forest into the silver mine. But I've kept my mouth shut, and it's saved me a lot o' trouble; now you and Pierre will have to do the same. We'll see you out of here at first light, my dearie: could you not try to get a proper sleep?"

But when morning came Pierre Franchet was adamant: he would not take flight while there was any danger of reprisals falling upon the friends who had sheltered them.

One long day passed, and another, and no company of Juaristas came to arrest them, nor was there any disturbance among the peons in the mine. On the third morning Pierre consented to set out, wearing a ranchero suit and sombrero like any small farmer using the highway for his lawful occasions. Sally was lent a costume left behind by Nannie Halkett when she went to school in Edinburgh, of the style just coming into fashion among the younger rancheros' daughters. The skirt, not unduly full, was divided, and fell gracefully to the tops of the wearer's riding boots, allowing some freedom of movement, and Sally declared it even better for riding than the Otomí skirt of the Las Flores days. Nannie's sidesaddle was also on loan, and was fastened on a neat dun mare, with no tricks, which Sally had ridden once or twice already.

All these preparations kept thought at bay, and then there was the anxiety of watching Pierre handle a very restless Rataplan with his left hand only, and of thinking how they would get through the village of Río Frío.

Both Mrs. Halkett and Ann were in tears when they started, and John, with his Scotch bonnet in his hand, wore his most portentous look. But young Tony created a pleasant and helpful diversion by mounting barefoot and bareback on one of the mules which turned the beam of the ore-crusher, and trotting after them to the village and beyond—looking, to a stranger's eye, very like an Indian mozo riding behind his master and mistress when they went to town. He went with them as far as his friends the woodcutters on the Llano Grande, who were able to tell them positively that Mexico was still holding out for the Empire, and that Diaz had shifted his headquarters outside the city to the Villa de Guadalupe.

"Guadalupe, where the Shrine is?" asked Sally.

"Yes," said Pierre. "I've never been there, but I know it's near Texcoco. It's a long ride, Sally, are you sure you can manage it?"

"If you can," she said briefly. He was sitting slumped in his saddle, rather flushed, but the mischief was out of Rataplan by now and he was going along easily and well.

"*Caballo alazán tostado, primero muerto que cansado,*" said Pierre contentedly, giving the reins a little shake.

" 'Rather die than give in', eh?"

"Yes. Rata boy, last time you and I had a promenade together, we didn't think we'd go riding with Madame again, did we?"

"Oh Pierre—but you really do feel better, don't you?"

"After two months of devoted nursing, I should do. But I'm beginning to wonder if I'll ever lift my right arm above my head again."

"You will, when the straps are off. Besides, what do you want to lift your right arm for? To rob an orchard?"

It was so exhilarating, to be cantering across the Llano Grande, and into the dark forest pass, and come out on the other side, and be on the way back to Mexico! They met few people on the road, and those they met paid little attention to them; the days of the great rabble seemed to be at an end. At eleven o'clock they turned aside into the woods and ate the cold ham and *jitomates* Ann had put in their saddlebags, and drank a little wine.

"Are you carrying your gun, Sally?" Pierre asked suddenly.

She nodded, speechless.

"You'd better give it back to me."

She took the Bayard from the pocket of Nannie Halkett's riding habit and handed it over.

"Don't you trust me with it, Pierre?"

"I don't want you to fire it again until I've put you through some target practice. Do you know you fired twice with your eyes shut?"

At the expression on her face he burst out laughing.

"And that night on the causeway, darling, with old Mora's horse pistol—why, your friends will never know how lucky they were not to be blown into eternity. It was a lucky fluke you missed them, just as it was a lucky fluke you hit Marina before she knifed us both."

"Are you sorry for what I did, Pierre?"

"I? Not a bit. Are you?"

He waited for her answer with a graver look than usual on his face.

"Oh—*sorry!*" It was like a sob.

"It was in self-defense, Sally. She might have killed us both—"

"How did *you* feel, after that night in the tavern at Montpellier—"

Pierre thought back across the killing years to the boy lying under sentence of death in his prison cell.

"I was heartbroken," he said. "But La Malinche—that was a different thing . . . You'll come to realize that, in time."

"Meanwhile I have to live with the knowledge that I killed a woman, don't I?"

Pierre was silent.

"Silvia's sister!" said Sally on a long breath. "Don Antonio Mora, La Malinche's father! Who always swore by noble blood as the most important thing in life! He wasn't too noble to go to the gipsy girls, even after he was married to Doña Mercedes—

"Silvia and La Malinche both dead, and by whose fault? What destruction Andrew and I brought with us, when we came down this road so confidently a year ago, to begin it all!"

He saw tears in her eyes and put his arm around her.

"This is the true beginning, my heart's heart—"

"It will be . . . when I have told my story to Diaz."

"Tell Diaz that you shot Malinche?" incredulously.

"I must, Pierre. If I don't, I'll always have it hanging over me. The dread of discovery—I couldn't live with that. Or the Halketts might be blamed, and suffer for it. And I *must* have everything absolutely clear and truthful—"

"I remember," said Pierre with his wry smile. "But *I'm* going to do the talking when we see Diaz."

He felt her trembling.

"Pierre, do you think General Diaz will be like the Emperor Napoleon? Will he require me to give a life for a life?"

Pierre tightened his clasp and said,

"After the fight at Atascadero, an old priest said to me, 'Only God requires a life for a life, not man'."

"Was it he who gave you the thornwood Cross?" she said shyly, and saw a sudden, painful flush on the face she loved.

"No, that was given to me earlier, at Aranzazu . . . 'Among thorns, You.' Some day I'll try to tell you what that has begun to mean to me . . . But now—don't be afraid of Diaz, Sally. He likes courage. And if there is a price to pay for ridding Mexico of La Malinche—I'll pay more than half of it for you."

The great highway, empty of travelers, stretched peace-

fully enough before them until they came to the inn at Xoquiapan. They avoided the public room and had food and wine
brought upstairs by a chattering servant. The girl said that only
a week before, the posada had been full of Juarista officers,
celebrating the marriage of General Diaz to Doña Delfina Ortega
y Reyes.

"Who but Diaz would hold his wedding in the middle of a
siege?" said Pierre admiringly. He made Sally laugh again; he
teased her until color and gaiety came back to her face, and that
night the husband was once again the lover when darkness fell.
The inhibitions of the Mine House, the nameless fears of the
underground galleries belonged to time past. They came together in new ecstasies which Sally had not dreamed of, and in
more deeply shared joys of the body, on the night of their journey
in hope to Porfirio Diaz.

It was on the afternoon of the second day that they rode
into disaster. They were not many miles from the outskirts of the
capital when Pierre decided to call a halt. They were both hot
and tired, the dun mare in poor shape, and a short rest in the
shade was advisable before they rode into Guadalupe. Pierre
had his serape off, and his jacket, and Sally had removed the
slings to let him exercise his arm a little, when a file of noisier and
more aggressive soldiers than any they had yet met came whirling
down on them, the army hacks strung out across the road and
raising a great cloud of dust.

"Don't look at them, dear. Don't worry!" Pierre said
quickly. But the leading trooper shouted, not ill-naturedly,

"Look at the love birds, men! See the *chica,* taking her boy's
clothes off beside the road!"

They were surrounded in a minute, jeers and good humor
turning suddenly to suspicion. Then Pierre's sombrero was
snatched off. The fair hair, hacked rather than cut, and the gray
eyes betrayed the Gringo; something in his bearing when he
sprang up, something in his accent when he damned their im-
pudence, gave the whole thing away. They cried,

"A Frenchman! A Frenchman! *Mueran los Franceses!*"

They had him down on the roadway, his wounded shoulder pinned against a boulder, and as Sally shrieked, and struck with ineffectual hands at the ruffian next to her, Pierre shouted out an order,

"Sally, ride! Ride Rataplan to Diaz!"

She could never have mounted Rataplan without a stone beside the road which served as a horse block. Even so she sprawled rather than sat on the saddle, half lying over the startled horse's neck, clutching mane and reins together, and struggling to sit upright. Rataplan gave a loud neigh, and fled. Two of the Juarista troopers started in pursuit. But Pierre's great charger, with the light weight on his back, outdistanced them easily, and Sally, looking back in terror, saw them turn and rejoin the group around Pierre.

She was too furious to think of danger. He had told her to ride to Diaz, and she would do it if she could, but the empty stirrup irons were banging at the horse's sides, and she herself could hardly perch upon the military saddle. Some cool lucidity of mind forced her into stopping, into wasting five minutes to gain what might be many more, as she dismounted near a fallen log and shortened the stirrup leathers to something nearer the right length.

"Now, Rataplan!"

She had mounted from the log and flung one leg over the saddle in the way that always seemed to her so natural. Riding astride for the first time she felt the chestnut lengthen his step, and shake his head, and cock his ears back, as if he liked this light neat horseman with the gentle hands and knew that he too must do his best. And this, of course, was riding; better by far than those canters on the turf or in the Bois, riding that was like floating, that bore her along like a feather in some new harmony between the human and the beast. She had never jumped in her life, but when she saw a low gate leading to a traveled track she put him at it, and Rataplan took it like a bird, saving two miles of highway and landing her in a quiet village street where she saw a group of soldiers riding ahead. Instinctively she checked

Rataplan. But in a moment she realized that there was no
danger here. These horsemen were singing together, in unmistakably American voices:

> *"John Brown's body lies a-moldering in the grave*
> *His soul goes marching on!"*

Heads were turned in amazement as Sally pulled alongside.
"Are you Americans?" she called. "Will you help me? I
want to know the way to Guadalupe."

"You're on the road to Texcoco, ma'am," a voice called
back. "Take the left hand turn at the crossroads. 'Tisn't far."

"Oh, thank you! And when I get there, how shall I find
the general's headquarters?"

"There's a whole slew of generals up there, ma'am—"

"Be quiet, man! The lady means Diaz."

The man who had spoken last pushed his horse up to
Rataplan.

"We're on patrol," he said, "we can ride by Guadalupe
just as well as not, and take you straight to headquarters. It
might save you a bit of trouble—"

"I'm very much obliged to you."

Sally spoke mechanically, impatient to be gone. The American wheeled into place beside her and they set out. Rataplan,
after his gallop, seemed glad to slow to a canter, and make one
of a familiar procession of moving animals.

"I'm afraid you're in some kind of trouble, ma'am."

Sally looked at the man riding by her side. There was something vaguely familiar about his bearded face.

"My husband was fighting with the Imperialists," she said.
"We were on our way to Diaz when he fell into the hands of
some of *your* men, a few miles back; I'm so afraid they'll—hurt
him."

He made a concerned sound. "Were they wearing any insignia that you could recognize?"

"Two of them had a 9 and a P on their collars."

"The Ninth Puebla—they're quartered near us at Texcoco. They'll have taken him in there, I guess—to Texcoco."

"*If* they've taken him—"

He saw from her set face that she had heard of summary executions, and said hastily,

"It'll be all right, ma'am—if he didn't put up too much resistance."

"He would resist if he were dying." Tepayac Hill came up ahead of them, and the towers of the Shrine of Guadalupe. Sally gave an exclamation, and urged her tired horse forward.

"You don't remember me at all, do you, ma'am?"

Recognition at last came to Sally.

"You're the officer who came to the manse, the night the Bummers set fire to Fayetteville . . . Lieutenant Fenton."

"And you're the young lady who stopped us at the gate—"

Sally thought of Andrew in Querétaro, and his long resentment at her meeting with this man; and the tears she had struggled to hold back came to her eyes.

"I've often thought of you since that night, ma'am, and with great admiration, may I say? Fate has brought you a long way from the Carolina woods—"

"You too," said Sally. "Or did you enjoy arson and pillage so much you felt you had to continue south of the border? Sherman must be proud of his pupils."

"We take this track to headquarters. To the left— I don't know about General Sherman, ma'am. I'm here serving in the American Legion of Honor, with Colonel George M. Green."

"The Legion of Honor!" repeated Sally. "Is *that* what they call it?"

He said no more. But she was secretly glad of his company and of the American platoon riding behind her, as they rode through the crowded street of Guadalupe, and the Mexican soldiers stared and pointed at a woman riding astride.

When they came to the adobe building between the cathedral and the town where Diaz had his headquarters, the American briefly told her not to dismount.

"I'll go in and have a word with the aides," he said, "it may help you to get to the general quicker. And if he's not there we can ride on at once."

It seemed a long ten minutes before he came out again. Sally was conscious, now that the ride was over, of her divided skirt and wind-burned face, and Rataplan stood with sweat on his neck and drooping head. At last the American appeared.

"I've talked to Colonel Felix Diaz, the general's brother," he said, "and I've told him where I hope—think your husband may be found. The general is very busy, but Colonel Diaz will try to get him to see you for ten minutes. I wish you good luck in your interview."

"Oh, thank you," said Sally from her heart. He helped her to dismount, as if helping a woman from a man's saddle was an everyday occurrence, and laid his hand on Rataplan's bridle.

"I'll put your animal in the headquarters stable," he said, "and tell the stable sergeant to rub him down. He looks to me at the end of his tether."

"Thank you again," said Sally. "And please forgive me for what I said . . . Lieutenant Fenton."

"It's all right." He took her outstretched hand. "Just try to remember—the broken men were not all on the Confederate side."

. . . At the end of his tether. In the anteroom to which an orderly led her, Sally felt as if she had reached the end of her own. Stiff from two days in the saddle, trembling after her burst of speed across the fields, she pressed her chafed hands together and forbade herself to ask for a drink of water. She had to deny herself even that small comfort while Pierre was in his captors' hands.

Yet she arranged her hair as best she could with her fingers —there was no mirror in the room—and shook the dust from her sleeves and skirt. There was something in that anteroom, where four clerks were writing industriously, which she had not expected to find in the headquarters of Diaz. "Rabble" and "ruffians" were the mildest descriptions she had ever heard of his followers; she was not prepared for this atmosphere of methodical work and discipline. The box files and japanned deed boxes which lined the walls obviously held all the papers and details of a complex military organization, and also—Sally knew by instinct—plans for a future stretching far beyond the capture of the City of Mexico.

She did not hear the door behind her open, and jumped quickly to her feet at the words,

"Madame Franchet? I am Colonel Felix Diaz."

She had heard Pierre speak of the younger Diaz, known to the French troops as El Chato, and felt she would have recognized the broad, snub-nosed cat's face which had earned him his nickname.

"Be pleased to come this way, señora. The Supreme Commander will see you now."

It was the rank and style once given to Bazaine, and Sally had seen Marshal Bazaine several times, as well as Maximilian, and many of the men who had ruled the Empire. Yet, when she went before Porfirio Diaz, she recognized that for the first time in Mexico she stood in the presence of a great man.

"General, my husband was on his way to you, when he was set upon by some of your men and taken prisoner."

This was the opening she had planned while she waited in the anteroom. But when Diaz stood up courteously behind his plain deal table and motioned her to a chair, the stiff aggressive words went out of her head at once. She sat down and looked up at him in silence.

Porfirio Diaz, in his thirty-seventh year, was a man of medium height, wearing a dark-blue uniform without gold cords or epaulets, and high black riding boots. A sweeping black mustache hid the wide flat mouth which was the only evidence of his Indian blood; to his Spanish father he owed his shapely head and the brilliant dark eyes which had nothing of the opaque Indian look. Those eyes now took Sally in from head to foot.

"In what way can I serve you, señora?"

"General, my husband was wounded after the battle of

Puebla, while defending the Imperial Army's retreat to Mexico. He set out, as soon as he was able, to see you and—and make his position—correct and regular. But some of your men attacked him as we came along, and—and I don't know what has happened to him now."

The stammered sentences, the sob in Sally's voice, did her no harm with Porfirio Diaz. He approved, indeed, of the tawny hair escaping from beneath her sombrero, and the creamy skin flushed with hard riding, and the slim strong shoulders in the fawn-colored shirt. He said:

"Your husband's name is Franchet, señora?"

"Yes, sir. Captain Pierre Franchet of the Imperial Cazadores. He was Sergeant Franchet, serving in the Foreign Legion, when he tried to stop you escaping from Puebla."

A gleam of humor came into the eyes of Diaz.

"I remember Sergeant Franchet. He was incorruptible. But you—you are not French, señora?"

"I am an American. My brother is Dr. Andrew Lorimer, who had—has a practice in Mexico. He is now in Querétaro with—with the Emperor."

Diaz moved some of the papers on his table.

"He *was* with the Archduke," he said. "The Archduke Maximilian was executed three days ago."

Sally rose involuntarily from her chair.

"You did it? You had him killed? That poor, weak, silly man?"

"The President made the decision, and not I, señora. But —it was the only one to take. You see those men out there?"

He motioned her to the window. Below headquarters, on the slopes of Guadalupe and beneath Tepayac Hill his army swarmed, waiting for the final attack on the besieged capital.

"If we had pardoned Maximilian, we would have lost control of all those men," he said. "We have trained them to the idea of vengeance for their wrongs. If we had showed mercy instead of vengeance to the Archduke, they would have turned on *us*."

"And you are going to go on, exacting vengeance?"

"There are some men, the men who brought the Archduke here, who must be punished—"

"Oh then," cried Sally, "your Republic will be no better than the Empire, and all the Republics that went before it!"

"Does the Archduke's execution mean so much to you, señora?"

"It means nothing at all to me! But Mexico matters! This beautiful country—this kind and gentle people—and you are proud of training them to vengeance, and turning them into wild beasts who live by mutilation and execution! General"—for she saw the truth in his eyes, and plunged—"*you* would have pardoned Maximilian! You are a soldier—you know your men would never mutiny against *you!*"

"Don Benito Juarez is the President of the Republic, Madame Franchet. He made that decision, and all the others affecting the men around the Archduke."

"My brother, sir?"

"Your brother is on his way to Tampico, señora. He has been deported from Mexico, and his property in the capital is forfeit to the Republic."

Sally thought of the parlor where the pictures and furniture from Scotland held so many memories of their old home, and anger made her say,

"The city hasn't fallen to you yet."

Diaz smiled.

"We expect to enter—there—not later than the day after tomorrow."

Sally followed the direction of his eyes. Not much more than two miles away, with every tower and belfry etched against the blue, Mexico lay at the feet of Diaz, as the ancient Aztec city had once lain at the feet of Hernán Cortés. Sally looked up at the controlled exultation in the Spanish face.

"Yours will be a triumphal entry, general."

"Not quite yet," he spoke abstractedly. "A soldier's entry,

for this time . . . The present triumph belongs to Don Benito—to our President."

"But he's an old man! He won't be President forever! *You* may be President, before very long! You have to think of how the world will regard you, Don Porfirio, and show some mercy now, if you are to be admired then!"

She was flushed and very beautiful, he thought, as she went on,

"I once heard a man ask of my brother, as I ask of you, 'What will you be in the year nineteen hundred—' "

"I shall be the master of Mexico!"

The words came quickly, firmly, with the most absolute assurance.

"Yes, I believe you will be," said Sally slowly. "I wish I was as certain of our future, as I am of yours."

"I think you need have no fear for the immediate future. I have sent to Texcoco to see after your husband—you see, Madame Franchet, I do believe in clemency; and I gave orders, as soon as we came here, that there were to be no reprisals against the men who fought against us. There are incidents, from time to time, beyond my control; but I hope all is well with Sergeant—with Captain Franchet, and you shall both be given safe conducts to the coast."

"But we have come to ask your permission to stay in Mexico."

Diaz dropped back into his chair.

"Now that surprises me," he said. "The foreigners have been hurrying out of Mexico."

"We both want to stay here, sir. I have a hacienda at Cuernavaca, and I hope—oh, I hope so much, that nothing has happened to it in the fighting; and we would live there quietly, and grow sugar, and help the peons—"

"Help the peons!" said the general sharply. "I remember now. My brother Felix reported it to me. Your place suffered no damage when Cuernavaca fell, or very little, because the peons told our men you had been good to them, and forgiven them their debts—"

"As the Empress Carlóta wished to be done throughout the land."

"I know she did. She meant to do well by the Indians; so did he. They might have been excellent rulers in their own country. Only . . . we could not have them thrust on us at the point of French bayonets."

Sally was silent. The hacienda safe! It was a joy, but was Pierre safe? Was she?

"Your husband carried one of those French bayonets, señora. His position here, in the future, might be very difficult. Would it not be wiser for both of you to go home?"

"Mexico is our country now, señor. And you said yourself that my husband is incorruptible. Of how many of your lieutenants can you say the same?"

She saw that the shot had gone home. But he countered with,

"He fought against us; your brother went to Querétaro with Maximilian and has been deported for his pains; you may have been generous to your peons, but—"

"But I went to Paris with Carlóta, and I killed a woman called Marina Perez, who was one of your supporters. Now you know the truth about us both, sir, and it is better, it's right you should. We still ask for a safe conduct to Cuernavaca, and the right to live in Mexico. Because you will never be the master of Mexico without the help of people like Pierre and me."

"You think Mexican help will not suffice?"

"But what have the Mexicans done?" cried Sally. "*All* that has been achieved in this country since the Spaniards left has been done by foreign aid! The French built the railroad and the telegraph. The Scots run the mines. The Americans lend you money! *You* cut each other's throats!"

She stopped, appalled.

Diaz said: "Captain Franchet has a very eloquent advocate . . . But then all you ladies are eloquent! You are all active,

intriguing, cajoling—what can a man, whose trade is fighting, do
against you?

"You see that army, Madame Franchet. I built it up from
the three men who followed me when I escaped from prison.
Today I have twelve thousand followers. And all the time, while
we men fought our way to the capital, this has been a woman's
war. Carlóta—she began it. Carlóta and Eugénie were at the bottom of the fighting. Then Carlóta and Eugénie fought each
other—"

"Carlóta and Alicia Iturbide," said Sally.

"So? You see, women everywhere. You and La Malinche.
The Marquesa de Vega and her cuckolded husband. Women
preventing us from carrying on the war—"

"But we heard on the way here," said Sally, "that even you,
general, found time to get married here, last week."

He threw back his head and laughed, such full-throated
laughter as no Indian knew.

"You argue well, Madame Pierre Franchet. So well, that
I think we must keep you in Mexico a little longer."

Diaz broke off as an aide came into the room and whispered
something. He nodded; dismissed the man, and turned back to
Sally.

"I have already given orders," he said, "that foreigners
wishing to remain in the country—there are not many who do—
are to be given residence permits on the parole system. They will
be required to report regularly to the local authorities, and keep
an unblemished record of good conduct. In your case I think
we must add to the parole some form of punishment."

"For La Malinche?" Sally breathed.

"*Quién sabe?*" For an instant Diaz was all Indian, reserved,
fatalistic. "My decision is that you must remain on your hacienda, visiting Cuernavaca only to report to the alcalde, for
the space of twelve months. No traveling, no visits to Mexico,
no lamenting with your neighbors the rancheros, no plots, no
politics, nothing but hard work—you understand? You boast
that I can only rebuild Mexico with the help of foreigners like

you. Rebuild your own small part of Mexico, and prove to me that you are right!"

"Our new sugar canes were planted last January," said Sally. "They will be ready for cutting very soon."

Diaz looked from her radiant face to the distant city.

"When the first year has ended, bring your husband to me in Mexico," he said. "There is much to be done—much to be said, I think, between us three."

It was solemnly spoken, as if Porfirio Diaz had had an instant's prophetic vision of the long life which stretched before him, when in the triumph of absolute rule, with all its cruelties and corruptions, he might be glad to have truth and courage by his side.

"I must leave you now," he said. "My Chief of Staff is waiting. I would take you to my wife—to Doña Delfina; but I know you want to see your husband first. He is on his way here from Texcoco. Go up on Tepayac Hill and wait for him!"

Chapter Twenty-five

LA GUADALUPANA

FROM THE Plaza Mayor, from the recesses of the silver mine, she had come to the third place, which Carlóta had said was the true heart of Mexico.

Sally crept into the church of Guadalupe quietly. It was full of worshipers: humble poor people from the town which had grown up round the great cathedral, and peons from the country districts, praying that peace might return to Mexico.

Under the dull blue ceiling, sooty with candle smoke, there was little light except for the blaze of wax candles round the Shrine. Sally knelt down and covered her eyes. In the hour when she must ask pardon for a great sin, the stern God of her fathers had brought her, at last, to her knees.

She asked for pardon, but she said prayers of thanksgiving too. For Pierre's love. For the life beginning for them both, in peace and work and happiness.

She prayed for Andrew, wherever his feet should turn.

She prayed, with tears, for Carlóta. And with the memory of Carlóta vividly present, she opened her eyes on the Shrine of Guadalupe.

She saw, stretched and framed in gold on the high altar, the miraculous cape on which the image of the Virgin appeared to the poor Indian. Her face, brown-skinned like the faces of those who worshiped her, looked benignly down on Sally.

"I am the Mother of all you who dwell in this land."

The words written beneath the image came to Sally like a benediction.

Presently she left the cathedral, and passing by the Chapel of the Little Well went up, as Diaz had directed, on Tepayac Hill. It was there the Virgin had given the roses to the Indian, and there, in the scrub and rocks, life seemed to flower again for Sally. The City of Mexico lay before her, Diaz' great prize and her future home, and she counted the familiar towers and named the aqueducts, the surrounding hills, the twin volcanoes, with love and dedication.

She heard a shout. Far down the hill she saw Pierre Franchet stumbling towards her.

She ran through thorn and cactus to his arms.